Allan Alexander

CHECKMATE RUN

A NOVEL

Paradigm Shift Press

Checkmate Run
All Rights Reserved.
Copyright © 2015 Allan Alexander
v4.0 r1.0

Cover Photo © 2015 thinkstockphotos.com. All rights reserved - used with permission.

Paradigm Shift Press

ISBN: 978-0-9915786-1-0
E-book ISBN: 978-0-9915786-2-7

Library of Congress Control Number: 2015902527

PRINTED IN THE UNITED STATES OF AMERICA

To my wife,
my love, my strength, my inspiration, and my toughest critic.

*

To our son,
my closest friend, my brother, and my confidant.

*

To our two grandchildren,
the indisputable reason for this story to see the light of day.

"It is important that we know where we come from, because if you do not know where you come from, then you don't know where you are, and if you don't know where you are, then you don't know where you're going. And if you don't know where you're going, you're probably going wrong."

— TERRY PRATCHETT

Preface

Why now?

Plainly speaking, it is just the right time.

We were driving home from Jacob's Shorecrest Preparatory School graduation, and nothing could wipe the smile off my face. My wife caught me by surprise when she squeezed my hand. I looked at her. She was smiling as well, full of pride and joy for our grandson, who just had graduated as a member of National Honor Society, the same way his sister Leah had graduated three years ago.

"I am so proud of our little boy," she said.

"He's not a little boy anymore," I replied. "Hard to imagine that our young man will be moving to Columbus to attend Ohio State in a couple of months. Time flies . . . "

"Time flies. . ." she echoed. "Ohio State University, class of 2018… Leah will be graduating from the Ohio State next year. Can you believe it? Wow!"

By all means, everything felt right, and my story was ripe to come out. I tried to start writing it a few years ago, starting and stopping on numerous occasions; again and again, tying bits and pieces together, trying to create and re-create some characters, places, and situations that existed in my life . . . or maybe just in my imagination. Time and again, it seemed almost implausible to separate my dream from reality, to the point where the lines began to blur and mix so thoroughly, even I couldn't tell the difference. Reality started to feel like a dream in which we currently exist; or maybe it became reality from a dream cherished and nurtured so tenderly that it did, indeed, materialize somehow.

What is this story about? It's the story of our struggle to escape from the Soviet Union, our unkind and heartless motherland, bitterly intoxicated with hatred for dissenters and nonconformists. Even now, so many years later, I still occasionally wake up in cold sweat in the middle of the night, lost in the labyrinth of the same endless run, trying to escape my pursuers by jumping over the abyss of that last seemingly insurmountable cliff, hoping that it was just a bad dream.

Once and for all, the story was primed to be told. This is the story of our survival . . . The story is real. Everything in it did happen. Some of the names and the dates here and there had to be changed so others may survive, or stay safe wherever they are. I want to tell this story to our grandchildren for their future sake so that they can fathom what life is all about and how all of us got to where we are right now. At last, they are mature enough to figure out why we had to run and what we had to run away from.

The time is precious and the memory is not limitless. This chaotic cacophony of thoughts inside my head is ready to explode if I won't start laying everything out in writing. Otherwise, it may choke me with tears of uncontrollable emotions or overwhelm me with gratefulness to the point of blissful insanity.

So, here it is . . .

Prologue

The single lightbulb above the cell door suddenly came to life. He instantly woke up and sat on the edge of his cot. A few seconds later, the heavy door swung open. He jumped to his feet and reported as required by prison rules, "Prisoner #14352 is here!"

The guard on duty stepped in, followed by Captain Chayko, the chief interrogator. The captain brought the prisoner a suit, a shirt, and a pair of shoes—the same ones he remembered wearing the day of his arrest only a few months ago. He had lost his sense of time, and he didn't know exactly how many months had elapsed. Nevertheless, he had come to realize that something was changing; the interrogations had become less frequent and not as violent. Lately, the prison docs had started to see him daily, taking care of his seriously bruised face and severely swollen lips, the lasting remnants of the relentless beatings he had endured.

"Clean up and get dressed," the captain ordered. "Your trial is starting today, and you will be transferred to the courthouse jail until the day of your sentencing." He gestured to the guard and shouted down the corridor, "Bring in a barber! Right now, on the double!"

When the guard left, the captain moved closer to the prisoner and whispered into his ear, "If you try to complain to the tribunal about your interrogations and our ways of making you more cooperative, you will bring upon yourself a gruesome death sentence. I will personally beat the living shit out of you, and when I get tired, my assistants will continue until your chest cavity is filled with your own black blood. There will be no bruises; we know how to do it correctly.

"The same docs who made your face presentable will try to prolong your miserable life for a couple of weeks, but we will keep up our 'treatment' day and night until you beg us to kill you. You will be coughing up small pieces of your own lungs, shivering in fever and horrible pain with every single breath you take, until the pronouncement of your untimely death, most likely 'caused by' pleurisy or pneumonia. You will become a perfect case study for the medical students on the dangers of heavy smoking. Did I make myself clear?"

Without waiting for an answer, the captain turned to the brought-in barber.

"I want a clean face. No cuts, no nicks!" He then added, before walking out of the cell, "You have twenty minutes to be shaved, washed, and dressed."

Shortly thereafter, Prisoner #14352 was escorted across the prison courtyard, which was covered with a thin layer of wet snow. He quickly looked up, trying to absorb just a little bit of the blinding sunlight, and took a few deep breaths of the chilled February morning air before being shoved into a windowless van dubbed the "Black Raven."

During the bumpy ride to the courthouse jail, he recalled the last conversation he'd had with his attorney:

"There is a great deal of commotion in the foreign press about this trial. The other day, Lev Smirnov, the Chairman of the Court, announced that the proceedings would be closed to the public and the foreign press. There is a belief that they will not be able to convict you. Article 70 of the Criminal Code has never been applied to literary fiction. Supporting case law does not exist. You wrote an absurd satirical novel totally removed from the realm of social realism. You described the absurd world of isolation and its absurd inhabitants, which have no meaning or bearing on reality.

"Yes, you did mock the life of imaginary party apparatchiks. Yes, your characters are asinine and stupid. Yes, there are some suggestive innuendos. But it is a work of fiction! Fiction! How can anyone transmogrify the work of literary fiction into anti-Soviet agitation and propaganda? Article 70 deals specifically with 'propaganda conducted for the purpose of undermining the state.' Your fictional characters are idiots

and charlatans. The neighborhood party boss is an incompetent half-wit. The protagonist is a laughable impostor. The mythical town does not exist. The whole thing is absurd. It is a grotesque fable—not propaganda. There is not even a chance of it undermining the state.

"The only delicate issue is publication abroad. But there is no law prohibiting it. It is kind of inimical to the unwritten rules, but that does not amount to a felony. In the worst-case scenario, it's a misdemeanor. The prosecution will try to force you to enter a guilty plea. If you do, they will rip you to shreds regardless of what they promised beforehand, and you will be sentenced to at least seven years at a Siberian labor camp. The accepted routine is to enter a guilty plea and beg for leniency. Not in your case. Forget it. The charge is preposterous. You have to plead not guilty."

The van stopped, and he suddenly heard the roar of a crowd through the now wide-open door. He squinted, blinded by the bright morning sun, and stepped out to be surrounded by the uniformed State Security standing as a human barricade between him and a swarm of supporters. Guards hustled him through the chorus of reassuring screams and encouraging shouts as picket lines of outstretched arms and raised fists flanked them to the towering entrance of the Superior Court.

Once inside, he was placed in the cold silence of a holding cell.

Will I see Masha today? Will they let her in? he asked himself. He had not seen his wife since the day of his arrest. "I think I hugged her for the last time on September sixth, last year—nineteen sixty-five," he muttered, before closing his eyes to collect himself.

The trial lasted for three days. A parade of so-called "experts" and "analysts" was presented by the state to berate, lambaste, and castigate the only available but sealed evidence—his latest novel *Lyubimov*—which had been printed abroad and which none of the witnesses had even been permitted to read.

Talk about absurd! he thought.

He tried in vain to block it out—to ignore all the senseless vitriol. He occupied his time by looking at his wife, who was sitting kitty-corner from him a couple of rows behind and to his left. Their opportunities to make eye contact were brief and infrequent since she was fiercely documenting all the courtroom proceedings in her green leather-bound notebook. The three-day trial turned into a three-ring circus, the only difference being that there was no laughter.

After the last witness finished his diatribe, the chairman of the court, Justice General Smirnov, ordered the defendant to stand up and read his prepared hour-long speech. In concluding, he addressed the defendant.

"After the evidence presented, do you realize the

damage you've inflicted upon our motherland by making a mockery of its people? You did not act alone, but your refusal to name your colluders and conspirators who smuggled that trash work of yours across our borders has proved to the court your total disregard for the well-being of our society. You put your singular, individualistic, selfish aspirations above the collective needs of our nation. Nevertheless, it is never too late to accept your culpability, come up clean, and beg this court for mercy. You have the final word. Do you accept responsibility for your criminal conduct? How do you plead?"

Prisoner #14352 cleared his throat, looked at the presiding judge, and quietly but firmly replied, "You did not show any evidence in support of the crime I am accused of committing. None of your 'experts,' and, I guess, neither of the other two judges, has even read *Lyubimov*. I resolutely declare I am *not* guilty!"

"Take the prisoner away!" Lev Smirnov ordered. "The court will reconvene for sentencing in fifteen minutes."

Fifteen minutes later, the prisoner was brought back into the courtroom to hear the verdict. He looked back at his wife. Masha's eyes were wide open, full, and brown, and her hands nervously squeezed the already-closed green leather-bound notebook. He could read her trembling lips as she mouthed, "I love you. Be strong."

He simply nodded in response.

Justice General Smirnov, flanked by the two other judges, loudly announced, "The Supreme Court of the Russian Soviet Federative Socialist Republic finds the defendant guilty as charged and sentences him to an incarceration for the term of seven years to be served at the strict-regime forced labor camp. This sentence is final and is not subject to an appeal. Handcuff and remove the prisoner. Court is adjourned."

Chapter One

The Salvaged Hope

H appy New Year! Happy 1965!
The headache was unbearable. I was nauseated
and wanted to die. The walls were slowly closing in on
me with little hope of escape. She was sitting on the
edge of the bed, changing the damp cloth on my forehead. What was her name? I knew it, but for the life of
me, I couldn't remember. Her hands were smooth and
pleasantly cold, and it felt so good when she touched
my burning skin. I tried to remember how the last
evening had started ... or maybe it had started a couple of nights before when we'd celebrated my first
poem published in a popular avant-garde magazine
New Word.

Man, it had all started out so cool, when I had
opened that coveted rugged blue magazine cover. I
had seen the list of contributing authors with my name
near to those of famed and respected writers enjoyed
and known by any Russian with a brain! With trepidation and utter disbelief, I'd had to close my eyes and
take a few deep breaths. Then, I had looked again. It
had *still been there* among the other names in the same
font and in alphabetical order. I hadn't been dreaming.

ALLAN ALEXANDER

I had opened the magazine to page 127, and there it was—"The Salvaged Hope"—word for word, one line of my poetry after the other. It had felt like a ladder descending into the depths of the unrevealed, leading down the page in some weaving, accelerating motion with the rhythmical staccato of punctuation marks. Then, the final word, the end of the last syllable, and the silence of understanding. I had shivered with pride when I had called Svetlana to break the news.

On New Year's Eve, we had stopped at a small restaurant across from Pushkin Square, joined by a couple of Svetlana's friends. Several toasts of Champagne later, many others, whom I could not recall, had commingled with us to celebrate the occasion. After a few more drinks, the whole bunch had decided to move on and crash a New Year's party at someone's apartment down the street. I *think* we did it. At that point, my memory went blank.

Now my head was pounding. Between the waves of pain, I could hear a quiet, soothing melody—a rhythmical monologue of a sorrowful singing man in the background of occasionally arguing strings and brass. If only I could understand the English words.

"What is he singing about? Who is that singer?"

"Frank Sinatra," she said.

"What day is today?"

"Saturday, January second."

"It's gonna be a lousy year," I moaned. "I'm so shitfaced."

"Yes, you are definitely three sheets to the wind," she confirmed.

It suddenly hit me that I had been drunk for two whole days. For the first time in my life, I was drunk ... terribly drunk. What a way to start the new year or say goodbye to the old one!

My senses were slowly waking up. Even with my death wish still present, I suddenly recognized that I was feeling the warmth of her body next to mine. It didn't seem to me as if I'd met her a couple of days ago. No! Her face was almost a face that would make me stop and do a double take if I saw her on the street, and when she talked, the sound of her voice covered my skin with goose bumps. I was possessed by the magical power of her hazel eyes, which permeated the space around us with an almost shamanistic, ineffable glow. She was so indefinably gentle. I could sense the waves of her breath on my chest. It felt so familiar, and the scent of her skin was causing my troubled head to spin ... Cowardly, I stretched my hand into the darkness and touched her breast.

She suddenly straightened her back, slowly removed my hand, and leaned closer to me. "I don't think so," she whispered and moved away.

I wanted to die!

Her incantation was so disarming. I had never felt that way about any other girl. Had there been other girls? I was not a virgin, but the desire for Svetlana was so dominant that it felt like I was. It made my mind tumble. Had we been intimate the other night? I could not recall ... Maybe? Had we? We'd stayed alone in her friend's apartment filled with soft music and intriguing darkness. Had it been her, the shadow sitting far away on the other edge of the bed?

The sudden thunder of her whispered words—*I don't think so*—kicked me right back into the misery of my pounding headache and poisonous nausea. The sad man was still singing, and I did not remember his name.

"What is your name?" I asked, burning with shame.

"Why wouldn't you try to sleep ..." Svetlana answered.

I closed my eyes ...

January in Moscow is usually cold. The morning air was crisp in my mouth. I was running on a slippery sidewalk, trying to beat the clock. Class starts at 8:30. Physics. The New Year's break had come to an end. For the last few days, Svetlana and I had stayed together, hiding from the rest of the world in her friend's vacant apartment.

I'd shown up at my parents' doorway the previous night to admit that I had not stayed with my Aunt Anna and to declare that I was insanely in love. There'd been a long and unpleasant conversation with my dad, who had been vehemently irate about my poem being published in *New Word*. First, it was "utterly insane and irresponsible" of me to write of such things people hadn't even dared to whisper about only a few years ago, jeopardizing everyone's safety and my own future. Second, I was too immature to become involved with a girl I had only recently met and was stupid enough to be lured into her bed. One of us obviously refused to understand that I was mature enough to think for myself and to fall in love.

The "responsibility" argument, which I had heard so many times before, did not sound any more convincing than it had on previous occasions. I realized that I was in trouble and that some harsh reprimand was on its way, yet I was ready to endure the punishment. Suspense, on the other hand, was a harsher form of torture.

That morning, my dad just shook his head and said, "What an idiot!" in response to my "Good morning!" He refused to say another word.

I have to talk to Aunt Anna tonight; she will help me deal with my folks, I thought in an effort to calm myself down.

My physics teacher, Ivan Petrovich Maximov, who was also the school's principal, never missed a chance to confront me. His hatred of me was slightly more obvious than my hatred of him. The closer I came to graduating, the more vicious his verbal affronts became.

"This ill-minded, word-rhyming abysmal friend of ours is planning to apply to medical school," he'd announced sarcastically to the class a couple weeks prior. "You will be accepted to medical school over my dead body!" he had hissed sadistically, flashing his torturous smile.

"*Your* dead body?" I had mumbled under my breath. "I wouldn't mind."

He had heard me, and I had been suspended for the rest of the final week. My dad had been furious.

What does Maximov have for me today? I wondered. *Today is Friday. I like physics but dislike my teacher.*

I was late, but the classroom door had not yet been shut. Maximov looked at me as I slipped in, and before I could open my mouth to apologize, he pointed to an empty seat in the front row. I sat and quietly began unpacking my book bag.

A long and unpleasant silence prompted me to look up. I was still somewhat hung-over from the last few nights and was in no shape to stir up trouble. I bumped into Maximov's angry stare. He held the latest issue of *New Word* in his hands.

Whoever blinks first loses, flashed in my head. I felt like that terrible New Year's headache was ready to burst between my eyes.

"The Salvaged Hope?!" he exclaimed, shaking the magazine open. His eyes were filled with rage. "Well, well, well ... There is *no* hope left for you in *our* world!" He smacked the *New Word* against my desk and threw it on the floor. "Am I right, class?"

I heard a single, lonely chuckle coming from behind me; the rest of the class remained silent. I leaned forward to pick the magazine up, but Maximov kicked it away from me.

"You wanna try that again, punk?"

As if what my dad had started the other night hadn't been enough, now I had to deal with Maximov. *Why are they so adamantly against my poetry? And why do I have to take more crap from this moron?* I was no longer a child. I would be graduating in four months.

Our eyes met again. I refused to blink first.

"Why are you staring at me like you're gonna eat me alive?" he fizzled.

"I am a Jew," I replied, still not blinking. "We do not eat pork."

"Get out! Now!" Maximov went ballistic. "You're finished! Get the hell out! You Jew bastard! Out of here! Out, out, out!" He was foaming at the mouth, stomping his foot on the floor, repeatedly pointing his right index finger in the direction of the classroom door, and going almost apoplectic in his 'righteous indignation'.

I slammed the classroom door, but the echo of his shouts rolled after my footsteps in the empty hallway. "Out of my class! Out of my school! Out of my life!"

I was standing transfixed outside the school door. *What the hell just happened? How will I graduate? How will I break this news to my dad? Why is everyone at odds with me?* I felt lost. Was my demeanor symptomatic of my yet unrealized maturity, which had suddenly gotten off the ground on the other side of that doorway? I did not know for certain then, but one thing I was sure about … I'd been expelled.

Happy New Year!

Chapter Two

Aunt Anna

Aunt Anna, my mom's younger sister, was the one and only friend I could trust.

"Happy New Year, my dear!" she said as she hugged me. "Come right in. I saw the new issue of *New Word*. Reading your piece of poetry in print was simply breathtaking. Attaboy! You never cease to amaze me. I am so proud of you. Congrats!"

Like my mom, she was short and stocky, and she was by far the smartest and warmest person one could ever find. She was the brilliant and adroit head editor of the publishing house Arts. Three years before I had been born, her only son, my cousin Felix, had passed away from a blood infection at the age of fifteen. That had happened during World War II, also known as the Great Patriotic War. Three months prior to the end of the war, I had come into the world to be engulfed by my aunt's unconditional and endless love.

"By the way, why didn't you call? Where have you been for the last few days? Why do you look so unhappy? What's going on?"

She was my protector, my mentor, and my dearest friend. Whenever I got in trouble, she defended me selflessly. She was my shield from the righteous anger of my mom and dad. My biggest fear was the fear of upsetting her. Instead of punishment, there would be a calm, reassuring talk as she coached me on how to control my emotions, how to use my God-given ability to think, how to be reasonable, and how to use my common sense to handle the intractable waves of my rebellious juvenile imagination. Rather than a reprimand, what I would get were her conciliatory pearls of wisdom, which I would never forget.

Her apartment was situated on Garden Ring just a few blocks away from my parent's place. The century-old estate, which had been the residence of the famous Russian opera bass Fyodor Shalyapin, had been converted to a communal apartment after his death in 1938. A heavy granite memorial plaque in his honor decorated the exterior wall next to Aunt Anna's study window. The building was dwarfed by a ten-story Stalin-era architectural behemoth next door, which hosted the American embassy.

That day at the end of the first week of January, I stood in my aunt's doorway and breathed heavily. "Ha-happy New Year, Aunt Anna!" I stuttered. "I w-was expelled ..."

She knew about my numerous bouts with Maximov and had always warned me to be careful with people like him. After listening to my version of the day's events, she took my hands in hers, looked straight into my eyes, and quietly drilled into me another pearl of her wisdom.

"Alex, your poetry aside, is it so difficult to remember that God gave you a tongue *to conceal* your thoughts? When will you man up? You should never pick a fight until you are prepared to win."

"I lost my cool, Auntie."

"You lost your school as well … and just four months before graduation, thanks to your sharp tongue. Where did it get you this time? In trouble … again."

"What can I do?" I felt totally addled.

"It's what *I can do* to save your butt."

"There will be no medical school without a high school diploma first," I said.

"We have to plan something to salvage your graduation without jeopardizing your admission to medical school."

"If nothing works out, I still have my writing to fall back on. My poetry—"

She interrupted me without giving me a chance to finish my thought.

"What in the world are you talking about? Most of the time you act like an adult, but sometimes, when you blurt out things like this, I suddenly see the remnants of your immaturity. Do not even think about giving up your career in medicine for your poetry. You never know what can happen in our country. Our 'comrades in charge' can take your poetry away!"

She then lowered her voice. "They can close magazines, stop publications. It has happened here before. They can take everything away from you … everything but your knowledge. Get accepted to medical school. Study as hard as you can. Graduate. Become the physician you've dreamed of being since you were a child, and … keep writing."

I felt that day's events finally catching up with me, and I was horrified by the realization that medical school could slip right through my fingers, giving way to the inescapable and glum reality of a compulsory military draft. "I am EXPELLED!" I screamed. "I'm screwed!"

"First, don't freak out. Pull yourself together, and learn what not to do next time. Second, don't dwell on a problem—search for a remedy. I am expecting one of my writer friends, Andrey Simyavsky. You have met him here before. He might be able to help us."

"I remember talking to him more than a couple of times. He is the famed Moscow State University professor of Russian literature, isn't he? I remember he liked my poetry, but how can he help me with high school now?" I was confused.

"He is not at the university any longer. He teaches

a Russian literature class at a nearby high school right around the corner from here. I happen to know the school principal there too. If we can talk your parents into allowing you to move in with me, you will be in that high school's jurisdiction."

"Auntie!" I cried out. "You are a genius!"

"Hold your horses, young fellow," she said, cutting me short. "We have to persuade Andrey Simyavsky and your parents first. In less than an hour, he will be here to meet with Alexander Tardovsky, the head editor of *New Word*, to discuss some serious matters. Are you staying or going home?"

"Can I stay?"

"Of course, you can; just call your mom."

The doorbell rang.

"I hope Andrey gets here first. Wait." Aunt Anna went to answer the door.

"How are you, my fellow writer?" Simyavsky walked in with the energy of a steamroller. "I read the latest issue of *New Word* and your new poem 'The Salvaged Hope.' Awesome! Impressive stuff! It's abrasively sharp and dangerously honest. Kudos to you, my friend! Now, after your head stops spinning from all the accolades and congratulations on becoming a published author, take a deep breath and promise your aunt and me that you'll be extra careful. I can bet you've already aroused a particular crowd and pissed off some powerful people at the same time. Welcome to the world of passion and poison."

"He got his portion of poison today," Aunt Anna said. "He lashed out his sharp tongue at his high school principal, Maximov, and got himself expelled."

"Ouch," Simyavsky frowned in disgust. "I know who Maximov is. What did you say to piss him off?"

"He implied that I wanted to eat him alive, and I informed him that we Jews do not eat pork."

"That's funny and right on target," he chuckled. "Maximov, I know, is a typical academic, lowlife, anti-Semitic pig. I knew a few Jewish writers who spent a number of years in labor camps during Stalin's reign because of Maximov and his buddies. They were the first ones to offer testimony at every trial dealing with cosmopolitan ideology, Jewish conspiracy, and anti-Soviet agitation and propaganda."

"Throwing Alex out before graduation," my aunt intervened, "could jeopardize his admission to medical school."

"Still thinking about medical school?" Simyavsky slowly leaned against the wall, stretching out his right hand, and suddenly, I saw the famed Russian literature professor everybody talked about so much.

"Good for you! I am passionate about your poetry, but I am even more excited about your persistent desire to become a physician. Actually, this is great, Alex. Look back at the history of our literature. Dichotomy, it is not. The great Anton Chekhov, for example, was a physician. He gave us a paradigm of how to cure the human body as a physician and how to dig deep into the human soul as a writer. His efforts should not be squandered, and you have the capacity to ensure that doesn't happen. You will write and you will heal. Pursue your goals with an open heart. You can do it. Nothing will stop you! Nothing—not even Maximov."

"Thank you for the accolades, Andrey. But come back to Earth," Aunt Anna interrupted him. "What we need from you right now is to transfer Alex to your school to graduate. You won't be sorry. The kid has an amazing, almost photographic memory and unbelievable retention ability. He will be your star student. Trust me. I am asking you to help us."

"You do not have to ask, Anna," Simyavsky replied without hesitation. "It would be my pleasure to help your nephew. Our principal is a good man and a friend of mine as well. Consider it done. Alex," he turned to me, "come to my office on Monday at eight o'clock sharp. We will take care of the necessary paperwork. Just between us big boys, keep your mouth shut. You don't need to create any more false friends and true enemies. Be smart. I mean, be smarter. Are we on the same page?"

"Thank you. I do understand," I replied gratefully.

"You are a dear friend, Andrey," my aunt said. "Keep an eye on him, please."

"Will do; will do," he replied while checking his watch. "Is Tardovsky still coming? I have to give him a piece of my mind."

I turned to my aunt and hugged her. "You are the best! I love you, Auntie."

She was the one who believed in my writing, helped me to develop my poetry skills, and inspired me to write more. She had also introduced me to Alexander Tardovsky, the head editor at *New Word*, a year ago and was totally responsible for my literary success.

"Now," she said, "do me a favor. Be quiet for a couple of hours. You can sit and listen if you want. Andrey, you don't mind, do you?"

"Not at all," Simyavsky answered. "Let the youngster learn about his new mentor, Tardovsky, who I'm sure won't mind either."

She opened the door to her study. I followed her in and melted into my favorite corner. I was so grateful for the opportunity to experience countless long evenings in her study, surrounded by piles of books and open manuscripts.

I witnessed the most unbelievable readings, presentations, and fiery discussions among the best writers, poets, and critics of that time. I was like a kid in a candy store, quietly sitting in a shadowed corner on the second step of an old library ladder that leaned against ceiling-high bookshelves, mesmerized by moments of brilliance and inspiration. Lately, discussions were becoming increasingly intense, opinions were being expressed unapologetically, and loud arguments were beginning to turn into finger pointing and, sometimes, bitter whispering quarrels.

Aunt Anna answered the doorbell, and a moment later, Tardovsky was in the room.

He nodded in my direction. "Your piece created a lot of chatter over the last couple of days, kid. Enjoy the moment, and do not lose your head."

He shook hands with Simyavsky and quietly said, "I don't know how to break it to you gently, Andrey. But it was dangerously stupid to send your manuscript abroad. It was dangerous, and it was stupid. I know that you did it a couple of times before. Do not deny it, please. What good came out of it?"

Tardovsky and his editorial board did not support Simyavsky's efforts to find ways—short of underground self-publishing, dubbed Samizdat—to print his novel abroad. Today, Tardovsky was the bearer of even more bad news. Despite his earnest efforts to gain censorship consensus to publish just a couple chapters of Simyavsky's latest novel, *Lyubimov*, in *New Word*, his request had been denied.

Although Simyavsky's temper was well known, he could control it most of the time, but not this time.

"I write to be read," he exploded, "not to be lectured by some idiot in the ideology section of the Writers' Union about my inability to follow the principles of social realism and my unpatriotic motives, and not to be banned from publishing!"

"And how do you think printing your book in England or Switzerland under the pen name Avrum Hertz will change this idiot's opinion? Like he doesn't have a clue or will never find out who Avrum Hertz is."

"What a dumb thing to ask! Why would I hallucinate about changing the censor's opinion? I just want to print my book abroad and then smuggle it back a few copies at a time. There are some brave souls among the foreign press corps who are willing to help; they're working on it as we speak."

"Have you ever thought about the consequences?"

"What can they do? Shoot me?"

"Actually, they can."

"They've already shot me right in the balls. They've castrated me, creatively speaking. For more than five years, I've been writing in-the-desk. Do you know what that means? It means that all my work is useless; it has nowhere to go. Not one publisher is allowed to even talk to me. How can a writer exist this way?"

"You have to wait a little longer. Be a bit more patient. Things are changing. It's going to be better … soon. Publishing your work abroad is like pitching red meat to vicious dogs. It will only delay that long-awaited change. You are not alone in your struggle."

"If I am not alone, where are my freedom-loving brethren?"

"Be careful. Do not shout," Tardovsky said.

"Careful?" Simyavsky went postal. "Careful? You and your bunch of fuckers! Where are all of you? Why couldn't I hear your angry voices at Writers' Union meetings? Where are all of you hiding? Get your heads out of your rectums! Is your courage limited to just fearless whispers and valorous ass kissing?"

"Come on! Being brave does not always mean being bold, direct, and dumb …" Tardovsky kept his calm, resisting the urge to use expletives. "It takes a lot more skill and a lot more patience to subvert restrictive censorship by quietly spreading the word and influencing the public opinion of the free world. We have to build the pressure from the outside. And we have to be smart about it."

"Those bastards will outsmart you ten times over before you know it. We have to raise the boiling point from within. More and more people are listening to *Voice of America, Radio Free Europe*, and *Deutsche Welle*. Our people are hungry to know the truth. We have to bring the printed word back to them. It's not for my own satisfaction that I'm willing to put everything on the line."

"I am not questioning your motives. I am questioning your methods, my friend. We all have the same goal, but what you are doing makes this goal harder and harder to reach. You are provoking outright editorial terror as a consequence of your actions."

The point of contention was intensified censorship at every level. For the last few years, there had been palpable hints of the iron fist relaxing its grip on creative freedom, but "Khrushchev's Thaw" did not last long, and it existed now more in our dreams than in the grim reality. A few works of Solzhenitsyn, including his *Cancer Ward*, and then many others were denied printing rights after a brief mysterious publication of *One Day in the Life of Ivan Denisovich* in Tardovsky's *New Word*.

As a result, a few brave writers snuck their typescripts out of the country. After a couple of them were published abroad and the printed books were smuggled back, the authorities went mad and unleashed the wrath of surveillance, intimidation, and persecution at every level of cultural, if not political, discourse. The goal was to squash ideological opposition.

"Did it help your late mentor Boris Pasternak when Isaiah Berlin smuggled his *Doctor Zhivago* manuscript to England and then to Italy, where it was finally published?" Tardovsky argued.

"His Italian publisher, Giangiacomo Feltrinelli, only did it because your editorial board at *New Word* didn't have the balls to publish it first. Did you put your life on the line to fight for it?" Simyavsky fired back.

"Easy, my friend, easy. I was not in charge there at that time. What about his Nobel Prize in literature that he was not even allowed to travel to receive?"

"What about it?"

"Did it help him? Did it save him from the government's wrath?" Tardovsky was trying to plead his point. "Has it helped any of us since? No, it has not! If you want to become a martyr, go ahead, but your martyrdom will negatively affect all of us who are collectively trying to bring change ... And then I can't help you!"

"And then," Simyavsky went ballistic, "you and all of your Writers' Union cronies can collectively kiss my ass! I do not need your magazine, and I do not need your help! I'll see you Monday morning, fella!" he said to me on his way out before slamming the door.

"As always," said Tardovsky, "leaving with a bang."

Chapter Three
Friends

The following Monday at eight in the morning, I walked into the principal's office at City School 114. Andrey Denisovich Simyavsky was already there waiting to introduce me to his old friend, Principal Gleb Sergeevich Golov. I found out later that they had met in the Army during the Great Patriotic War somewhere near Stalingrad. Both men had been wounded on the same day, decorated with the Red Star Order for heroism on the battlefield, and had become close friends while supporting each other during the few months they'd spent in the military hospital, recuperating from their injuries.

After the war, both men had been sent to study at Moscow State University, and five years later, they had graduated with honors on the same day. Golov had received his master's degree in education and Simyavsky in philology. Golov had been sent to rebuild a couple of failing schools in Moscow's Krasnaya Presnya neighborhood, while Simyavsky had been asked to stay on at the university as an adjunct professor in the Department of Russian Literature.

Both men were the epitome of professional success.

In a few years, in what was nothing short of an academic miracle, the failing schools had been transformed under Golov's tutelage, and Professor Simyavsky's university course on the history of Russian literature had become an intellectual feast. Andrey's lectures had captivated the prodigious audience that overcrowded the largest lecture hall of the main campus at Lenin's Heights. His class had been a phenomenon; like a magnet, he had attracted every intellectual interested in the roots of early Russian surrealism and its transformation through the art of creative writing. His own publications, columns, and critical reviews of contemporary Soviet literature had not been habitually barbed but delicately and skillfully keened. He had almost virtually dissected the works with a surgical instrument capable of precisely carving the human mind. In a short while, the enigma of Andrey Simyavsky had been heedfully revered by some and resentfully regardeded by others.

A few years had passed, and Golov had been offered a promotion to the State Department of Education. He had declined, expressing his dislike for the bureaucrats and refusing to join their ranks; instead, he had chosen to be a real educator and a staunch advocate for children. He had accepted the position of principal at City School 114, which was situated near Rebellion Square, the same school from which he had graduated before the start of the Great Patriotic War.

In the meantime, the growing academic and literary influence of Simyavsky—his lectures, publications, and the overwhelming number of applicants to his class—had drawn the watchful eye of the State Security's Department of Ideology. His perceived notoriety had prompted authorities to unleash a campaign of brazen reviews in *Pravda, Izvestiya*, and *Literaturnaya Gazeta*, describing him as the enemy of social realism and the oracle of hostile Western ideology. Shortly after the appearance of those articles, Simyavsky had been dismissed from Moscow State University for "irresponsible and deplorable academic conduct." It had been at the end of "Khrushchev's Thaw" and marked the beginning of "Re-Stalinization" and the "nut-tightening" era of Brezhnev's new rule.

Golov had proven to be a real friend. A couple of days after Simyavsky's dismissal from Moscow State University, Golov had gone out of his way to secure a position for him as a Russian literature instructor at City School 114. The Regional Board of Education had vehemently opposed such an appointment. To overcome the resistance of the Board, Golov had enlisted the support of an influential group of Veterans of the Great Patriotic War and the Fraternity of the Cavaliers of the Red Star Order, including a few of two- and three-star generals and even a couple of deputies of the Supreme Soviet. The Regional Board of

Education had reluctantly succumbed to the pressure and approved Simyavsky as the head of Russian literature department at City School 114.

All this had taken place less than a year ago.

"Are you ready?" Simyavsky asked, pushing me through the open door of the principal's office without waiting for my answer.

"Good morning, Gleb Sergeevich. I'd like to introduce you to my young friend, Alexander Loevsky. As I briefed you earlier, after an unfortunate encounter last Friday with one notorious high school principal, Alexander was expelled from City School one-twenty-eight. I think you know my old and trusted friend Anna Amchislavsky, the head editor of Art Publishing House. Alexander is her nephew, and she pleaded with both of us to help the kid so he can graduate this academic year. His application to sit for the medical school entrance exam has already been accepted, but Anna was afraid that Maximov's shenanigans could put it all in jeopardy."

Golov leaned back in his chair and, after a pause, said, "So, Alex, looks like Maximov is not one of your favorite people." There was a hint of a smile on the principal's lips, and it felt as if his sharp eyes were drilling into my face.

"Andrey's introduction was quite compelling, and I happen to know your aunt rather well. She is the most wonderful and resilient person I've ever met. I assume it's not easy being under her guardianship. How good are you, academically speaking? We don't have your transcripts yet."

"For the last four years, I've never gotten a 'B.' I've been a straight 'A' student so far." I answered proudly.

"And what exactly did you do to get expelled?"

"I made a few sarcastic remarks to Comrade Maximov against my better judgment."

"Is that your assessment or your aunt's?" Golov was still smiling while his eyes continued to explore my brain. "Please be honest, young man," he added.

"My aunt's," I responded humbly.

"And what about your assessment, Alex, if I may ask?" continued Golov.

"I am sorry, but I could not resist the temptation. Maximov had been on my case for quite a while, looking to pick a fight, tempting me to insult him, taunting me to turn thuggish. He stated in front of the whole class that I would become a physician only over his dead body. He couldn't stand me for being a Jew, like I could do anything about it."

"What do you think you can do?" Golov was probing. His sharp eyes took over my brain, and I suddenly opened up.

"I do not understand what I can do. I recognize that I was born this way, but I don't believe that I am different from any other Russian. I speak Russian, I think Russian, I live Russian, I write Russian, and still I am called a Jew. I am disliked for I don't know what. I am ashamed to a degree for not being like everybody else, but I think I am like everybody else, and I don't know how to make my point ... how to bring it across."

"Do you have to bring it across?" Golov continued calmly.

"If I don't, how can I stop Maximov from mocking me?" I asked in quiet desperation.

"I don't believe you can stop him," Golov responded in a soft tone, "people like Maximov will always exist. You don't have to prove anything to their kind. Nothing will satisfy them. My advice to you is to learn what you are. Knowledge is your best weapon. Learn about your history, regardless of how difficult it is. Study your people's past. The realization of your roots will bring you pride instead of shame. It will make you stronger.

"Trust me, the overwhelming majority of Russians, me and Andrey included, do not share Maximov's views. We defeated Nazi Germany in the Great Patriotic War, but we still have to defeat the fascists in our midst—the ones, like Maximov, who poison the surrounding air with their vitriol toward Jews. Dismiss them. Learn about yourself. Forget about their kind and become proud of what you are."

"Alex happens to be one talented poet, already published in Tardovsky's *New Word* magazine," Simyavsky added.

"You see," Golov replied, "there is a lot for you to be proud of. Got it?" He paused for a moment, and his eyes warmed up into a gentle smile. "Welcome to our school, Alex. You will find it quite different. We have some awesome folks over here. Make yourself at home."

He got up and shook my hand for a few long moments while still drilling me with his sharp and slightly squinty eyes. "I have to confess ..." He put both of his hands on my shoulders and quietly continued, "I think I know why Maximov flipped. I read your 'Salvaged Hope' the other day. It's truly brave. Surprisingly strong for a man of your age. Be careful, but rest assured that you are among friends here. I will ask Andrey Denisovich to take care of you personally."

"Thank you, Gleb Sergeevich," I said, opening the door. I was startled by his revelation, and at the same time, comforted by his protecting kindness.

"I do appreciate your help, Gleb. I'll call Anna right away. She is waiting," Simyavsky added. He then got up to leave the room.

"My pleasure," Golov replied. "Send Anna my regards. Tell her we have to get together soon for old time's sake."

I heard the office door softly squeak closed behind us.

"Let's go to my office and try to set up your schedule, young fellow." Andrey Simyavsky put his arm around my shoulder, and we started walking together through the labyrinth of corridors at my new school.

"How do you like my old friend and your new principal?"

"I do like him; he is not Maximov, for sure," I replied.

"Not at all. I would dare to say he is quite the opposite. Honest. Direct. Great man. Loves the kids. This school is his life."

"There is something in the way he looks at you. You know… It's something in his eyes. It feels as if he is looking right through you, like putting you under his spell. I tried to be careful and not to show what I really felt deep inside, but somehow he made me open up."

"That is my friend Gleb at his best. He reads people; he knows how to bring out their very essence. It's a gift. Some students love him, some are afraid of him, but all respect him," he concluded at the end of our walk as he opened the door to his small office.

It didn't take long to go over the schedule and my class assignments. We were done in less than an hour.

I was ready to leave when Simyavsky gestured for me to stay.

Out of nowhere, he said, "I would like to get together sometime to talk about your poetry, if you don't mind. It could be a fascinating journey, young fellow, if you do it right. Your writing is bold and gutsy, but I know only one side of it—the published side. Indeed, you express your social attitudes pretty well. What about a softer, more lyrical side? Have you ever been in love? Have you written anything romantic?"

"Yes, I have, but it's personal. I don't know if I want to reveal it. I'm afraid it wouldn't be interesting to anybody but a few Peeping Toms. This sort of public 'lovemaking' might be entertaining for a couple of voyeurs, but certainly demeaning for the rest of those involved."

"I understand why this could unnerve you, but let me take it to a different level. I am talking about art, not pornography. I can show you the way to learn the mastery of expression; to mesmerize your readers; to make them feel, see, and touch through you, through your senses. You can become their medium, their key to the mystery of human passion, to the yet unknown universe of unrealized emotions. Think about it for a while … Let me know."

"I will … I definitely will," I hurried to respond.

"I have to go teach my class in a few minutes,"

Simyavsky said, "and you have to locate your class-room in the meantime. I think it's on the second floor. Can you find it on your own?"

"I sure can. Thank you, Andrey Denisovich," I said as I left his office, feeling grateful and a bit over-whelmed by his unsolicited interest in my poetry. How did he know that I was of two minds about sharing with Tardovsky all that stuff I'd written about Svetlana and me? How did he sense it? His words about learning "the mastery of expression" were so in keeping with my quest for his guidance. For me, he was a literary giant—the celebrated Moscow State University pro-fessor of Russian literature whom everyone had been talking about just a few short months ago.

I stood motionless outside his office, holding the door handle, downright bewildered by his offer to be my literary mentor. It felt like divine providence. At that very moment, I realized that some inordinate and unfamiliar force was about to change my destiny. It had transplanted me to a new school, connected me with kindhearted people, and surrendered me to the capti-vating influence of Andrey Denisovich Simyavsky.

Chapter Four

Entrance Exams

Winter was pretty much done. Spring had pushed it away, warming and refreshing the cold, gloomy air that had been hanging over Moscow for nearly five lengthy months. It almost felt as if people's hearts were also waking up and thawing out. Here and there, one could see hints of sparse and unexplainable smiles occasionally dressing up the faces of the previously gray and seemingly indifferent street crowd. By the time final exams were over, the basswood trees parading the streets in their naked glory had started to doll up in green, filling the fresh air with the flirtatiously sweet aroma of fleeting but powerful blooms. In a little while, white petals covered the sidewalks, pretending to deck out the city streets for graduation day.

The new school was like a breath of fresh air. Everything seemed different. Without exception, teachers and students appeared to be a notch smarter and far friendlier than at the old school. The graduating class was much more mature, and the great majority of us were studying genuinely hard to be ready for the universities' entrance exams, which were coming up barely a few short weeks after graduation.

For the most part, in the rest of the civilized world, four full years of college preceded entry into any professional school. This gave high school graduates plenty of time to mature and make up their minds about what to do with their lives. In the Soviet Union, the structure of higher education, along with everything else of importance, was quite different and, most of the time, did not make any sense.

Here, on the contrary, decisions and choices about one's life journey had to be dealt with during the last couple years of high school by the "ripe" age of eighteen. Only a few among us were mature or lucky enough to make the correct choice and to endure the following years of professional school without having regrets in the midst or at the end of our studies. Contrastingly, the rest of the flock hated everything about their hastily chosen métier and had to struggle with boredom and mediocrity for the remainder of their unfortunate lives.

I had dreamt of being a physician from as far back as I could remember, so my choice had been very clear to me for a long time. Medicine and poetry could co-exist forever, so I thought. There was no doubt in my mind that I would ultimately ascend to become an accomplished physician, but somehow, the struggle to climb the poetical Mount Everest on my own proved to be quite daunting and despairing.

My unbelievable luck had led me to Andrey Simyavsky, and not surprisingly, his mentorship had significantly improved my writing skills and unleashed a real poet in me within just a few short months of our collaboration. With his help, I felt like I could finally see the peak of that mountain; my Everest was almost conquered. I was totally enthralled by the seemingly endless view from the imaginary top of my literary future, which was filled with a burning desire for upcoming recognition and well-deserved fame.

Little did I know then …

Andrey and I spent a lot of time together. My aunt was worried that I would neglect my studies and that it could have a negative effect on my grades.

"Alex, you have to keep your grades up. Only straight 'A's will guarantee your acceptance. There is a quota on the number of Jews allowed to be accepted into medical school. It is not just a rumor. It's our sad reality… an unspoken directive coming from above. You are a Jew. The odds are stacked against us. Getting the very top grades are your only insurance, your only chance to tip the 'scales of justice'. I know that you are a good student, but you spend too much time with Andrey, honing your poetry. Do not neglect your studies, I beg of you."

"Auntie Anna, stop tormenting yourself," I argued. "I get straight 'A's, and I will continue to do so, trust me, but I love my poetry, and Andrey has opened my eyes to such an intricate side of it. I've had unbelievable time writing under his tutelage. And yes, I've heard the stories that, in the past during Stalin's reign, there was a Jewish quota, but Stalin's been dead for more than ten years. Times have changed. People have changed. That rubbish is over."

I hugged her, and she looked back at me as if she were ready to give up. "Yes, things are different," she breathed out, shaking her head, "but chieftains are still the same. I worry about you, my dear boy. Medicine is still much safer than poetry around here. I am going to talk to Andrey anyway."

The next day, I overheard Andrey saying to my aunt, "Anna, cut him some slack, please. He is not a kid any longer. You don't need any other proof; just read his work. He writes like a fully ripened author— as well if not better than any of us. I'll make sure he does not neglect his studies. Stop worrying; he will do fine. Be proud of him; he is turning out to be an inspiring poet. Let him loose."

Shortly thereafter, because of Andrey's insistence, I was finally welcomed into a small circle of my aunt's literary colleagues and friends, where I spent much of my time listening and learning.

Andrey pulled out of me a bunch of unfinished poems that I had written to Svetlana and had kept secret.

We started to work on them together, uncovering new styles and trying new structures and cadences. The improvement was so physically palpable that Andrey insisted on showing my new work to Tardovsky. I agreed, although, initially, I was hesitant. To my disbelief, Tardovsky was enthusiastic about my newly discovered genre.

"Your rebellious political poetry would sound much sharper and more abrasive if it were interlaced with personal, lyrical works of yours from time to time. Let us continue to mix it up. Our readers are looking for the unexpected ... for surprises and challenges," he concluded, nodding his head approvingly.

From that point on, with his patronage, my poetry became almost a regular monthly feature in *New Word* magazine. Within a very short time, my alliance with Andrey Simyavsky had turned into an invaluable creative camaraderie.

All other things aside, graduation day came and went like a single breath of spring air. The traditional school assemblies were all decorated in the same red banners, and chest-thumping, patriotic speeches reminded us all that we were forever indebted to our glorious Communist Party and all its distinguished leaders for the gift of knowledge. Then, at home, never-ending renditions of popular jokes mocked and belittled the same leaders behind closed doors.

The traditional endless shots of vodka were drunk around tightly seated tables covered with crisp white tablecloths and an assortment of appetizers artfully crafted from what was seemingly the same staple foods—cabbage, potatoes, onions, and herring. Friends and relatives gave incessant toasts to health, success, happiness, and the hope for an immediate, long-lasting, and better future. At the very end, competing voices of the inebriated delivered old patriotic war songs intermingled with the angry lyrics of newly written guitar ballads, like a descending lullaby finally tucking in neighborhoods on the verge of sleep.

Nevertheless, the next morning came, bringing nothing new or better—only massive headaches and hangovers accompanied by a ghastly smell permeating trolleys, buses, and subway trains.

Anyone getting ready for the universities' entrance exams had to skip or limit the punishing part of that celebration and submit themselves to another few weeks of grueling studies and review sessions. I managed to escape early that night to join Svetlana in her friend's vacant apartment to indulge myself in everything that a horny eighteen-year-old shaver could only dream about.

Svetlana was the perfect lover; her slim body,

velvety skin, and long, silky curls of aureate hair were obviously created in heaven. Her green eyes were mesmerizing, and the sound of her soft voice always covered my skin with goose bumps. She was a perfect love goddess—beautiful, passionate, playful ... and insatiable.

Svetlana looked eighteen. When we'd first met, she'd told me that she was a few years older than I and that she was attending Moscow University, where she was studying at the Jurisprudence School. Never one to show passion for her studies, she'd recently explained to me that philosophy or theory of law did not excite her and that she'd only chosen to pursue a law degree because of her dad's tenacious insistence.

I was astonished and delighted, however, by the unanticipated depth of her knowledge of history, literature, and the arts. She could talk on the subject of ancient Rome and discuss Cicero's oratorical gift forever. Sometimes it felt like her erudition was nonchalantly spontaneous and had no limits, and that alone made me feel hopelessly possessed by her.

Our *libidinous getaway* had been emotionally exhilarating and ardent. On the last night of our stay, in the darkness of the room, Svetlana was sitting naked on the windowsill. Held spellbound by the streetlights, she slowly recited a few translated stanzas of Omar Khayyam:

"... *and none there is to tell us in plain truth* ..."

I interrupted her, finishing the next line:

"... *whence do we come and whither do we go.*"

Startled, she froze and then slowly turned my way, shaking her head as if attempting to recover from her daze. Suddenly, she leapt across the room and lunged back into the bed. She wrapped her arms and legs around me, shivering in titillation.

"I can't believe it. I didn't think you knew Omar Khayyam. I'm shocked," she muttered in my ear.

"What are you so shocked about? I love Khayyam a lot, and I know most of his work by heart, sweet cheeks," I whispered back.

"Are you trying to enrapture me?" She jokingly pushed me away, got up on her knees, and towered above my head. "Khayyam is my favorite poet. Got it?"

"Favorite? He is your favorite? How about another poet—the one you just made love to? What about him?" I protested.

"Calm down..." She kissed me on the forehead. "He is my favorite only second to you, silly." She kissed me again and laid her head on my chest. "I feel so different around you... You are my escape from this world filled with boredom and stupidity. Is that about us? Is there a chance we are made for each other?"

"What do we know?" I mumbled.

Suddenly, she feigned a frown and challenged me

again. "How about this one?" Her daring eyes darted at me from under her eyebrows,

"*... there was a door to which I found no key ...*"

I was ready and fired back,

"*... there was the veil through which I might not see.*"

She rolled around, leaned over, and kissed me slowly. I was fading away in the sweetness of her lips, which were spiced by the salt of her tears. We devoured the rest of the night, lost in each other's arms, laughing and crying between the sheets, making love and reciting verses from Khayyam's "Rubaiyat" over and over until the calm of the morning twilight lulled us both to sleep.

It was the last time we spent a few days in a row together. I thought I was deeply in love with her, but at times, it felt as if she were playing me by disappearing off the face of the earth for days or weeks at a time.

In the morning, she vanished again without even a phone call. In a way, it was a blessing in disguise. I spent the next month studying for the entrance exams without any interruptions, and the time passed swiftly.

A couple of days before the exams, Svetlana called from out of nowhere to wish me good luck. She apologized for her absence and told me that she'd left to tend to a sick uncle somewhere near Leningrad and that she'd been thinking of me the entire time. She said she hadn't wanted to interrupt my studies with her phone calls.

I was glued to the phone, mesmerized by the sound of her voice and unable to respond coherently. It seemed I could feel her breath.

"You should've called, but I was talking to you every day anyway, and I was writing every word down," I said. "When you come back, there is a lot of poetry waiting for you. I miss you, Svetlana."

"I will call you the moment I return," she promised.

"I love you," I said.

"Same here," Svetlana replied before hanging up the phone.

Peculiarly, I was becoming more and more attracted to her.

It was Friday, and I had to go to the Admissions Department of the medical school to find out what my group number would be and which room I should report to on Monday. When I got to the school lobby, it was already crowded. A sea of applicants were trying to make their way to the back, where entrance examination schedules and group allocations were placed inside the few locked glass displays hanging along the wall. The groups were broken down in alphabetical order. I tried to get through the crowd to the middle one, designated by the letters "K - L - M."

"Do you have an extra pen on you?" The girl

standing in front of me looked over her shoulder. "Somebody borrowed mine and disappeared with it a moment ago. Now I have nothing to write my schedule down with." A pair of big, intelligent gray eyes looked at me from an adorable face, which was covered in scores of tiny freckles.

"I happen to have a spare one." I smiled at her, trying to peel my eyes away from her innocently revealed cleavage. "You can have it if you want."

"Thank you much!" She smiled back. "I promise to return it to you as soon as I write down my schedule. What's your name?" she asked.

"I'm Alex, Alex Loevsky."

"I think I've heard your name or seen you somewhere before," she pondered.

"Anything's possible," I said, sidestepping a direct answer. "What's yours?"

"Lara Katz. Come to think of it, we could end up in the same group."

"It's quite likely; 'L' is right after 'K.' We should know shortly, but this line is moving too slowly," I said impatiently while studying her.

"What's the rush?" she replied. "We'll get there sooner or later, and our names will still be there."

In a few minutes, we finally stopped next to the "K - L - M" display case and looked at the group allocations. I scanned the list a couple of times, jumping back and forth from line to line, but I could not find my name.

"Did you find it?" Lara looked perplexed.

"I don't understand this." I looked at her. "My name is missing. It's not on the list."

"Neither is mine."

"Yours too? That's strange. How could this happen?" I wondered in disbelief. "Let's look again ..."

"Alex, you can stand right here and dwell on it until the wee hours. Nothing will change. We need to act ... straighten it out. I'm going to the office to get an explanation."

She quickly made her way through the crowd to the open door of the admissions office. I unsuccessfully tried to keep pace with her. I was halfway there when she came out of the door, found me in the crowd, and waved, signaling me to follow her to the very right end of the back wall.

"The secretary told me," she announced when I finally caught up with her, "that if a name is not on the general schedule, it's most likely on the additional list. She gave me no reason. It should be right here. Let's look."

She led me to the last display case on the right. The additional list was there, and it had about fifty names in alphabetical order.

"I found it!" Lara announced happily. "Look! Here I am!" She pointed to her name.

I read aloud:

"*Katz, Lara*

Klein, Bertha

Kogan, Michael

Kurtz, Rosa

Levi, Maya

Levin, Boris

Lieber, Fanya

Loevsky, Alex."

"It's creepy," she commented. "I kind of sensed that we might be in the same group." Lara stopped smiling and now looked seriously concerned.

"Are you unhappy that we are?" I raised my eyebrows.

Lara looked at me silently for a few seconds and then asked quietly, "Alex, are you Jewish?"

"I am; so what?"

"So am I," Lara said. "Now, look at this list again. Look!"

"Okay." I looked again and instantly got it. "Everyone on this list has a Jewish last name. I see what you mean. It's odd ..."

"It doesn't look right." Lara was biting her lip. "There's something sinister here."

"Maybe it's just a coincidence?" I tried to release the tension and continued with a smile, "What if it's simply a list of gifted students who all happen to be Jewish?"

"Not funny. I do not believe in coincidences," Lara replied with a concerned sigh. "I don't like it, but we can't do anything about it right now. I have to go study. It was nice meeting you, Alex. I'll see you Monday at the biology exam," she briefly looked at the schedule, "at eight thirty in the main building. Room one-oh-three. Here's your pen. Thank you."

"Before you return it," I said, "can you write down your phone number for me?"

"Get a life, Alex. That pickup line is so lame." She shook her head and squinted at me. "You look like a nice guy, but dating is not on my short list. I'm fighting to get into medical school right now."

"Lara, I didn't mean that. I'm sorry if it came out wrong. I just want us to stay in touch. I wasn't trying to hit on you. I am not looking for a date; I'm involved with somebody else."

"Really?" There seemed to be a hint of disappointment in her response. "Okay, then," she said, brushing it off. "My apologies; I didn't know. Let's stay in touch. Here it is." Lara wrote her phone number on a page that she tore from her notebook. "I have to go. See you …"

"Thanks. See you Monday," I answered.

I watched her as she walked away. The girl was as tough as she was beautiful.

I found Andrey Simyavsky at my aunt's place.

"Greetings, young man. I bet the first exam is physics. Right?" he asked.

"Wrong!" I replied testily. "It's biology …" Realizing immediately that my response sounded rude, I calmly corrected myself, "I'm sorry, Andrey. It's biology, on Monday morning, at eight thirty."

"Alex, what's wrong, my boy? You don't seem yourself." Aunt Anna came closer and looked me straight in the eyes.

I opened up, "I was so wrong … wrong and stupidly naïve about the whole thing. Remember when you told me that there was a Jewish quota, and I just foolishly dismissed it? I thought that times were different now … But guess what! There was a quota then, and as sure as hell, there's still one now! I can't stand this! Why can't we be like everyone else? Why are we always at fault? What did we do wrong? Why do they feel the need to make us the scapegoats? Look in the freaking mirror, you communist bastards!" I was shivering with the anger that had finally materialized and had started to surface.

"Calm down and stop screaming! You did nothing wrong!" Andrey got a hold of my arm. "Nothing! Stop blaming yourself. Tell us what happened at the school. What in the world ticked you off?"

"I was trying to get to the group breakdowns and

exam schedules at the Admissions Department. It was like a zoo over there. A lot of applicants and everyone was trying to get to the lists first, like it was a race of some sort.

"In the crowd, I met a girl; her name was Lara Katz. We exchanged a few words while waiting. We even bantered that since 'K' and 'L' are next to each other, we might end up in the same group. She was one feisty, skinny little thing with a pair of huge gray eyes and a cute freckled face.

"When we finally got to the posted list, neither of us could find our names. She went to the office, where she was told about 'the additional list' hanging at the end of the hall. We finally found our names on that list, and I was content enough. Suddenly, Lara asked me if I was Jewish, and after I confirmed that I was, she pointed to the list and asked me to look again and check it over. In total disbelief, I realized that every one of the fifty plus names on the list was most likely Jewish. We were all grouped together.

"Something ill-omened was in the works. Lara's eyes were filled with desperation and anger, and I caught a reflection of my own pain in them. I tried to act like it was nothing worth paying attention to, but my blood was boiling. This was the first time in my life that I've ever been confronted with institutional evil, and I felt defenseless. I didn't feel sorry for myself; I swear I didn't. I will beat those anti-Semitic bastards academically any time, and I'll get top scores! But this poor girl ... I cannot be complacent. She didn't deserve to be walloped like that."

Andrey was holding me by the arm; his eyes were red, and he seemed on the verge of tears. "Real folks are not complacent, my dear friend."

"I've been fighting against it all my life," Aunt Anna cut in. "Andrey is fighting his fight and he isn't even Jewish. Sit down for a moment, Alex, and take a deep breath. Let's figure out what can be done."

We sat quietly for a while, drinking the hot tea that Aunt Anna had poured into our cups from a whistling teapot she'd brought from the kitchen.

In the meantime, Andrey went to the next room to make a phone call. When he returned and sat down, he sipped a bit of his tea, cleared his throat, and said, "I just talked to my wife. Masha's sister-in-law, Nina, is working part-time in the document section of the Medical School Admissions Department. She is off this weekend and has to return to the school on Monday morning to proctor one of the exams. Masha is trying to reach her as we speak. Let's see what these two can come up with."

Suddenly, the phone rang in the adjacent room. Aunt Anna went to pick it up. "Hello? Hi, Masha, how are you? I know it's past dinnertime. Don't worry; I'll make something for him to snack on." She brought the phone, which had a long cord, and placed it in the middle of our table. "Yes, he's right here waiting for your call. Hold on." She passed the phone to Simyavsky.

"Hi, dear, what's the plan?" He listened for a while, periodically nodding his head in confirmation of what he'd just heard. "Does she think it's gonna work? We'll be here waiting for your call. Tell her to be careful. Love you, dear." He hung up the phone.

"What are they up to, Andrey?" Aunt Anna could not hide her nervous curiosity.

"Here's the deal," he explained. "Masha and Nina are on their way to the school right now. Nina has the main gate pass and the set of keys to the whole document section. She will find Alex's dossier and will move it from its present location to his alphabetical 'K - L - M' group.

"The tricky part is to remove his name from the present list and retype it in proper alphabetical order into the existing sets of group breakdowns and exam schedules. There could be three or four sets of them over there, and she better get hold of them all, so all of them will match. Luckily, most of the security guards are on the fifth floor of the school, monitoring the officially sealed and locked examination tests. In the meantime, Masha will stay on the first floor, keeping watch at the document section doors. It should take them about an hour. We just have to wait for their phone call."

"I'll fix something for you boys to snack on, as I promised," Aunt Anna said as she went to the kitchen. She soon returned with a loaf of dark bread, a plate of cold cuts, and a jar of pickles. We chewed on our snacks and sipped our already cold tea in total silence, watching the phone sitting in its cradle in the middle of our table, which was now covered with fresh breadcrumbs. The loud ticking of the grandfather clock in the corner added a third dimension to the eerie stillness.

An hour and twenty minutes later, Aunt Anna picked up the teapot, walked out to the kitchen, and put it on the stove. Suddenly, the phone rang, breaking the nervous silence that had engulfed the room.

Andrey grabbed the receiver. "Masha? Are you girls okay?" He listened for a couple of minutes while Aunt Anna rushed back into the room, looked at us both, and tried to guess the outcome. Suddenly, Andrey's worried facial expression melted into an enormous smile. "Got it! Room two fifteen. You two girls are my heroes. Hug and kiss Nina from all of us here. I'll be home in an hour. Love you, dear." He kissed the receiver and hung up the phone.

"It's all done. They're on their way home. The lists were the trickiest part, as expected. The fourth set of exam schedules and the group breakdowns were on the seventh floor in the dean's office, but they got inside somehow. Your group is now 'KL-seven,' and your room is two fifteen on the second floor. Screw the bastards! There's no way in the world they can catch the switch now. They are as dumb as they are vicious."

I sat at the table, unable to move. I tried to open my mouth to express my gratitude, but to my chagrin, my head dropped into my arms, and I couldn't stop the flood of tears running down my face.

I felt my aunt's hands caressing my shoulders. "You have to be strong, Alex. Life doesn't always bring you the laughter of success; most of the time, it adds some tears into the mix."

"Welcome to maturity, my man," Andrey added. "Get a grip! Stop! Do not give them the satisfaction. Stay strong. Here's a handkerchief; wipe your face dry. By the way, about that freckle-faced girl you met … Lara. Is there a phone where she lives? Do you have any way of getting in touch with her before Monday?"

I raised my head, wiped my tears, and swallowed the bitter knot in my throat. "She gave me her phone number. Why do you ask?" I was at a loss.

"You should give her a call. She was moved to 'KL-seven' with you. I really have to go now." He hugged my aunt, ran his fingers through my hair, and then made his way out.

I was stunned. An unknown feeling that bore some resemblance to guilt, however, overshadowed my sense of relief.

"What about the rest of the names on that damned list, Aunt Anna? What will happen to them?"

"The same thing that could have happened to you. There is only so much that can be done in one day, but it has to be done for as long as it takes ... one name at a time, until everyone is safe. That is our people's destiny, Alex. You should never forget it."

"I never will. I swear."

I unfolded the page torn from Lara's notebook and dialed her number. She picked up the phone.

"Hi. It's me—Alex."

"Do you know what time it is? Why are you calling that late?" she whispered angrily. "My folks are going to bed, and I'm still studying. Don't you have anything else to do? Go study! Or do you know it all?"

"Hey! Take it easy!" I interrupted her rebuke. "You and I have been moved to the 'KL-seven' group. The biology exam will take place on Monday at eight thirty in room two fifteen on the second floor. Be there."

"You better be serious." Her voice was quivering. "If this is a prank, I'll kill you. How did this come about anyway?"

"Someday you will find out. Now go back to your studies. Good night, Lara."

"Wait! Please don't hang up. This is for real, isn't it? I can't thank you enough, Alex."

"I had nothing to do with it. Have a good night." I finally smiled from ear to ear and hung up the phone.

Monday's biology exam was a piece of cake. I got an "A." The physics exam on Tuesday was the same—another "A." The entire month of uninterrupted prep was paying off. The third exam on Wednesday was Russian literature—three hours to write a composition on one of three topics that we were given that morning.

Literature was my strongest subject, and it should've been the easiest of all the tests since the writing process came so naturally to me. The grading method was what worried me. Of the four exams, this was the only one that would be graded subjectively. That's why, my aunt told me, the Russian literature composition was used by the authorities to give certain examinees lower scores or to outright flunk them. It was not syntax, knowledge of the subject matter, or writing style they were looking for; it was, in a way, an ideology test. It also depended on which examiner would be reading and grading your work and what instructions he or she received the previous day.

"You have to outsmart them," Aunt Anna repeated

over and over to me. Her words were right there, stuck in my head. "Always try to get into the examiner's mind and give him what he wants to hear from you today. It could be totally different tomorrow."

Out of the three listed options, I safely picked the "Evil of Money in *Crime and Punishment* by Fyodor Dostoevsky." I pretty much knew from the topic what I needed to write and where I had to lure the examiner's "inquisitive" mind. I adhered strictly to my Aunt Anna's composition "guidelines," and I was finished in less than the allotted three hours. At the end of the day on Thursday, the grades were posted. My aunt's instructions had worked; I got an "A."

An "A" grade was equal to five points, and after the third exam, I'd accumulated fifteen points, the highest score on a five-point scale. The last exam, chemistry, was on Friday. We all had to wait for a couple of hours after the test was over to find out our final grades and overall score. The passing score for admission had been announced a day earlier; eighteen was the magic number. I had a pretty good feeling that I was in a secure position. I needed only a "C" in chemistry to pass; nevertheless, I was still nervous about the whole process since I'd learned only a week before, on the previous Friday, that the system was rigged, and my innocent trust in fairness was forever lost.

When the scores were posted and I saw my fourth and final "A," I closed my eyes and proudly whispered to myself, "Screw you, scoundrels! I'm in!"

"Hey, Alex!" I heard suddenly. Lara ran toward me, her teary gray eyes unable to conceal a storm of emotions.

"Can I give you a big hug?" Without awaiting my response, she hugged me and kissed me on the cheek. "Thank you! Thank you! And thank you again! I would never have been here without your help. I'm in! I got eighteen out of twenty. I'm a medical student now! How did you do?"

"I'm in as well! We're medical students now!" I shouted a few times while picking Lara up off her feet and spinning both of us around.

"Put me down, please," she asked me quietly. When I stopped, she continued, "Not all of us, not really … A moment ago, I ran into Michael Kogan and Laura Friedman. They were on *that list* with us last Friday."

"How did they do?" I asked, feeling my heart tightening into a knot.

"Terribly … the whole group … all of them failed composition. Their scores were not released on Thursday. They were announced to them at the very end, half an hour ago, after the chemistry test results were posted."

"They flunked them all?" I uttered in total disbelief.

"Everyone in the group," Lara confirmed.

The celebration was over. I did not know what to say or do.

I had to be alone. Instead of taking the subway, I took a long walk home along Garden Ring. I felt as if the early evening twilight was following me, steadily overtaking the city and crisscrossing its busy streets with long, sharp shadows. An hour and a half later, the streetlights came on, driving the darkness away, into the labyrinth of soundless courtyards.

The steady rhythm of my own footsteps finally caught up with my racing mind, restraining the chaotic clamor of scornful emotions overtaking my entire being and slowly bringing me back to sanity. No immediate answer or solution was in sight. It felt as if the never-ending fight for survival would be my plight for the rest of my life. I remembered the words that my aunt had said to me the other day: *One name at a time, until everyone is safe; that is our people's destiny.*

I will never forget it, Aunt Anna. I swear.

I was just a block away from home when I saw a crowd of onlookers swarming a police barricade blocking the driveway that led to my old high school, number 126. Scores of policemen and firemen were running around the barricade, and a few fire trucks and a couple of ambulances were parked inside the school courtyard. From afar, I could only see a corner of the school building, which had been wrecked, turned into a huge pile of bricks and fragments of twisted metal. The crowd was swelling, and I saw a few of my neighbors among them.

"Hey, Alex! What's up with the med school exams?" one of them asked.

"It's all done. I'm in," I responded. "What's going on over there?"

"Looks like an accident," another one replied.

"What the hell happened?" somebody else yelled.

Assumptions and inferences were flying back and forth.

"Some idiot rammed a car into a corner of the school building."

"He was probably drunk …"

"Who knows? Maybe he was. One policeman told me that the corpse smelled like booze."

"Nobody knows. He's dead now; let him rest in peace."

"It was bad. He flew out of his car right into the wall. They are still removing chunks of his body from the wreckage."

"Did you see the monster he was driving?"

"It's an old wartime German-made Horch."

"I think I knew the old fogey who drove it," said one of my neighbors. "I heard that the car was his war spoil; he brought it from Germany some years ago."

"This Horch was huge! It demolished the entire wall."

"Yeah, this clunker was his precious possession. He was working on it all the time, fixing this and fixing that. I knew the guy who got the carburetor for him. Another one found the right pair of brake cylinders the next month. The poor soul was planning to take it for a test-drive and then finally paint it before the end of the summer break."

"That was some test-drive! Wasn't he that very school's principal?

"Yeah, come to think of it … Right, it was him. What was his name, do you know?"

"Maximov?"

"Yeah, Maximov …"

"That asshole? It couldn't have happened to a nicer man …"

What? Had I heard right? I couldn't believe it. It was Maximov! I just turned around and rushed away. The reality of fate suddenly struck me, and the echo of Maximov's voice reverberated in my head, "You will be accepted to medical school over my dead body! … Over my dead body!"

What goes around comes around... It could not be simply a coincidence on a day like today. I felt riveted for a moment. The whole thing was too eerie not to be taken as a sign. It was bone-chilling.

Beware of what you wish for, creep! You just got your wish fulfilled. There is justice in this world!

I reached the entrance of our apartment building, and instead of waiting for an elevator, I ran upstairs to my parents' fifth-floor apartment.

My dad answered the doorbell and let me into the entryway. I closed the door behind me and leaned against it, trying to catch my breath. Mom and Dad were standing still in restless expectation, frightened that they might hear bad news.

"You are killing us!" my mom timorously broke the nervous silence. "Say something! Did you make it?"

"Yes, Mom! I did! It's over! I got the top score—twenty! I'm a medical student!" I squeezed the words out of my tightening throat as I walked straight into my parents' open arms.

"There is justice in this world," whispered my dad.

Overwhelmed, all three of us snuggled into one big hug and quietly stood together.

Chapter Five
Passion and Poison

O nly a few weeks were left before the beginning of the new school year. I had to buy a bunch of textbooks, anatomy manuals, some lab supplies, dissection instruments, and a couple of lab coats. Lately, I'd started to get some modest but continuous payments from *New Word* for whatever had been published so far, and I'd managed to save some money to buy almost everything I needed to start the medical school year on my own without my parents' help.

I moved to a dorm, and the first couple of months flew by. I was preoccupied with my medical school studies and successfully passed my first set of exams during the last week of October. My scores put me at the top of my class. Mom and Dad were finally happy, and Aunt Anna was beaming with pride.

It felt like my literary success was also paying off in different ways. I was trying not to pay attention to the fact that some of my classmates had gotten wind of my writing career and were beginning to discuss it openly. I caught some flattering buzz from a few friendly newspapers, as well as the repudiation of many not-so-friendly ones. On the spur of the moment, I was invited to appear on two television shows to talk about contemporary poetry—mine in particular. Regrettably, on both occasions, the time allotted was too short, and the anchors were cautious and scripted. The questions they asked were dull, and I was not allowed to read what I'd wanted to read—not on camera anyway.

Nevertheless, the very next morning, I learned that my obscurity was over, and not of my own volition. The rustle of "It's him; it's him!" was following me. It seemed that now nearly everyone knew my face, and there was nowhere for me to hide. I was frequently stopped and asked to sign a copy of *New Word* or just to autograph a blank piece of paper; that felt really cool.

But now and then, someone in a crowd would greet me with a sharp elbow to the ribs, or I would feel the sting of a passerby hissing and dubbing me "a motherfucking traitor kike." That didn't feel cool at all. I remembered Simyavsky's *"Welcome to the world of passion and poison"* phrase, and I quickly learned that fame was not always pleasant and that it came in many different forms.

That night, I was going to the Expression Club, a highly trendy café near Mayakovsky Square, to read my poetry. Mila Siegel, a young TV show producer whom I'd met at the Ostankino TV studio the previous week, invited me there. She was well known for being one of the founders of "Nights of Discoveries" at the sought-after, edgy Expression Club. "Nights of Discoveries" had gained instant popularity by inviting young writers, actors, poets, songwriters, and artists to showcase their work and submit themselves to fiery discussions with the audience. Incidentally, she happened to be the sister of renowned film director and screenwriter Yakov Siegel, which added even more to her clout.

When I arrived, she hugged and kissed me nonchalantly on the cheek and then led me to her table. Her brother was already seated there among some other people whom I did not know. On the opposite side of the table, I recognized the bald and slightly chubby popular bard, Yuri Vizbor.

Right away, he noticed me, reached across the table, and shook my hand. "Alex the Poet! Nice to see you, man. Welcome to the Expression Club. Mila told me that you might be here tonight. I'm so glad you made it. I just love your poetry ... love it."

My head was spinning. The famous Yuri Vizbor had recognized me! Mila introduced me as an old and trusted friend, and I was seated next to her brother. She filled my champagne glass and raised hers as she addressed the table, "A toast to never-ending talent! To the Expression Club and its friends! To us—the expressionists of the New World!" She sipped her champagne, put her glass down, and took a seat to the right of me. She stretched her arm around my shoulder, leaned in closer, paused, and then looked straight into my eyes. As she looked at me, I studied her slightly open and quivering lips for a few awkward seconds. It felt unwittingly intriguing and strangely flattering.

"I was worried you wouldn't come," she said quietly, looking at me. "Fame is poisonous."

"I can assure you I'm not poisoned yet, and I'm far from being famous. I'm honored to have been invited to the Expression Club. It was so nice of you. I promise I won't let you down." I was trying to conceal my newly discovered emotional vulnerability.

"Don't be silly! Everyone here is honored to hear you. I'm flattered that you accepted my invitation after that terribly concocted interview at Ostankino." She hugged me again and kissed me on the cheek, this time dangerously close to my mouth. Then she paused, looked straight into my eyes, and suddenly erupted in a meteoric soliloquy, "I could've talked to you right there, right away, apologized, and explained the restrictions imposed on us by those damn censors and cowards in charge, but you just vanished without a trace. It took some effort to locate you later at the med school dorm."

She was talking up a storm, and I was looking at

her with curiosity, hearing only every other word of her diatribe about the momentous change of creative attitudes billowing on our horizons. I was slowly falling under the spell of my surroundings and her more than intellectual seductiveness.

"What would you like me to read?" I broke in.

"Anything! Just anything you dare to share. At this place, you can let loose. Just do it!" she encouraged me. "This is our venue ... our Montmartre, if you wish. We are at the Expression Club. We are the expressionists! There is no censorship here. These folks are eager to hear it all—raw and uncensored. Just let it out the way you feel. Yasha," she suddenly addressed her brother seated to my left, calling him by his nickname, "I hope you recognize Alex, the poet I spoke to you about a couple of weeks ago."

"Yes, you did indeed." Yakov Siegel looked at me with a friendly smile and stretched his arm forward. "It's my pleasure to finally meet you in person." We shook hands as he kept patting me on the shoulder. "She hasn't stopped talking about you since last Thursday. What did you do to my baby sister, Alex? I hope you guys are not involved. Nobody can tolerate that nonstop blabbermouth for more than a few days. How long have you two known each other, may I ask?"

"Not long at all, I can assure you." I picked up his sarcastic tone.

"I hope you will last, for my sister's sake."

"I'll give it my best shot ..."

"Don't even try; she will drive you nuts in a couple of hours."

"I'll still try."

"Don't say I didn't warn you."

"I won't. I promise."

"Here comes another sucker." He slapped my shoulder again and playfully pinched my cheek. "After she dumps you, let's stay friends. Deal?"

"Sure!"

"All jokes aside, I love your poetry, man. How old are you?"

"Twenty-one," I suddenly lied.

"Come on. Really? I would never have guessed. Your writing is way too mature for your age. And so is she, by the way. My sis is twenty-seven going on forty. Didn't she tell you the truth?" He was laughing loudly like a little kid.

"I'm gonna kill you, asshole!" Mila screamed, turning red. Then she looked at me and asked, "Does it actually matter?"

"Does it?" I rebutted.

"Not to me," she answered.

"Cool. I feel better now," I replied and then hastily finished the rest of my champagne.

Then we all talked ... about everything and

nothing. We exchanged jokes, and there were tears of laughter. We made toasts as we drank champagne, and we made fun of each other.

I was introduced to Edward Steinberg, Misha Schwartzman, and Vladimir Weysberg—so-called "metaphysicists" and well-known avant-garde artists—who were among the guests at the table next to ours. A couple of weeks earlier, they had instantly become the talk of the town when their "unauthorized" outdoor art exhibit in the park on the outskirts of Moscow had been closed down by the authorities merely an hour after it had been opened. Before the artists could collect their work and leave, they had been overrun by a bunch of organized hoodlums who had destroyed and burned everything they could get their hands on. Tonight, this trio was lionized by everyone here at the Expression Club, which was a haven for nonconformists.

Edward came to our table to welcome me and compliment my recent publications in *New Word*. It really felt as if I did belong there in this warm Bohemian circle of creative souls bound together by nothing but their artistry and the common quest for freedom of expression.

Impetuously, Mila put her arms around my neck and whispered in my ear, "Now! It's time to introduce you to everybody. Don't be nervous. Just get up and follow me."

We approached the small platform in the corner of the café. Mila tapped the microphone a couple of times to get the audience's attention. "Good evening to all of you, our old and new friends. Tonight, the Expression Club wants to welcome the well-known bard and balladeer, Yuri Vizbor, and introduce to you our latest discovery, the talented and already controversial poet Alexander Loevsky, mostly known to you as Alex the Poet. Please make both of them feel at home."

While everyone applauded, Mila brought Yuri Vizbor up to the podium and stepped down. She grabbed me by the arm, pulled me slightly to the side, and asked quietly, "Have you ever heard him sing?"

"Not in person," I answered.

"I always get goose bumps when he sings. Listen ..."

Yuri sat down on a high stool, adjusted the microphone, and touched the strings of his old, gypsy-style seven-stringed guitar. He sang *"My Dearest," "You Are the Only One I Have,"* and a few other songs that everyone seemed to know by heart. The lyrics of his songs were interwoven with the soft, melodramatic chords of his guitar, casting an unexplainable spell on the audience.

I looked around. Couples and groups around the tables melted into one monolithic assembly, breathing the same air and eagerly anticipating every sound. Everyone was captivated by his lyrics; some were lip-syncing along, and some were on the verge of tears. By the last few couplets, everybody was singing together.

Two adjoining tables near the entrance door caught my attention. The eight guys there were dressed alike with red armbands on the right sleeves of their sport coats. The group leader appeared to be a seven-foot-tall albino giant. I leaned toward Mila. Pointing with my eyes, I quietly asked, "Did you notice Snow White and the Seven Dwarfs over there?"

"Not funny," Mila said, her face registering concern.

"I'm not trying to be funny. That tall dude looks ominous. Do you know any of them? Who are these people?"

"You don't want to know. They are the Civil Order Watch, a sort of self-appointed militia. They're supposed to assist local police with petty crimes and civil disturbances."

"They don't look like they belong here."

"They don't," she whispered back. "A couple of weeks ago, the regional Committee of the Communist Youth Union directed us to accommodate them at Expression Club gatherings. It seemed ridiculous, but nobody argues with the committee. Please, don't pay any attention to them. They are just a bunch of ya-hoos. Screw them! They don't understand even half of what's happening here. Fucking morons!"

"Those morons will not be happy with my socio-political stuff that they're about to hear," I warned her.

Mila shrugged it off. "They're too stupid to catch it anyway. Ignore them. Just pretend they don't exist."

"But they do ... unfortunately. And I doubt they're all that stupid." I sensed that Vizbor was just about done.

The café suddenly erupted into loud applause. Vizbor stepped down from the podium. "I warmed them up. Now it's your turn, Alex. Good luck! You're on your own. Go ..."

"That's not fair, Yuri," Mila scolded him. "Come on. It's his debut tonight. Be nice. Be helpful."

"Relax; I'm just pulling his leg. Here we go ..." Yuri returned to the podium and took the microphone. "Thank you, thank you very much, dear friends, for your more than warm reception. But now ..."

I could not believe what I was hearing. Vizbor played a few chords and then lowered his guitar. Suddenly, he started to recite the opening verses of my "Salvaged Hope." I was mystified and looked at Mila. She gave me a warm smile, took me by the hand, and walked me up to the podium.

Yuri stopped reading. "That wasn't mine," he announced, pointing at me. "It's his. He is known to most of you as Alex the Poet. He is the one who wrote 'Salvaged Hope.' Dear friends, please extend your

ALLAN ALEXANDER

warm welcome to our new friend, the young poet Alexander Loevsky!"

Everyone stood up and applauded. I was stunned. How did he know the opening verses of my poem well enough to recite them by heart?

"Was my introduction a bit better this time around?" Yuri's face was all smiles.

"Did you two rehearse the whole thing?" I asked.

"No, no, we didn't," he answered. "I wish I was the one who wrote your poetry. One day, Alex, I promise I'll write the music and sing it myself. The podium is yours now. Go get 'em!"

Yuri and Mila stepped down, and I took the microphone.

"What should I read first?" I started.

"Begin with 'Salvaged Hope'!" someone in the audience shouted. "Not from where Vizbor stopped, but right from the very beginning."

I read a collection of my sociopolitical poems without interruption for more than forty-five minutes. This was followed by close to an hour session of questions and answers. I then signed autographs. I was exhausted by the time Mila came up to the podium to rescue me. She thanked everyone and closed the night. We went back to our table, where Yakov filled my glass with champagne and began speaking.

"Something extraordinary just happened over

there. You and Vizbor totally captivated that crowd. The desire to listen to both of you was insatiable. The audience couldn't get enough. Amazing, simply amazing! With that said, I would like to raise my glass to the magic of this night, the talent both of you possess, and to you, Alex, for joining our circle of devoted friends."

Everybody at the table got up and clinked their glasses over the middle.

"Bottoms up!"

The café crowd eventually started to melt away. It was getting late, and as people were leaving, some were stopping at our table for an autograph and some to say goodbye. We were still seated when the Civil Order Watch at the other end got up and left.

"What in the hell were they here for?" Yakov asked, shrugging his shoulders. "It didn't look like they enjoyed the evening at all."

"I already explained to Alex that they were forced on us by the regional Committee of the Communist Youth Union," Mila said apologetically. "We had no say."

"They were here for no good reason," Yuri Vizbor added. "It's getting late. Time to call it a night and go home, my friends."

"I saw a similar group of goons flaunting their red armbands at our burned-down open-air art exhibition the other week," Edward Steinberg confirmed.

"Those motherfuckers torched us down. I know it was them; I just know it. I recognized one of them ... that seven-foot-tall albino Neanderthal."

The Civil Order Watch presence tonight was a put-down, I thought as we all gathered our belongings and headed for the exit.

The late-night air felt nippy. The sky was dark and studded with a myriad of bright stars, and the streets were already empty in preparation for tomorrow's busy workday.

"Hey, guys, do you want to stop at my place for a nightcap?" Mila asked.

Before anybody could utter a word, the group of eight appeared out of nowhere and surrounded us. It dawned on me that their notorious red armbands were now gone. The albino Neanderthal grabbed Vizbor's guitar and smashed it against a wall, shattering it to pieces.

"What the hell are you doing? Are you out of your mind?" pleaded Vizbor.

"Listen carefully, you bunch of cocksucking Jews," the Neanderthal retorted, "the next time you get together to poison the minds of our Russian Soviet youth with your fucking provocative intellectual crap, I will personally bust your heads instead of that shitty gypsy guitar. Do I make myself clear? Any other questions? Have a great fucking night!"

With that, *Snow White and the Seven Dwarfs* disappeared into the darkness the same way they'd appeared.

After a long pause, Vizbor slowly said, "It had never even occurred to me," as he picked up the scattered pieces of his demolished guitar, "Siegel, Steinberg, Loevsky, Schwartzman, Weisberg ... what a group! Holy shit! I never saw it that way. How did that happen? I'm the only one here who isn't Jewish." He then shouted into the darkness, "I am a Catholic of Lithuanian decent, you bunch of assholes!" He turned around and quietly added, "You know what, I take it as an honor to be assaulted as one of you, my friends ... as one of us."

We all stood speechless. Breaking the silence, Yuri hugged me and said, "Nobody promised it was gonna be easy. Welcome to the Expression Club, Alex."

Is that right? I pondered. *It felt more like some overexpressed sobering welcome to the Club of Passion and Poison.*

"Come on, guys. Luckily, nobody got hurt. What a miserable finale to the otherwise great evening!" Yakov Siegel said, breaking the unwieldy silence, and then rushed to flag down an approaching cab. "Get in the car, Mila. I warned you that the whole thing would bring us nothing but trouble. Who needs that shit? Time to call it a night."

Chapter Six

Was It *Lyubimov?*

That night's experience put a serious damper on my short-lived euphoric perception of limitless literary freedom and the mystical bohemian union of artistic souls... and that was just the beginning. Everything unraveled rapidly from that point. The iron fist of the authorities wasn't wasting any time.

The Expression Club was closed by the end of the same week. I tried to get in touch with Mila Siegel to find out what was going on, but she didn't return my calls. The following Monday, the KGB's Second Directorate, the State Security ideological surveillance apparatus, started to summon most of the "Bohemians" one by one for questioning, warning them about repercussions and daunting nearly all of them into oblivion.

A handful stood defiant but kept quiet and isolated for the time being. After a few random arrests, many "enthusiastically" and publicly conceded and denounced the rest of the dissent, to save their own hides and to be left alone. Some turned out to be fly-by-nights or just cowards. The self-aggrandizing founders of the crumbled Montmartre were nowhere to be found.

Contrary to my worst fears, and to my obvious relief, somehow regime's dragnet seemed to miss me—at least for now. I tried to get in touch with Svetlana, but mercifully, she was unreachable being with her dad at one of the remote military bases at the Soviet Union's far east border near China. I did my best to suppress my desire to find somebody I could talk to about all that tormented me... about that night at the Expression Club and about my dread of becoming a quarry of the Second Directorate. I did not want to agonize my aunt or my mother, or to be mercilessly lectured by my dad's apropos "shoulda, coulda, woulda," so I got the hang of keeping my angst and uneasiness to myself.

Be that as it may, I suddenly learned what creative loneliness was all about. Fortunately, my medical school studies occupied most of my time, and my weekends were spent in the company of Aunt Anna and Andrey Simyavsky. Mysteriously, *New Word* continued to publish my work, but not as frequently as before, and the poems chosen by the editorial staff were not my best edgy political ones; rather, they were from the soft and melodramatic love collection of my earlier poetry written to Svetlana. That editorial malaise drove me nuts, but Aunt Anna reassured me that things like that had happened before and that I was not the first one to experience it.

"Patience is a virtue, my dear. You have to learn

how to be patient, how to wait. It's a strategy of sorts. Keep writing, but do not think that you are writing in-the-desk. Persuade yourself that you are working on a compilation for a future book of your poetry."

"I am in the middle of a month-long writer's block, Auntie. Not a single verse for the whole month. It's killing me. I talked to Andrey Simyavsky about it, and he responded the same way you did. Wait! But for how long? He didn't have an answer.

"He promised to get in touch with me, but he hasn't been returning my calls. He always had returned my calls before. Now it feels like he's avoiding me. This is totally not like him. He's not himself; he's changed. Have you noticed? Something isn't right, and it's bothering me. What's going on?"

"Andrey is very concerned about something you need to stay away from for now. You are way too young for that stuff."

"Is that about his new book?" I probed.

"I told you, it's not for you to know."

"But I do know! It's about the book he's trying to publish abroad, right?"

"Where did you come up with such a demented idea?" Aunt Anna raised her eyebrows and looked away.

She was obviously trying to skirt the issue, but I was searching for the right answer.

"I am not making it up. I was in your study almost

a year ago when Andrey walked out on Tardovsky and slammed the door. I heard when Tardovsky said that it was a dangerous and stupid idea to publish his novel abroad. I even remember the title. It was *Lyubimov*, wasn't it? Am I right? Was it *Lyubimov*? Come on, tell me the truth."

Suddenly, my aunt's expression turned stern. She moved closer and grabbed me by the arm. Her dour voice was trembling.

"Listen to me very carefully! Stop digging. You did not hear a thing about that book; you do not know the title; you never saw either of them here. Erase it from your brain forever. Got it? You know nothing, you heard nothing, and you saw nothing! I implore you, shut your mouth for your own good, and do not argue with me. Remember what I told you so many times? Your tongue should *conceal* your thoughts. *Conceal!* I am not blind, nor am I stupid. I am well aware of what's going on. I have good reasons not to talk to you about it. I had survived much the same subjugation before, but you have a lot to learn. Your naïveté is dangerous. The repressions, which have been set in motion right now, are extremely perilous. Many lives could be ruined. The last thing you need is to be dragged into it. Step away. Go back to the dorm and study. Do not talk to anyone about Andrey or his book. Call me tomorrow after school … and use a payphone."

"But, Auntie Anna, I don't understand …" I was totally lost.

"Enough! You will understand at some point. Go now; leave!" She cut our conversation short and walked me out the door.

Masha and Andrey Simyavsky lived just a couple of blocks away. On my way to the dorm, I decided to stop at their place to check if things were all right.

I took a brisk walk along Garden Ring, trying to figure out why Aunt Anna had become so apprehensive about my knowledge of Andrey Simyavsky's new book and his attempt to publish it abroad. How could she forget that I had been there when Tardovsky had tried to persuade Andrey not to do it? I had witnessed it firsthand! She had always kept me in the loop when it came to what was going on … until today.

Something had happened. What had I missed? What could it be? I couldn't come up with any reasonable explanation. Could it be that someone had told her about that night at the Expression Club and my unfortunate acquaintance with *Snow White and the Seven Dwarfs?* I hadn't told her about it because I hadn't wanted her to worry. I couldn't un-ring that bell. Whatever had taken place outside the Expression Club had been out of my control, and so far, the Second

Directorate hadn't summoned me. Maybe I'd lucked out ... or maybe not. But why should I bring unnecessary apprehension to my aunt and my parents beforehand? If the proverbial shit hit the fan, we would all finally deal with it then.

I reached my destination and walked into Simyavsky's apartment building. The circular stairway wound along the walls of the five-story-high shaft of the stairwell, and on every floor, a wide landing interrupted the spiral curve. The space was dimly lit, musty, and ghostly quiet until it was filled with the loud echoes of my footsteps. I stopped at Simyavsky's door on the third floor and rang the doorbell.

A woman, whom I did not recognize, looked at me through the cleft of the slightly opened door, which was protected by a safety chain.

"I am here to see Andrey Denisovich. Is he home?" I asked.

"No, he is not. Who are you?" she responded.

"Is Masha home?" I insisted.

"Nobody's home. Who are you?" she repeated.

"Where are they?" Something didn't feel right. "I am Alex Loevsky."

The moment she heard my name, she rushed to unlock the chain and whisked me inside.

"Come right in! Quickly!" She let me in, looked outside and checked the stairwell, and then closed and double-locked the door. "I know who you are. You are close friends with Andrey, aren't you?"

"Yes, and you are?"

"Do you remember that Friday night, the weekend before the medical school admission exams last summer?"

"Are you Nina?" I hesitated.

"Yes. I am Masha's sister-in-law. Why did you come? You shouldn't be here now. It's dangerous."

Suddenly, I realized that the apartment had been ransacked. Everything had been turned upside down. Broken glass and piles of books were everywhere, and feathers from ripped pillows were scattered across the floor.

"What the hell happened here?" I freaked out and began firing one question after another. "Are they okay? Was it a break-in? A robbery? Did anybody call the police?"

"It's not what you think, Alex. It's a lot worse. Nobody had to call the police. They arrived here on their own at six in the morning. Andrey was arrested and taken away. Masha called me and asked me to rush over here. The moment I arrived, she bolted after them; they were heading to the KGB headquarters. The rest of the thugs stayed and proceeded to pillage the place. They had the guts to deputize me to be a witness of record for their execution of a search warrant. Look what they've done here. It's atrocious."

"Why did they arrest Andrey?" I asked.

"I don't know, and I didn't ask," she replied.

"Where is Masha now? Have you heard from her since she left? Has she called?" I wanted to know.

"No, she hasn't. It was your aunt who called a few hours ago, after everyone left."

"My Aunt Anna called a few hours ago?" I was startled.

"Yes, she did. We talked for a while. Neither of us had a clue where Masha could be right now or when she will return. I am waiting for her to come back, and in the meantime, I'm trying to clean up the mess those savages left behind. Poor Andrey ... This is so horrible." Nina covered her head with both hands and leaned against the wall. Then she slowly slid down to the floor and started to sob. I crouched over her, put my hand on her shoulder, and tried to calm her down.

"Please don't cry. I'll stay here with you and help you clean it up."

Nina kept quietly sobbing. She appeared to be deep in thought. From time to time, she would shake her head, as if trying to rid herself of the dubious daze of sinister reality. A few moments later, she stopped crying and got to her feet.

"No, no, no! It's way too dangerous for you to stay here. You never know; they could return at any moment. The bastards left this apartment quite angry 'cause they couldn't find what they were looking for."

"What were they looking for?" I questioned.

"They took all Andrey's notes, his typewriter, his address books, a few manuscripts, and they were still looking for more. Then they found the letters—the ones he received from his students, friends, fellow writers, and publishers. They took the box full of Andrey and Masha's letters from the wartime when he was in the Red Army. Everything he collected through the years, they took it all."

The magnitude of my aunt's reasons for worrying slowly started to sink in. Andrey was my mentor, and we had become ideological soul mates. My understanding of creative freedom came from him. Some of my published poetry alone was reckless enough to get me in trouble. My aunt knew what was going on and was trying to shield me from the suffocating grip of the Second Directorate. Did she already know about that night at the Expression Club? Why hadn't I thought about that before tonight?

I picked up a fistful of goose feathers from the floor and let them go as I watched their slow descent. "How many pillows did they manage to massacre?" I asked.

"All of them," Nina said. "Everything they could find, they destroyed. They carved up all the mattresses, the couch, and the chairs. They said they were looking for Andrey's last novel."

"His last novel ... Did they mention the title?"

I feared it would be what I thought it was. Maybe Tardovsky had been right that night in my aunt's study when he'd warned Andrey about the consequences of circumventing the authorities and publishing his illicit anti-Soviet novel abroad.

"They were looking for the original manuscript and copies of the printed book. I overheard them say they were searching for *Lyubimov*," Nina replied.

"Oh no! Exactly what I feared the most! Damn it! Tardovsky was right." I couldn't find the words to express my feelings. I just stood there aghast and dumbfounded.

They were looking for the printed book. I realized now that *Lyubimov* had finally been published and then smuggled back into the country. Andrey hadn't ever mentioned it to me. Some time ago, he'd allowed me to read the typed manuscript with the handwritten editorial comments all over the pages; that's all it had been. I'd been fascinated, but since then, he hadn't said a word about publishing the novel abroad … not one word. Maybe he had been protecting me, as my aunt was doing by keeping me out of the loop.

Nina interrupted my awkwardly culpable silence.

"Alex, you really have to leave now. What if they return? You are also a writer. You don't want them to see you here. Please, go. I'll be okay." She unlocked the door and let me out.

As I walked down the stairs, I thought about the fact that this was the second time of the day that I had been told to leave—earlier by my aunt and now by Nina. I was convinced that Aunt Anna had anticipated my visit to Simyavsky's apartment and had asked Nina to show me out as quickly as she could. Why was she so overprotective of me? Did all of them really think that I was unable or not mature enough to comprehend what was going on around me?

In so many discussions with Andrey, I'd come to appreciate his subtle and sagacious way of teaching me about the historical waves of ideological and political suppression, which were sanctioned by the Communist Party apparatchiks every time the party changed its ruler. Andrey did it almost nonchalantly—not to instill fear in me, but to develop my awareness of those waves, prepare me to fight for what I stood for, and coach me on how to survive if all else failed.

It was obvious to me by now that he'd entered into his last fight some time ago when he'd adopted the pen name Avrum Hertz. The publication of *Lyubimov* abroad had been put in full motion, but Khrushchev's sudden demise had caught everybody by surprise. Everything had changed rapidly. Publication had become inevitable, and it had been too late to stop what had already been started. *Lyubimov* had been printed in

Washington, and I guessed that, in the last months, a few books had made their way back home.

By the time I reached the exit, the door swung open, and I nearly collided with Masha.

"Alex, sweetheart," she paused, trying to catch her breath, "how long have you been waiting here?"

"Not long... It's not important!" I retorted impatiently. "I want to know what happened to Andrey. How is he? Tell me, where is he now?"

"He was arrested this morning, as you probably already know. They took him to the KGB prison at Lubyanka Square. As I was told, by the end of the day, he will be incarcerated at the Second Directorate's detention center for the time being for the initial interrogation. There will be no visitors, and he won't be allowed to see his attorney for a month—most likely even longer. Andrey's fellow writer, Yuli Daniel, was arrested this morning as well. I already contacted a couple of lawyers, and they are 'working the system' as they put it."

"Oh my goodness," I groaned. "How bad is it?"

"It doesn't look good at all." Masha shook her head. "It looks like Andrey will be indicted on anti-Soviet propaganda charges."

"I'll do anything to help; just tell me." My head was spinning, and I didn't know what I could do to be of assistance.

"It sounds harsh, and I know that you're such a dear friend... There's no doubt in my mind that you'd do anything for Andrey, but I beg you now, stay as far away from it all as you can," Masha pleaded. "That is how you can help. It's what Andrey told me to tell you before they took him away."

"But how can I stay away if he's in trouble? I know that all of it started because *Lyubimov* was published abroad and smuggled back home. Nina told me earlier that the agents who stayed behind and did the search couldn't find anything. They left totally pissed. Are the manuscript and the printed copies safe? I can help you to hide them, Masha."

"Shhh ... Learn to be quiet! Walls have ears!" she whispered and continued in a hushed tone. "Thank God it's all in a safe place by now. For a week, Andrey had a premonition that he would be arrested any day, and sooner rather than later. Luckily, we took care of everything just last weekend."

"Maybe I can——"

Masha quietly interrupted my relentlessness by pressing her index finger over my lips.

"Stop it, my dear. You are still wet behind the ears. You are unprepared for this fight. It's out of your league. You have to forgive me, but I'm tired as hell right now. The last thing I need is to argue with you. Learn quietly. I have to relieve Nina, take a shower, and get some sleep. I have a ton of work to do tomorrow. I promise I'll be in touch and will keep you informed. Go home, Alex." She gently pinched my cheek, spun me around, and pushed me toward the exit.

Chapter Seven

Demonstration

A couple of days later, the authorities broke the news about the recent arrest and indictment of two "renegade" writers—Simyavsky and Daniel—for the dissemination of anti-Soviet agitation and propaganda abroad. For the next few weeks *Pravda, Izvestiya,* and *Literaturnaya Gazeta,* the three leading newspapers, were set to churn the official spin that aimed to frame public opinion. The Politburo made the decision to close the court proceedings to the public and the press and to use the Simyavsky and Daniel trial as a pivotal point to reverse the gains of Khrushchev's Thaw.

It seemed the ideological bulldozers of the Second Directorate had started to lay down the groundwork to return to the show trials of the worst years of Stalin's reign by sanctioning a denunciation campaign to distort and destroy Simyavsky's and Daniel's literary works. Anyone trying to express an opposing view was immediately belittled and ostracized. Any attempt to defend either one of them, or just to ask for leniency, was portrayed as a part of the greater conspiracy to undermine the very foundation of the Socialist State.

For all that, times were different now. Nikita Khrushchev had recently been ousted, but in the interim years of his reign, he had inadvertently let the Freedom Genie out of the bottle, and many of us had hoped that it would not be so easy for General Secretary Brezhnev's new rule to shove it back into servitude. The memories of mass repressions and Stalin's atrocities that had been brought to light were still too raw to be simply ignored.

The dissent was not so silent anymore, but the old style of collegial betrayal and ideological cruelty, as in the past, displayed no limits. Recent Nobel Prize laureate in literature, Michael Sholokhov, went as far as to demand that the defendants be executed as "Enemies of the People." Sholokhov's cronies in the Writers' Union came up with a collective condemnation letter, which was signed by nearly two dozen "patriots" of the social realism breed.

It was getting uglier and uglier every day.

At the same time, the numerous petitions in defense of the two writers, signed by prominent Soviet intellectuals, academicians, scientists, writers, composers, and other luminaries, began to get through to General Secretary Brezhnev. A group of prominent Writers' Union members who opposed the Sholokhov faction's condemnation signed a letter addressed to the standing executive committee of the Communist Party. The letter argued that the trial itself would do more harm to the international reputation of the Soviet Union than the work of the writers themselves.

Out of the blue, I received a phone call from Yuri Vizbor.

"Alex? It's Yuri. Can you talk?"

"Hey, Yuri. Are you okay?" I responded.

"Has the Second Directorate summoned you yet?"

"No, not yet. Still waiting. Did they talk to you?"

"You bet your ass they did. I need to see you. Can we get together?"

"When?"

"Now!"

"Where are you?" I asked

"Near Arbat Square," he answered.

"We can meet at Alexander Gardens, to the left side of Kutafia Tower in thirty minutes."

"See you in half an hour," he said and hung up the phone.

Thirty minutes later, I exited the subway station, crossed Manezhnaya Square, and headed in the direction of Trinity Tower, which dominated Kremlin Hill. The green roof of the Arsenal building and the round cupola of the Supreme Soviet were hiding inside behind the tallest tower of the Kremlin Wall. The downhill bridge over Alexander Gardens connected it to the squat Kutafia Tower at the very edge of Manezhnaya Square.

I spotted Yuri nervously pacing back and forth at the entrance to the gardens, to the left of the Kutafia Gates.

"Sorry, I'm a little late. How are you?" I greeted him.

"I'm so happy to see you." Yuri shook my hand and gave me a bear hug. "How have you been?"

"Trying to survive," I answered.

Yuri diverted his gaze to the Kremlin and said, "Not the friendliest place to have a meeting. Why here? Why Alexander Gardens?"

"Let's go inside and you'll see," I answered. "I love to come here. It's the safest and quietest place in Moscow. All the State Security agents around here are too busy guarding the Kremlin. That leaves very little room for snooping and eavesdropping."

We walked through the gate and dived into the shadow of Silver Fir Alley. The Gardens ran along the exterior of the Kremlin, hugging centuries-old walls in an almost full circle, starting north of Red Square and stopping at the foot of the ancient Saint Basil's Cathedral to the south. With the Kremlin Wall to the right and tall, thick, fragrant evergreens to the left, we were somewhat shielded from the damp December nip coming from the nearby bend of the Moskva River.

"You're right, Alex. This place is very quiet and totally secluded. I'd never have guessed that there'd be no one around at this time of the day."

"This is my uninhabited island. I come here to write or just to be left alone. It is like a sanctuary for me ... a spa for my mind."

"Yeah, some spa," Yuri said, raising his coat collar and shaking a few fresh snowflakes from his hair. We quietly walked together along the alley, and I patiently waited for him to tell me why he'd needed to see me right away. Suddenly, he stopped and looked around, making sure that we were still alone. Then, he asked quietly, "Alex, I heard that you and Andrey Simyavsky were very close, were you?"

"Yes, we were. He is my mentor and my dearest friend."

"Well, then how did you take his arrest? How do you feel?"

"I am not getting it, Yuri." His question flustered me. "What do you mean, how did I take it? I am devastated. I feel shocked. I am horrified. Is that enough for you? I hate those fuckers who put him away. I feel helpless! How else would I feel?"

"Calm down; don't get angry. I'm sorry for putting it that way. I'm much older than you are, and I've learned to be cautious. We don't know each other well enough; that's the only reason I had to ask. Please, don't be upset; I had to see how you'd react. People have started acting so strangely. The worst is coming out of them at the most unsuitable time. The number of humans worthy of my trust is rapidly dwindling. You and I have met just once, and I only know you for your poetry. Your poetical honesty is what moved me to call you, and I hope you are what I think you are. Plenty of so-called 'friends' in the last month have turned out to be strangers. I don't feel that I'm making that mistake with you."

My initial burst of anger started to dissipate.

"This is not a mistake, Yuri. I won't turn into a stranger." I looked at him calmly as I cautiously tried to figure out what he was expecting from me. "So, why are we here? Just tell me," I said softly.

"Do you remember what day tomorrow is?" Yuri asked.

"December fifth," I answered. "Is that why we're here?"

"Good guess," Yuri continued, "December fifth— the Constitution Day. Let's party!"

"Are you inviting me to a party to celebrate fuck- ing Constitution Day? Are you for real?"

"Come on, Alex. Drop it. Sarcasm obviously isn't your strong suit."

"I wasn't trying to be sarcastic. The Soviet Constitution is a sham." I backed off.

"Come to think of it, you're right. That's why I came here to invite you to a party of sorts. There are a couple hundred people planning to get together at Pushkin Square to 'celebrate' Constitution Day at the foot of the monument to the great Russian poet Alexander Sergeyevich Pushkin."

"You've totally lost me, Yuri. Pushkin died over a hundred years ago. What does he have to do with Constitution Day? Help me decipher this ... please."

"Think, Alex! What did Pushkin's poetry mostly deal with? It dealt with the struggle his generation faced for the choice they had to make. *Monarchy or Democracy. Tyranny or Liberty*. A century and a half later, it is our turn to take a stand for liberty. Tomorrow at Pushkin Square, we will raise our banners quoting the Soviet Constitution—where it guarantees liberty of expression. We will be protesting the arrests of Simyavsky and Daniel and demanding an open trial in accordance with existing law. It will be presented to the foreign press as 'The Meeting of Openness'—the first demonstration of its kind not sanctioned by the regime."

"Holy shit, Yuri. This is serious. Public protests are illegal, aren't they? Won't we all be arrested?"

"Most likely some of us will, but not for long. They will have to let everyone go free before night-fall," Yuri responded with a smile. "What will be the charge? What crime will be committed? Quoting the Soviet Constitution and demonstrating in its defense? It may be insane, but it's not criminal. If it's criminal, then the Constitution is a sham, as you put it, and the authorities would never have the guts to admit it. The same Constitution guarantees us freedom of assembly, doesn't it?"

"Sure, it does. It's the KGB and its Second Directorate who don't see it the same way," I answered. "What time did you say tomorrow?"

"Three o'clock. Are you in?"

For a moment, I felt like the snow and the sudden gust of wet wind coming from the river had hit me right in the face, nearly choking me. I caught my breath and was instantly relieved, knowing what my answer would be. My newfound courage had not been blown away with that wind. I felt guilty about my initial display of anger.

"You don't have to ask twice, Yuri. I owe it to Andrey. Of course, I'm in!"

"For a moment, I was afraid I was losing you, kid. But now I'm proud you didn't disappoint me. Keep your head up. You're in good company. Be at Pushkin Square tomorrow at three p.m. I'll bring your banner for you. The banners are made out of thin fabric, so they can be easily rolled tight and hidden away until the moment we're all ready to unfurl them."

"How long do you think we'll stand there? Till dusk?" I asked.

"Alex, you're such an optimist," Yuri answered with a simper. "Short of a miracle, we won't last longer than half an hour. It would take about that much time for the local police and the Second Directorate to summon their troops. We just have to make sure that the foreign press will be there to snap as many photos as they can for the world to see how the Second Directorate operatives will break us down, tear up our banners, and chase everybody away."

"You know, Yuri, Andrey was so convinced that pressure from within would bring needed change, but it looks like Tardovsky got it right when he told Andrey that pressure has to be built from the outside. Now it makes total sense to me. Correct me if I'm wrong, but the goal for tomorrow is to gather the foreign press corps at Pushkin Square so they can witness and document our protest for the whole world to see, right?"

"I'll make it simple for you," Yuri dismissively shrugged off my reasoning. "The 'whole world' does not exist. It is a parable and a fractured myth. Our civilization is split into two different worlds. There is a free world somewhere, and then there is ours, which is full of injustice and despair. Inside, outside ... Who the hell cares in the end? We have to build up the pressure to save those two men. If we don't, then all of us could be next."

"That's simple enough," I said. "See you tomorrow."

Sunday was the only day of the week I allowed myself to turn off my alarm clock and sleep late; but that day I woke up early. The neighborhood bakery next door was open, and the smell of freshly baked bread being loaded into delivery trucks penetrated my dorm room through a slightly opened small window leaf. I felt instantly hungry and got dressed to walk downstairs. There was a "secret" passage, once shown to me by the dorm's stoker, from the boiler room right into the bakery's backyard loading dock. That early on Sunday morning, I could always get a couple loaves of bread or a box of breakfast pastries from one of the "entrepreneurial" truck drivers for only a buck. I got the box of just-out-of-the-oven pastries and decided to take a thirty-minute-long walk to my aunt's apartment for a cup of coffee. A morning walk and fresh air should clear my head and give me time to figure out how to break the news to my Aunt Anna about what I was planning to do at three o'clock that day at Pushkin Square.

It was a typical Moscow Sunday morning in early December. The streets were almost empty, and the air was drizzly and frosty. The wind coming out of no-where was dancing in circles along the streets, making it feel even colder, and I had to raise the collar of my old leather jacket to cover my neck. The box of hot pastries and the brisk walk kept the rest of me warm. The skies above the city looked gloomy and gray, but the lampposts along the sidewalks were decorated in bright red colors of flags and banners running along and across the streets, reminding everyone that it was today we were supposed to celebrate the Soviet Constitution Day.

Aunt Anna answered the door and gave me a long, conciliatory hug.

"I was harsh on you the other day. I treated you like a nettlesome child, and I'm sorry for that. It is quite hard for me to get used to the fact that you grew up very fast and are not a kid any longer. I probably should've listened to Andrey and stopped being so protective of you, but honestly, I cannot promise that I will change very soon. It will take some time. In a lot of ways, you are still a kid to me."

"Aunt Anna," I said, "just forget it, please. I love you, and I do understand. Look what I got—some fresh pastries. Can we have a cup of coffee and a little chat? I know that you were trying to protect me from the terrible news about Andrey's arrest that day."

"I did not know how bad the situation was then,

and I hoped that it would resolve itself rather quickly. I was wrong, unfortunately. Let's go to the kitchen; we'll have a cup of coffee and talk it over." She seated me at the kitchen table, opened the box of pastries, and poured two cups of coffee.

"I don't want to keep any secrets from you, Auntie. I'm reading all that crap the newspapers are making up about Andrey. It's horrible, totally dishonest, and making me sick. I shared my feelings with some people I respect and trust. They taught me a great deal about the Brezhnev's regime determination to undermine what Khrushchev's Thaw succeeded in doing, even accidentally. The authorities went all out in their attempt to choke our newly discovered creative freedom, and they are now threatening all of us with repercussions. The paradigm is changing. We cannot succumb to the threats. We have to act. If we allow Andrey and Yuli to be locked up and put away for their writings, then nobody will be safe anymore."

"Is there something else? What are you up to?" Aunt Anna quietly asked, looking straight into my eyes.

"I cannot sit still and do nothing while Andrey is in trouble."

"What are you trying to tell me?" She pretended to be calm but locked her fingers together, and her knuckles turned white.

I took a deep breath.

"A group of people will participate in a peaceful demonstration at Pushkin Square this afternoon. They will be holding a few banners quoting the articles of the Soviet Constitution where it guarantees the liberty of expression and the freedom of assembly. They will be protesting the arrests of Simyavsky and Daniel and demanding an open trial," I ventured to explain.

"And that is how they plan to 'celebrate' the Soviet Constitution Day publicly? Did I get it right?" Aunt Anna interrupted my explanation.

"How did you know that?" I was stunned.

"It doesn't take a genius to figure it out," she replied. "You're planning to be there as well, aren't you?"

"Yes," I said quietly, "I'm planning to be there."

"Have mercy on me, Lord," she whispered. "I assume you realize that you and the rest of your group will be arrested."

"I do, Aunt, but ..."

"But what? Are you willing to risk everything you worked so hard for? You will be kicked out of medical school, and then you will never become a physician. Your poetry will be banned. You will never be published. Are you willing to sabotage your entire future?"

"Aunt Anna, please, hear me out," I pleaded.

"Go ahead," she said. "I'm listening." Her hands were trembling.

"Why is everything about me? My school, my career, my poetry, my future ... You and my parents did not bring me up to be selfish. This is not about me; it is about all of us. Throughout your entire life, like most of your friends, you were trying to cope and survive. You were trying to beat the odds and outsmart the system. All of you hated the regime, but you never resisted it. Andrey is different. He took a stand. The rest of you exerted yourselves to be quiet, to stay away from trouble, away from stirring the pot, never taking chances, thinking ahead about your every move, as if your life were some sort of a timed chess game. Is that how you want me to live my life?" I said in frustration.

She interrupted my short soliloquy. "I lived my life the way I did in hope that your life would be better. There are some things you have not experienced, fortunately, and I hope you never will. You do not know firsthand how severe Stalin's reign was ... how many millions he slaughtered to rule the rest of us in terror and fear. You do not know. It is not something I just read about. I experienced it.

"Your mother and I had two brothers—your uncles you never had a chance to meet. They were in the military. More than twenty-five years ago, one of them lamented about the destiny of his commanding general who had been wrongly accused and later executed. Somebody overheard his lament and reported on him.

Both of my brothers were arrested and charged with treason.

"As a rule, the rest of the family bearing the same last name would also be taken away. Luckily, your mother and I were married by then, and we used our husbands' last names. We were spared, but we never saw our two brothers and their families again.

"Then the war started, and it was another fight for survival. We experienced the bombs falling on our heads and the mass evacuation from Moscow to Siberia. There, we learned firsthand about the massive labor camps of the GULAG. We overcame disease and famine. I lost my husband. Your mother and I each lost our sons. Our lives were not easy.

"In the late nineteen fifties, when Nikita Khrushchev unveiled Stalin's atrocities, we filed an inquiry and later received an official apology letter stating that it was a 'tragic mistake,' and the names of our brothers were rehabilitated posthumously. However, nothing could bring them back. As a tribute to my two brothers' memory, I changed my last name back to my maiden name—Amchislavsky.

"Our unfortunate life experiences taught us to shield our loved ones from even a hint of danger. You can compare my life to a chess game if you wish, but I do not want you to become a sacrificial pawn in your own game of chess. You have to think over every move and every step you take far in advance to avoid the traps and pitfalls placed there by your ruthless opponents. Evaluate the danger. Do not get trapped. This game can be deadly if you lose."

"We are not planning to lose," I reassured her, feeling that she was ready to give up. "We invited a number of foreign press correspondents to document our peaceful protest and let the Western world know of what will transpire at Pushkin Square this afternoon. We thought everything over. Indeed, initially, we will be arrested, but the authorities will be forced to let us go shortly thereafter.

"What are they gonna charge us with? The celebration of the day of our 'beloved' Soviet Constitution? The 'illegal' banners bearing the quotes of the same Constitution guaranteeing us the freedom of assembly? That would be close to impossible. We are going to let the world know that there is a struggle going on in our homeland—the struggle for freedom—and that there are brave people over here who are willing to put everything on the line."

"Did you say 'brave'? Let me break some news to you—one can be brave only when he has nothing to lose," Aunt Anna said, squeezing my hand. "How many of you at Pushkin Square will have nothing to lose? I hope you are right. I cannot stop you. Just do not tell your mom and dad. Go now, and please be careful."

Time was really flying today. I did not realize that my conversation with Aunt Anna had lasted that long. I had less than a couple of hours left to run a few errands. The closer it got to three o'clock, the more restless I became. At a quarter past two, I boarded a trolley running along Boulevard Ring in the direction of Pushkin Square.

I had nothing better to do than just to survey the passengers boarding and exiting our trolley at every stop. Obviously, nobody had a clue what would be happening at Pushkin Square in less than an hour. If Pushkin Square was their final destination, then some of them might witness our rally, and a few of them might be a part of it.

I could not spot any potential participants, but the two guys standing at the front doors caught my attention. Both of them were sporting identical windbreakers and camera bags. They looked like they belonged to the foreign press corps Yuri was counting on so much to be there. I hoped that my presumption was right and that they would get off the trolley at the same stop as I did—Pushkin Square. *Without their timely reporting, it occurred to me, our undertaking would be doomed from the get-go, and our optimistic hope for a brief arrest could turn into one unpredictably prolonged disaster.*

Two more stops were left before the final destination, and my anxiety started to build up.

"Pushkin Square," announced the driver.

I was out first, as soon as the rear doors opened. To my relief, I saw windbreakers and camera bags leaving through the front door a few seconds later.

The square was not any more crowded that day than on any other Sunday. Most of the people were at the rear of the square standing in line for the box office of the Rossia movie theater, and some congestion could be seen at the top of the square around the bronze statue of Alexander Pushkin. The rest of the crowd was evenly milling around the square.

I spotted Yuri next to the monument and rushed in his direction. "Hi, Yuri, I'm here."

"Alex, I'm glad you made it. Here's yours, as I promised," he said as he handed me a tightly folded piece of white cloth. "Hide it under your jacket for now and watch me. When I give everybody the signal, you will pull it out, unfold it, and raise it above your head. Make it very visible. Got it?"

"Everybody, you said? How many are coming? Where are they?" I wondered.

"They are here. So far, about fifty mixed in the crowd around the monument. We have five more minutes."

"I saw a couple of photographers just arrive. They looked like foreigners."

"There are about twenty members of the foreign

press positioned on both sides of the monument. Most of them are photographers. They will start shooting as soon as the police confront us."

"Aren't you nervous?" I asked.

"Honestly?" Yuri answered. "I'm a little nervous. We thought through every move, but it's like a fucking unpredictable chess game. I hope that our game plan will work. The authorities will be trapped. They cannot lock us up for too long. They will be forced to let us go as soon as our embassies abroad start flooding the Kremlin with reports. The foreign media coverage about the disastrous fate of our peaceful Constitution Day Rally for Freedom at Moscow's Pushkin Square will be damaging. Nevertheless, I'm scared shitless that some little detail of our game plan is missing and it will not work as designed for some reason; that we could mess it up somehow; or that we grossly overestimated the sensitivity of Brezhnev's administration. What about you? Are you scared?"

"I have to take a stand for Andrey. I just don't want to think about how scared I am." I looked at my watch. "By the way, we have no more time left to be scared. It's three o'clock sharp," I answered.

"Let's start it then!" Yuri put two fingers to his lips and whistled loudly.

We unfolded our banners simultaneously. About fifty more banners jumped in the air. The square went silent for a moment, and then the crowd started to roar louder and louder.

It did not take too long for the sound of a few police whistles to cut through the roars. Some people sensed trouble and started to pull away to the periphery of the square, while others, overwhelmed with curiosity, were trying to get closer to the monument to see what was going on. A few photographers began to make their move inside the crowd, randomly snapping pictures and firing blinding flashes. Everybody holding a banner started to move closer to each other, forming a nucleus surrounded by a couple hundred sympathetic bystanders.

Some started to chant, "We want freedom, we want freedom, we want freedom ..." More and more voices joined in, and the chants turned louder and louder. "Give us free press! We demand open courts! Free Simyavsky and Daniel!"

Then someone screamed, "Cops!"

I looked to the right, where the voice had come from, and there they were at the corner entrance to the square—a squad of cops leading truckloads of internal security troopers. They charged the crowd, and the mayhem began, accentuated by the strobing lights of camera flashes.

The assault was swift and lasted just a few minutes. The troopers attacked our banners first. The hand-painted constitutional quotes were torn from our hands and taken away by the first line of assailants. Then the second wave of them came in and cut inside of our group as we were trying to stay tightly together. The attackers finally succeeded in separating our pack and dragging us away one by one.

I noticed two guys with familiar windbreakers and camera bags. Both of them hastily left the scene, running in opposite directions. Then the police reinforcements arrived and took care of the bystanders by pushing them away from the square and onto the side streets. The vocal ones who tried to resist were punched and clubbed into obedience. About a dozen covered police trucks were standing ready, idling at the corner entrance of the square. All who were arrested were unceremoniously shoved inside the trucks, locked in, and driven away.

Yuri and I ended up in the same truck. Nobody talked. About ten minutes later, our truck came to a stop inside an unknown internal courtyard.

"Looks like we are at the infamous Lubyanka Prison," somebody said.

We were ordered to step out, escorted as a group into the main building, and locked inside a stinking cage already filled with protestors.

"It does not look too bad so far," Yuri said.

"Really?" I replied. "What does not look too bad? Lubyanka isn't bad enough for you?"

"Think, Alex," he continued. "They placed men and women inside the same cage. We still have our belts and shoelaces. Nobody searched us or took away our documents. Strange, isn't it? The only answer is—they do not know what to do. They will not keep us here for long. They've never dealt with anything like this, so they are feverishly trying to get orders from their superiors. They don't know how to deal with the situation. Nobody wants to be at fault and take responsibility. I can bet on it! In an hour or so, *Voice of America* will start broadcasting the news about our protest at Pushkin Square. Give or take another hour and we'll be out."

"We'll see. I wish I shared your optimism," I replied and then sat on the floor in the corner of the cage, resting my back against the iron bars. A thought crossed my mind: *Andrey's cell could be somewhere nearby, maybe even in the same building.*

A couple of hours passed before two uniformed guards and a second lieutenant approached the cage and unlocked the door.

"Women come out first ... one by one," the second lieutenant announced, and he started to escort the women, one every couple of minutes, through a tall green door into the adjacent room. After the last woman left the cage, he ordered, "Men now. Same way ... one by one, as I said."

I squeezed Yuri's elbow and whispered, "We are all in deep shit! They are separating the men and women now. Next, they'll take our belts and search us."

"Think positive," Yuri replied. "I'm telling you; they're letting all of us out."

"I hope you're right," I whispered back.

Soon it was my turn to go. I knew that I was shivering when I walked out of the cage, following the second lieutenant through the tall green door. He led me into a small room where a female sergeant was sitting behind the desk at the opposite set of doors.

"Your documents," she said in a flat, unemotional voice.

I gave her my student ID. She studied it for a moment, entered my name into an open folder, and then asked, "Where do you live?"

"In a dorm," I answered.

"Which campus?"

"On Pirogova Street."

She marked it down and gave my student ID back.

"Your pass number is L thirty-seven. Proceed through the door to the checkpoint on your right." She gave me a round token and buzzed the door open. I turned right and walked alone down the narrow corridor to a checkpoint equipped with a full-height turnstile placed in front of the exit doors. It was reminiscent of a medieval torture device.

"Stand close!" commanded the guard attending the rotogate. "Give me your token. What is your pass number?"

"L thirty-seven," I said and passed my token to him.

He punched the number into a keypad, inserted the token into a slot, and pressed the button. "Proceed!"

The turnstile clicked and swiveled me through. I pushed the exit door open and walked outside. There, I took a deep breath of the cold, misty night air and slowly exhaled, trying to calm myself down as I looked around. "Furkasovskiy Pereulok" read the street sign.

I was standing alone, outside the back wall of Lubyanka jail next to the KGB headquarters on the opposite side of Dzerzhinsky Square, hesitant to believe that our plan had worked.

Chapter Eight

The End of *New Word*

It was way past midnight, and the metro, trolley, and tramlines were closed for the night. Other than the ever-present taxicabs, a few bus routes had been kept open, but the buses were running on a sparse, late-night schedule. I did not have enough money for cab fare, so I had to settle for a one-hour bus ride to my aunt's place.

At 2:30 in the morning, I finally rang her doorbell. The door swung open instantly. Wearing a terry robe over her nightgown, Aunt Anna stood there wide-awake, as she'd been waiting for me to show up at her doorway. She grabbed me by the shoulders and broke down crying.

"I was worried sick about you." She wiped her tears with the back of her left hand while pounding my shoulder with the right one. "You're such a bastard!" she wept. "A grown-up bastard whom I love so much. I knew the day would come when you would do something crazy like that ... something out of my control. But I'm not quite ready for all that stuff yet. I'm not ready to take it."

She continued to sob quietly while burying her

face in my chest and caressing my tousled hair. It felt for a moment as if she were lost, despairingly trying to pull herself together. I'd never seen her so upset.

I tried to calm her down. "Auntie, I love you too. Stop crying. Compose yourself, please. I might be a bastard, but I'm a lucky bastard. I'm here, and I'm safe. Everything went according to plan. We were let out of Lubyanka jail shortly after midnight."

"Lubyanka? Of all places? Oh my God!" She stepped back and wiped her face with the sleeve of her robe. "All evening long, I was glued to my short-wave radio, listening to *Voice of America* and *Radio Free Europe* describing the gory details of what was happening at Pushkin Square. Most of the frequencies were jammed, and I had to jump from one station to another all evening long, trying to hear more news. All the broadcasts painted quite a gloomy and terrifying picture. I didn't know how much of it was true, embellished, or exaggerated. While you were there, I was at home listening to my shortwave radio and being scared to death for you."

"Did you talk to my parents?" I asked. "Do they know where I was?"

"No, they do not. I talked to your mom earlier and told her that you were probably at the dorm studying. You are making a liar out of me, my dear."

"I'm sorry, Auntie, but you warned me not to

share my whereabouts yesterday afternoon with Mom and Dad. You are the only one in my family who understands what is going on and wouldn't throw a fit. My parents, on the other hand, would go ballistic for sure if I even attempted to level with them."

"Throwing a fit," Aunt Anna replied, "would do no more good than it would have done to argue with you yesterday. It is admirable that you acted selflessly and stood up for Andrey, but you have to learn how to be a bit more pragmatic. Emotional decisions, most of the time, will render undesirable results."

I became defensive. "How can you ask me to be pragmatic and void of emotions if Andrey is in prison? He is my mentor and my dear friend. You are asking way too much of me. By the way, he is your friend as well. What is your plan?"

"I do not have a plan yet, but I'm working on one. I'm exploring every connection of mine, every contact I have, everyone who owed me a favor in the past, and anyone who can be useful. It is not that easy. As I told you so many times before, we are in a deadly chess game. You do not know the scale of the evil we are up against. There is no second chance. You have to make the right move on the first attempt and not get trapped. What good can it do for Andrey if we all fail and become useless? I might not find the answer right away, but I will not give up until I have one."

"Aren't you tired of making futile plans and looking for viable answers all your life and finding only quixotic solutions? How many pawns have to be sacrificed in this chess game of yours? How many lives do you need to live to defeat the evil you are talking about?"

"It is not my game, Alex, and I'm not in it willingly. I have only one life, and I will not stop trying for as long as I am breathing. It is our destiny, my boy. We have to fight not to become one of those sacrificed pawns, even if we cannot figure out how to win for now. There is no escape from it—no way out." She suddenly looked at her wristwatch and swung open the door to her study. "You will sleep on the couch. Enough talking for tonight. You do have classes in the morning, don't you?"

"No way out? Maybe there is. There has to be… somewhere," I said under my breath, and then gave Aunt Anna a good-night hug.

December whisked by swiftly. Unbeknown to any of us yet, the Constitution Day demonstration at Moscow's Pushkin Square would become an annual human rights event that would later be dubbed Glasnost (Openness) Meetings. In the meantime, the year 1965 was rapidly coming to an end. It had started carelessly well with Svetlana and the youthful euphoria of falling in love, *New Word* magazine and the inebriation of my fleeting literary success, and Andrey Simyavsky and his life-changing mentorship. Then, on the flip side, the year had hastily succumbed to the sobriety of a never-ending struggle with injustice, hatred, arrests, persecution, and the doldrums of our glum and exitless reality. I came to understand how much the past twelve months had given me and how much more it had taken away. A year later, I was definitely more mature and far less innocent.

As New Year's Eve came and went, I was in a somber mood. I was thinking of Svetlana all night long as I looked through the window of my dorm room and watched the snowflakes dancing slowly in the wind. Exactly a year before, I'd been looking at her sitting naked on a windowsill, gazing at the falling snow, and reciting verses of Omar Khayyam; but now I knew that she was far away, both literally and figuratively.

It felt like we had grown apart. Svetlana had called me a couple of times in the early summer, but I had not heard from her since. She did not know how much my life had changed in the last few months. I'd never spoken to her about Andrey, and I doubted now if I ever could. She'd left Moscow to live over four thousand miles away with her dad, with whom she was very close. Knowing that he was a one-star general holding a very high position at the Space Center, I would never venture to share with her my innermost thoughts of dissent and the level of my frustration with our regime and how oppressive it had become. Nevertheless, some part of me inexplicably missed her a lot, and I felt wretched.

Another month passed, and Andrey's incarceration and upcoming trial overshadowed everything else. Masha Simyavsky called Aunt Anna one night to inform her that Andrey's trial was scheduled to start in a week—on the 10th of February. The next morning, I bumped into a shivering Yuri Vizbor, who was waiting for me at the main entrance of the medical school.

"I've been standing here freezing my ass off since seven o'clock looking for you."

"My class starts at eight. Why didn't you call?" I asked.

"I'm afraid our phones are bugged. The State Security is most likely tracing all our phone calls now. I heard a rumor last night that Simyavsky and Daniel's trial is scheduled to start in a week."

"It's not a rumor. My aunt talked to Andrey's wife, Masha, last night. Yes, the trial will start on February tenth, but you did not come here to wait for me in the cold for almost an hour just to say 'Hi'. What's up, Yuri? Are you plotting another protest? Let's go ahead. I am so frustrated with being helpless that I'm ready for anything. Just tell me, how long will we be arrested for this time? Cut to the chase."

"Your guess is almost right, Alex, but hear me out. I'm trying to assemble a sizable group of people to show support for the defendants in front of the Superior Court every day of that trial. Since the trial will be held behind closed doors, all the foreign press will be gathered at the entrance steps of the Superior Court, separated from the rest of us by police barricades. We will be standing behind those barricades peacefully in front of the press corps cameras. There will be no arrests, no banners, no protests—just a massive show of support. We have to gather a lot of people there. I need your help."

"I'm in! What else can I do?" I fired back without even a pause.

"Can you get in touch with all your acquaintances you trust and ask them to join the rest of us outside of the Superior Court building for the duration of the trial? Will you do that?"

"You know I will, Yuri."

"Since our phones are bugged, phone calls are out. You must do some legwork. You have to contact people personally. We do not want to alert the State Security's hound dogs," Yuri warned me.

"How do you know for sure that our phones are bugged?" I asked.

"I am more than certain of it. Those bastards are listening in on the phone calls of every one of us who was arrested at Pushkin Square last December. Didn't they ask for your name and address before letting you out? We are certainly on their watch list and under surveillance now."

"I'll be careful, I promise. Thank you for the invite, by the way. I'm sorry; I have to hurry to my class now. I'll recruit everyone I can. I'll be in touch, Yuri," I said and firmly shook his hand.

That day's lectures flew by, and not a single word registered. I just could not concentrate; instead, I tried to think of which like-minded people I could trust. Regretfully, by the end of the school day, I had only been able to come up with a couple of names. *Better than nothing*, I said to myself.

Over the next few days, I had to get in touch with Mila Siegel at the Ostankino TV station. Next would be Edward Steinberg, whose art studio near Arbat Square I had visited once. Artist Misha Schwartzman and sculptor Vladimir Weysberg were sharing a loft above Edward's art studio. I'd seen all three of them on a couple of occasions since that night at the Expression Club. I'd also learned not long ago that Misha had been at our protest at Pushkin Square but that he'd come late and had been on the opposite side of the monument when the police had charged the protesters. He'd been lucky enough to be able to run away to avoid being arrested.

On my way back to the dorm, I suddenly thought of Lara Katz. I actually smiled thinking of that feisty, freckle-faced girl. I felt that after what had happened with both of us at the medical school entrance exams the previous summer, she was definitely at odds with the regime, and I could trust her.

From the beginning of the school year in September, all three thousand students in our freshman class had been separated into smaller study groups. Lara and I had ended up being assigned to different groups, and, until now, our paths had not crossed. We'd only seen each other peripherally on a couple of occasions. I looked up her schedule and decided to wait for the end of her anatomy class.

As I waited at the exit of the lab, the door swung open. I saw her coming out with a group of students. I walked up to her. "Hi, Lara! How are you?"

"Hey, stranger," she greeted me with a smile. "What are you doing here? Waiting for someone?"

"Actually, I'm waiting for you."

"You're waiting for me?" A blush spread across her freckled face. "What's the occasion?"

"Are you done here for today? Can we talk?"

"Sure," she replied. "Let's grab our coats and you can walk me to my trolley station, okay?"

We checked out our coats at the cloakroom downstairs and stepped outside. The courtyard was covered with a fresh layer of snow. We passed through the gates and kept walking silently down the street.

"Why are we here?" Lara broke the awkward silence. "What did you want to talk about?"

"So, how's school going for you?" I was not sure how to start.

"Same as for you, I guess."

"Have you made any new friends here?" I continued.

"Some, but I mostly keep in touch with a few girls from our infamous 'Jewish group.' Remember, the one you rescued us from last summer, the weekend before the admission exams? How about you? Any new friends?"

"Not at the medical school. I've made a few good acquaintances in some different circles ... outside of the medical school. You know ..."

"What circles?"

"Different ones ..."

"Alex, stop talking in riddles. You don't have to be so sly with me. I'm not dumb; I know who you are."

"For real? Then who am I, Lara?"

"You are Alex the Poet. I recognized you the first time we met. I do read *New Word*, and I know your poetry. Stop being so clandestine," Lara unloaded and jokingly pushed me away. "Everyone at school knows who you are."

"Are you kidding me?" I had not realized that, and it took me by surprise. "Seriously, what else do you know about me?"

"I know that you are not looking for a date and that you're involved with somebody else." Lara blushed again.

"Who told you that?" I protested.

"You did, when we first met. I remember it very well."

"Did I? But that was then—almost eight months ago. It's a bit more complicated than that. I mean, a lot more complicated. Never mind …" I mumbled, trying to figure out how to change the subject and get to the point.

Somehow, right from the start, Lara had taken charge, and she did not want to relinquish it. Her inner strength was almost palpable. I remembered it from our first encounter, and that quality of hers had never failed to amaze me.

"So, why are we here?" She broke out laughing. "Come on; tell me. The suspense is killing me!"

Her laugh was so contagious that I started to smile back.

"Can you stop it for a second, please?" I begged her. "Can you let me talk? I'm serious."

"Start talking then … seriously." She suddenly stopped laughing and looked at me, waiting for my response.

"Do the names Simyavsky and Daniel sound familiar or mean anything to you?" I asked.

"Are you talking about the two writers arrested not long ago who'll be put on trial soon?"

"Yes, I am talking about them. So, you are aware—"

Lara interrupted me impatiently, "Of course, I am. Correct me if I'm wrong. Those two 'unlawfully' published their books abroad since the censorship expurgated them as anti-Soviet propaganda and barred their publication at home. Is that what it was?" Lara paused, waiting for my response.

"You got that right, Lara ..."

"... and the point is," she continued, "that the newspapers' campaign orchestrated by the authorities against those two writers was the most despicable and cruel propaganda offensive against anyone I have ever witnessed."

Suddenly, she squinted her eyes, stepped up to me, and said, "Why did you ask me about it? How are you involved? Don't tell me you know both of them; do you?"

"I don't know Yuli Daniel personally, but Andrey Simyavsky is my mentor and my dearest friend."

"Alex, I'm so sorry for laughing earlier. I wasn't aware ..."

"You don't have to feel sorry, but I'm here to ask you for help."

"Tell me what I should do," Lara fired back.

"The trial starts next week. My friends are trying to assemble a sizable group of people to show our support for Simyavsky and Daniel on the steps of the Superior Court for the duration of the trial. There will be a lot of foreign press there. The photographs of massive support outside the Superior Court printed in Western newspapers would hopefully apply enough pressure on the Communist Party Central Committee to influence a lenient outcome of the trial."

"Count on me. I will be there," Lara assured me.

"I know you will, but we need as many people as we can get. Can you get in touch with your friends and get them to come there as well?"

"I'll talk to my girlfriends—the ones from that 'Jewish list.' I bet they will be eager to join us."

"It's a long story, Lara, but you have to believe me—the State Security's Second Directorate is monitoring most of the phone calls, and we do not want to alarm them. You have to contact your friends in person. No phone calls. Can you do it in the next couple of days?"

"I will, Alex ... definitely will." She suddenly gave me a big hug and added, "I'm so glad you found me."

"So am I, Lara. Please, stay in touch."

"I will." She turned around and dashed down the street to her trolley, which was about to leave the station.

Early the next morning, instead of going to my classes, I stood guard at the entrance of the Ostankino TV station, looking for Mila Siegel. After more than three hours, my feet turned cold and numb. *Maybe I missed her in the crowd*, I reasoned to myself. I took a tram back to school with the intention of returning to Ostankino at the end of the day. However, a few more hours of waiting rendered the same result later. It was very late when I finally decided to cut my watch short and return to the dorm. *It could've been her day off today*, was my concluding thought. *I'll try again tomorrow.*

My patience was rewarded the next morning when I spotted Mila exiting the subway station. I rushed to intercept her before she approached the TV station's checkpoint gate. She saw me right away and greeted me with a hug.

"I haven't seen you in so long," she said almost apologetically.

"I called you a couple of times and left messages, but you didn't return my calls."

"That's quite unusual," Mila said, looking past me. "Nobody gave me your messages. So, what's up?"

"I want to ask you a favor," I said.

"Hurry up; I don't want to be late. What is it?" Her response did not sound encouraging; it was short and almost rude. She seemed to be a different person;

not the same one I had met before. I decided to cut right to the chase without spilling any of the details.

"Will you be willing to join me in front of the Superior Court next Thursday morning?"

"What for?" Mila asked.

"To show support at Simyavsky and Daniel's trial." I assumed she knew what I was talking about, and it seemed I was right.

"Who else is coming?" she asked without making eye contact. Somehow, I did not like the tone of her voice.

"A few of my medical school friends will be there. I don't think you know any of them."

"I would consider being there, Alex, but I have to be honest with you … I'm afraid to put my career in jeopardy for some childish show of support. What good will it do anyway? Both of those writers did some stupid shit, and now all of us are paying the price. Come to think of it, I'm out."

"Come to think of it, you were never in!" I replied and hastily walked away.

I spent the rest of the day at school. I could not stop thinking about my morning encounter with Mila Siegel. What a great disappointment she'd turned out to be. I remembered that evening at the Expression Club when she'd raised the toast *to us—the expressionists of the New World*. I had trusted her sincerity then, but this morning,

I'd sensed right away that something had been wrong, and luckily, I'd stopped short of revealing to her that our common friend, Yuri Vizbor, was in charge of the whole thing. It was hard to believe that someone who was so altruistically involved in avant-garde arts and literature could be so selfish and callous. *What a deceptive bitch she'd turned out to be. Live and learn*, I said to myself.

I had only one day left, and I decided that the next day, right after school, I would pay a visit to Edward Steinberg at his studio. Since the other two "metaphysicists," Misha Schwartzman and Vladimir Weysberg, occupied the loft in the same building, I would be able to see all of them on the same night. Deep inside, I was almost sure that it would not turn into another disappointing meeting, but, after what had happened that morning, everything had become questionable, and I'd learned that it was not prudent to vouch for anyone anymore.

The next morning, I decided to head to school a little earlier to glance through my notes before my biochemistry test. To my surprise, I bumped into Misha Schwartzman at the medical school entrance. He grabbed me by the elbow and pulled me away.

"I have to talk to you, Alex. It's urgent and extremely important. I know that your class will be starting in fifteen minutes, but it won't take long."

"What's going on? Is everything okay? I was planning to visit your studio tonight anyway."

"Don't be alarmed. Everything is fine. I just wanted to ask you to join us on Thursday morning on the steps to the Superior Court to show support for Simyavsky and Daniel. Bring as many friends with you as you can. By the way, were you planning to visit my studio tonight for any particular reason?"

I broke out laughing. Misha looked at me curiously, as if I were losing my mind.

"Why are you laughing?" he asked. "Did I say something funny? I don't think I did. What's wrong with you?"

"Nothing is wrong," I answered. "Everything is fine. You just made my day. Believe it or not, I was planning to visit your studio tonight to talk to you, Vlad, and Edward about the same thing—about Thursday morning. I'm so glad you came here first."

"Isn't that something!" Misha exclaimed. "Great minds think alike. I have an idea. Don't change your plans. Come over to my studio tonight anyway. Some of my friends will be there. I just sold a couple of my paintings, and we're gonna celebrate together. Go to your classes now. See you tonight around seven o'clock." He shook my hand and disappeared around the corner. I turned back and walked through the school doors, smiling from ear to ear.

February in Moscow is routinely adorned with cloudy gray skies, cold, and snow, but on that Thursday, not a single cloud could be found. The sun was shining, trying to soften up the gelid air. However, as a reminder to everyone that winter was still here to stay for at least another couple of months, gigantic piles of dirty snow accentuated the crooked nakedness of the linden trees sashaying along the sidewalks of the city streets.

Police barricades crisscrossed the square in front of the Superior Court. It resembled a gigantic tic-tac-toe board and extended uphill to the entrance steps of the main building. A sizable crowd had been building up for the last couple of hours on both sides of the barricades fencing in the single-lane driveway leading to the court entrance.

When the black, windowless van backed into the driveway, the crowd came alive and started to roar. They pushed against the barricades, slowly moving them closer to each other. Unable to negotiate the suddenly narrowed driveway, the van came to a complete halt, and a platoon of internal security troops rushed from the court's entrance to the back doors of the stalled "Black Raven."

The doors slowly swung open, and Andrey Simyavsky stepped out. He looked up and around, as if searching for someone in the crowd, before being encased by the guards. They swiftly threaded him through the shouts of support, in and out of pickets of outstretched arms and raised fists, up the steps, and in through the doors of the Superior Court building.

I did not have a chance to fight my way through the crowd to get a little closer to him. My heart sank when, even from where I stood, I saw Andrey's withered body and his hollow-cheeked, ashen, exhausted face.

I spent all three days coming to the square and standing there. Surrounded by likeminded rabble, I was an insignificant piece of a hopelessly unsolvable puzzle. Frozen by the irremediable despair of the inevitable outcome, I was unable to talk to anyone. Then, at the very end of the third day, the appalling news of the final verdict descended upon us. The crowd was stunned and slowly dissipated without a sound.

When I finally came to my senses, I found myself sitting across from my Aunt Anna at her kitchen table. "I am a wreck, Auntie." My voice was quivering. "Everything is destroyed. There is no hope in sight."

"Pick yourself up," she said calmly. "Do you remember the closing verses of your poem 'Salvaged Hope'?"

"Of course, I do!" I exclaimed and recited it aloud:
"At the end of the thorny rope of betrayal and disgrace,
We did salvage our hope at a price of our faith...

"But what does that have to do with anything?" I wondered.

"A lot if not everything! Be true to your poetry. Do not turn it into a simple slogan. Live by your words. Never surrender your hope. Never give up! What is happening right now around us is destroying your faith in a just society, but it should only strengthen your resolve to protect your soul and to be a survivor. Keep your hope alive! One day, when you feel that you have nothing to lose but yourself, your hope will carry the day, and you will set yourself free. Live for that day, my dear Alex. Live for that day."

"Easier said than done, Auntie. I think I'll go to see Masha Simyavsky now and spend this evening with her. She should not be left alone."

"She is not alone! Where do you think she spent the last two nights? She was here. We ate dinner together, and then she went to my study, opened her notebook, and worked on it till way past midnight. I talked to Masha not long ago, just before you came, and offered to keep her company, but she wanted to be left alone.

"During the trial, she was documenting every-thing that took place there. Being trained in the past as a stenographer, she recorded in shorthand every witness, every statement, and every word. She is at home now working, transcribing her notes, and does not want to be disturbed.

"I want to level with you and dispel your notion that nobody cares, that everything is over, and that nothing else can be done. Just keep what I tell you to yourself, promise?"

I nodded in response.

"We are developing a contact who is willing to help us set up the right channels to smuggle the transcript of the trial proceedings abroad. The free world has to know all the details of that trial."

As I sat down looking at my aunt, my jaw dropped. As she opened up to me, I saw a side of her that I never knew existed. She was a sly, crafty, and surreptitious fighter contriving her next moves like a bona fide chess player. I was ready to jump. The fight for Andrey was not over. She had not given up. Now she was escalating it to recruit the support of the free world.

Stunned by this revelation, I headed to the dorm encouraged, enlivened, and relieved.

A couple of weeks later while at school, I was suddenly called to the dean's office, where a message was waiting for me. Claudia Petrovna, the dean's secretary, informed me that I had been requested to make an immediate appearance at the main office of the *New Word* publishing house.

"The dean wants you to cut your classes short and

comply with this request at once," Claudia Petrovna said, looking at me above her eyeglasses.

"What is this all about?" I was totally taken by surprise. What was the connection between my medical school and my publishing house? It did not make any sense. "Why is the dean involved?" I asked Claudia Petrovna.

"Dean Dubinin told me to give you this message just before he went into a meeting. I do not know any details. You better do what he said right now." Claudia Petrovna returned to her typewriter, indicating to me that her mission had been accomplished and that our short conversation was now over.

I left Pirogova campus and jumped into a trolley traveling along Boulevard Ring. I could not figure out why I'd been summoned by my magazine so urgently. Twenty minutes later, I walked into the *New Word* lobby. The very moment I crossed the doors, I was confronted by a group of uniformed State Security troopers.

"Your documents!" Before I could react, my book bag was taken away, and two of the guards frisked me and emptied my pockets. I was then escorted to the second-floor conference room.

A man dressed in a civilian suit was seated at the head of the conference table, and a major and a colonel with State Security epaulettes were standing behind him at the window.

"Take a seat, young fellow," said the man as he pointed to a single chair on the opposite side of the long table. I sat down, still trying to figure out what was going on.

"My name is Nikita Kirilovich. Do you know why we're all here?" the man asked.

"I honestly have no clue," I answered. "I hope you will explain it to me." To my surprise, I was calm and collected.

"Your poetry is almost a regular feature of *New Word*. It is quite powerful, and I would venture to say even a bit provocative. You undoubtedly have talent and the support of your slightly misguided fans. Obviously, Tardovsky also likes your work. That's what sells his magazine. Right? Where did you learn to write like that? Was there anybody who influenced your development as a poet? What do you think?"

His patronizing tone of voice and demeanor projected authoritative power, but somehow, I did not feel like I was falling under his dominating spell so far.

He suddenly changed the subject. "What do your parents do?"

"My dad is a barber, and my mom is a seamstress."

"Do they write poetry, if I may ask? Do you have any siblings?"

"No, my folks do not write. Siblings ... My older brother was killed in nineteen forty-four, fighting

Nazi Germany, a year before I was born. I never met him. I do not have any more siblings."

"I am sorry to hear that. I lost my older brother in that war as well. Many people died to protect our lives. Now back to your poetry ... I learned that you did enjoy some literary mentoring from Andrey Simyavsky in the not-so-distant past. Tell me about your interaction with him. Do you think he influenced your political ... I mean your *poetical* development?"

I knew whom I was dealing with now. This man was a smooth operator. Switching subjects in the middle of a sentence, interchanging words, giving accolades, at times acting sympathetic and then redirecting the guilt to someone else was nothing more than his interrogative style. It was a technique designed to play on one's emotional and psychological feebleness. Andrey had taught me how to use a similar approach in creative writing for when an author wants to lure his reader into the trap of an unexpected finale. *Why couldn't I try the same?* I thought.

"What was your brother's name?" I asked.

"What brother? Oh, you mean my *late* brother. His name was Vladimir. What was *your* brother's name?" he asked in return. This man was slick.

"Are you serious?" I looked straight at him and saw nothing but a bit of surprise and a cold look of irrelevance in his eyes. "What a coincidence! My brother's name was Vladimir too," I continued. "Second Lieutenant Vladimir Loevsky. He was just nineteen years old when he died."

"Yeah … War is a tough business," he replied. "Why don't we return to the subject of your poetry?"

"I'm sorry; I kinda went off on a tangent. What did you ask me about my poetry before?" My resolve to play his game only strengthened.

"How close were you to Andrey Simyavsky?" Now I could see that my interrogator was starting to get a bit irritated. "Were you his friend, his confidant?"

"I wish I were, but he was in a different league. No, we were not close at all. Occasionally, he helped me to work on my style, rhymes, rhythm, cadence … You know, all that technical stuff. I do not know if he had any friends. He was almost an introvert, a loner." I lied with such conviction that I almost started to believe myself.

"Who introduced you to Simyavsky? How did it happen?"

I know what you're doing, pal. I paused for a moment. *You are way too transparent. Try harder next time.*

"Nobody did. We met last year. He was my Russian literature instructor at the high school I graduated from." I was figure skating around the truth, carving my answers in a way that ensured they were very close to it. I could not afford to be caught in a blatant lie.

"And how did both of you end up here at *New Word* together?" He was still trying to entrap me.

"Andrey Denisovich suggested to me that I show my poetry to Alexander Tardovsky. You probably know that he was this magazine's literary critic a long time ago."

"Did you have a chance to read Simyavsky's latest novel *Lyubimov*? What do you think of it, honestly?"

Take it easy, fellow, I thought. *I'm not that stupid.* "Did he write a novel? I didn't know he was a novelist. I always thought he was just a literary critic."

"You did hear about his trial, didn't you? It was in all the newspapers."

"I thought he was on trial for his articles published abroad, not for a book."

"Did you ever meet his wife ... what's her name?" His style of questioning was becoming increasingly aggressive, and he was probing everywhere.

"Yes, I did. Her name is Masha. I saw her on a couple of occasions when Andrey Denisovich was helping me with my poetry and invited me to his apartment."

"How recently have you seen her?"

"I think it was last year ... maybe in April," I said, hoping he did not know the truth.

"You haven't seen her since the trial, like in the last few days, have you? I am giving you a chance to be honest with me ... to come clean."

I felt relieved. Now I was sure he did not know the truth.

"I am being totally honest with you. I have not seen her in the last few days. That's the truth."

"Okay then. I believe you." He turned his head to the window. "Major, you had a question, didn't you? Go ahead."

"By the way, Loevsky," the major said coming forward all the way from the window and putting a heavy folder on the table in front of me, "can you check this folder out? See if you recognize any of the writings. Whom do they belong to?"

There was a label on the folder's spine—*Loevsky, Alexander. Poetry (sociopolitical). Pending publications.* I looked through the pages slowly, feeling that something sinister was about to happen.

"Yes, I did write all of it." I looked at him, pondering what to expect from this one. "All of this belongs to me."

"Not anymore!" the major yelled back, ripping the folder from my hands. "It belongs to us now. This garbage should never again see the light of day. You and all your motherfucking collaborators who helped you to concoct and circulate this anti-Soviet malice, who published all that bitter venom of yours, will be held equally responsible for the dissemination of this poison." He angrily returned to the window mumbling, "bunch of ungrateful cocksuckers…"

Nikita Kirilovich was quietly studying my reaction from across the table and softly drumming the top with his fingertips. "You can go for now, but we are not done." He got up and dismissively gestured for me to leave.

On my way back to school, I tried to make sense of what had just happened at *New Word*. What had prompted the State Security to take charge over there? What was all that bullshit about my talent and my misguided fans? Why had they tried so hard to establish the extent of my connection to Simyavsky? They had already managed to convict and sentence him a couple weeks ago without my "assistance." What about that screaming major ripping my poetry folder away and spewing threats and expletives?

Suddenly, it came to me. I recalled the warning Aunt Anna had given me a while ago: *You never know what can happen in our country. Our "comrades in charge" ... they can take your poetry away ... they can close magazines, stop publications. It has happened here before ...* If only I had realized then how prescient her premonition had been. I now understood why that moron had told me that my poetry would never see the light of day. I didn't think that Tardovsky would ever abandon me as long as he was in charge of *New Word* ... But what if he wouldn't be in charge of it anymore? What if they ordered the magazine to close? Then what? I figured I would find out soon.

Somehow, instead of uncontrollable panic, my mind went into a rationalized survival mode. I stopped at a payphone booth and dialed the number for Simyavsky's apartment. I was concerned about my interrogator's attempts to find out if I'd seen Masha after the trial. I had to let her know. Where had he been trying to lead me? What had he been looking for? I couldn't explain it, and that bothered me.

The phone rang for a while, but nobody answered. *I'll try again later*, I thought.

I returned to the school's anatomy lab and rushed through my assignment. I was done in less than three hours and then headed toward my aunt's home. On the way, I stopped at the payphone and dialed Masha's number again. This time, the line went dead.

"Masha is missing," Aunt Anna told me when I arrived. "Nobody knows where she is. We've been looking for her for the past three days. I've already arranged for her neighbors to report her disappearance to the local police by noon tomorrow if she doesn't show up tonight."

"Maybe that's why they were asking me if I've seen her since the trial." I recounted to Aunt Anna every detail I could remember of how I'd been summoned to *New Word* and of the interrogation to which I had been subjected.

"I was afraid it would happen sooner or later," she said. "The bastards will close *New Word*. I just sense it. Those thugs are on an all-out assault now. They are ruthless."

"But, Aunt Anna, why are they looking for Masha? Does her disappearance have anything to do with it?" I was baffled.

"It does, Alex. Trust me. As I told you before, Masha was documenting everything that happened in court during Andrey's trial. The authorities kept the trial closed for a reason. Brezhnev's goons did not want the world to find out how mercilessly they squash intellectual dissent. The real truth told about the trial would be a huge embarrassment for the regime.

"A few days ago, Masha was set to meet with someone who would try to pass her transcript of the trial to a third party capable of smuggling it out of the country to Andrey's publisher in Switzerland. I am not totally sure, but I think the young man's name was Mark Levine or Levitt, and she felt she could trust the people who introduced him to her. They gave her assurances that he would find a way to make it happen."

"So this interrogator of mine, Nikita Kirilovich, was beating around the bush while actually trying to find out if I knew where Masha's notebook was?

Freaking scoundrel! He really knew how to weave a tightly convoluted web. I hope Masha is safe."

"I hope she is …" Aunt Anna looked up and added, "Please, dear God, help us all …"

Chapter Nine

Missing Notebook

L ate that night, on my way to the dorm, I stopped at Simyavsky's apartment to see if Masha was back. Nobody answered the doorbell. Just to be sure, I knocked on the door a few times—same result; she was not there.

Suddenly, the neighbor's apartment door opened a crack, and I heard a woman's voice whisper, "There is no reason to knock. Nobody is there to answer. Masha has not come back yet. I know that you are their friend. I've seen you visit many times before. I am worried sick for her. She would never leave for more than a day without letting me know—especially since the day Andrey, her husband, was arrested.

"I'm afraid something bad had happened. I just sense it. Her sister-in-law came here a few hours ago. She had a key, but the very moment she unlocked the door, she was arrested and dragged away. You have to be extremely careful, young man."

The woman stretched her hand out through the opening into the murky light of the stairwell and gestured me into her apartment. "Come inside. Quickly. I'll let you through the service stairs and out through the back door."

In total silence, I was threaded through the darkness of somebody else's apartment and out the back door to a narrow stairwell leading to a dark courtyard and then to the backstreet. I cautiously looked around and did not see anyone following me.

I returned to the dorm way past midnight and went straight to bed. My mind was mulling feverishly over everything that had happened that day, but I was dead tired to concentrate on anything. The very moment my head touched the pillow, a deep sleep befell me, calming my troubled mind and wiping away all the boundaries of reality.

I dreamed that I was in an empty theater, hiding deep inside the orchestra pit next to a set of huge barrel-shaped drums. The orchestra was rehearsing Tchaikovsky's *1812 Overture*. The conductor turned his head in my direction, graciously waved his baton, and pointed it at me screaming, "Louder! Open up! Now!" The percussionist started pounding the living hell out of the drums so loudly that it started to hurt my ears to the point that I had to wake up.

I then discovered that someone was indeed pounding on my dorm room door.

"Open this fucking door at once! That is an order!" The door was ready to give way and almost flew off its hinges.

"Give me a second!" I shouted back, as I turned

on the light and hurriedly attempted to don a pair of pants and a T-shirt.

When I finally unlocked the door, I was pinned against the wall by a couple of policemen. I then saw the familiar face of the State Security major whom I'd had the "pleasure" of meeting in the *New Word* conference room. Without warning, he buried his fist in my stomach.

"Where did you hide that fucking notebook? Answer me, motherfucker!"

For a moment, I lost my breath and became nauseous. He then whacked me again and again. I tried to squeeze out my response before he could punch me once more.

"What notebook? Don't hit me again, please. I really don't know what notebook you're talking about. Please, don't. Just explain to me what notebook you're looking for."

This time, he hit me across the face.

"The green leather-bound notebook, fuckhead! The same one that bitch, Simyavsky's wife, gave you before she was hit by a car the other night! Where is it? Who did you give it to? I will punch you again if you don't open up. Move your fucking lips and say it! Where is the notebook?"

Masha was hit by a car?! Had I heard him correctly? I was crouching down in pain and agony.

"I didn't know she was hit by a car. You didn't make that up, did you?"

"Oh, *you didn't know it*, you little piece of shit. Why did you ask me if I made it up then? You just couldn't hide that you were much closer to her than you would like us to believe. Do you care to find out what happened to her? For real? Well, she is dead now. Dead! What I care to find out is where you hid that green notebook! Will I really have to beat the fucking answer out of you, or will you cooperate?" His fist flew right into my face and split my lips open. I was now swallowing a steady stream of my own blood.

"Comrade Major, I *am* being honest. I do not know …" I was unable to finish my sentence before he began to pound me in the stomach repeatedly until I fell to my knees and started to vomit.

"I am not your comrade, you fucking wimp! Drop this worthless piece of shit on the floor. Let him choke on his own vomit. We will get to him later!" he ordered both policemen, who were still holding me by the arms. "Start searching his room. Look inside every crevice. Turn all his stuff upside down and inside out if you have to. That notebook of hers has to be hidden somewhere. Report to me after you're done." The major left the room, kicking me in the stomach one more time on his way out.

The search lasted for more than a couple of hours.

All my books, notes, and handouts were torn from their jackets and thrown on the floor, blanketing it in multiple layers. My mattress and pillows were meticulously dissected into pieces, rendering them totally useless. I watched how senselessly everything was being destroyed as I sat on the floor, supporting my head against a corner wall.

Luckily, Masha's notebook was not in my possession. The only conciliatory thought that entered my mind while those fuckers searched my room in vain was that, hopefully, the green leather-bound notebook was in good hands and on its way across the borders of the Soviet Union. The world must be told of how Brezhnev's regime was trying to roll back the clock and return the country to the gruesome years of Stalin's reign with millions of people vanishing without a trace. The truth must be unveiled about Andrey Simyavsky, Yuli Daniel, and the many others who risked their lives to resist the miserable, totalitarian lack of freedom choking our land.

While I tried to keep my eyes on the two policemen going through my stuff, my mind drifted unsteadily along the razor-thin edge of consciousness. I was striving to keep my eyes open and not to pass out, but I think at some point I did. When I opened my eyes, I was alone, and an early morning light was coming through the window of my dorm room. The state of mayhem left behind brought me back to reality. I tried to get off the floor and take a deep breath, but a sharp pain grasped my chest, telling me that, most likely, a couple of my lower ribs were broken.

I slowly sat up and looked around. Again, much like the other day, what had happened earlier did not bring a wave of panic—maybe because none of it had been totally unexpected. Yes, I was very upset and even scared, but I was not paralyzed by fear. My brain was still functioning in that rationalized survival mode that I had discovered inside me the other day. I needed to plan, to work out a strategy. I had to talk everything over with my aunt.

Out of nowhere, the major's voice came thundering inside my head—*Do you care to find out what happened to her? She is dead now. Dead!*

Masha had not simply disappeared; those scumbags had murdered her in cold blood! The realization of her horrific demise squeezed my chest so tightly that I could not take another breath. When I finally managed to inhale some air, the pain of loss was far more excruciating than the pain of my possibly broken ribs.

I had to get out of the dorm and lie low somewhere for a few days to get myself together and figure out what to do next. I tried to open the door, but the doorknob was gone. The door had been locked from the outside. Shit!

Then I remembered that I had a small toolbox under my bed. I'd brought it to the dorm a while ago to mount a couple of bookshelves, and I'd never taken it back home. I held my breath and cautiously crawled under the bed. Yep, there it was. Fighting the pain, I slowly pulled the toolbox out and armed myself with an ice pick and a flat screwdriver.

A few minutes later, I quietly managed to remove all the hinge pins. I jimmied the door just a little and looked out into the hallway. It was empty. I pried it a bit more, grabbed my old leather jacket off the hook, and, trying not to faint from the agonizing pain, I slithered out. To calm myself down, I took a few short, shallow breaths. Then, using the same set of tools, I leaned the door back on its un-pinned hinges inside the doorjamb and rushed down the hallway to the back stairs leading to the boiler room. I moved a few boxes away from the wall behind the boiler and opened the hidden door to the bakery's courtyard. Nobody was there—just a couple of parked bread trucks.

I left the bakery yard through the back gate. The narrow street was empty, and I was alone. I walked away from there, unsure of where I was headed. Somehow, I had to find a way to break the gruesome news about Masha to Aunt Anna, but was it safe for me to go to her place?

Had my "jailbreak" been pure luck, or had my

captors let me escape on purpose? What if they had staged the whole thing? Was I being used as a lure by the major and his buddies who were now going to watch my every step? Perhaps I'd become a new open page in their file and they would try to fill in the blanks by finding out whom I would contact. Most likely, they were looking for ways to entrap me so I could inadvertently lead them to Masha's notebook. I knew that it was preposterous since I had no clue where the notebook was, but they were of a different opinion.

I remembered when Aunt Anna had told me about her brothers' arrests years ago. She'd mentioned that when she'd gotten married, she'd taken her husband's last name. Because her last name at the time of the arrests had not been the same as her brothers', she'd been spared and had not vanished along with some of her relatives.

The authorities had been sloppy, acted in a hurry, and, luckily, had not connected the dots then. I hoped that they would not make the connection between my aunt and me either, and I was determined that I would not be the one to help them. I had to be vigilant and cover my tracks. I couldn't lead those snoops to my aunt or to anybody else who could've known or been associated with Andrey and Masha Simyavsky.

I realized that, most likely, the KGB already knew

who my parents were and where they lived. If I went there, I would not open a Pandora's box of new leads. I was feeling worse by the minute and had to get to my mom and dad before it was too late. I had to get some help, warn them, and talk a few things over face to face.

Chapter Ten

Arrest

On the way to my parents, I stopped at a 24-hour drugstore to get a few elastic bandages. I knew that applying support to my injured ribs would ease the nagging, nonstop pain. The store was empty—probably due to the early hour. I approached the checkout window and rang the bell. After some commotion behind the frosted glass, I suddenly heard a familiar voice and was stunned by it.

"What do you need? I'll be with you in a second."

Lara was staring at me from the other side of the counter through the open window of the frosted glass partition.

"Alex? What the hell happened? Oh my God! Look at your face! It looks horrible! Come right in." The door next to the window suddenly swung open, and without waiting for my response, she unceremoniously pulled me behind the counter. I cringed from the pain.

"Easy, please. What in the world are you doing here?"

"What does it look like? Working! Follow me; we have to take care of this right away." She led me through a narrow hallway between stocked cartons of various sizes to the back room, where she sat me down at a desk covered with familiar-looking class notes.

"Who did this to you? Wait; stay here." She left for a moment and came right back. "Do not say a word if you don't want to." She brought a pack of gauze sponges, a bottle of hydrogen peroxide, and a small jar of iodine. "Hold on tight," she warned me. "It's probably gonna sting and burn like hell, but it has to be done."

Lara soaked a piece of gauze in peroxide and applied it to the deep gash on my cheekbone.

"Hold it with your left hand. Apply some pressure. Shit, the blood is still oozing. Keep the pressure while I wash some blood off your lips. Holy crap, Alex! The cut on your upper lip is really bad. If it doesn't stop bleeding in the next thirty minutes, I think it has to be sutured. Squeeze this gauze pad between your lips and hold it tight."

She gently lifted the gauze off my cheek and started to apply iodine to the cut. It burned so badly that I had to take a deep breath, but as soon as I tried to do it, the bubbling mixture of blood and peroxide ran right down my throat, provoking a bout of unstoppable coughing. I scrunched down in agony and nearly passed out.

"I think my ribs are broken, Lara," I croaked, trying to suppress my cough.

"I have to remove your jacket and shirt to look at your ribs," Lara stated, without giving me a chance to quarrel with her. I just made a gesture for her to be careful.

She ignored it and quickly removed my jacket and shirt. "Don't be shy. Both of us are medical students." A second later, her jaw dropped as she saw my naked torso. "Who is the son of a bitch that did this to you?" she exclaimed. "You are bruised all over. Let me bring a few elastic bandages to wrap your rib cage and apply some compression to it. You don't have shortness of breath, do you?"

"No, I don't. I just have a lot of pain when taking a deep breath, and this cough is killing me."

"I'll be right back." She left the room, returned with a glass of water, and dropped a couple of pills in my hand. "Take them both right away."

"What is it, Lara?"

"It's codeine. It will suppress your cough and ease the pain."

"Where did you get it?" I asked.

"Are you dazed?" she retorted. "We are in a drug-store, silly. I pulled it right from the pharmacy."

"I did not see the pharmacist there."

"It's too early. Nobody is here yet."

"But it is a narcotic. Won't you get in trouble?"

"I couldn't care less about that right now. You need

it. Besides, I will not get in trouble. The pharmacist is my second cousin; that's how I got this job. I am moonlighting here twice a week. Stop arguing and take it right away!"

I chased the two pills with the full glass of water, realizing how thirsty I was.

"Now, sit up and raise your arms. I will wrap your bruised ribs."

After Lara finished bandaging my chest, I lowered my totally exhausted arms.

"How does it feel now? Not too tight?" she asked.

I carefully tried to take a couple of deeper breaths, and to my amazement, the pain was much more tolerable.

"It does feel better. You have a magic touch, Lara."

"My touch has nothing to do with it. Could be the codeine, could be the bandages, or could be both … as long as it works."

She sat down behind the desk, silently looking at me and rubbing her temples for a couple of minutes. She then quietly asked, "Will you tell me what happened, finally?"

I looked at her, feeling thirsty and slightly light-headed. The codeine had started to take effect.

"I would really appreciate some more water," I said.

Lara brought me another glass. I gulped it and

unexpectedly lost my guard. I told her in detail about everything that had happened to me over the last couple of days. It felt like a confession, but somehow I did not care. I just had to trust someone at that moment, and it felt like she was the right person.

"You are not going to your parents now," she countered. "It's too dangerous, and you do not want your mom and dad to see you like this. I will take you to my folks' place. They live in Obiralovka, a small town about an hour away from the city. You can spend a few days there to recuperate and weather the storm. We will have to take a train there."

"Lara, I'm really grateful for your offer, but we won't even make it to a railway station. Don't you think they're looking for me right now? I don't want you to get involved."

"It's too late, Alex. I'm already involved. We are going to my parents. Period! Better yet, I'll get in touch with my older brother Valery. He drives a small utility truck, and he can give us a lift. I'll tell him to pick us up right from the drugstore's backyard, so we can sneak away unnoticed. Let me get you to the stockroom at the very back of the store before the day shift arrives, and you can wait for me there. I'll give him a call right away, and then I'll clean up after us in the meantime."

The codeine had worked its magic; I felt too loopy

to argue. Lara took me to the stockroom, put me down on a small cot, and locked the door behind her as she left. An hour later, her whisper woke me up.

"Valery is waiting outside. Let's get out of here quietly." Lara led me to the back door, through a loading dock, and into the open rear door of a capped truck bed. "Lie down on that piece of foam rubber and rest. It will take us a little over an hour. I'll sit in the cabin with my brother. Here's a bottle of water for you." She then slammed the door without even giving me a chance to say anything.

The truck took off. I could not lie down; it was too painful. So, I propped up the foam rubber and sat up, leaning against the cabin wall. That felt a bit better, and I knew I had no other choice; I had to brace myself and stomach the ride for another hour.

After a dozen sharp turns and a couple of abrupt stops, we evidently reached the highway, and our truck gained a steady pace. Within a few minutes, I started to doze off while muttering to myself, "What an awesome girl … just awesome …"

Lara's family occupied the bigger section of a large log cabin with an apple orchard in the front. When we finally reached our destination, Lara got out of the truck and opened the gate in the wooden fence surrounding the entire yard. Her brother parked the truck inside the yard, closed the gate, and they both helped me to get out of the vehicle.

I looked around and, cringing in pain, tried to take a deep breath. I quickly realized that I was in no shape to do anything but lie down and recuperate. Lara's plan had been the only viable alternative for my survival. I was afraid that the next "interrogation" by the major or his cronies would most likely end my life if not cripple me for the rest of it.

"Let me help you get to the second floor. There's an extra room there that will be perfect for you to rest away from the noise and commotion." Lara dived under my arm, and Valery grabbed me by the belt as they helped me up the stairs. I started to feel nauseous and light-headed again. Lara touched my forehead with the back of her hand.

"Alex, I think you're running a fever. Let me get a thermometer." She left, and Valery helped me to bed, propping my head and chest high on a few pillows. "Hold on, man," he tried awkwardly to encourage me. "You're in good hands. My sister can bring the dead to life."

"Thank you, Valery. Fortunately, I'm not dead yet. But you're right; your sister is one doughty chick!" I said in quiet admiration.

Lara came back and shoved a thermometer under

my armpit. She also brought a cold, wet cloth, which she placed on my forehead. It felt so good until she retrieved the thermometer and exclaimed, "Thirty-nine point seven degrees Celsius! I'm afraid this could be the start of pneumonia or, God forbid, pleurisy."

I really felt like shit but responded facetiously, "Doctor, you're not a real doctor yet. How would you know?"

"You want a real doctor? I'll bring the real one to you later today. You're such a knucklehead. Lie down, try to get some sleep, and don't be a smart-ass," she responded. "Valery, come downstairs with me, please. I have an idea." They left the room and closed the door.

A couple of hours later, Lara was shaking my shoulder, trying to wake me up.

"Wake up, brother," she repeated a few times. I looked around baffled. Who was she talking to? Her brother was not in the room. Lara was standing next to a woman in her late thirties who was wearing a parka over her white lab coat and a stethoscope around her neck. Lara was talking to me.

"Say hello to your doctor, Valery." She winked at me as she emphasized *Valery*, and then she turned around to address the woman. "I really appreciate you coming here on such short notice, Doc." Lara was firing her words at the speed of a machine gun.

"Let me tell you what happened, since this

knucklehead brother of mine can't talk due to his messed-up lips. Late last night, he took the last train home from a party with his buddies somewhere in the city. He was a bit tipsy and had dozed off in his seat when he was assaulted and robbed by a gang of hoodlums. I don't know how he got back here; I found him lying in our front yard this morning. His documents and a little money he had are all gone. Thank God, he's alive and managed to get home.

"I'm a medical student, and I've already taken care of his messed-up face and bruised ribs, but he started to run a fever not long ago. I was already on my way to our regional policlinic to book him for a house call when, luckily, I ran into you doing your house-call rounds on our street. I am so grateful you agreed to come see him right away."

"No problem, young lady. I was almost done in your neighborhood anyway. You just saved me a trip here later in the day after my clinic hours. What is your name again?"

"I'm Lara, Lara Katz, and he is Valery Katz, my older brother." Lara faced me and winked again. "Valery, let me help you take off your shirt so the doctor can examine you."

If I had been asked to speak, I would have been unable; I was totally speechless, looking at Lara in admiration as she took charge.

"Can I address you by your name, Doctor?" Lara asked.

"Sure you can. I am Tatiana Pavlovna, Lara. What medical school do you go to?"

"The First Moscow Medical School."

"It's a great school. I was lucky to get into the First Med years ago too. Most of my friends had to settle for the Second Medical School. Competition there was not as tough. Where can I wash my hands?" she asked.

"Right here." Lara opened a washroom door and got a fresh towel from a closet.

Tatiana Pavlovna washed her hands as she continued the conversation.

"Is any particular specialty on your mind?"

"It's too early. This is my first year. Surgery ... maybe radiology ... I'm not sure yet."

"Good thinking, girl," Tatiana Pavlovna responded. "Don't repeat the mistake most of us made. I chose family medicine, thinking it would be the easiest route. I didn't want to be a hospitalist. But I was wrong; it's the hardest one. For half the day, you see twenty to twenty-five patients in the clinic; the other half you spend making twenty house calls, rain or shine. Five years into it and you get burned out. Sadly, by that time, it's too late. Power to you; be a specialist. Smart! Now, let's take a look at your poor brother."

She approached my bed. "You don't have to talk, Valery, if it's too painful. Just nod or shake your head, okay?"

I nodded in response and sat up.

Lara helped to unwrap my rib cage, and I felt a cold stethoscope traveling along my chest and my back.

"Breathe in … breathe out. Breathe in … breathe out. Can you take a deeper breath?"

I shook my head, thinking *No!*

"He almost passed out the last time I asked him to do that, Tatiana Pavlovna," Lara added.

Tatiana Pavlovna hung her stethoscope around her neck and re-bandaged my ribs.

"His lower ribs are definitely broken. We need an X-ray to see the extent of the damage and to find out if he has pneumonia. The good thing is that he doesn't have shortness of breath, so I don't think his lungs are punctured. You took good care of his cuts and bruises. I don't think the cut on his upper lip has to be sutured; let me secure a butterfly right there. Just keep all his wounds clean from now on and apply some antiseptic a couple of times a day.

"I am writing a prescription for penicillin and codeine. Fill it right away. Also, here are the stat orders for the labs, X-ray, and fluoroscopy. Make sure to bring him to the policlinic before tonight, and call me tomorrow morning. If his fever hits forty or higher, bring him to the emergency room right away. Any questions, colleague?"

She then looked at me and added. "Valery, you have the best sister in the world. She did everything right. Follow her orders and stay in bed. Promise? Please, walk me out, Lara."

I nodded again, and both of them left the room.

A moment later, Lara returned with Valery following her. "Get ready," she said to me. "Valery is giving us a ride to the policlinic right away."

"I don't know how I can ever repay you both for what you've done. How did you come up with this idea?" I asked, choking on another wave of coughs.

"My brother, like the rest of my family living here, has his chart on file at our local policlinic. Tatiana Pavlovna has a lot of patients assigned to her geographically, and she most likely doesn't remember everyone's face. If you are Valery and you live here, she cannot turn you down; she has to take care of you. Later, when she returns to the policlinic, she will request *your* chart from the file room and will enter the record of today's house call.

"The idea was not to leave any new records in your name. That's how you became Valery's double. Valery is injured and he needs help. If anyone asks for an ID, it's gone because he was robbed last night. It's documented in the chart. End of story. This way, you can't be turned away, and no one can trace your whereabouts."

"Ingenious!" I said, trying to catch my breath.

"It's four thirty already. Let's get your tests done and fill your prescriptions. Go start the car, Valery. I'll help Alex get downstairs."

"Whatever you say, Lara. I give up," I said.

"Don't be so easy." She smiled back.

We arrived at the policlinic at five minutes to five. My lower ribs were indeed broken, but there were no signs of pleurisy. A couple of hours later, on the way home, Lara filled my prescription, and I took a painkiller right away. We returned to the log cabin, where Lara and Valery helped me back upstairs. I was shivering. Lara helped me to bed and brought me a cup of chicken soup.

"My mom made this for you. She knows that you're here and that you're sick. I told her you need a place to stay for just a few days to get better. She remembers that if not for your help, I wouldn't be in medical school now. I did not tell her anything else; I just asked her to keep it to herself.

"After you're done with your soup, take the penicillin, and here's some aspirin for you as well. Your fever is getting worse. Try to sleep, Alex. I'll be downstairs and will keep an eye on you through the night."

She left me alone in the room and turned off the light on her way out.

"Good night," she said, standing in the doorway. "If you need me, knock on the floor. My bedroom is right below."

"Good night. Thank you for everything, Lara." I put my head down on the pillow, and before I knew it, I was asleep.

"You slept for twelve hours straight." Lara walked into the room with another cup of soup. "You have to have this right now," she commanded. "How do you feel?"

"I think I'm better," I said. "The cough is gone, and so is my fever."

"I checked on you in the middle of the night and gave you more penicillin and codeine. Do you remember?"

"No."

"Come on, Alex. Really? You told me that you had to talk to your aunt, and you gave me her phone number."

"Did I? I can't recall a thing."

"Never mind. I called your aunt this morning. She invited me to come over. I went to her place, and we talked for more than an hour. She was worried sick about you. I had to tell her everything you told me regarding your ordeal and about our early-morning escape to Obiralovka. She was obviously relieved.

"You're lucky to have someone like her in your life. Your aunt is such an interesting woman. Like, she lives in a totally different and mysterious world. She gave me a tour of her place. What an apartment! What a beautiful library! There are so many old books and so much history on those shelves. There are walls covered with photographs of your aunt with famous writers, artists, and celebrities. She even told me that you knew some of them personally.

"I felt like I was in a museum; my head spun. She revealed to me that, many years ago, it had been the famous Fyodor Shalyapin's place and that his study was where her library is right now. There is something notable about your aunt. She made me feel like I was her old friend. I was simply overwhelmed by her aura."

"That's my Aunt Anna. That's exactly how she is," I replied.

"She's coming here to see you later today, by the way."

"You are too much, Lara ... Thank you for going there."

"Trust me, the pleasure was mine."

At the end of the day, I heard a strange commotion downstairs, and without warning, the door flew open and Lara ran into the room in a panic.

"I don't know what the hell is happening down there!" She was pale, and her lips were quivering. "Two military Jeeps and a black Volga sedan just arrived. They are parked outside the fence, on the street, blocking the gate. Your aunt is standing there, escorted by a one-star general, and they are demanding to see you. Look out the window. They're right there. What did I do wrong? Why the Jeeps? Who is the general? What's going on? Did I screw up? What should I do now?"

I got up and looked through the window. I saw my aunt accompanied by a one-star general wearing the raspberry epaulets of the Interior Ministry troops.

Aunt Anna saw me in the window. She smiled and gestured to me not to worry.

"Lara, I'm completely lost. I don't know what to make of it. I don't know who that general is, but my aunt doesn't seem nervous at all. We have no other choice but to let them in."

"Are you sure?" Lara asked.

"What else can we do? I trust my aunt. We will find out shortly what all this is about."

Lara went to the door and shouted, "Valery, open the gate! I'll be there in a second!" She then looked at me and added, "I'll be right back."

I looked through the window and watched as Valery opened the gate and Aunt Anna walked inside the yard. She gave Lara a big hug and then waved to the general, inviting him to join her. A moment later, all three of them walked into my room.

Aunt Anna ran up to me and studied my bruised face while gently holding my shoulders. She then turned to the general and said quietly, "Pavel, look what that sadistic asshole did to my boy's face! Look! It's horrible!"

The general approached me and offered a handshake.

I shook his hand. "Comrade General ..."

"Alex, call me Pavel Sergeevich. I wish we had met under different circumstances." He then sat down and removed his fur hat, revealing a headful of curly black hair. "I've known your aunt for many years. Anna and I are time-tested friends. We know each other from way back when both of us went to the same high school in Kremenchug, the city of our youth. That's how long we've known each other. My uniform should not frighten you and obscure who I am and why I am here. I am your aunt's friend, and I am here to help."

"I guess ..." I answered, not convinced.

"Alex," Aunt Anna said, "you can trust Pavel like you trust me."

"Aunt Anna, I have to break the horrible news for you. I have to... Masha Simyavsky... She is not any longer with us... She was murdered the other day..." I said chocking in tears.

"I know it, Alex. I do know it... Her funeral is

tomorrow," Aunt Anna answered with a deep sigh. "To survive, we all have to stay strong. Wipe off your tears, my dear."

"Can we talk in private?" Pavel Sergeevich asked and looked at Lara.

"I'll wait downstairs," Lara said as she rushed to the door.

"Lara, stay put," Aunt Anna stopped her. "Pavel, she is one of us. She is a Jewish kid ... a member of the tribe, just like the rest of us in this room. Her family name is Katz. Alex and I trust her, and so can you. She will stay if you don't mind."

"Well, young lady," he looked at Lara as if measuring her up, and then he seemed to welcome her in, "just remember—everything said here stays here, inside of these walls. It's imperative, got it?"

"I do. Thank you." Lara nodded in response.

"Alex," Aunt Anna said, "listen to what I have to say to you very carefully. This is dead serious. Andrey is in prison and Masha is murdered. The State Security's Second Directorate is vicious. When they start going after you, they never stop. What you have tasted is barely even the start. Pavel and I hope that it was a pure coincidence. They picked the *New Word* as a fallout of the Simyavsky and Daniel trial since Andrey was closely associated with the magazine and Tardovsky had tried a couple of times in the not-so-distant past to get the censorship consensus to run a couple of chapters from Andrey's novel *Lyubimov*.

"That day, they summoned more than a dozen authors whose work was regularly published in *New Word*. Their goal was to intimidate and browbeat everyone into submission, as they were shutting down the magazine anyway. It was, most likely, just a fishing expedition, but somehow that asinine major picked up on your association with Andrey, and the whole thing unraveled in the wrong direction. We have to get you off their radar and out of their reach. Pavel and I spent some time trying to come up with a strategy, and Pavel has a plan."

"The whole thing might sound too far-fetched and risky for you, but it can be done, and you have to accept the risk and make the move," the general said. "We have to hide you away for a while ... away from the Second Directorate and away from that hog-wild major. Your case is a career builder for him. I know the way it works over there. He thinks he's onto something. Most likely, he will act on his own because his kind don't like to share the glory with anyone else. He thinks you're the one who will lead him to that notebook."

"I honestly don't know where this notebook is, Pavel Sergeevich," I interrupted.

"I know you don't! I also know who does. That's

why I have to help you to disappear off the face of the earth. I have to hide you in the only place the major doesn't have access to. Where do you think that place is?"

"I have no clue," I said. "The moon? Where is it?"

"It's much closer. Right under his nose. In the Interior Ministry jail. I'll take you into my personal custody and put you under concealed arrest. While you're incarcerated, I'll use my connections in the higher echelons of their command to find a way to transfer that moron major to somewhere at the Far East ... to the southeastern frontier, where he will be 'helped' to bite the dust in one of the cross-border clashes with the Chinese army. After everything quiets down, we will make a deal with the state prosecutors and set you free. You will be able to start with a clean slate."

"How long will it take for everything to quiet down?" I asked.

"It's hard to predict. It might take a couple of months, give or take."

"What's gonna happen with medical school in the meantime?" I wondered aloud.

"Most likely, you will be expelled, but we will make it plausible for the school to reinstate you later on," Pavel Sergeevich calmly explained.

"Will I be able to write again?"

"Stop acting like a spoiled child, Alex! Your life is at stake! Who is thinking about your poetry now? We are trying to save your life! Wake up to reality!" Aunt Anna exploded.

"Anna, cool it, my dear," Pavel Sergeevich said softly. "He's asking a question. He wants to know. He will understand. Remember how you were at his age. It's hard to be rational and trusting after what he's encountered lately."

"Forgive my outburst, Alex. I am as frustrated as you are," Aunt Anna continued. "But this is our only chance. Grab it! Do you remember how we used to compare our daily struggle to the strategy of a chess player? We have to make a few deceptive and unexpected moves to disorient and confuse our opponents. Let's fool them by sacrificing a couple of pawns and neutralizing one of their bishops. It will buy us enough time to escape the inevitable checkmate."

A heavy and quiet pause sat over the room for a moment. I looked at Lara—at her pale, freckled face, tightly squeezed lips, and wide-open gray eyes. I then looked at the trembling fingers of Aunt Anna's hands and at the general's curly black hair. Everyone was waiting for me to respond.

"What I understand," I said slowly, "is that one way or the other, I will end up in jail. I do not understand why I deserve it, and I don't think anyone here can give me an explanation. That's just the way it is. That's how our convoluted, bastardized system works. It is insane, unjust, unforgivingly cruel, and nobody gives a shit. There is no life around here. Everybody just exists ... just trying to get by ... just trying to run away from a checkmate.

"Now more than ever, I understand your chess-game analogy, Aunt Anna. Now I know why you put so much effort into teaching me how to survive. We are all prisoners here. The whole country is one lousy jail. This isn't even a country we're living in ... It's a stinking colony of deceit! What kind of life do I have to live from now on just to survive? I have to think over my every step ... every word I say. I have to doubt everyone I come across and can't trust a single soul I come in contact with until proven otherwise.

"It may be a chess game all right, but it is not a life I wish for myself or anybody I care about! I'm willing to make that move ... put my life in your hands and go to jail. I know there is a risk involved, but I have to trust you, and, fortunately or not, there is no other choice left for me. Let's play this ghastly chess game. Let's run away from that checkmate. Let's make that risky move ... Damn it!" Frustrated, I hollered the last sentence and leaned against the wall totally exhausted.

"Well, I'm glad you got it off your chest, Alex," Pavel Sergeevich said. "But that was the last public speech of this sort that you will ever make for your sake and your aunt's. You will keep your mouth shut from this point on. When all of us understand each other, words are not necessary.

"Let's go downstairs, get in the car, and go to the city. Right from the start, I'll put you in the jail's infirmary for a couple of weeks until you recover from the damage inflicted on you by that major. We will make a record of the reckless abuse you were subjected to earlier, just in case. Then, we will play it by ear. Are we on the same page?"

"I'm sure we are, Pavel Sergeevich," I responded.

Lara nodded in agreement as I looked at her. Suddenly, she came closer and gently gave me a quick hug.

"I'll keep my fingers crossed for you," she whispered in my ear. Then she turned to the general and asked, "Can I visit him over there, Comrade General, please?"

"Here's my card," Pavel Sergeevich answered. "Call me in a couple of days. I'll help you to arrange visitation."

"Thank you, Pavel," my aunt said. "I owe you one."

"This isn't the first time I've heard that, Anna. I still wonder when I'll be able to collect on all your promises." The general smiled, and then the three of us went downstairs.

We crossed the apple orchard on the way out. Valery shook my hand, wishing me well, and closed the gate behind us as we got into the general's black Volga sedan.

The trip to the city was silent as we traveled in darkness. When the car finally came to a halt inside the Interior Ministry's inner court, Pavel Sergeevich, who was in the front passenger seat, sent the driver out and then turned to face Aunt Anna.

"Anna, you are staying in the car. My driver will take you home." He then turned to me. "Alex, here's what you have to do. You will get out of the car, and the guards will handcuff you. You will be escorted to the intake ward to be booked. When the guards bring you inside, wait for a few moments and then say that you don't feel right. Ask for a cup of water and for permission to sit down. Without waiting for anybody's response, you are going to faint. When you fake it, be as genuine and graphic as you can. Stay on the floor until the medics arrive. I'll be right there a moment later, and I will take care of the rest of it. Got it?"

"Yes." I squeezed my aunt's hand and got out of the car.

A squad of Interior Ministry troopers, who had accompanied the Volga all the way from Obiralovka, dismounted their Jeeps and stood waiting for me. I was handcuffed and taken inside the building. They handed me to a gray-haired sergeant in charge of three other guards and left.

The guards showed me to the bench near the wall and ordered me to sit down. I did so and then asked for a cup of water. I got no response and asked again, adding that I did not feel well.

"Fuck you!" the sergeant responded calmly continuing to look through his paperwork. "Nobody feels good around here. It goes with the territory."

At that point, I rolled my eyeballs, made a gurgling sound, and slowly slid to the floor. On the way down, I bit my damaged lip and it started to bleed again, covering my entire chin with a mixture of blood and saliva.

"Shit!" the sergeant exclaimed. "The fucker was serious! Call the medics right away, and do not touch him. Make sure he's breathing; he could be an epileptic and might be having a seizure."

I started to cough through my slightly opened lips, causing saliva to foam around my mouth.

"What the hell is going on over here?" I heard the thundering voice of the general, who had just walked into the room and was now towering over me, studying my face. "What did you do to this prisoner, Sergeant? Look at his face! Are you up to your old antics again? Are you eager to be demoted? Didn't I explicitly order your captain to stop that crap? We are not the KGB over here. We do not treat prisoners this way anymore. I will not allow that to happen under my watch. Do I make myself clear?"

"Yes, Comrade General, sir."

"Did you call the medics?"

"They are on their way, sir. Comrade General, I swear to you, nobody touched this perp. He arrived here like that. He just fainted all by himself a second ago and fell off the bench. Ask the guards; they saw the whole thing. I did nothing ... honestly."

"Stop wailing like a woman. You don't want those assholes from Amnesty International to pay us a visit again, do you? You are out of your mind! When the medics arrive, tell them to take the prisoner to the infirmary right away. We will take him off site and lock him up there, for the time being, until his face heals. I am doing this for you, Sergeant— to save your butt. You are about to retire in a couple of years, aren't you? You don't want to fuck up your pension, do you?"

"No, Comrade General, sir. I do not."

"Then seal his record, assign him a number, and keep your mouth shut. Do we understand each other?"

"Roger that, Comrade General. I'll do exactly as you ordered."

"Report directly to me when you are done, Sergeant."

"Yes, Comrade General, sir!" the sergeant responded, standing at attention.

"Better yet, Sergeant ... I want you to take personal responsibility for this prisoner. Who is your commanding officer?"

"Lieutenant Primakov, sir."

"Very well, Sergeant. I'll talk to Lieutenant Primakov to arrange your transfer to the infirmary as soon as tomorrow morning."

The general left and the medics arrived. They cracked an ammonia capsule and shoved it under my nose. I almost choked, and my tears forced me to open my eyes. I went through the motions as if I were coming around and returning to my senses. The medics removed my handcuffs and placed me on a stretcher. One of them slid a blood pressure cuff onto my left arm while the other unbuttoned my shirt and studied my bandaged rib cage.

"Who put this bandage on? Do you have broken ribs? How did this happen?" the medic asked.

"I blacked out," I answered. "I don't remember a thing."

"What is your name?" he continued.

"I cannot recall ..." I replied slowly, after a long pause, pretending that I was ready to faint again.

"Let's take him upstairs now," one medic said to the other. "We'll hook him up to oxygen and an IV line right there in the ward. He looks like shit, but his vitals are stable. Let the morning shift deal with him tomorrow. Are you done here, Sergeant?"

"I'm done," the sergeant replied. "Go right ahead, guys. Hurry up."

We took an elevator to the fourth floor. After passing a couple of long corridors, the stretcher stopped, and I heard the door being unlocked. I was wheeled into a small cell and placed on a hospital bed.

One of the medics stripped me of all my clothing, covered me with a hospital gown, and took my temperature. The other one applied a few electrodes to my chest, hooked me up to a monitor and an IV line, and then covered my nose and mouth with an oxygen mask. Both men then left, locking the door behind them on their way out.

I looked around. To my right, I saw a couple of small windows very close to the ceiling; they were covered with a wire mesh and painted steel bars. Against the wall to my left was a stainless steel toilet bowl. The cell door dominated the opposite wall at the foot of my bed. The small circular eye of the observation window had been left open, and I felt as if it were staring right at me all the time. The lightbulb above me was on. The ordeal of the last few days finally caught up with me, and for the first time, I consciously allowed myself to relax, ignore the light, and fall asleep.

I was awakened by the squeaky sound of a cell door. I noticed the morning light coming in through the windows. A woman wearing a white lab coat and a stethoscope around her neck walked into my cell accompanied by someone who was already known to me—the gray-haired sergeant.

"Let's see ... what do we have here?" She picked up a clipboard from the foot of my bed. "How old are you, young man?"

"Twenty," I replied.

"What do you do?"

"I'm a medical student."

"Interesting," she said, looking over her eyeglasses at my face. "Would it be too much trouble for you to tell me why you are here?"

"I don't remember anything, Doc. I blacked out," I replied.

"I'm talking about the infirmary. Is your messed-up face the only reason you're here? What else is wrong with you?"

"I think I have a couple of broken ribs, and I ran a fever the other day."

"Let me see your chest." She unwrapped the bandages and examined my bruised rib cage. "Wow! Who beat you up?"

"I said I don't remember. I blacked out."

"Guard, can you leave us alone for a moment?" she asked. "I'll call you when I'm done." When the guard left the cell and closed the door, she leaned toward me and lowered her voice.

"Don't answer if you don't want to. It was just a rhetorical question, mostly for the guard. You can trust me. I am a friend. I talked to the general a short while ago. I'll do my best to keep you here for as long as you need to be, but you have to level with me as well. I have to know what's going on with you to be able to treat you right. The general instructed me to document all the damage that was previously—how can I put it?—inflicted on you. You don't have to tell me who did it; just tell me how all of it happened."

"I was woken up in the middle of the night in my dorm room and was interrogated right there until I lost consciousness. It was three of them. Two were holding me by the arms, and the third one did all the beating. I'm lucky the animal didn't kill me. When I regained consciousness, I was on the floor in a puddle of bloody puke, unable to breath and in horrible pain. I managed to escape, and then I was helped by one of my friends, who gave me shelter and procured some painkillers and antibiotics for me. I took those pills for a couple of days until I was brought here."

"I'll get you back on your feet, Alex. I promise."

My eyes almost popped out. "How do you know my name?"

"The general told me. Besides, I would have recognized your face a bit later anyway. I know who you are. I saw you on TV some time ago. I had a subscription for *New Word*, and I love your poetry. Everything will be okay. I'll take good care of you. You have one powerful friend upstairs."

"In more ways than one ..." I replied.

Chapter Eleven
Freedom?

I spent a few long weeks at the infirmary. My face returned to normal, and my broken ribs were almost healed. The monotonous boredom of solitary confinement was finally broken when Lara was allowed to visit me. One evening, I was taken by the gray-haired sergeant to the visitation room, where I saw Lara staring at me from the other side of a table.

"Come on," said the sergeant. "Comrade General told me that she's your sister and that I can allow you to give her a hug and sit next to her if you wish. I'll leave you two alone for a few minutes," he said. He then added with a wink, "If she isn't your sister, then keep your hands to yourself. No hanky-panky allowed over here."

Lara and I gave each other a long hug.

"Thank you for coming," I said. "How did you manage to get permission?"

"You have to thank your Aunt Anna and her friend, the general. How do you feel?"

"Thank God, I'm almost where I was before I met that so-called 'friend' of mine, the major."

"I was asked to convey to you that soon after your

arrest, your 'friend' the major was transferred to a combat unit on the Sino–Soviet border and that he vanished without a trace during one of the skirmishes with the Chinese on some small island on the Ussuri River about a week ago. Nobody could find his body, so he is listed so far as missing in action."

"I can't believe he's gone …"

"Believe it. The general said that he talked to a couple of border guards who were there at the time and witnessed the major wander off into our own minefield."

"Ouch…" I said. "That wasn't too smart. I wouldn't wish that explosive finale on anyone, but what goes around comes around…"

"The general thinks that, in a month or so, it will be safe to proceed with your case. Your Aunt Anna is on a mission now to find a lawyer brave enough to represent you. I have so much to tell you. Please, let me talk, and do not interrupt me. Your mom and dad are okay. I visited them every other week. I don't think your mom liked me at first. Now I feel that she is warming up to me little by little, and I think we are getting closer to each other since she did invited me to come and spend some time together more often. I don't know what did it, or why, but since we grow closer together right now who cares why… As long as it works.

"I see your Aunt Anna quite often, and she sends

her love. I'd like to think that we're going to be good friends. She is an amazing person. She wants you to be kept up to date on all our studies, so she asked me if I could help by keeping detailed class notes for you. I was allowed to bring my notes from all the lectures you've missed so far. The sergeant took them from me to check them when I arrived. I will keep bringing them to you from time to time so you won't miss anything."

"Was I officially expelled from school?" I asked.

"Unfortunately, you were. There were a lot of rumors going around, but the official version was that you were expelled because of your poor attendance record."

"Is that the best explanation they could come up with? It's kinda lame."

"The student body is still trying to connect the dots, and, in spite of what they have been told by the administration, most of our classmates think your disappearance had everything to do with the arrests of a few other writers who were frequently published by *New Word* before the magazine was shut down. Our guys are not that stupid. Well ... some of them are, but the majority can think and read between the lines.

"The word on the street is that you are among the ones who were arrested for their 'inflammatory' writings circulated by *New Word*. The rumor mill is churning out all the gossip in full throttle, but I'm trying to stay away from it. I just shrug my shoulders dubiously when asked if I've heard anything new. By the way, I asked Aunt Anna if your reinstatement would be achievable later on. She said that we'd fight one battle at a time. Our goal right now is to set you free. I tend to agree with her."

As I looked at Lara's freckled face and big gray eyes, I realized that her wholehearted friendship and devotion, not just her beauty alone, had incessantly enthralled me. I would be indebted to her forever for everything she had done. At that moment, I discovered an unexplainable and overwhelming sense of closeness to her that was bursting inside me, ready to come out.

"You have to be careful, Lara," I said. "I could fall in love with you—"

"Keep dreaming," she cut me short. "Didn't you tell me way back then that you were involved with someone? I remember that very well. I am not getting between the two of you. I don't know who that girl is and, frankly, I don't care. We will not let it happen, Alex. You are my friend and I am yours. Period. Friends should not fall in love."

The very second Lara finished her sentence, the gray-haired sergeant opened the door and walked into the room.

"We are done, Sergeant," Lara said quickly.

"Thank you for giving us a few minutes to talk to each other. Okay, brother," she added, looking at me with a strange twinkle in her eyes. "Be a good boy, feel better soon, and read all the notes I left with the sergeant. See you soon." She gave me a hug, quickly kissed me on the lips, and rushed to the door.

"Let's get back to your cell," the sergeant said. "Pick up that box of notes your sister left and bring it with you. That sister of yours, she's a pistol."

Shortly thereafter, Simeon Yakovlevich Gurevich, a well-known criminal attorney, paid me a visit to inform me that the Court had appointed him to be the counsel for the defense. When he saw the expression of total disbelief on my face, he confided that some people who wanted to remain anonymous had actually arranged his appointment and that he was, therefore, not at liberty to disclose who they were. "I refused to be paid for your defense. I just had to do it pro bono as *a member of the tribe*, so to speak... Did you get my drift?"

"Simeon Yakovlevich," I replied with a smile, "Of course I did. With a last name like yours, I kinda figured that you were most likely Jewish. Regardless, I want to express my gratitude to you for taking my case."

"You are quite welcome, Alex. I owe it to myself and to the people who trusted me to defend you," he replied. "Here's my plan, though I must warn you that it won't be easy sailing. Most likely, you will be charged with 'Proliferation of Western Ideology' or 'Anti-Soviet Agitation and Propaganda.' Either one of those charges would fall under Article 70 of the Russian Soviet Federative Republic Criminal Code. "

"Trust me, I understand my predicament."

"I hope you do. The moment we unseal your records, the prosecution will demand to transfer you to the KGB's jurisdiction. I am positive that we will prevail and that they will drop their demand and back off the very moment I show the court evidence of your 'interrogation' by the late major. I am glad the general thought of it beforehand.

"For your own good, I will try my best to keep you in solitary confinement though, since the Interior Ministry jail is somewhat different from the KGB's Lubyanka Prison. The general population at Lubyanka consists mostly of political prisoners, but this place is filled with all sorts of human garbage. They are all criminals here. Most of them are hoodlums, muggers, and killers.

"Knowing how the KGB operates, I don't want to give them a chance to take out a contract on your life and pass it on to one of their moles among the inmates here. The possibility of this is quite remote, but it's better to be safe than sorry. Solitary will not be as comfy, so to speak, as your cell upstairs at the infirmary, but you will be safer in it, and we will try to keep the time you spend there to a minimum. I'll request to expedite the proceedings and will offer a plea bargain right away. We'll take it from there."

A couple of days later, I was transferred from the infirmary to a solitary confinement cell in the main prison block. My new cell was tiny and had no windows. If not for mealtimes, I could only guess what time of the day it was at any given moment.

My food ration consisted of two measly meals per day. Typically, in the morning, it was a cup of hot water, a thin slice of rye bread, and a cup of diluted, tasteless grits or porridge. In the evening, it was some thin stew of unknown origin or stinking boiled cod and pickled cabbage with a square of coarse pumpernickel bread. At least the food served at the infirmary, which had initially been loathed by me due to its absence of taste and unpalatable appearance, had been served hot three times a day in amounts sufficient to keep me just short of being hungry. Now, it seemed like a distant and sumptuous object of gastronomic excellence.

Now, I was hungry all the time and had to learn very quickly how to prevent that feeling from driving me insane. I also figured out how to carve away and stash a few small pieces of bread, which I would consume slowly throughout the day to cheat the hunger.

Another few weeks passed, and I did not hear a word from my attorney. Lara never came back to visit me after I left the infirmary. Over and over, I read all the notes she'd brought for me, and by now, I could recite them by heart.

The guards were constantly changing. Without exception, they were irresponsive and indifferent. When they entered the cell for the nightly row calls, they never made eye contact and took no notice of my attempts to communicate with them. Every question I asked was ignored and left unanswered.

The psychological torture of total isolation started to feel crippling. The heavy feeling of emptiness and the unknown started to crawl under my skin and into my soul. I started to understand the infinite cruelty of solitary confinement and how it could drive someone to insanity even after a short time. The only way for me to survive was not to give up.

I remembered that, some time ago, Aunt Anna had brought to the fore the meaning of the closing verses of my poem "The Salvaged Hope":

"At the end of the thorny rope
Of betrayal and disgrace,
We did salvage our hope
At a price of our faith ..."

"Live by your words," she had said. "Never surrender your hope. Never give up!"

I had to keep my hope alive. That was the only chance left for me to pull through. In my darkest moments of the last few weeks, I reminded myself again and again of Lara's selfless help, the general's pledge to "take care of the rest of it," Attorney Gurevich's plan of action, and my acceptance of his premonition that "it won't be easy sailing." Gurevich's foreboding had proven to be more than correct; the sailing had been far from easy. It had turned into a tormenting storm, shredding my sails to threads, attempting to throw me against the rocks of my cell walls, and turning me into a helpless wreck.

With all that said, deep inside of me, I nurtured the perpetual belief that as long as I had Aunt Anna somewhere outside of the prison walls, I could not allow despair to get the best of me. I was more than certain that she would not give up until I was set free.

At first, I thought it was the middle of the night when the guards dragged me from my cot. They ordered me to get dressed and, without explanation, led me through a labyrinth of seemingly endless hallways to the stairwell. I suddenly felt frightened and numb. On the way there, to my surprise, I noticed rays of light coming through a few small windows near the ceiling. Now I knew that my perception of time was totally skewed.

I was taken outside to the prison courtyard. We crossed it and entered the doors leading to the vestibule of a familiar building adjacent to the massive entrance gates. It occurred to me that it was the intake ward. That ward was connected to the courtyard to which I had been brought in the general's black Volga sedan a few months earlier.

The guards showed me to the room and left.

Simeon Yakovlevich Gurevich came forward from behind his desk and greeted me.

"Alex, my goodness!" He rubbed his bald head. "You've lost a lot of weight, my man. Sit down, please."

I sat in the chair on the other side of the desk, and he moved another chair around and sat next to me. "You must be starving," he said. He then opened his briefcase and pulled out a paper bag containing a homemade sandwich. "This is for you. Eat first; then we'll talk."

I took a big bite of the delicious white bread and salami creation.

"What day is today?" I asked him with my mouth full.

"Today is Thursday, August eleventh. Tell me, how do you feel?" Gurevich asked as he watched me devouring the sandwich at the speed of light.

"August eleventh? I am losing my mind, Simeon Yakovlevich. Six months have passed. How much longer—"

"It could be over today," he interrupted with a smile.

"Today?!" I gasped in disbelief, almost choking on the little that remained of my sandwich.

"You are correct. Today, if you cooperate."

"Cooperate? I don't understand," I said, swallowing the last bite.

"Let me brief you. It took us longer than we thought because we tried to get the correct combination of participating parties—the Unholy Trinity, so to speak—and to make at least two of them dance the same jig."

"I don't get it. What Trinity? Who's supposed to dance with whom? I think I'm losing my mind indeed."

"No, you're not losing your mind. I was speaking allegorically. Let me dissect it for you. As you're most likely aware, in all our courts, the cases are heard by a collegium consisting of a presiding professional judge and two people's assessors, who are elected laypeople rotating in and out every couple of weeks. I call those three the Unholy Trinity—just between us. Then, there is me—the advocate on your side—and the prosecution on the other.

"The prosecutors, as I warned you beforehand, did charge you with Anti-Soviet Agitation and Propaganda because of your writings. They are accusing you of disseminating blatant slander of the state with the goal of undermining the tenets of the Soviet regime. They are asking for a minimum five-year sentence under Article 70 of the Criminal Code. We can do nothing about the charge. The prosecution is following the KGB's Second Directorate orders, and it will stand."

"Are you telling me that I'm going to a labor camp for at least five years?" I jumped to my feet.

"No, don't panic. I am not telling you that. Sit down! Be patient and listen carefully. The hearing for your case was rescheduled many times in the last few months. I was running out of more or less legitimate reasons to request another postponement. Your case was placed on a court docket for today, and we finally got lucky.

"The stars aligned, so to speak. The presiding judge knows the general. That is huge. The judge's decision, however, has to be supported by at least one people's assessor. I found out the other day that the wife of one of them is in dire need of your aunt's help. The woman is dreaming about publishing her book about tasty, healthy cooking, and I promised her husband that your aunt's publishing house, Art, would cooperate with her in exchange for his cooperation in court. Get it? Can I continue?"

"Got it, Simeon Yakovlevich," I assured him. "Go ahead."

"I had a private meeting with the judge and the general late last night. We made a deal. Your poetry appeared in *New Word*, which was, at that time, a legitimately published magazine. Nothing out of the ordinary. It was not printed abroad or in the underground press, like the so-called *Samizdat*. There is no aggravating evidence that warrants sentencing you to the full term requested by the prosecution. The judge is going to consider your young age as a mitigating circumstance and will only sentence you to time served. Six months. Period."

"That's hard to believe. Sounds great ... but what's the catch? You mentioned a couple of minutes ago that I have to cooperate. Who do I have to cooperate with?"

"There is the presentencing agreement that you have to sign. It requires you never to engage in creative writing in the future. Sign it, face the court, and you will be sentenced to time served. You will be set free on your aunt's recognizance today. You do not even have to return to jail."

"Did you say *never*?! Are you serious?" I cried out.

"That is the only restriction the judge imposed on your freedom."

"Only? But poetry is my life! Who needs that kind of freedom?"

"Do you want to waste five years of your life in the hard labor camps? Don't be stupid, young man. 'Never' is quite a flexible term. You never know how long this 'never' will last in our land. One day, there might be a changing of the guards around here, if you know what I mean. It's now or *never*. Take the damn deal." He pulled the agreement from his briefcase and placed it on the desk in front of me.

"I'm sorry. I just don't know if I can do it, Simeon Yakovlevich," I said. "What will Aunt Anna think of me when she finds out?"

"You are a smart kid, Alex, but right now you sound stupid. I am totally startled. How can you be released on your aunt's recognizance if she doesn't know about it? Does that make any sense? We all— your aunt included—worked so hard on this deal for so long; do not screw it up now. If not for your own sake, do it for your aunt's. 'To avoid the checkmate and save the game, we are going to castle the king, shield him with the rook, and distract our opponents by sacrificing one of our knights.' That's what your aunt said to me when we parted after the meeting last night."

"Are you telling me that she was at that meeting with the judge, the general, and you? Is that right?"

"Yes, she was at the meeting. Will you sign this agreement now, please?" Gurevich pulled a fountain pen from his pocket and awaited my response.

"Give me your pen," I said and quickly placed my signature on the dotted line.

"You will thank me for many years to come, young man." He placed the signed agreement into a folder and put it into his briefcase. "Let's go and face the judge now. Guard!" he yelled through the closed door. "We are ready to move."

"Thank you, Simeon Yakovlevich," I replied and shook his hand.

The ride to the courthouse was short. I arrived there in less than twenty minutes. But then I was locked in a dark holding cell for more than an hour before being brought into the courtroom.

To the right of me, the oversized coat of arms of the Soviet Union dominated the wall above the court's podium. The tall, heavy wooden chair in the center behind the podium for the presiding judge was decorated with the same coat of arms carved into the wood above the leather-covered backrest. Two similar, slightly scaled-down chairs were positioned on both sides of the central one; they were to be occupied by the two people's assessors.

To my left was a barrier separating the court from the members of the public who were already seated.

I saw my parents and Aunt Anna sitting next to each other in the front row. Lara and Valery sat in the row behind them.

When I entered the defendant's dock and sat down, my parents' eyes filled with tears, and Aunt Anna's hand covered her mouth. They had not seen me for a while, and my appearance had visibly shaken them. Simeon Yakovlevich Gurevich approached the barrier from the court side and quietly briefed them, trying to calm everyone down. The two prosecutors sat at the table across from the defendant's dock without even looking in my direction.

Suddenly, the bailiff walked in and loudly announced, "Stand up! Attention everyone!"

The judge and the two people's assessors entered the courtroom and took their seats.

Then the bailiff continued, "The People's Court of the Central District of the City of Moscow is in session. The presiding judge is Sookharev, Georgiy Gavrilovich. The people's assessors are Petrosian, Arsen Ashotovich and Shatunovsky, Dimitry Evgenevich. Now, everyone can take their seats. Quiet in the courtroom! The criminal case number 78-621/1966; State vs. Alexander Loevsky in accordance with Article 70 of the Criminal Code of the Russian Soviet Federative Republic. Prosecution, state your case."

One of the prosecutors got up and addressed the court. "Comrade Presiding Judge, the state charges the defendant with agitation and propaganda directed at undermining the ideological foundation of our Soviet system and subverting the minds of our youth by creating and circulating slanderous fabrications for the purpose of defaming the Soviet State and our social system."

The presiding judge looked at me and then addressed Attorney Gurevich, "I am aware of the agreement reached with the prosecution, where the defendant is accepting responsibility for his actions and pleading no contest to all charges. Do you want to add anything to the agreement presented by you and signed by the defendant?"

"No, Comrade Presiding Judge. I have nothing to add to it. Again, I am pleading with the court for your indulgence and mercy to the defendant in consideration of his young age. My client was never before charged with criminal or subversive activities nor did he ever wittingly participate in such. He was mistakenly influenced by the extraneous tendencies to deviate from his life plan of service to society by becoming a physician.

"Recognizing such a mistake and realizing the predicament he placed himself in, the defendant assures the court that he will never indulge in creative

writing and will concentrate all his efforts on his studies and his future medical career to repay all his debts
to society. His aunt, Comrade Anna Amchislavsky, an
exemplary citizen with an impeccable reputation and
proven public and professional trust, is pleading with
the court to place the defendant under her recognizance upon completion of his incarceration in confor-
mity with the sentence you are about to impose on
him."

While my attorney was speaking, the judge was
looking at me, measuring me up. I obviously did not
want him to read my eyes, which were filled with the
rebellious repulsiveness that I felt toward the socialist
justice charade and the lawyerly exercise in meaning-
less semantics. I looked up at the judge momentarily,
and it seemed to me that a spark of sympathy was in
his eyes. I did not want to disclose to him that I was
privy to the meeting of the previous night, so I tried
to look down and occupy myself by imagining that the
courtroom floor was a gigantic chessboard where the
abstract strategy game was being played. Somehow,
I saw the judge, looking like a bishop piece, being
dragged to our side of the board by a knight piece,
who closely resembled my attorney.

The judge addressed the prosecution, and I looked
up. "The court is assuming that the state is a part of
this pretrial agreement presented by the defense. Since

the defendant accepted the charge and is not going to contest it, what is the prosecution's position regarding expeditious sentencing?"

The prosecutors quietly and visibly argued with each other for a couple of minutes, and then the older one addressed the judge. "With your approval, the prosecution will not challenge the pretrial agreement presented to the court by the defense in the aforementioned case and will not object to your consideration of the immediate sentencing of the defendant according to the sentencing guidelines approved by the Supreme Court of the Soviet Union on September seventeen of last year."

The presiding judge stood up and announced, "The court will reconvene in ten minutes. Due to the brevity of this recess, the defendant shall remain in the courtroom."

The judge and the two people's assessors left, and two policemen stood guard on both sides of my seat. Attorney Gurevich approached me.

"No communication allowed. Stay back!" ordered the bailiff.

Gurevich simply shrugged his shoulders and stepped back without argument.

In ten minutes, the bailiff ordered everyone to stand up. The judge and the two people's assessors took their seats.

"Sit down, everyone," said the judge. "Defendant, remain standing. After reviewing the aggravating and mitigating circumstances of the case, the court agrees with the prosecution request and sentences the defendant, in accordance with Article 70 of the Criminal Code of the Russian Soviet Federative Republic and the sentencing guidelines approved by the Supreme Court of the Soviet Union on September seventeenth, nineteen sixty-five, to the term of five years ..."

Everything inside me dropped. The murmur of the public filled the courtroom. I heard my mother cry out and my Aunt Anna gasp loudly. I felt weak at the knees. I then looked at Attorney Gurevich. He was rubbing his bald head and maintaining a poker face, showing no emotion.

"... served as follows," continued the judge. "Incarceration shall be limited to the six months of time served, and the remaining four years and six months should be suspended in lieu of probation and the personal recognizance of Citizen Amchislavsky, Anna Abramovna."

One of the people's assessors jumped to his feet.

"I categorically object to the last part of your sentencing! We did not vote back in your chambers for any suspended sentence. You did not bring that up. I disagree—"

The judge interrupted him authoritatively, "I do

not give a damn what you object to. Before jumping to your feet and interrupting the presiding judge, familiarize yourself with courtroom decorum, the law at hand, and the approved sentencing guidelines. Now shut up and sit down! We had the majority decision here. It is final," concluded the judge while the second people's assessor nodded approvingly. "Bailiff, after Citizen Amchislavsky signs the recognizance order, release the defendant."

I couldn't believe my own ears. I took a deep breath and looked at my attorney again. Simeon Yakovlevich Gurevich was looking at me, smiling from cheek to cheek. He was no longer rubbing his head; instead, he was giving me the thumbs-up.

Aunt Anna came to the bailiff and signed the order. The policemen on both sides of me disappeared, and I found myself in the arms of my mom and dad, sobbing like a little kid.

Chapter Twelve
General's Deal

While I'd been in prison, I had been expelled from medical school, and my room at the dorm was now occupied by someone else. It's not as if I would have needed it anyway; to comply with the court order, I had to move to Aunt Anna's place until I was reinstated in med school. I was actually looking forward to spending most of my time in my favorite room in my aunt's apartment—her library.

The morning after my release, Lara ran into the library to greet me.

"Yesterday, I almost fainted at the courthouse when the judge read the first part of the verdict, sentencing you to five years. I came to my senses as soon as one of the people's assessors started to argue with the judge. Only then did I realize that the second part of the verdict about your release and your conditional sentence was for real. I didn't want to interfere with your reunion with your parents, so Valery and I left the courthouse right away. I couldn't wait to see you again this morning."

"Here I am," I smiled and opened my arms. "Come and get me."

Lara rushed to give me a hug and a peck on the lips.

"Watch out!" I warned her. "I told you some time ago that I might fall in love with you."

"Not a chance!" She hastily pushed herself away from me. "I told you before, and I'm telling you again now—friends do not fall in love with friends. Besides, for your information, you are not my type. So, stop it once and for all. Period!" She squinted at me, trying her best to look angry, but her freckles gave her away by suddenly becoming more noticeable against her blushing cheeks.

"I give up," I said. "But just for now ..."

"Good boy," she replied. "I brought a load of class notes for you. You'll have one hell of a time catching up. When will you request reinstatement?"

"Request is a very strong word. Don't you realize I'm a convicted felon? How about an appeal instead of a request? In reality, I am ready to beg for my reinstatement. Medical school is the only important thing left in my life since I'm not allowed to write anymore. Aunt Anna was dead right when she urged me not so long ago to stop relying exclusively on my poetry and to pursue my other calling—a career in medicine."

"I'm just curious, Alex ... Since doctors and teachers are the lowest-paying professions in our country and, for that reason alone, ninety-five percent of our physicians are women, why in the world did you want to do medicine?"

"That's a loaded question. How many students were in our freshman class?"

"About three thousand," Lara replied.

"And how many males were among them?"

"Just a few ... I didn't count. How many of you were among us girls?"

"Just twenty-six," I answered proudly. "It was like being in the Garden of Eden filled with beautiful angels. We were just twenty-six lucky, over-sexed medicine-loving idiots. Are you happy with my assessment?"

"Why should I be happy?" Lara asked, shrugging her shoulders. "I don't know how many of the guys in our class were real men. Maybe most of you were just a bunch of pansies. I knew one real man, but he was involved with someone else outside of the school, if you know what I mean."

"Stop being such a tease, Lara. I do know what you mean. But I haven't seen that girl in over a year. As far as I'm concerned, it's over."

"Is it, honestly?" Lara asked in return. Her question was so direct and straightforward that it caught me by surprise. She was looking at me, waiting for an answer.

"Honestly? I don't know."

"You see, that's why I value you as a friend. You are honest with me."

"Rest assured, Lara, that I am and always will be honest with you. I'll be your loyal friend forever. I'll never forget what you did for me when I was on the run and down in the dumps. You saved my life, for God's sake! Nobody else would have done what you did."

"Wrong. A lot of people would have done what I did. I was just in the right place at the right time. Both of us got really lucky."

"Got lucky? That part, I do not remember," I foolishly tried to make a joke.

"You're such an asshole, Alex." Lara pushed me in the chest and turned away. "Don't ever joke about us that way."

"I'm really sorry, Lara. I didn't mean to upset you. Not another word, I promise … Peace, sister?" I stretched out my hand.

"Peace, brother," Lara answered hesitantly, "but you're still an asshole … sometimes!" She slapped my hand in reconciliation. "Let's change the subject."

"Okay. What about my reinstatement? Aunt Anna is not wasting any time. She informed me before she left for work this morning that the general, whom you met once at your parents' place in Obiralovka, my aunt's friend Pavel Sergeevich, is coming tonight to brief us on the meeting he's supposed to have today with Dean Dubinin. Aren't you staying?"

"Since you can't show up at school, someone else has to go there to the library to work on all those class notes for you, pal," Lara replied. "I have to compile my own notes with some of our classmates' to arrange them all in order. I'll come back in a few hours if you don't mind."

"Please, come back. Thank you for everything," I said, walking her to the door. "See you tonight."

For the rest of the day, I was immersed in the pile of class notes that Lara had left for me. While going through it all, I confirmed to myself again and again that she was an awesome notetaker. Reading her lecture notes felt like being in the class and listening to the instructors in real time. She highlighted every significant nuance and every important detail of the subject being covered. After studying her class notes, reviewing and understanding the corresponding pages of the available textbooks felt quite simple. In fact, it was almost too easy—a walk in the park.

By the end of the day, I took a practice test to find out how much I had retained of all the material I'd studied so far, and I got a perfect score. The most amazing part was that, in just one day, I'd managed to cover the equivalent of at least a couple of weeks of the regular class workload, and I had not been overwhelmed by it at all.

That evening, Lara returned with a huge box of notes.

"Is that all? How much more left?" I asked.

"That's it," Lara answered. "All of it is here. It covers all the lecture material till the end of the spring semester. How are you doing so far?"

"You won't believe it," I said. "Almost an hour ago, I finished going over a couple weeks' worth of notes. In the end, I took a practice test and got a hundred percent."

"That's impossible," Lara responded. "Did you cheat? Maybe just a little?"

"I swear I didn't. And I actually enjoyed it."

"You are such a masochist, Alex. How could anyone enjoy cramming? That's really hard to believe. I have nothing else to do over the next couple of weeks until the start of the new school year. We can study together. I can be your study partner if you wish. I want to witness your hundred-percent scores in action."

"Hey, don't threaten me with a good time! I'll take any help I can get. Please, be my guest … join me."

"It's a deal!" Lara answered. "By the way, do you want your study partner to faint? I'm starving. Do you have anything to eat?"

"I'm such an idiot," I said. "I didn't even ask if you were hungry. I'm sorry. Can I boil some pasta and warm up a couple of hamburgers for you? I think there are some left in the fridge."

"That would be great. Can I help?"

"Let's go to the kitchen. You can watch," I offered.

When the pasta was on the table, I realized that I was starving as well. We both devoured the food, eating with two forks from the single plate I had put on the table in front of Lara. The plate had slowly migrated to the middle of the table between the two of us. I cannot explain how close to her I felt at that moment.

Suddenly, I heard the sound of a key in the lock of the apartment door. Seconds later, Aunt Anna walked into the kitchen accompanied by the general. Lara and I jumped to our feet to greet them.

"Hi, kids," Aunt Anna said, looking at our empty plate. "Do we have any food left? Pavel and I are dead hungry, aren't we?" She looked at the general, who simply nodded in agreement. "Pavel arrived here at the very same moment I did. We have not even had a chance to talk."

"Good evening, Anna Abramovna," Lara rushed to answer. "It's good to see you again, Pavel Sergeevich. It's my turn to cook now. Let me make some home fries and prepare the rest of the hamburgers I saw in the fridge. Can I?"

"Sure you can. It will be awesome. Make yourself at home, Lara," Aunt Anna replied.

"I'm happy to see you both here," said the general. Wearing a gray suit, he looked completely different in civilian clothes. "Let's sit down and have a little chat."

Lara started to peel some potatoes and onions, and then she put a large frying pan on the cooktop. Aunt Anna opened one of the cupboards and retrieved a bottle of red wine, a corkscrew, and four wine glasses. The three of us sat down while Lara was peeling and frying potatoes and onions in the large pan and preparing half a dozen hamburgers in a smaller one.

The general poured the wine and said, "Lara, whatever you're doing over there smells wonderful, my dear. So, this afternoon," he continued, turning back to Aunt Anna and me, "I paid a visit to our 'friend' Dean Dubinin at the medical school. He happened to be one stubborn, hard-to-the-core cookie. It took some effort to soften him up."

Aunt Anna interrupted him, "What was the effort, if I may ask?"

"You would never guess ..."

"Try me," she replied.

"I initially asked the dean to do me a favor and reinstate Alex in his class at the medical school by the start of the new school year. He instantly refused and became 'righteously' offended while subtly hinting that he would expect some sort of reward in return. I didn't bite. Waiting for my response, he went back and forth for about an hour, taking the hard-line approach and playing the role of 'moral guardian of the future generation of Soviet physicians.'

"He visibly grew more and more frustrated for getting nowhere with me. Then he finally proclaimed that his duty was to be a father figure to all his students and that, like every father, he was fully responsible for the morality and socially responsible conduct of his 'children.' In the end, he pulled out his pocket watch and looked at it, indicating that our meeting was coming to an end.

"I then pretended to question him innocently about whether he had any kids of his own, and he told me that he had two sons. He proudly informed me that the older one, Evgeny, had just received his Ph.D. in Biology and was waiting to be confirmed as a junior member of the Academy of Science. I asked him if Evgeny, by any chance, drove a car.

"Suddenly, he turned red and emptied a glass of water in a couple of gulps. His forehead was now covered with multiple beads of sweat, and his hands began to shake. His glass was clinking as it vibrated against his teeth. I paused for a moment to let his fear sink in deeper.

"Then I quietly asked him if he thought I could somehow be helpful to the parents of a young and promising scientist who had been involved in a hit-and-run accident less than a year ago. I informed him that the parents didn't yet know that one specific department of the Interior Ministry knew who the perpetrator was and was ready to issue a warrant for his arrest. With tears in his eyes, the dean confessed that earlier this year, he had paid a large sum of money to Colonel Trubin, the head of the Moscow Section of the State Motor Vehicle Division of the Interior Ministry. Colonel Trubin had assured him that nobody would ever find out what had happened.

"Unfortunately, Trubin had been foolishly certain that no one knew about the bribes he had frequently accepted. I calmly told the dean that Trubin was now under criminal investigation and house arrest. I also reminded the dean that receiving as well as offering bribes to state officials was a serious criminal offense punishable by imprisonment of up to fifteen years.

"The dean slumped in his chair. I thought at first that the poor man was having a heart attack. I loosened his tie, unbuttoned his shirt collar, and told him nonchalantly to calm down since my office was holding all the strings to the investigation. Then I offered him my help and another drink of water. His shallow, rapid breathing slowly became somewhat closer to normal, and his teeth stopped rattling against the glass when he drank from it.

"I reassured him that his cooperation in Alex's

reinstatement would help me to steer Trubin's brib-ery investigation and the hit-and-run case away from him and his family. The dean was trying to express his gratitude but could not squeeze a word from his tight-ened throat in response and instead unsuccessfully at-tempted to kiss my hand."

"That's bizarre. What a coincidence," Aunt Anna said.

"It was bizarre, indeed, but it was not a coinci-dence at all," Pavel Sergeevich smiled and continued. "Do you remember what I said when we first met, Alex? I told you that we would make it plausible for the school to reinstate you later on. Well, I empha-sized the word 'plausible' because, a month earlier, I had been informed that the dean's older son had been involved in a hit-and-run accident, which was some-how connected to our Internal Affairs corruption investigation involving the medical school dean and the head of the Moscow Section of the State Motor Vehicle Division.

"To put it simply, I am always trying to keep up to date with what is going on with some people of in-fluence. You never know when some of that dirt will come in handy. So, I kept the whole thing idle, just waiting for the day we would need to use it. Today was that day.

"Here's what I got at the end of the day from our

'beloved' dean. You will be allowed to sit for the last year's final makeup exams, which he will schedule strictly for you a couple days prior to the beginning of the school year. You will have to get a passing score in each course on your first attempt. The school year is about to start in a couple weeks. If you don't get a passing score, you will have to retake the exams next fall, but then you will be set back a year.

"Since the State Department of Education is supervising the exams, you have to get the passing scores for real and on your own. That part is out of the dean's hands. He swore to me that he could only help you to sit for the makeup exams; he can't influence your grades. That is outside of his realm. What do you think? Can you do it? Can you get prepared and be ready in less than a couple of weeks?"

"Yes, he can!" Lara jumped into the conversation while putting a dish with home fries and a plate filled with sizzling hamburgers on the table. "You do not even know how smart he is. I assure you that he can do it. Today he finished reading two weeks' worth of study materials, and, to my surprise, he got a hundred percent—a perfect score—on his first practice test!"

"That was quite an enthusiastic endorsement, Lara. I am impressed," Pavel Sergeevich responded and then turned to me. "Alex?"

"Pavel Sergeevich, will I have any other choice?" I

asked rhetorically. "I have to do it, and I will. I won't let you down, and I can't afford to lose the whole year."

"Pavel," Aunt Anna said, "I know my nephew. He is tenacious, and he is smart. If anyone is able to do it, it's him. Thank you for everything you did to save his life and for this chance you're giving him now."

"Stop it, Anna. That's what friends are for. Years ago, you saved my butt. This time, it was my turn."

"Let's have a toast to our friendship, to Alex's success, and ... to Lara's cooking. Let's eat, finally. I'm starving!" Aunt Anna finished clumsily, covertly wiping away a single tear, which incidentally sneaked away and slowly rolled down her cheek.

"Good luck to you, Alex," the general said, raising his glass. "Do not let us down." He then lowered his voice, looking at each one of us seated around the kitchen table, and added quietly, "L'haim, members of the tribe! To life! May all our dreams come true."

I got ready for finals in less than the allotted two weeks and felt fully prepared to tackle them head-on. The exams were split equally between Monday, August 29th, and Tuesday, August 30th. If I passed, I would begin my second year with the rest of my class on September 1st. *Wouldn't that be awesome?* I thought, as I entered the medical school building that Monday morning.

The security guard accompanied me to the auditorium, where the two proctors from the State Department of Education were waiting for me.

"Do you have anything in your pockets?" one of them asked.

I had come prepared, knowing what they would be looking for.

"No," I answered. "I just have a couple of pencils and my ID. Would you like to see it?"

"Of course," the other proctor replied. "Empty your pockets. Put everything on the table, and turn your pockets inside out so we can confirm that's all you have on you."

I did what I was told and then patiently awaited further instructions.

"Your pants pockets should remain inside out for the duration of the tests. If you need to go to the bathroom between exams, one of us will escort you there and back. If there is any appearance or suspicion of cheating, the test will be immediately terminated and the rest of the exams will be cancelled. Do you understand?" the proctor almost screamed at me.

I had not even had a chance to open my mouth to reply when I heard an angry voice behind me at the entrance doors.

"That sort of conduct should be stopped at once!" The voice then angrily continued, "This is not a prison, for Pete's sake!"

I looked back and saw Dean Dubinin marching commandingly to the front of the auditorium.

"You are inside a sanctuary!" he declared loudly. "These are the walls of the First Setchenoff Moscow Medical School. This distinguished scientific and teaching institution I am in charge of is more than a century and a half old. I am the dean here, and you will obey my orders! I do not know if the kind of acrimony you have expressed so far is a result of your own zealotry or somebody else's vehement instructions, and, frankly speaking, I do not give a flying fart. You will do your proctoring job in compliance with the accepted standards and regulations, and I myself will be present in this auditorium at all times to make sure that this ugliness that I had witnessed here a moment ago will not happen again!"

"I'm sorry, Comrade Dean. I was under the impression that this ... Can we talk in private?" started the other proctor, but the dean didn't let him finish.

"This discussion is over, and your impression will lead you somewhere you do not wish to be. The top brass of the Interior Ministry is watching us." The dean looked around demonstratively. "Do you want to deal with them ... the top law enforcement authorities?

Don't be a fool. Start the test, and I will stay here to monitor you, my friend."

The dean then turned to face me. "Alex, you can put your pants pockets back in. Pretend all this never happened, my friend."

"Take your seat, please," the proctor offered politely and put the first test booklet in front of me. "You have two and a half hours to answer all the questions."

I opened the booklet and started to register my answers on the score sheet. I was done in forty-five minutes.

"Do you wish to take a break?" the proctor asked.

"Not really. Can we start the second one?" My response took him by surprise.

"Can we?" Both proctors looked at the dean, awaiting his permission.

"Of course, you can. Why not? What are you waiting for? Go ahead!" The dean, nevertheless, sounded intrigued as well.

I finished the second test in one hour and fifteen minutes.

"I don't need a break," I said. "Can I have the third test booklet, please?"

Startled, the proctors were now staring at the dean.

"Do it. Give it to him now!" the dean ordered.

At twelve thirty, I pushed away the finished booklet and score sheet for the third test.

Both proctors and the dean looked at me without blinking.

"Are you sure you didn't miss anything, Alex?" The dean's voice reflected his perplexity. He sounded completely puzzled.

"Can I have a bathroom break now?" I asked. "I just need a few minutes."

"What do you mean?" one of the proctors asked, shaking his head in total disbelief. "We're done for today, aren't we?"

"Go to the bathroom, Alex. Take your time. The three of us will have a little chat in the meantime."

I was on a roll and felt almost euphoric. Lara's notes had been excellent, and my memory was as sharp as it had ever been. *What if I do have a photographic memory? Maybe Aunt Anna is right*, I said to myself as I stood in the bathroom, zipping up my pants. I started opening the bathroom door and stopped halfway when I heard the dean's voice resonating in the empty auditorium.

"Let him take the rest of it now. He will fail for sure. There's no way in the world he can be that sharp for another few hours. We'll put a time limit on him; let's say that five o'clock is the cutoff time. You can offer to him, *It's all or nothing. Come back and try your luck tomorrow or be done with everything right now.* He'll take the bait; I'm sure of it. He'll be afraid that after you submit your reports tonight, tomorrow could be a different scenario with different rules imposed from the top. Let him race against the clock. This is our only chance to satisfy your people at the Second Directorate and blame the failure on him."

What a frigging snake! I thought. *He's trying to screw me. The hardest test was the second one—biochemistry. The remaining tests are a piece of cake. I don't need more than three hours to take them all. Go ahead, you bastards. Let's play this chess game.* I opened the bathroom door, crossed the short corridor, and entered the auditorium.

"Alex, my friend," the dean immediately addressed me softly. "It's all up to you. I conferred with my colleagues over here while you were on your break, and they graciously agreed to stay to give you the opportunity to finish all the remaining tests if you wish. There's only one caveat—you have to be done with the three remaining tests by five o'clock. What do you think?"

"It's almost one o'clock now, so I would have just four hours left for the three remaining exams, right?"

"That's perfectly correct," the dean affirmed enticingly. "I bet you can do it. What do you say?"

"I really appreciate your offer, Comrade Dean. But I'm kinda afraid to gamble with my future. It's not enough time for me. I don't think I can do it. Can we break now? I'll have the rest of the day and all night to cram. Can we continue with the three remaining tests tomorrow?"

"What if we add an extra hour today? Will that suffice?" one of the proctors asked, looking at the dean.

"Yes! How about six o'clock?" the dean offered eagerly. "Can we shake hands on it right now?"

"I don't know," I responded, slowly rubbing my temples. "It's tempting … What about seven o'clock?" I haggled.

"Six thirty, and that's our final offer," the dean countered, raising his eyeglasses upon his wrinkled, sweaty forehead as he looked at me impatiently.

"How long will it take for you to verify and finalize the score sheets?" I suddenly addressed the proctors.

"The six single score sheets?" the second proctor started to think aloud. "I have all the matrix cards in my briefcase. To match the scorecards against the windowed matrix cards, to grade them, to complete the report, and to certify it shouldn't take me longer than fifteen minutes—maybe twenty minutes max. Why did you ask?"

"Here's the final deal," I said. "You can take it or leave it. I will try my best to finish by six thirty, but if, for any insane reason, I'm done before five o'clock—and I do realize that I will have to rush like a madman to finish it all—you will have the certified grades for me twenty minutes later."

"Make it thirty minutes," the proctor said in a hurry.

"Only if you're done before four thirty," the dean upped the ante and wiped his forehead with a hanky, "and only then!"

"Is that a deal now?" I asked.

"It's a deal. But you are my witness, Alex, that I did try to talk you out of it," the dean answered. "It's a deal, but those two gentlemen will attest to the fact that I did warn you not to rush."

"Let's start then," I said, taking my seat.

I was done at four fifteen and got up. My adrenaline was maxed out. The dean sat at the head table speechless, shaking his head in total disbelief.

"A deal is a deal," one of the proctors said, retrieving the six windowed matrix cards from his briefcase.

"You are an amazing test taker, young man," the other one added. "I'm guessing you'll end up with all passing scores; regardless, I have never met anyone capable of doing what you just did. I'm really sorry for being rude to you earlier this morning. Friends?" He extended his hand and offered me a handshake.

"Sure, why not . . ." I said, accepting his handshake.

My bladder was on the verge of bursting, but I did not want to leave the auditorium before my scores were announced.

"Twenty-nine out of thirty!" exclaimed the second proctor. "Five 'A's and one 'B.' That's unbelievable! Let me fill in the certification form right away."

"That one 'B' was for biochemistry, wasn't it?" I asked.

"Who cares at this point, dear Alex?" Dean Dubinin descended the podium, hovering in my direction. He was spreading his arms wide like eagle wings, getting ready to give me a hug. "Congratulations, my friend!" The fake sweetness of his voice was utterly nauseating. "Now you are officially a second-year student. Keep your grades up, and do not let me down. I would like to embrace you, my dear friend"

I stepped back, looking at the auditorium exit door. "No offense, Comrade Dubinin, but my bladder is ready to give out. I have to run to the bathroom immediately. I'll be right back."

I bolted out of the auditorium at the right time; another moment and I would have wet my pants. It seemed to me that I stood smiling at the urinal for a while. When I returned to the auditorium, no one was there—just a certified copy of my final scores waiting for me on the table.

Chapter Thirteen
Confession

The first day of my second year of medical school had flickered down like a birthday cake candle, turning into a tasteless, colorless wax and melting into the surrounding chocolate and vanilla sweetness. Those parts of a cake were, figuratively speaking, left on the plate with no one willing to touch them. For understandable reasons, I felt like that leftover part of the cake—a pariah who was unsavory, odious, and simply too risky a person to be associated with.

Over the next few months, my academic standings added to my isolation. Becoming a "curve breaker" was never meant to gain friends and popularity among one's fellow classmates. I had to deal with an additional unhealthy mix of envy, rejection, and disdain.

But for me, school was not a popularity contest; it was a fight for survival. I couldn't care less for those people who admired me one day for my poetry and then turned on me the next day when the authorities proclaimed it too dangerous and too provocative. I was despised by others who could not step up to the plate to compete with me honestly, who were constantly cheating, and who, when caught, blamed "the prodigious Jewish conspiracy" for their academic inadequacy.

Unfortunately, for them, the latter could not explain the essence of their grievance. It was too laughable to be taken seriously. As a result of the subtle but strict compliance with the limiting quotas, a very insignificant number of Jewish students were in attendance. I guessed that, besides Lara and me, there were maybe five or six more Jews among the almost three thousand students in our class.

The Jewish conspiracy theory could not fly; nevertheless, it loitered around notoriously, waiting for another chance to strike. Right from the start, I understood that only solid knowledge would lead me to a successful medical career, and that was the only way for someone like Lara or myself to survive in the prevailing environment.

Lara proved to be a devoted friend. She never abandoned me. We were like Siamese twins joined at the hip.

Somehow, she managed to establish the strict boundaries of our relationship—no lascivious innuendoes, no sultry jokes, no inappropriate touching. None of these was permissible. The relationship was as asexual as the life inside a convent or a monastery could have been. Nevertheless, we spent a lot of time together, enjoying each other's company—studying our brains out, eating between studies, going to the school library together, and, on rare occasions, visiting the theaters, the ballet, and the opera.

But the greatest treat for us both was listening to the fiery discussions happening inside the walls of the private library of my Aunt Anna's apartment. Lara and I were allowed inside Aunt Anna's circle of friends. Each and every one of them had their distinct perspective on the common concerns of the destiny of our generation and a plethora of opinions about that generation's future. We sat quietly, listened, and learned...

I should not say that this sort of relationship was easy for me, because I really experienced way more than just friendly feelings for Lara. But she kept me at a distance, insistent on maintaining a strictly platonic relationship. She did not allow me to get any closer in my infrequent and timid amatory exploits because of my admission to her long ago that I was involved with somebody else and was not sure whether it was over.

For the life of me, I could not lie to her, because Lara was not who occupied my nights. My dreams were involuntarily permeated with memories of the sensual encounters with Svetlana and with her mind-numbing seductiveness. I was waking up in the middle of the night inhaling the scent of her skin and feeling the taste of her lips. I would close my eyes and imagine being entangled in her long aureate curls spread all over my pillow.

I saw us lying intertwined in each other's arms, making endless love, and reciting the same verses of Omar Khayyam's "Rubaiyat" repeatedly, as we had done the last night we had spent together. I still could not purge it from my memory. I was stalked almost every night by the awe and dread of our unfinished love affair. It almost became a sort of psychotic obsession, and the frightening part of it was that I did not care how long it would last, and I was not looking for a cure.

Coming back to reality, and to be completely fair to the rest of the flock, a couple of our study partners, Paul and Andrew, had also never turned away from me. They were also treated like a couple of pariahs, rejected by the rest of the class under the suspicion of being gay. If proven to be true in our time, that would have constituted a crime punishable by five years of imprisonment. In the long run, who the hell among us cared whether Paul, Andrew, or both of them were gay or not? But the rumor mill churned that they were because they did not publicly mix with any class members of the opposite sex. Because of that, the common opinion was that they were most likely involved with each other.

Actually, I didn't think so, and I wouldn't care

if they were. To the best of my knowledge, none of them ever made a weird move on me or acted in a strange manner. The way I saw it, they were just a couple of complete nerds mustering all their efforts to memorize and systematize every little detail of the study material they crammed at all times. That alone was enough for me to dismiss all that other nonsense. Inside the intense and busy life of a medical student, who had the time to be concerned about what any one of us did or did not do between the sheets?

Another couple of years passed. The lectures started to give way to clinical rotations, but the four of us were still stuck together studying after the clinics and on weekends.

One late Saturday afternoon when we were done for the day, Lara and I decided to go to a movie. Knowing what the answer would be and just to be polite, we invited Paul and Andrew to join us.

They looked at each other, and after a short pause, Andrew said, "We were actually planning to ask both of you if you would like to join us this afternoon."

Lara was caught by surprise. "We've known each other for more than three years, and this is our first invitation from you. What's the occasion, if I may ask?"

"Simhat Torah," Andrew answered, and he blushed.

"Did you just say Simhat Torah?" I asked again, hardly believing that I had heard him correctly.

"Simhat Torah," Andrew repeated slowly. "That is the happiest Jewish holiday ... when young people get together and celebrate. You know ... They sing, they dance ... We were quite sure that you and Lara were Jewish ... Aren't you?" Andrew looked completely embarrassed.

"Yes, we are," Lara rushed to his rescue. "But we never thought that you two were."

"You are correct; we are not," Andrew started to explain with a stutter, blushing even more. "I mean, you are only partially ... just about seventy-five percent correct. I, myself, am not Jewish. Our last names, Polyakov and Voronin, are very Russian indeed. Paul got his last name from his late father, who was Russian Orthodox, but his mother and his sister are Jewish, and he was raised by his mom as a Jew."

"Andrew has a crush on my sister, poor boy," Paul cut in. "I took him with me to the synagogue at Arkhipov Street on the same occasion last year, and that was where he and my sister met for the first time. Now, he is a lost soul in love."

Andrew's face was red but wreathed in a smile.

Lara and I looked at each other and responded simultaneously, "To hell with the movie!"

"We are joining you," Lara said.

"What's the plan?" I asked.

"What are we doing?" Lara echoed.

"We are going to Arkhipov Street to the syna-gogue," answered Paul. "You know where Moscow's Grand Choral Synagogue is, don't you?"

"I have no clue. I've never been there," I answered and looked at Lara.

"I used to live nearby a few years back. I know where it is," Lara shrugged her shoulders, "but I was never been inside of it either … Isn't that the only one in Moscow?" she asked. "Alex and I, we are kinda … not religious … Am I right, Alex? We are not observant, if I may say so. I don't know how to explain it. We know that we are Jews because if everyone around us has a chip on their shoul-der, they'd tell us that we are. It's complicated …" She looked at me as if asking for my help.

"You don't have to explain," said Paul. "Been there, done that … if you know what I mean."

"I've never been inside a synagogue," I said. "It would be interesting to see."

"I don't think we'll be able to get inside. By the time we get there, the place will be packed," Paul ex-plained. "Traditionally, the men pray in the main sanc-tuary downstairs, and the women have to go upstairs to the balcony. I don't think you and Lara want to be separated at this point. Way too many people will be there tonight."

"How many?" I was curious. "A few hundred or more than that?"

"It's impossible to explain, man. Thousands. You would never believe me. You have to see it with your own eyes. It's literally packed from wall to wall and all the way to the doors. That's where all the young people congregate, right on the street in front of the synagogue, and everyone outside there has a blast!"

"Thank you for the offer. I'm all excited to see it. Let's go."

"Remember what day today is, Alex," Paul said.

"Today is Saturday, October fourth, nineteen sixty-nine," I replied. "Why do I have to remember it?"

"I'll tell you later." Paul smiled in response.

We left the dorm, and the four of us walked to the subway station. We took the train to Revolution Square and then continued to our destination along the labyrinth of old, quiet streets, tree-shrouded parks, and noisy intersections until we suddenly stopped at Pokrovsky Gates.

"When we get to the next intersection," Paul explained, "You and Lara should close your eyes and turn right onto Arkhipov Street. Andrew and I will be right behind you. All of us will be standing at the top of a long, narrow decline bending to the left. The synagogue is located about two-thirds of the way down on the right-hand side of the street. Take a couple of steps and then open your eyes. You will remember this moment forever."

I took Lara's hand, and we closed our eyes and turned right. After a couple of steps down the street, we opened our eyes and immediately froze, numb. Lara squeezed my hand hard and pressed herself tightly against me.

In front of us was a rolling, long, and narrow street demarcated by two rows of century-old two- and three-story buildings. As far as I could see, the street was filled with a tightly packed and constantly moving crowd. An unending sea of smiling, singing faces shone like little pieces of a lively, bright mosaic incessantly morphing as they hovered above the now invisible canvas of the cobblestone pavement.

Now and then, suddenly appearing and disappearing, the rotating rings of perpetual horah dancers were leaving their traces throughout the crowd, flying like round cookie cutters over the flat surface of a rolled-out cookie-dough sheet. As we started moving down the street, drawn deep inside the crowd, as if by some gigantic magnet, we instantly became entangled in the rhythm of those simple and invitingly appealing dances, the sounds of previously unheard songs, and the unexplainable euphoric feeling of belonging.

Spontaneously, through the splashes of laughter, we started to sing along with the lyrics yet unknown to us.

Hava nagila, Hava nagila, Hava nagila, Ve'nismeha ... Let's rejoice and be happy; the words of the ancient song felt so sweet and soothing on our already ruffed vocal cords.

"Do you feel the same thing I feel?" I shouted in Lara's ear.

"Look around!" she yelled back, spreading her arms as if trying to embrace the whole crowd. "We are not alone! I could not have imagined that there were so many of us! Together ..."

We were moving around from one horah ring to another, making new friends and bonding in small talk. Out of nowhere, Paul and Andrew appeared, holding hands with a pretty, busty redhead.

"Meet my sister, Kira," Paul introduced the girl. "Lara and Alex, our study partners. My little sis broke his heart," he added laughingly, pointing at Andrew.

"Stop teasing him!" Kira commanded, stepping in front of a completely embarrassed Andrew. "My brother is such a goofball. I've heard so much about you, guys. It's nice meeting you both, finally."

"Nice meeting you as well," Lara answered.

Paul looked around and said to me, "Isn't it awesome? Isn't it invigorating?"

"Thank you, Paul, for bringing us here. You were absolutely right! I'll remember this day forever ..."

"Mazel tov!" Paul replied.

"What does it mean?" I wondered aloud.

"It means 'good luck, good fortune' in Hebrew. What a beautiful night it is! It's almost palpable … Can you feel it?"

"I feel like I was just born tonight," I answered.

"Mazel tov! Happy birthday, man!" he responded.

"I feel like …" Lara said suddenly, "… like my leg is on fire. Let's step out to the sidewalk. I have to check it out. It feels like my right nylon has a huge hole over my calf and is melting right into it."

I took Lara by the arm and pulled her to the side. On the sidewalk under a streetlight, I looked at the back of her legs. One of her nylon stockings had melted away, and the skin under it had started to turn red, showing signs of a chemical burn. I saw a water spigot protruding from the wall. I rushed to open the valve and let the water run over her leg.

"Stay still," I said. "I know the water is cold, but let it run over your calf for at least a few minutes. We have to wash that chemical off for whatever it is to be at least partially diluted or neutralized."

Lara raised her skirt, unfastened the damaged stocking, and took it off completely.

"It's stopped burning now," she said, looking around.

"What the fuck do you think you're doing, asshole?" A few feet away from us stood a tall, athletic-looking guy in his thirties wearing a white-and-blue kippah pinned to the top of his wildly flying red hair. He was holding high the twisted wrist of a short man wearing a trench coat with the red armband of the Civil Order Watch on his sleeve. The short man, whose arm had being twisted and stretched, was writhing in pain, as he was trying to hide a large plastic syringe in his captured hand, squealing vehemently.

"You just wait, Jew bastard! You're gonna pay for this, you piece of stinking shit! Let my arm go, you motherfucking kike!"

The crowd rolled back slightly, surrounding the men in a tight barrier.

"Look what you did to my pant leg, you son of a bitch!" The back half of the tall guy's left pant-leg was gone.

"I hate you, you fucking kike!" The short man continued to squeal, trying to pry his hand holding the syringe free.

"Do you still think that we, the Jews, are easy targets for raging bigots like you? Not anymore! You ran into the wrong Jew, pal! Do you think it's fucking funny? Do you? Now, go and laugh all the way to hell!" The tall guy shouted as he ripped the syringe free from the short man's hand. He grabbed the short man by the hair, almost lifting him off the ground, aimed the syringe at the man's face, and emptied its contents in a single squirt. The short guy desperately twisted himself free and immediately fell to the ground, holding his face while screaming his lungs out and convulsing wildly as the acid burned his eyes.

"Have a taste of your own fucking medicine, pig!" The tall guy threw the empty syringe on the ground, pulled off his kippah, and quickly started to make his way through the crowd and down the street.

At the very same moment, I heard the sound of police whistles and saw a few hordes of familiar-looking members of the Civil Order Watch wearing red armbands on their sleeves. They were running from the adjacent courtyards and charging the crowd, which then started to roll downhill, accelerating in the direction of the wide-open intersection with Solyanka Street. The police followed the crowd, methodically handcuffing and dragging people away.

"There's no way in the world I'll let you get arrested tonight," Lara said, pulling off her other stocking and throwing away her drenched high heel shoes. She led me in the opposite direction, uphill. She turned sharply to her left and into the darkness of a narrow opening inside the picketed fence. "Let's run to a nearby subway station. I know the way."

"Are you sure?" I asked.

"Just follow me," she answered.

Lara guided me down a few long and murky alleyways, through a number of squeaky gates, in and out of dark courtyards, and across some tramlines. We ran along the backstreets until we were totally winded. Then we threw ourselves on a bench in a small park to catch our breath.

Suddenly, Lara turned to me and threw her legs over my thighs. She climbed onto my lap and buried her face in mine. As I cradled her in my arms, she rewarded me with the most ardent and trembling kiss I could have ever expected from her but could only have wished for in my dreams.

Suddenly, she stopped cold and pulled herself away as if nothing had happened. She then calmly said, "What? Stop staring at me! It was just a decoy, silly. Didn't you see a couple of Civil Order Watch goons running by us a moment ago? Let's take the subway to your aunt's place now and weather the storm there. Do you think she'd mind?"

"I am sure she won't. But how will you make it barefoot through the streets of Moscow on a cold October night without drawing any attention?" I asked. "I have a few bucks on me. Let's flag a taxi cab instead."

We climbed into the backseat of a cab a minute later. I was fully occupied during the ride to Aunt Anna's place thinking of that kiss as I held Lara in my arms, trying to keep her warm and rubbing her tired and bruised feet.

"Happy birthday to us, Alex," Lara whispered in my ear and then slowly kissed me on the lips.

I shut my eyes and whispered back, "Happy birthday to us, Lara ... Mazel tov!"

"You weren't at the Grand Synagogue, were you?" was the first thing Aunt Anna asked when she opened the door.

"Yes, we were there tonight," I answered.

"I knew it!" she exclaimed. "I just sensed it. I was worried sick. Are you two okay?"

"Yes, we are. What were you worried about, Auntie?" I asked as innocently as I could.

"I'm not dumb. I hope you've figured that out by now. Lara, it's nighttime in October. We're way past the Indian summer. It's chilly outside. Why in the world didn't you wear shoes? And where are your stockings, if I may ask, young lady?"

"Anna Abramovna," Lara started, "please don't be angry with us."

"I'm not angry, Lara," Aunt Anna interrupted. "I was a nervous wreck! Almost an hour and a half ago, I was listening to *Radio Free Europe* on my shortwave radio. They started to describe some disturbances happening at that very moment near the Moscow synagogue, where, as they said, thousands of Jewish youth celebrating Simhat Torah were assaulted by the Civil Order Brigade followed by the riot police.

"They reported that dozens of people were attacked with some kind of acid to provoke the confrontation and that a lot of participants were being rounded up and arrested. At that very moment, the station became jammed. I began turning the dial like crazy, but every news broadcast from abroad was also jammed. Was what I heard an exaggeration, or wasn't it?"

"No, it did happen exactly as it was reported," Lara answered. "My leg was sprayed with acid. My stocking started to melt into my leg. Alex pulled me to the sidewalk, where he saw a water spigot on the wall. Luckily, he washed the acid off right away, and my leg stopped burning in a couple of minutes.

"Then we saw someone from the crowd confront the assailant and wrestle away a syringe from him. The syringe was filled with acid, and he emptied it all straight into the man's face. At that very moment, the Civil Order Watch charged the crowd, and the police started to arrest everyone they could get their hands on.

"Some time ago, I'd spent a couple years living in that neighborhood, so I knew my way around and knew how to slip out of there in a flash. I dumped my already beat-up high heels, and then Alex and I made our way out of there unnoticed, running through the network of abandoned courtyards and deserted back-streets. We flagged a cab and came right here."

"You're still nervous, my dear girl," Aunt Anna said, giving Lara a hug. "I can feel you trembling."

"I'm just cold, Anna Abramovna ... and I'm shivering because ... because ... I was afraid ... that he would get arrested over there. I'm scared to death of losing him now ... because I feel that we've grown so close that I just can't imagine my life without him."

"Without *him*?" Aunt Anna asked with a smile, pointing at me.

"Yes! Without him ... I am falling for him ... for Alex ... for your nephew, Anna Abramovna," Lara repeated a few times, as if trying to nail her point to make sure we understood. She then buried her face in Aunt Anna's chest and began to cry. I was standing next to them, frozen, shocked by Lara's unconcealed confession and her sudden tears. I had never seen her so distraught.

"But, Lara, you're the one who told me so many times that friends don't fall in love with fiends. You're the one who kept me at a distance and didn't allow me to get closer to you," I argued.

"I know ... and I was right. I was fighting myself, resisting falling under your spell for the last few years. But you were always near, and you somehow tricked me and made your way into my hea-a-a-a-rt," Lara sniveled.

"Lara, my girl, that's life. You're both falling for each other. It's wonderful, and it should make you feel like you are in seventh heaven. Why in the world are you crying your eyes out?" Aunt Anna asked, caressing Lara's back and trying to calm her down.

"Because I am very happy-y-y-y-y ..." Lara yowled. In a few moments, she stopped crying, wiped her eyes with her sleeves, and then looked at Aunt Anna and me.

The three of us broke out laughing.

"I'm sorry I lost it, Anna Abramovna," Lara finally said, wiping her eyes with her sleeves again and fighting a sudden wave of hiccups.

"Please, call me Aunt Anna."

"I will. I just have to get used to it," Lara said, hiccupping every few seconds. "It's getting late. I have to go."

"You are in no shape to go anywhere. Why don't you stay here tonight?" Aunt Anna offered. "I'll put you in the guest bedroom, and Alex will stay on the couch in my study. Alex," she suddenly addressed me, "bring a glass of water for Lara, please."

I opened the door to the kitchen and heard Aunt Anna continue, "Get some much-needed sleep, my dear girl, and you'll pull yourself together by morning.

Anyhow, tomorrow is Sunday; there's no school. We can have a late breakfast together. What do you think?"

"Thank you, Anna Abra ... Thank you, Aunt Anna. You're very kind. I'm sorry I allowed my emotions to get the better of me earlier."

I was standing on the other side of the kitchen door, holding a glass full of water, trying not to interfere and, at the same time, not to miss a single word of their conversation.

"It happens to the best of us," Aunt Anna continued. "We are women. You are young, and your emotions overwhelmed you tonight. When I was your age, it used to happen to me every month at the same time, if you know what I mean."

"Yeah," Lara lowered her voice, "it's almost that time of the month ... I'm seriously falling in love with him, Aunt Anna."

"I couldn't wish anything better for both of you. In my humble opinion, you two were made for each other. He is very smart and talented, but he needs a cool head like yours in his life. You have my blessing if you are looking for it." With those words, Aunt Anna took Lara's head in her hands and kissed her on the forehead. I could not hide behind the kitchen door any longer.

"Here it is, Lara. Please take a few sips." I came out from the kitchen with the glass of water.

Lara drank a little and gave the glass back to me.

"Thank you, Alex. My hiccups are gone, but I feel exhausted."

"Are you hungry?" Aunt Anna asked. "Would you like a little bite before bed?"

"Thank you, Aunt Anna," both of us answered at the same time. "But we're not hungry."

"Let me show you to your bedroom, my dear." Aunt Anna took Lara by the hand. "Alex," she said ceremoniously and with a conspiratorial smile, "you may now kiss your bride ... good night." Before closing the bedroom door, she turned to me and added, "Wait for me in the library. I have to have a word with you."

I felt thirsty and finished the rest of Lara's water. Aunt Anna returned, and we sat on the couch in her library.

"You stood there like a piece of furniture when the girl was saying that she's falling in love with you. That was not the reaction I expected to see from you. What's wrong?"

"I don't know, Auntie. I think I just got scared. I know what I feel. Lara is my best and dearest friend. I want to spend the rest of my life with her. I have no doubt about that. She is the most beautiful and giving person I've ever met. She does not do anything halfway. If Lara says that she loves me, it's all the way ... totally and unconditionally. How can I, in return, give her most but not all of me? I am so not ready to deal with all that stuff."

"I don't understand, Alex. What's the problem? You don't think you love her?"

"No, it's not that. I know I've been head over hills for Lara for a long time … Maybe it is love. But there is another part of me that I am unable to control. When I close my eyes at night, it's not Lara I dream about making love to. I can't get Svetlana out of my dreams. She is the one I wrote all my love poetry about if you remember. I know it might sound crazy to you, but I think I've started to lose my mind. The other day, as I looked through a trolley window, I thought I spotted Svetlana walking down the street. I'm sure I was daydreaming, but I broke out in a cold sweat.

"She left Moscow for Turatam a few years ago, and she is there with her dad almost five thousand miles away. It's like a lingering disease. How can I get that intrusive fixation out of my life? How can I clear it from my brain? I can't hurt Lara, and I can't lie to her. Help me please, Aunt Anna."

"Stop living in the days of yore, Alex. Look ahead and dream ahead. Do not turn back. Leave what happened a few years ago behind you. Set yourself free. Do not try to relive it. It never works. It will only bring you pain and despair. I'm telling you this from my own life experience. Do not turn yourself into a mental wreck!

"The fling with Svetlana is in your past. I can assure you that it was not love. It was just an infatuation that was powerful enough to keep you engrossed in it on and off for a few years. Your feelings were obviously accentuated by the poetry you wrote about her. The magic of poetry makes it feel like it was real love. That's why it appears to you now as an obsession.

"You were too young to understand what love is. You have to mature enough to be in love. There is a wonderful young lady in your life now, and you will share your future with her. Don't you dare to lose her. Do not be a fool.

"Take it slow … one day at a time. What's the rush? Don't think that Lara will let you into her bed before the two of you are set to tie the knot. Not a day earlier. You have plenty of time to liberate yourself from that Svetlana reverie.

"Let's talk like two adults. Metaphorically speaking, men have just enough blood in them to supply only one head at a time. Use the head that is up on your shoulders—not the other one that's up in your pants. Do not let your heart be fooled. By the way, does Lara know about Svetlana?"

"Yes, when Lara and I met for the first time and she thought I was hitting on her, I told her that I was involved with someone else. She asked me a few times if that was over, and I replied that I had not seen or spoken to the other girl for a few years but that I still wasn't sure if I was over it. I couldn't lie to her."

"You are smart enough. Wake up to reality. Love is like a campfire. A slow flame will keep you warm for a long time, but a spontaneous, out-of-control inferno will die out as fast as it started, leaving you burned-out and destroyed. Life sometimes throws a few curveballs at you. Don't just stand there waiting to get hurt. Hit them out of the park. Get it?"

"I think so …"

"Good! It's getting late. I'm going to bed now. Make yourself at home, my boy."

Aunt Anna got up and left me in her library alone with a lot to think about.

Chapter Fourteen

Alexander Gardens

As usual, the night before that daunting final surgery exam the four of us were studying together at the small dorm room occupied by Paul and Andrew. We were cramming for a few nights, and I could not concentrate any longer. Every time I looked at Lara my mind was drifting away. All those thoughts about the past, the present, and the future were lingering inside my head intertwining with an increasing intensity. I needed to sort them out.

It was three o'clock in the morning when I finally gave up and pushed the surgery handouts away. I was exhausted.

"I have to go for a walk," I said.

Paul looked at me as though I were plagued with a severe mental illness.

"Are you nuts?" he asked. "The exam starts at nine, and we haven't gotten through the first half of the syllabus yet."

"I can't think straight anymore," I said as I grabbed my jacket and my notes. "I'm going for a walk."

"Leave him alone, Paul," Lara jumped to my defense. "Let him get some fresh air. Alex, don't stay away for too long, please. It's chilly outside, and we can all use your help."

"I'll try …" I replied and raised the collar of my jacket on my way out.

The old-fangled building that housed the medical school dorm was located in close proximity to the Moskva River. At night, it was the most tranquil site of the old city—the city I adored so much. Cobblestone sidewalks slowly rolled along the century-old houses and velvety quiet courtyards. Dimmed lights under the arched passageways elicited some unexplainable intrigue over the mysterious, endless corridors of sleeping, communal apartments. A nippy night breeze removed the remainder of the day-staled air and breathed new life into the old buildings.

The street whirled down to the greatness of the granite river embankment. It no longer cuddled you but instead gently pushed you out into an open space lined with slow-moving black water. As I approached the bridge, the soft echo of muffled footsteps now changed to the sound of a snappy, brisk metronome.

A small incline led to the crest of the bridge, lazily unveiling the perpetual, starry sky. On the other side of the river, the oak alleys of Alexander Gardens weaved their way along the Kremlin Wall. My favorite spot was the last bench in the alley next to the Trinity Gate. It was the deepest, darkest corner of the garden, where the bricks of the wall were covered with thick somnolent moss, and the air was filled with the wintry scent of pine trees.

The streetlights paraded along the uphill drive, cutting through the garden to the gate. The narrow beam of a streetlight above the wall penetrated the leafless crowns of tall oak trees and majestic evergreens, creating a small, shiny island at the very edge of the bench. I loved to come here and sit alone in the quiet of the night to read, or just think, without sharing the untroubled darkness with anyone else. That was my retreat and my escape.

I zipped up my jacket, opened my notes, took a deep breath, and tried to concentrate.

Suddenly, the silence of the night was cracked open like an eggshell with the sound of nearby hedges being crushed. The sharp blast of a police whistle echoed on the other side of the park. I looked back.

The shrubs gave way to a dark figure who swiveled his body across the bench and sat next to me. He held his right hand against his chest, trying to catch his breath, while motioning to me with the left one to sit still. His pale face looked frightened.

"Are you okay?" I jumped.

"There's not enough time." He shook his head and grabbed my arm, pulling me back to the bench.

"The KGB's goon squad's gonna be here in a few

moments. I don't know who you are, and I'm most likely mad, but there's no other choice. Give me your hand! Quickly!"

He reached into his pocket and removed something wrapped in tissue paper. He hastily put the object into my open hand. Then he rolled my hand into a fist and pulled himself closer.

"Listen, you don't have to do this, but if you do ... there's a phone number there at the very end. Call this number and tell them you have it."

"Have what? What is it?"

"Just take it and call. No time to explain. You can save more than three hundred lives. Innocent lives. The proof is in your hands. They are not all insane."

"It is you who is insane! Who are 'they'? Who are you? What proof are you talking about? You don't know me, I don't know them, and I don't know who the hell you are!"

"I beg of you, please take it. Please," he moaned.

"Okay," I gave up, "I took it. Okay? It's in my hand. But how do you know that I will call?"

"I *don't* know," he growled, holding his chest and gasping for air, "but I hope you will. I have no other choice. And those who are locked up ... you are their only chance. The goons are gonna get me any minute now. Those sons of bitches are not looking for you. It's me they're after.

"I feel the noose getting tighter, but this noose is set up just for me. You can slip away. They're everywhere. They're really close. Do you hear? If what I gave you gets into their hands, then nobody will know; nobody will help. Nobody! You, and only you, can save those lives … or you can do nothing and just save your own hide."

The sound of police whistles was getting closer and closer.

"Oh shit!" He suddenly got up and looked around, checking out the darkness. "Those dogs are near … I am so fucked. Do not let these people vanish in vain. You are the only chance they have. Three hundred and forty-six souls … Fucking bastards! Fucking bastards! Please, do it. Call that number. I'll draw the goons away. I beg of you, help!"

He let my arm go, and before I could say a word, bolted to the right and melted away in the shadow of the oak alley. He ran toward the darkness in the direction of the fast-approaching cacophony of police whistles, screaming, "I'm right here, shitheads! Come and get me, you bunch of cocksuckers! Right here! Do you see me now? Fuck you! Fuck you all! Oh, shit! No! Argh …"

The whistles suddenly stopped, replaced by a chorus of angry voices and mad shouts. I could hear the noise of a scuffle, which sent chills down my spine. He didn't stand a chance. The end of the brawl was punctuated by the cold click of fastened handcuffs, and after a second of silence, I heard the monotonous sounds of weighty blows, like those of a boxer hitting a heavy bag in the gym. I froze.

Suddenly, someone yelled, "Enough! You will break his fucking neck. Stop it, you fucking morons! I'm ordering you to stop! He needs to be interrogated. Don't you fucking hear me? Let him loose! Stop it now! Step back! Let me in!"

Then, after a few quiet moments, the same commanding voice spoke. "Shit, he's dead already, you bunch of half-wits. Someone will be in serious fucking trouble because of this, and it will not be me, I swear. Sergeant, search the body. Now!"

A few minutes later, when the silence returned and took over the gardens, I found myself shivering behind the bench, hiding in the thick shadow of the Kremlin Wall. When I finally opened my cramped fist, I saw a shiny brass key wrapped in the thin paper. Once unfolded, there were two pages revealing a numbered list of three hundred and forty-seven names. The last name on the list was Zamoker—the only one without a first name—followed by a phone number.

The thin crimson edge of the early morning skyline started to light up.

I'm gonna flunk this darn exam. The thought pounded in my head while I ran back to the dorm. Cold wind was blowing from the river, and I was shivering and frightened. I looked at my watch. It was five thirty in the morning. *I have three and a half hours left until the exam; I have to get myself together!*

I was petrified—big time! Would they now be looking for me? I hoped they would not. How could they know that I was there? They had screwed up, and he had died. They had killed him, and then they had rushed to wrap it up. I could just imagine how this squad of angry and disappointed bruisers had dragged his body into the Black Raven, jumped into their cars, and left.

My heart pounded as I ran. My right hand was clasped tightly around the brass key and the small square of folded tissue papers for which someone had been murdered that morning.

Chapter Fifteen
Phone Call

The test was long and draining. I immersed myself completely in it, and that calmed me down. Nevertheless, that phone number did not leave my mind. In the evening, I finally got to a payphone. Nobody was in sight. The phone booth, like most of them in Moscow, was permeated with a nauseating stench. My heart was pounding, and my palms were sweating. With every attempt to take a deep breath, I choked on the heavy, mephitic air.

I deposited the coin and dialed the number. Somebody with a squeaky voice answered.

"Hello?" I said in a trembling whisper. "Zamoker? I have the list."

"Who is this? Who are you?"

"It's irrelevant. I am a stranger."

"What list are you talking about?"

"The list of names ... I got it this morning."

"What names?"

"Are you Zamoker?"

"No. Where did you get that list? Who gave it to you?"

"In Alexander Gardens ... somebody I didn't know ... I have to talk to Zamoker."

"Who is this Zamoker you're mumbling about? Do you have that list now?"

"Yes."

"Can you read from it?"

I unfolded the list and started reading.

"Oh my God!" the voice responded with muffled anxiety. "He did it! Why are you calling instead of Mark? Where is he?"

"If we are talking about the same man, he was … murdered early this morning in Alexander Gardens."

"Murdered? How do you know?"

"I heard it … I witnessed it. The KGB squad beat him to death."

"Were you there?"

"Yes, I was."

The voice froze for a few moments before asking, "What happened?"

"It was a chase … sort of a manhunt …"

"Who are you?" The voice was probing.

"I was just a bystander. The man stumbled into me just a few moments before they got him."

"What is your name?"

"He gave me a key and the list of names, typed on tissue paper, and he begged me to save it and to call this number."

"Where are you calling from?" the voice kept probing.

"From a payphone, damn it. Stop interrupting. Let me explain. He took off and ran right into a group of KGB hounds; it was as if he was trying to lure them away from me. Are you listening?"

"I am. Who is Zamoker?"

"*You're* asking *me?*"

"Who else do you think I'm asking?"

"I don't know ... Let me finish."

"Just get to the point."

"In a couple of minutes, they got him. It sounded like they handcuffed him first, and then he was mercilessly punched and kicked over and over. In the end, they broke his neck. He died. Instantly."

"Why did you decide to call?"

"I read the list. I recognized some of the names."

"What names?"

"Some people I came in contact with when I was arrested a few years ago."

"You were what? Why? Who are you?"

"Do you remember the Simyavsky and Daniel trial? Remember the demonstration on Moscow's Pushkin Square? I was arrested there for the first time. I met some of them there and then again at our three-day support vigil at the Superior Court during the trial."

"Who are you?"

"Do you recall the end of New Word magazine? Some of the writers and editors were rounded up. I used to write for New Word. I was arrested again and spent six months in jail. I was lucky ... I was let out, but there're many others still doing time."

"Drop the charade. What is your name?"

"Alex... My fans and my friends used to call me *Alex the Poet*."

"Can you come right away to thirty-five Donskaya Street, Apartment four seventeen? Please, hurry up. We are all waiting for you." I heard a couple of short beeps and then the line went dead.

About an hour later, I walked into the five-story apartment building on Donskaya Street, took the stairs to the fourth floor, and looked down the stairwell. To my relief, there were no signs that I was being followed. At least, so I thought. Trying to catch my breath after that rapid ascent of eight flights of stairs, I looked around to find apartment 417 and rang the doorbell.

"Who is it?" asked a familiar squeaky voice from behind the closed door.

"It's me—Alex," I answered.

The door was opened a crack and was then instantly shut. A split second later, I heard the sound of the chain being rapidly unlocked. The door swung open.

"You weren't followed, were you?"

"I do not think so," I replied.

"You can never be sure, young man. I think that our phone has been bugged for at least a couple of months, but as long as you use a public phone to initiate the call, the authorities are unable to connect the dots right away. I think we are safe."

I was rushed across the darkness of a tiny hallway into a dimly lit room. A soft desk light warmed up a tiny circle around the dining room table. About a dozen faces floated amid heavy cigarette smoke. They looked familiar, although I didn't recognize them instantly. When I entered the hazy island of light around the table, I heard a sigh of relief.

"It's really him," somebody muttered.

"What a small world! It's really him; it's Alex Loevsky," another voice confirmed.

"Alex the Poet! I was among those arrested at the demonstration on Pushkin Square. We were inside the same holding cage with you and Yuri Vizbor at Lubyanka." The woman in her late fifties, got up, pulled me close, and gave me a hug.

"It's a miracle that he ran into you," she sobbed. "It's simply a miracle."

A few hands stretched out from the smoky darkness, seeking a handshake.

"Thank you," a man in thick glasses said. "Thank you for being there for him."

"Who was he?" I asked.

"Mark Levitt ... He was a research fellow at the Serbsky Institute of Forensic Psychiatry. He was one of us... A true patriot with a great heart. When he saw the KGB guards en masse at the newly formed hospital ward, he became suspicious of what was going on inside. He used his research as a reason to obtain access to additional archives located in that ward.

"He discovered a number of well-known jailed dissidents who were declared insane and locked up indefinitely. They were continually injected with heavy doses of chlorpromazine and insulin, and after a few days, they were in an almost vegetative state, ready to be presented to the International Red Cross if an inquiry were made. They would appear to be severe psychiatric cases. Their families were not informed of their whereabouts, and every one of them would become another unsolved case... a mysterious disappearance."

There was a silent pause. Bluish smoke from a few cigarettes slowly climbed to the lightbulb.

"Mark was trying to compile a list of every dissident there. 'Every name,' he used to say, 'every single name, whatever the cost is.' He swore he would get the list out ... and now he's dead. Damn cowards! Animals! If you were not there at Alexander Gardens, if you hadn't saved the list, he would be just another vanished name."

"It is all here," I said, handing over the key and the thin piece of paper to the man. "What difference does it make after all? He's dead! He is another vanished name. What good can come of it all now?" I was exhausted and felt hopeless.

"Would you like some tea?" someone asked.

"Do you have anything stronger?" I replied.

"Vodka?"

"Please."

A couple of minutes later, I was ushered into a tiny kitchen. A bottle of Stoli as well as a few shot glasses, bread, pickles, and herring were on a small table. Someone pitched an open pack of cigarettes and a box of matches toward the middle.

Then the people started to introduce themselves. Their names were very well known. They were dissidents—the real soul of our seemingly soulless country.

"Now I can put names to your faces." I tried unsuccessfully to smile. "I've learned so much about you since my first time in jail. Over there, everyone knew someone who was a dissident or *refusenik*. It feels like I knew you all."

"Let's drink to better times."

"To our freedom!"

"To the late Mark's memory!"

The ice-cold gulp of nearly frozen vodka tightly

squeezed my throat, sending shivers through my entire body. A moment later, the fiery ball in my stomach was radiating a gentle, soothing warmth, caressing my brain with the numbing, weightless comfort of deep and disengaging sleep.

Chapter Sixteen
Eugene and Nate

I woke up in a strange place. I was thirsty and hung over.

"Thank goodness it's Saturday," I mumbled, trying to fall asleep again.

The early morning sun was shining through the window of a small room. A few timid light rays criss-crossed the dusty emptiness, probing the awakening space. I rubbed my eyes and looked around. Besides the old sofa on which I was resting and the dining chair across from it, there was nothing but rows of packed cardboard boxes of different sizes. The old, dark, and flowery wallpaper was torn in many spots, and cobweb hung from the corners of the ceiling. The stale air was pierced by the inviting smell of freshly brewed coffee coming through the door, which had been left open a crack. I got up and found my pants and my shirt, which had been carefully folded and placed on a lonely chair. I got dressed, and gingerly crept out to the noise of running water and clanking dishes. The place looked like an apartment that was waiting to be abandoned. There were packed suitcases and piles of books all over the neglected parquet floors of what looked like one of the living rooms of a century-old and formerly grandeur estates of the Old Arbat neighborhood.

I walked into the kitchen to be greeted by a friendly mutt of doubtful lineage and the smiling face of a tall, barefooted fellow in his late thirties who was wearing a sleeveless tank top and long swimming trunks. He turned around, shut off the faucet, and ran his fingers through the wilderness of his red, uncombed curls.

"Good morning and welcome to my humble abode," he announced, looking at my puzzled face. He somehow looked painfully familiar to me. "I'm afraid my name escaped your waning attention the other night. Let me reintroduce myself." He took a theatrical bow and announced, "Eugene Baras! My friends call me Zhenya."

"Good morning. I'm Alex."

"I know your name. We did meet last night, if you recall."

The mutt was licking my hand and wiggling his tail as a sign of acceptance of our acquaintance. The memories of the previous night were still scrambled in my head.

"What's his name?" I asked.

"We call him Reff," Zhenya answered.

"How did you... ? I'm sorry, did I get here on my own? I mean, how did I get here?"

"Don't worry; you weren't kidnapped. Last night, I took the liberty of assisting you to find the place of your inhabitance, but your innocent inebriation turned into militant unresponsiveness. You left me with the choice of taking you to my place or dumping you on the sidewalk. I hope you don't mind that I chose the former."

"Sorry." I was embarrassed. "It's been a tough couple of days. Usually I can hold my liquor, but last night... I was just dead tired."

"Don't be silly. I'm glad I could help. Cuppa coffee? Some water maybe?"

"Yes, that would be nice. Water and coffee, please?"

"Pull up a chair, relax, and make yourself at home."

Zhenya filled my cup with steaming coffee, put it next to a glass of water on a small kitchen table, and opened a cardboard box of sugar cubes. I guzzled down the water. Reff looked at me with pleading eyes and licked my hand again. After receiving a sugar cube, he retired into a corner to enjoy it.

"You said Reff? Kinda unusual name for a dog."

"Reff is short for Refusenik. We named him in recognition of the third denial of our continuous but unsuccessful attempts to get exit visas to emigrate to Israel."

"You are the first refusenik I've ever met," I said quietly. Suddenly, everything around me looked different and started to make sense. "I did learn about growing numbers of Jews being refused emigration permits when I listened to 'Voice of America' on the short-band radio."

"Thank God for short-band radios and 'Voice of America'!" Zhenya exclaimed. "Do you mind?" He pulled a cigarette from a pack and lit a match. Without waiting for my response, he took a hit and exhaled, suspending a perfect ring of smoke in the air in front of my face. Studying me through that vanishing ring, as if through a picture frame, he paused in quiet expectation of my response. It suddenly hit me.

"Come to think of it, I could've seen you somewhere a short time ago."

"Really?" Zhenya responded. "Where, if I may ask?"

"I know! I saw you at the synagogue on Arkhipova Street during the Simhat Torah celebration. You were the one who confronted the scumbag from the Civil Order Watch who sprayed some acid on my girlfriend's leg and then on your pants. I really felt vindicated when you gave him a taste of his own medicine."

"That son of a bitch did learn his lesson, but we all have to fight the rest of them. What do we have to lose? Freedom? We never had it. Let our people go, you frigging bastards!"

"A lot of young people I met at the synagogue

were chattering about emigration, about the escape. It all started to make sense when I saw the desperation on Mark's face when he ran into me at Alexander Gardens."

"Small world... So, what do you make of it?"

"Of Jewish emigration?"

"Drop it. Be serious... Of what happened in the park, of the late Mark Levitt, of the people you met last night... "

"I don't know what to make of it."

"Come on. Stop being so careful."

"I had never witnessed a murder before."

"Neither have I. I would've been scared and pissed."

"If you really want to know, I feel very angry about it... angry and helpless. A lot of repulsive stuff surfaced lately, laying bare what's going on. I guessed there was an opposition or an underground of some sort, but I thought it was imaginary, invisible... Somewhere... I never expected that this murder in the park and a piece of paper left in my hand would lead me to the reality of it... To you and your friends."

"Well, there you go. That's one reason not to feel helpless."

"Collective despair doesn't attract me."

"We aren't desperate. We act. Did you write your poetry out of hope or out of despair?"

"Why do you ask? Do you know my poetry? Does it sound desperate to you?"

"I used to like your poetry. That's my point. It was filled with hope. I couldn't wait for the next issue of New Word to come out. It was some serious stuff."

"That's very kind of you. Thanks."

"Do you still write?"

"I was admonished in quite strong terms by the court *to stay away from all this nonsense*. My aunt pulled all the strings—used all her connections—and, somehow, the authorities let me go free on her recognizance. I was warned, though, that if my writings ever resurfaced, my aunt would be severely punished as well. I still write a little, but between the two of us… only for myself, furtively. It's really tough to write in-the-desk. It's like talking to yourself. There's no feedback. It's lonely, like being in a vacuum. There isn't even an echo. It's frightening. Being in medical school helps a lot though. You can only dampen that dread by staying busy and being tired."

I took a sip of coffee and stopped talking, trying not to hover on the brink of elegiac lament. A moment later, Zhenya broke the silence.

"The other night when your phone call came out of nowhere, we all got frightened. Was it you or was it an impostor using your name? It could've been a KGB snitch. A turncoat of sort. In our circle, we've all become vigilant and, to some extent, paranoid. We don't trust anybody nowadays. There is so much betrayal going on. Everyone around is desperate to save their own hide at any cost. And who can blame them? Their hope was stolen, and without hope, there is no need for the soul. So, they would sell their souls next. We became a society of inveterate traitors, backstabbers, and informants. On the contrary, the group of people you met last night is the only hope for our salvation. They are the remaining conscience of this country's future, if she still deserves one."

"When I called last night, I was scared out of my wits."

"Trust me, it was a relief when some of us recognized your face. Then the news you delivered about Mark's murder overshadowed everything else."

"I felt it as well. I was totally drained emotionally. What will happen to Mark's list?"

"We have to bring it to the world's attention somehow. There were rumors and innuendoes in the foreign press that the State Security apparatus used psychiatric institutions as a weapon aimed at intellectual dissent in an attempt to suppress and intimidate political opposition. Yet, nobody had the hard evidence to prove it. Prominent dissidents started to disappear one after the other. It came out of nowhere. All our inquiries went unanswered. When Mark made his gruesome discovery at the Serbsky Institute, it confirmed our worst suspicions. He pledged to get evidence of what was going on and to compile a list of the victims. We agreed that doing nothing would put many more on the path to oblivion."

"How can you get the word out?"

"We want to talk to Nate Krimsky. He is a friend— an American raised in Great Britain and now working for Moscow's Associated Press bureau. In the past, he really helped us to get the news out about what was going on over here. We spent last night verifying every single name on Mark's list. Only one is still a mystery. We couldn't figure out who Zamoker is. Nobody has ever heard of him. There is no first name, no middle initial, and no address. There's nothing at all. It's like a freaking puzzle."

"What about the key? Do you know how it fits into this puzzle?"

"No one has a clue. Something isn't right; it's very strange. Mark was tediously methodical. Even his scientific research was very heavy on statistical details. Every single name on the list was followed by a first name, date of birth, address, and date of disappearance ... everyone but the very last one. Zamoker's name was followed only by a phone number, which didn't even belong to him. It was the phone number for Bonner's apartment."

"Bonner? Professor Bonner from the Academy of Science? The famous nuclear physicist?" I was startled.

"Yes, genius, it was his apartment you came to last night. It was Mrs. Bonner who recognized you first."

"Wow! I got wind that both of them had recently been ostracized by authorities for signing pro-democracy petitions. Then there was a press campaign orchestrated against them, but who would've thought that they were... You know... "

"Actively involved?" Zhenya finished. "They are more than involved. Both of them are like a couple of powerful nuclei, attracting more and more of us, like the particles of the same matter, together, guiding us to the right orbit and keeping us from bumping into each other."

"You talk like a physicist." I was still in disbelief.

"I am a physicist!" Zhenya responded fervently. "I used to work under Professor Bonner on the Deep Space and Black Matter research project."

"You worked at the Kurchatov Institute?" I was stunned. "Why did you say 'used to'? I would've expected that to be a very stable position."

"Why? Because, I don't work there anymore. Look around you. This is my dwelling. Do you see any signs of stability around here? What don't you see? Doesn't it look abandoned and desolate to you? You seem to be a smart fellow. You are Jewish, aren't you?"

"Yes, I am."

"More so then. Open both your eyes. You are not immune to it either! First, my PhD was blackballed. Then my promotions were stopped. Then I was banned from international conferences. One day, I was called to the office of the head of human resources. She greeted me with a guilty smile and confided that despite the fact that she liked me personally, she had to follow the directives from above. She said that they were working on improving the moral and ideological stability of the staff and were resisting cosmopolitan tendencies among their scientific labor force. To do that, she was instructed to 'clean up the stables'—to reduce the number of Jews employed by the institute due to 'their questionable loyalty and propensity to political instability.' She was so sorry, but my position had been terminated. I was fired!

"Bonner attempted to resist. He wrote letters and protested but got nowhere. They stole my future. I had no other choice but to apply to emigrate to Israel. Three months later, I was summoned to the Interior Ministry to get my rejected application back, adorned with a red stamp saying 'Refused.' The reason I was given was laughable. Black holes in the deep space had somehow become a 'state secret,' and the information I was in possession of was a matter of state security. Thus, as an emigrant, I would become a security threat. At that moment, I was dubbed a 'Refusenik.' As a physicist, I was deemed to be unemployable. A martyr to friends and a traitor to foes.

"Don't you see around here everything is packed and we are ready to leave? Over the first couple of years, we sold our stuff and our furniture bit by bit to buy groceries and milk for our kid. I am working nights now, sometimes as a janitor and sometimes as a watchman." Zhenya's eyes started to fill with anger. "For the last three years, we've been fighting to leave. I have been demanding to be allowed to reapply every year since. I will not give up, and I'll be ready to leave in an instant. I am striving for the moment the bastards throw me out of here, out of this living hell. If they won't let us live, then let us leave! The hope to prevail is the only thing left; it keeps my wife, my son, and myself sane! We are yearning to get out, just let us! Fuck your asinine loyalty; we do not belong here." Zhenya took a few brisk puffs of his almost-finished cigarette to calm himself down and sat quietly, almost paralyzed by frustration.

His emotional outburst was sad and moving at the same time. How could he survive such a fall from the pinnacle of his career to the pit of hopeless reality and still sustain the ability to fight for his and his family's future for three long years? To break the awkward silence, I asked, "Where are your wife and kid now? I'd like to meet them one day."

Zhenya extinguished what was left of his cigarette and smiled.

"Of course you will. They are not a 'state secret'. Rosa and Jake usually spend nights at her parents' place. It's just ten minutes away. They will be here shortly. Nate Krimsky is bringing them back; he loves a cup of my coffee in the morning."

Reff had finished his sugar cube and was calmly dozing off in his corner. The sound of the doorbell woke him up and led to an unstoppable barking attack that was directed at the entrance door.

A minute later, the door swung open, and Zhenya's four-year-old son, Jake, joined Reff in a geometrically unexplainable rolling frenzy.

"Stop it, both of you!" said Rosa as she and Nate walked in and locked the door behind them.

"Hi, I'm Rosa." Zhenya's wife came closer and gave me a hug as if she'd known me for a long time.

"Hi, I'm Alex," I responded.

"Nate Krimsky, Associated Press," Nate said with a slight British accent and shook my hand. "Get out of town!" he suddenly exclaimed. "I think, I know who you are. You are Alex, 'Alex the Poet.' Don't say a word. I know it's you. I covered the New Word trials for my agency. I was in the courtroom. I've wanted to meet you in person for so long now. How did you two run into each other? Zhenya, can I have a cup of your

magical coffee, please? So, how did this come about?"
He was a journalist to the bone.

"He was so eager to meet you, Nate, that he begged
me to let him in to spend the night here," said Zhenya.
After a pause he continued, "On a more serious note,
Alex witnessed Mark's murder at Alexander Gardens.
You most likely know about it by now. He's the one
who brought Mark's list to the Bonners."

"I learned last night about that murder, but I'd like
to hear a bit more from the horse's mouth, as we say
back home. Please, Alex, can you shed some more
light on your encounter with Mark and the people
who murdered him? I'd like to gather more details,"
Nate insisted.

"There are no real details. Everything happened
so fast. It took just two or three minutes."

"Hold on, guys," Rosa jumped in. "Stop it. Spare
the details for a bit. Jake and I will take Reff for a
walk. I want to keep Jake out of this discussion. He is
already starting to repeat some eyebrow-raising stuff,
which he absorbs like a sponge. We stopped at the
bookstore the other day. Every shelf was displaying
General Secretary Brezhnev's new memoir, *The Fire
Land*. I mean every single shelf. There was nothing but
copies of his book. Jacob decided to loudly announce,
'Mommy, look. On top of everything else, this loser
is a writer now.' I had to retreat from the bookstore

like a bullet because of the angry looks I got from the people inside. So, please, hold your thoughts until we are out of here. I'm glad I met you, Alex. See you later, Nate."

She attached a leash to Reff's collar, grabbed a protesting Jake by the arm, and closed the apartment door on her way out.

"Alex, please can you recount for me what happened that night in Alexander Gardens?" Nate continued.

I described to him what happened. Nate finished taking notes, closed his notepad, and, after a moment of silence, said, "Zhenya, were you able to confirm the names on the list?"

"All, but one."

"At first, I thought I would write an investigative report and put it through the AP wire service. But I have a better idea now. We have to arrange a press conference of all Western journalists accredited in Moscow. We'll invite the available family members to make a plea on behalf of their loved ones locked in psychiatric prisons for no reason other than to intimidate and silence the opposition. That will humanize the personal tragedies and build a much stronger case against the punitive use of psychiatry by the KGB."

"I like it, Nate! I think that press conference will resonate much louder, much stronger, if you will. We did identify most of the names, and the Bonners are getting in touch with the families as we speak. In the meantime, we are still trying to figure out Zamoker's identity. It's like an equation with two unknowns. First, who is Zamoker? None of us have ever heard his name, and we have no clue where to look for him. Second, why did Mark pass that key to Alex along with the list?"

"Maybe that key is for the Bonners' apartment door?" I asked. "How many locks are there, Zhenya, one or two?"

"No, it was not for the Bonners' door. There is one lock and one dead bolt on that door; that key doesn't fit either of them. I thought of that right away and checked it as soon as you passed the key to me last night. Wrong door, wrong locks, and wrong key."

"I got it!" exclaimed Nate. "It's simple. It's a linguistic riddle. Come on, guys. Key ... lock. Lock ... key. Think. Every key belongs to a lock somewhere, correct? Now, what is the Russian word for *a lock*?"

"*Zamok,*" I answered.

"You see? Zamoker is not a name. Take *zamok* from *Zamoker* and replace it with *lock*. What do you have now? *Zamok-er* is transformed into *locker*. I bet that key will open a locker somewhere. Did Mark try to hide anything more sizable?"

"Darn it. It is simple indeed. Why didn't this occur to me earlier?" I wondered aloud.

"Where is that locker?" Zhenya asked.

"I don't know, but you guys have the brain power-house over there," responded Nate. "Who was at the Bonners' apartment last night?"

"The usual group—Asbel, Bukovsky, Kahn, Ginsburg. Zeldovitch and Tamm came later."

"There you go. Put your heads together. You have to figure it out. Who knows Moscow better than you guys?"

"Sometimes, it seems to me that you know it better than we do. We will leave that to you, Nate. It's more natural for someone of your persuasion—a reporter—to look for that type of stuff than it is for Alex or me. I am too tall and stand out in a crowd. Alex is a poet and a physician. Those guys are known to be total wimps." Zhenya winked at Nate, coming to my "rescue."

"Stop pulling my leg," I protested. "Do you really mean that? I am not a wimp."

"Why don't you let Alex join forces with us?" Nate added.

"I think he already has." Zhenya gave me a sort of conniving smile while stretching his right arm across the table.

"I think I already have." I firmly shook his hand. "Count me in."

Chapter Seventeen

Unexpected Encounter

"You are looking at a very promising future, young man. Those steady hands and sharp mind of yours will make you a desirable addition to our department after you graduate," said Dr. Plotkin, the Head of the Department of Surgery and my professor of orthopedics, as he turned the pages of my personal file.

"How did a convicted felon suddenly become a desirable addition to your department?" I asked.

"I was informed that your conditional four-and-a-half-year sentence came to an end, and you are not a convicted felon any longer. Someone at the Interior Ministry ordered your personal file to be wiped clean. However, a slight problem still remains."

He lowered his voice. "Dean Dubinin told me that in order to get his support for your appointment to our faculty after graduation, you still have to rectify what happened some time ago and to affirm your loyalty to our institution. You know, a 'sincere public apology' in the next issue of the school's journal could be just right. That would make my task of helping you a lot easier. You still remember how to write?"

"I think I do, but I was prohibited from writing creatively, as you know." I nodded with a dejected smile. "A 'sincere public apology,' as you and the dean see it, would be a work of obnoxious fiction, the worst kind of creative writing to my taste, and totally inappropriate material for the medical school journal."

"Don't be a smart-ass, and save your sarcastic bile for your enemies, which I am not." He looked at the closed door and leaned across his desk. "I am not Dean Dubinin. I do not think like him, and I do not act like him, and unlike him, I do not report to the KGB.

"I'm a physician, not a bureaucrat. That's why I am here. I chair my department because of my expertise. I happen to like you, and I don't want you to be sent far away for a few years after graduation," he said in an undertone. "I need you here. I do enjoy working with you. Please, help me to take care of it. Trust me."

"I am running late for the clinic, Professor. Thank you anyway. I'll think about it," I replied on my way out.

I walked through the courtyards of Old Pirogova campus to the OB clinic, trying to suppress my anger. Dr. Plotkin did not irk me; maybe he did, in fact, wish me well. I was pissed off at the whole system.

"We don't trust anybody nowadays." Zhenya told me the other day.

Neither did I... I'd kept my mouth shut and stayed out of trouble. My grades were the highest in the class. I finished my research projects ahead of time, and the last two had been nominated for "The Scientific Project of the Year" award. What else did those bastards want from me? There was no way I would ever become an ass-kissing opportunist!

I took the service elevator to the fifth floor and slammed the door on my way out. *Sincere apology? Up yours, Dean Dubinin! You will never get one from me. I remember how you tried to double-cross me.*

The dim hallway of the obstetrics and gynecology clinic was packed. I had a little more than a month left on this rotation. I squeezed myself into the noisy drove of expecting women, trying not to hurt anyone on my way through. Holding the door handle to the office, I looked back. I suddenly thought I glimpsed Svetlana's face. My jittery eyes probed the crowd. *What a frigging mind game*, I thought.

"Good evening, Doc!" Poline, the head nurse, looked at me over her glasses. She pushed me into the office and pointed her raised finger at the clock.

"Poline, it's not evening yet; don't give me a hard time, please. It's one ten. I'm only ten minutes late," I pleaded.

"You're on your own today, Baby Doc."

"Great! Where is Doctor Rubin?"

"He's still in surgery. He said that by staying busy, you won't have enough time to kill any of his patients."

"Thanks. Can I see my appointment list?"

I looked through the list. Her name was not there.

Stop daydreaming! I said to myself. *Aren't having nightmares about her bad enough?*

"Time to go to work," echoed Poline.

I knew that I was not daydreaming when Poline brought me the chart for my last patient and led me into the exam room. Blood rushed to my head when I saw Svetlana's face. I did not have to pinch myself; it wasn't a dream.

It was more like a nightmare ... Her last name had changed; her chart said "divorced," and her clinical diagnosis stated "miscarriage." She was there for her follow-up visit.

With Poline in the room, I pretended that Svetlana and I did not know each other. I introduced myself, went through the routine questioning, and did a brief exam. Everything was in order. Poline left the room as soon as I was done.

I washed my trembling hands at the small sink while Svetlana got dressed behind the screen.

"Do you still write?" she asked nonchalantly, quite out of the blue.

"Time flies," I muttered. "You still remember?" I looked at her. My face was burning.

"How could I ever forget?" she answered.

"A few years have gone by …"

"A few, give or take." She came out from behind the screen. Our eyes met.

"I still remember," I said.

"Some things are not so easy to forget," she answered.

"I hope that what you remember isn't too odious, is it?" I suddenly broke out in a cold sweat.

"Not at all." She stepped closer and looked into my eyes. "I wanted to see you again. It just did not work out then. Are you working late today?"

"I'm done now. If you have time, we can go somewhere just to talk. Can we?"

We went downstairs to a little café across the street.

"Did you really want to see me?" I asked with trepidation.

"I did." She smiled and touched my hand.

I looked into her hazel eyes. They had the same warm glow, memories of which had kept me sleepless for so many nights.

"Of course, I did …" Her familiar deep voice brought out myriads of goose bumps all over my skin. "How could I forget? Do you remember our New Year's night?

"You were so hung-over. You kept waking up and

falling back asleep every hour. You asked, 'What is your name? Please tell me your name' again and again, like you didn't know me at all. You tried to explain that you had never met anyone like me. Then suddenly you got up, moved very close to me, and started reading your poetry.

"You read for almost an hour, looking straight into my eyes, and I hoped it would be endless. I'd never read nor listened to anything like that before. It was an unknown and unexplainable feeling. How could I ever forget?

"That very year, my dad was transferred to the Space Center. I had to move to Turatam with him ... Do you still write?"

"Not really; no one will publish my poetry, and I am not allowed to write anymore."

"I am well aware. I know what happened. I bragged to all my friends that I knew you. It's hard to believe how dramatic and brave your poetry was for someone your age. Learning that you, your publisher, and a couple other writers were arrested and that New Word was shut down came as a shock to everyone I knew. My dad warned me to stop talking about you. The Space Center was permeated with State Security spying on everyone. It became dangerous to even talk about those things."

"Didn't your dad coauthor a book on space telecommunication?"

"Yes, he did when he was still at the Moscow Institute of Telecommunication Engineers. Shortly after we moved to Turatam, he was promoted to one-star general and given the highest security clearance. Being the daughter of the Head of Telecommunications at the Space Center, I was forced to stop talking and even thinking about you, as I was fearful for my dad—not so much for myself but for his future and his career."

"What about your career?"

"Mine? To finish the law school my dad arranged for me to take a couple of correspondence classes and I received my law degree a year later. My dad found a position for me as a legal consultant at the Space Center Internal Security Department. I mainly did the paperwork on patent protection and personnel security clearance. It was the most boring thing I had to be involved in, ever."

She paused, looking into her espresso cup.

I patiently waited for her to carry on.

"Were you scared when you were arrested?" she asked, resting her chin on her folded hands. A tear, like a little sparkle, vibrated in the corner of her eye.

"I spent six months in solitary confinement. You bet I was scared. The charge was dead serious—'Anti-Soviet Agitation and Propaganda.' I was just twenty years old. The court showed leniency. I was sentenced to time served, plus a four-and-a-half-year suspended sentence, and then set free on my aunt's recognizance."

"When are you done with your medical training?"

"It's my last year."

"And then what?"

"I don't even want to think about that right now. Most likely, I will be sent far away for at least five years to some underserved area to pay my debt to society, but I know I will return eventually. I love Moscow; I do not know if I could live without it. What about you?"

"What about me? I was married and pregnant."

"Who's the lucky guy?"

"I don't think he's that lucky. You don't know him. Ironically, his name is Alex too. We got married about a year ago. We were dating on and off. It dragged on for a couple years. Then I got pregnant. It was so stupid. There was no love there—just an escape from boredom. Lately, everything has become quite complicated. We've been divorced for almost three months. I had to move back to Moscow."

"Is he in the military?"

"No, he's not in the service. He's a scientist. Nuclear physicist. He works for the Space Program."

"The Space Program? Isn't that where your dad is?"

"Yes. That's where we met—in Turatam, Kazakhstan, deep in the desert, more than six thousand kilometers away."

"I hope you didn't commute!" I tried to be witty.

"That's not funny... I was stuck there. Pregnant and bored. Then I had some medical issues. My father-in-law didn't want me to stay there any longer. He ordered me to leave and come back to Moscow. He didn't think there were enough good specialists outside of Moscow to take care of his future 'royal' grandchild," she said sarcastically. "Now he doesn't have to worry any longer."

"Royal?" I asked, puzzled.

"He is extremely powerful and acts like a little dictator. Comrade First Deputy Minister of Communications of the Soviet Union. He does not like me, and I do not like him. Now, after my miscarriage and divorce, he probably hates me to death and will take it out on my dad."

Something in the tone of her voice felt wrong. My throat felt like a coarse piece of sandpaper rasping the space under my chin.

Svetlana looked straight at me, paused, and then took a sip of her already cold espresso. A small line of foamed coffee was now decorating her upper lip. She licked it off and slanted her eyes, looking through the window at the fiery sunset hiding between the rooftops down the street.

I thought I realized what was wrong. Everything was! My head spun...

She had been married to a "genius physicist." She had been pregnant. She was now divorced. She was trying to get over her miscarriage, and she was lonely and lost in total emotionless emptiness ... And I was hell-bent on seeing her again.

I knew it was wrong. I knew it was stupid. I knew it was insane. I knew it was the last thing I needed.

"How did you get into this 'royal' mess?" I asked.

"Don't I look like a woman who is extremely interested in physics?" She smiled back.

"You do look like an extremely interesting woman, but physics ... I don't think so."

"And you are absolutely right. I flunked my final exam and decided to spend a couple of months with my dad. As I said before, he was a one-star general and was in charge of telecommunications at the Space Center in Turatam. A lackluster life in a mind-numbing desert.

"My dad is a workaholic, and I hardly saw him during the day. Then I was introduced to Alex. He offered to tutor me in physics, and I had nothing better to do over there. We spent a lot of time together. He intrigued me from the beginning. He was so in love with his work that he would talk about it all the time. And that was all he did. He talked about physics day in and day out.

"In Moscow, I had gotten used to being noticed.

There was seldom a guy who didn't try to pick me up. Here, everyone knew I was the general's daughter, and that meant 'trouble.' Nobody wanted to get on my dad's 'hit list.' When everybody around you is cynical and indifferent, you gravitate toward someone who at least acts irrationally and talks enthusiastically.

"Nights in Turatam were long … long, cold, and desperate. I was bored. One midnight, I knocked on his door."

"What about your dad?" I was curious.

"He's tired of being a bachelor. He misses my mom so much. He thinks that if she were with us, we would be a family again."

"Why did they divorce?"

"They didn't. She died. Breast cancer."

"I'm sorry. I didn't know."

I gazed at her in dead silence, watching the reflection of sunset in her hazel eyes and feeling as if I were falling in love with her all over again. She was the girl I'd spoken to in my dreams for all these years. My memory hadn't failed me. Not at all! I remembered the smell of her skin, the sound of her voice, and the taste of her lips. I'd written so many poems for her, though she'd never read them.

Had I been trying to find her? Should she ask if I did? Over the last few years, each time I tried to close my eyes at night, I'd see her face. She appeared to be so far, and I felt so much desire that nothing else seemed more lucid—nothing but my dreams of her.

"It's getting late. I have to go," Svetlana said.

"When can I see you again?" I didn't want her to leave.

"Any time. I am back in Moscow for good. Just don't disappear for another five years," she answered. "Here's my phone number." She wrote her number on a napkin, leaned across the table, and touched my cheek with her lips. "Let's get together soon."

I stared at the door slowly closing behind her and sensed the puff of outside air trying to stalk that vanishing dream of mine.

Trying to piece together what had happened over the last couple of weeks led me to the conclusion that everything around me was spinning faster and faster in an extremely snarled pattern. The I-am-sure-what-to-do feeling was missing, and an unexplored sensation of unsinkable emptiness paid me a disturbingly endless visit.

A few days passed and things were not getting any better. I had to place myself somewhere in the middle of this enormous puzzle, but so many pieces around me were missing. Did I belong there? The feeling was painful beyond belief. I was falling down the cliff, bracing myself for impact as my brain formed a tight knot. I was not my own self any longer, and there was nobody to talk to. Self-inflicted loneliness had finally caught up with me.

Was I missing her that much?

I think I was.

I'm gonna call her, I decided. *Today.*

After her divorce, Svetlana had moved into her father's apartment on the south side of Moscow. When I got there, the door was open. I knocked and walked inside.

Her apartment was small but very keenly furnished. Everything was organized in tiny functional islands. A huge, black-and-white portrait of Hemingway hung over the dark green sofa and dominated the front wall of the living room. The adjacent walls were covered with tightly packed bookshelves.

My eyes froze when I saw two of my poetry books and a few back issues of New Word proudly displayed on a corner shelf. That was more than bravery on her part. She was too smart to ignore the danger of keeping banned books and magazines. It was a punishable offense to possess them, yet she did so openly.

Why?

Slippery and quietly squeaky, light oak parquet floors glistened under the scarlet flow of sunset light pouring through the huge window and the glass door to the balcony. The open, unobstructed view of the river bend, Lenin Stadium, and the Moscow State University skyscraper was breathtaking. My mind was drifting when Svetlana entered the room wearing a bathrobe and a thick towel rolled like a turban over her wet hair.

"Your door was open."

"I left it open for you," she said, kissing me on the cheek. "I had to take a shower. It was an exhausting day."

"Aren't you afraid to keep it so out in the open?" I stepped back and pointed my eyes to the corner bookshelf.

"I don't give a damn what anybody thinks. I love your poetry, and I'm not concerned about the reper- cussions of having it in my guardianship. This is my apartment, and those are my books! That's the only thing I have connecting me to you. They cannot take away my dreams. I am tired of being afraid. I am sick of being alone. I refuse to play that game any longer!" she cried out. "I love what I read ..." She paused, stepped closer, and said quietly, "... and I love to see the one who wrote it."

I looked at her in awe.

The warm glow of her eyes and the hint of a smile on her lips were temptingly enchanting and disarming.

"I'm glad you called. I was waiting." Svetlana held

my hand and pulled me toward the kitchen. "You must be hungry. Are you coming straight from the hospital? Let me fix something for you. It will take just a few minutes, okay? What would you like?" She did not let my hand go.

Like before, the sound of her voice covered my skin with goose bumps. She was standing next to me—so close that I could discern the fragrant scent of her skin. I took her other hand and looked into her eyes.

"Svetlana …" I tried to clear my throat.

She let one hand go free and slowly pulled the towel from her head. Her aureate hair rolled across her shoulders, glowing in the crimson sunset.

"Don't say a word," she muttered under her breath. She leaned into me and rested her head against my chest. "Don't say a word," she repeated, her whisper trembling. "Why didn't you call for so long?"

"I didn't know if I could … if I should."

"I was waiting. I was waiting …"

I already knew that submissive feeling of being mesmerized out of one's realm.

"I will not let you go!" she said under her breath. She rested her arms over my shoulders, looking at me as she moved her face closer and closer.

"I'm not going anywhere," I managed to respond.

Finally, our lips met, feverishly quenching their long thirst for each other.

Chapter Eighteen
Dean's Office

T he words "not again" were pounding in my head. I was waiting to enter the dean's office. Doctor Plotkin told me that I was summoned to appear that afternoon, and every time you are summoned to the dean's office, it spells "trouble." While I was waiting, the "wheel of fortune" was loudly spinning in my head, and I was trying to figure out what I would be warned about or accused of that day. After the New Word trial, when I was freed and eventually reinstated at the medical school, the dean used to call me on the carpet every few weeks to remind me how grateful I should be for the "second chance" I'd been given. I was told ad nauseam "to stay away from those evil 'avant-garde' circles." Those people with their "pseudo art" had apparently brought me to the brink of total destruction and moral decadence, and they could still ruin my future if I chose that slippery slope again.

"You are going to become a much better doctor than you are a poet," the dean used to murmur to me while showing me to the heavy double doors of his office.

The rhythmical clicks of the imaginary wheel in my head could not stop at any peg of information that would even remotely implicate me of possible wrongdoing.

Click. My clinical rotations were impeccable.

Click. My patients were very happy with me and so were all my clinicians.

Click, click. I kept a low profile with the rest of the clinical staff and tried as hard as I could not to step on anybody's toes.

Click, click, click. I was not aware of any "extracurricular" activities of mine that had become known to anyone.

Click, click. I kept my connections to the other side of my life—the dissidents and our nighttime meetings—strictly to myself. The other night, Nate, Zhenya, and I had been at the Bonners' apartment holding one of our brainstorming sessions about the location of Mark's mysterious locker. I had recalled a locomotive symbol engraved on the key. The number on the other side of the key had been ground off. Only the first digit, "1," had been left untouched. The phone number I'd dialed had begun with the Leningradsky District exchange—251. I'd had to dial "1" first for a long-distance call. *Maybe it's locker number 1251.* I'd had to assume that it was the locker number and narrow the search to a few train station terminals around

Leningradsky District. I had a hunch that the locker we were looking for was somewhere over there.

"Interesting thought," Nate had said. "Wasn't Mark residing in Khimki?"

"Yes, he was, come to think of it," Zhenya had replied. "And if so, his everyday commute was through the Leningradsky Railroad Station. Khimki to Leningradsky Railroad Station..."

"Maybe we are onto something here," I'd surmised. "If he did commute via the Leningradsky Railroad Station, there are more than a few hundred lockers in and around that terminal. It would be quite logical to use one of the lockers inside to secure whatever he had to hide. Just think about it ... he gets off the train, walks through the terminal, puts whatever he has in a locker, and walks out to a subway station, melting into the rush-hour crowd. It's the most inconspicuous way to do it, if one had to."

"Wow, Alex," Nate had said. "I'm impressed. Are you sure you aren't a sleuth?"

"Yes, I'm sure," I'd rebuffed. "Give me the key. Let me find that locker."

"Be my guest. Knock yourself out!" Zhenya had stretched out his hand with the brass key in his open palm.

There'd been seven or eight of us in the room. No one could've spilled the beans. They'd put their trust in me, and I had to protect our alliance from any danger by keeping it secret. I touched the key in my pocket.

Click. I even kept my newly written poetry, unpublished and unpublicized, to myself, writing in-the-desk and not reading it to anyone—not even to Lara. I was also extra cautious not to reveal my comings and goings to anyone among my medical school peers.

Click. Click. Click ...

Stop! Wait a minute ... I take it back. Hadn't I shared my new writing with Svetlana? It had been a few nights ago when she'd almost begged me to show it to her. I had not, but I'd read a couple of my new poems. They'd been snappy verses, strong words—quite inflammatory, even for my taste—and a sort of lamentation of never-realized freedom. And she'd liked them. Oh my God, she really had. She'd been so excited and surprised and had seemed very happy that I'd started to write poetry again.

"Please, read more to me! More!" she'd exclaimed.

I'd read some more.

"It is so on the edge. It's so honest, so risky. Tell me what triggered it. You are a genius. If people read it, their heads will boil. You nailed it. You haven't read it to anyone else, have you? I hope you haven't tried to self-publish in the underground *Samizdat*. No, that would be too dangerous. I love it so much. I love you even more. When did you go back on your promise not to write ever again? What happened? Please, tell me everything. It seems like I know so little about you now. Your poems, your writing has brought us so much closer. I need to know you better. I want to be you ... to feel your heart, to touch your brain, to taste your breath. Please, help me. Tell me. Share everything with me, please."

I knew she liked poetry—mine in particular— but I'd never seen her get so excited about it so quickly. That night, she'd looked disarmingly beautiful. Her eyes had been moist with tears of desire and her quivering lips had been all over my face, showering me with a wild stream of never-ending kisses. I'd known that I was melting in her arms, succumbing to that sweet poison of submissiveness. Her loose curls had started to tickle my nose and, all of a sudden, I'd sneezed loudly. It had been so unromantically funny that we'd broken out in uncontrollable laughter ... The spell of the moment was instantly gone, and I hadn't told her anything she hadn't needed to know. Thank God I'd learned to be cautious.

Click.

The door swung open, and Dean Dubinin gestured me in.

He put his arm over my shoulder, closed the door behind me, and walked me to his oversized desk, which was oddly occupied by a man in his late forties. This man, who was unknown to me, had a shiny bald head, and his face was decorated with gold rimless eyeglasses. He greeted me with a warm smile and an outstretched hand.

"I want you to meet Yuri Sergeevich," the dean said.

Yuri Sergeevich's handshake was uncharacteristically soft and feminine for his otherwise projected "take charge" demeanor.

"I hope it will be a very productive acquaintance," the dean continued. "Yuri Sergeevich is an old friend of the school, its faculty, and the student body, and he is always interested in our star students like you. I expect nothing less than full cooperation from you, my friend. Yuri Sergeevich was the one who gave the final approval for your reinstatement four years ago," he murmured, looking straight into my eyes with a very cold expression. He squeezed my shoulder. "Gratitude is the greatest virtue." He let go of me before continuing, "I am late to a meeting with our research council now, so I will leave you two alone." He softly and quietly left his office, disappearing behind the closed door.

"Please, take a seat," Yuri Sergeevich said in velvety-soft baritone as he pointed to a chair on the opposite side of the dean's desk.

"We're meeting for the first time, but I know a lot about you. How are your studies? I've heard you're quite an academic success story." He impatiently awaited my response.

"I do study hard," I said, "and I like to stay busy."

"Busy, meaning what?"

"Study, clinics, tests ... you know ... "

"Library?"

"Library, of course ... "

"So, what was your reason for asking the librarian the other day if she could by chance locate some old issues of New Word?"

He caught me unprepared. How the hell did he know? "No particular reason... Just some nostalgia for my old stuff published there."

Yuri Sergeevich leaned back in the dean's chair, faked a friendly smile, and unbuttoned his camel wool blazer.

"You have to understand; there is no old stuff, and there is no New Word—not for you, not for anyone else. We removed every printed issue for good. It's not in circulation. It is closed. Finished! Done! Let me talk to you like a friend. My department was very pleased to know that you kept your word and kept yourself on the right track. I really hope you will continue to abide by this and not make my life and your own any harder.

"Believe me, it's hard enough to monitor all those

irresponsible hotheads among our youth who want to stir up trouble. Somehow it escapes them that they have become an instrument of Western powers and their intelligence services, spreading their rotten ideology like a disease, like the plague. They've forgotten who is giving them opportunities to pursue higher education, who fought for them against Nazi Germany, and who shed their blood for our collective bright future. You have to be on our side, my friend. You have to prove to me and to the entire department that you've parted ways forever with your questionable past and are ready to join the rest of us to cure the sick— to cure their bodies as well as their minds—and to help us to squash for good that poisonous ideological pathology proliferating in our midst. You're with me, aren't you?" He extended his hand toward me.

I had no other choice but to accept his handshake, albeit hesitantly.

"Very good," he said with the same soft, friendly smile. "I want you to keep your ears to the ground." He stood up and walked toward me from behind the desk. "I want you to be my eyes and ears inside this institution. Everybody knows who you are. Some of your friends will never think twice about telling you if there is some questionable meeting of any sort, some secret 'underground' art exhibit, or some unauthorized piece of literature published in Russian abroad.

Nobody will ever think that you are my man. I need to know if any of this happens, and I must know at once. And, most importantly, I must find out who the culprit is. Don't worry about anything else. Nobody but Dean Dubinin knows about our meeting. Count on him for any assistance, and if something comes up, here's my card. Call me at once. Day ... night ... it doesn't matter."

He walked me to the door and shook my hand again.

"I will be checking on you from time to time. You can go now," he finally said.

The hallway was empty, and I was alone. I looked at his business card:

Col. Shatura, Yuri Sergeevich

Regional Director

Second Chief Directorate

Committee of State Security

Phone: 213.32.64

The KGB ... I put my right hand into my pant pocket and tightened my fist around the brass key. I rushed downstairs skipping every other step on my way to the school lobby; I was in shock and disbelief.

Had it been a bad dream? Or had I just been recruited to be a KGB informant?

Chapter Nineteen
Kornilov

Some events seemed impossible to explain. I had learned over the last few years that the unexplainable was usually too dangerous to be just left alone. The unexplainable needed to be explained one way or the other, sooner or later.

Our class president, Peter Kornilov, was the last person on earth I would trust. He was a candidate member of the Communist Party and a staunch protector of the ideological dogma forced by authorities onto every aspect of our lives. His nauseating speeches, permeated with communist slogans, became a routine attribute of every scheduled class assembly.

When not at the podium, he tried very hard to pretend to be like everyone else and professed that the ideological hat he'd been wearing just a moment before was nothing but a career-advancing necessity. He would frequently tell a provocative joke to his fellow students and goad them into an analogous response. Luckily, most of us knew whom we were dealing with and tried to avoid him politely or respond to him in neutral, non-committal terms.

At the end of the day, Peter joined me on my walk from the clinic to the library.

"How's everything going, my man?" He smiled and patted me on the back. "You don't give us simple folks any room to breathe, you, the curve breaker. Can you just pretend for once that you don't know all the right answers and lose a couple of points on the next test? Give us some slack, dude."

I thought for a moment about what my response to him should be, and smiled. I then made a serious face and looked around, as if checking to ensure we were alone. Lowering my voice, I firmly expressed my concern.

"Peter, you're not suggesting to me that I should throw away all those people's money, are you? All that money our motherland is spending on our education, and you want me to cheat? Shouldn't we feel obligated to repay our debt to society by putting the most effort into our studies?"

"Hey, Alex," he responded seemingly without surprise, "are you serious? Cut the shit! You can't bullshit a bullshitter. Talk openly to me. You can. You're smart enough to understand what is what. Don't you see who I really am behind that fucking communist mask I'm forced to wear in public? I am one of us. That is my way to survive.

"Come on; give me a fucking break, man. I am not

stupid either, but I do envy you. You are the lucky one. You have the talent. Just look at your grades."

"Study hard; you'll get the same grades."

"I was always envious of you. Always."

"What are you talking about?" I was surprised and intrigued at the same time.

"After all that shit you were involved in ... after all that, a year later, somehow, you were not only rein-stated in our medical school, but you advanced to the next academic year. It was like you didn't even miss a beat. You don't have to tell me anything, but don't take me for a fool.

"I've been watching you for quite some time. You're trying to pretend you're a loner, but everybody is talking about you behind your back, and most of the students quietly admire you. Don't be surprised, but I did read all your poetry, and guess what? I liked it. I think and feel about everything the same way you do, man. I'm on your side. Someone like you just can't be simply a misanthrope."

"Why do you think I am?" I was curious.

"Because that's how you behave. I haven't seen you with your friends. Who are your friends, by the way, and where do you hide them? I want to be among them as well," Peter kept insisting.

"I don't have time for all this nonsense. I have to study to keep my grades up. The state exams are a few months away. I cannot disappoint your envy, Peter." I faked a smile as I tried to finish our conversation on a funny note.

"Please don't look at my friendship offer as nonsense. I'm not asking for anything in return. I really want us to be friends. Don't be surprised, but I do own an issue of the banned New Word; I have it hidden away. It's the one with your poem 'Salvaged Hope.' You can trust me, and I think I can trust you."

The library entrance was just around the corner. I lengthened my stride in an effort to get there faster as I struggled to put an end to the bizarre and provocative encounter. Peter walked briskly next to me, trying to keep up with my pace.

"I read some prohibited books that have been stealthily circulated lately. Please don't ask who gave them to me. You know I wouldn't tell."

"I'm not asking," I interrupted, but he kept going.

"I just finished Boris Pasternak's *Doctor Zhivago* and have just now started Solzhenitsyn's *Cancer Ward*."

"Why are you telling me all this stuff? I think you're making a mistake. A huge mistake," I said, reaching for the library door.

Suddenly, Peter pulled a small paperback from his pocket, and before I could step inside, he shoved it into my book bag. "It's Doctor Zhivago. You can have it for a week. Read it and give it to as many people as you can trust, but I have to have it back on time. Just keep your mouth shut. See you, man." Peter stepped back and swiftly walked away.

I entered the library and ordered a couple of text-books. My hands were shaking. When the books arrived, I signed for them and told the librarian that I would be in the study hall on the third floor in case anyone asked for me. I went to the third floor but quickly turned around, entered the back stairwell, and walked out. I was too disturbed to study.

I crossed the street, strolled around the corner to a nearby payphone, and dialed Eugene's number. "Hi, Zhenya. It's me—Alex. Something strange just happened. We have to talk. In person."

"Can you come to my place right away? Nate is here. Is that OK?"

"Yes. Even better. I'm on my way," I said and hung up the phone.

I had a couple of rubles on me and decided to flag a cab so I could avoid public transportation, where I knew I could be followed. The cab took me to Arbatskaya Café. I paid the fare, exited the cab, and stood at the front of the café for a couple of minutes, studying the street just to be sure I had not been fol-lowed. Then I entered the café, walked right through to the back door, and crossed the wooded courtyard.

A few minutes later, I was ringing the bell to Eugene's apartment.

"Hi, guys," I said, walking into the kitchen and trying to calm my heavy breathing and rapid heartbeat.

"Come right in, brother," said Zhenya, greeting me with a hug.

"Nice to see you, old man." Nate got up and acknowledged me with a firm handshake. "Sit down. Join us."

"What do you want—coffee or tea? What happened?" Zhenya was eager for any news.

"Cuppa tea, if you don't mind. I had the weirdest experience an hour ago," I started. "Our class president, Peter Kornilov, a well-known commie and, most likely, the chief fink of the medical school, offered me his friendship, trying to persuade me that he is not what others think of him … that he's just 'one of us.'

"To prove his loyalty, he confided in me that he has a source that supplies him with banned publications, which he is actively reading. Then he shoved a paperback into my book bag, telling me that I have a week to read it and to give it to as many friends as I want."

I pulled out Kornilov's paperback and put it in the middle of the table.

"*Doctor Zhivago!*" exclaimed Zhenya. "Where did he get it?"

"Don't touch it, Zhenya!" Nate blurted out. "Do

you have a pair of gloves? Any gloves ... Yes, where did he get it, Alex?"

"I don't know. He's the last person on earth I would trust with anything. I would never expect him to read Pasternak and Solzhenitsyn. Trust me; he's up to something, and it doesn't smell good."

Nate donned a pair of gloves and carefully examined the paperback. "About two hundred copies of Pasternak's *Doctor Zhivago* are in underground circulation right now," he murmured while inspecting the book. "I happened to have one in my possession the other month. It's a great read, by the way—the work of a genius. Feltrinelli Books printed all two hundred copies in Italy. They held the publishing rights. This paperback looks and feels different. It's not from the Feltrinelli edition."

Nate flipped a few pages and then looked through a single page, which he held up against a lightbulb. "Bingo!" he said. "It's a fake. Look through the page. The Feltrinelli version is printed on thin, plain tissue paper. This one is printed on tissue paper as well, but the paper is different. It has a watermark on it. Someone was not very smart leaving evidence like that."

"What evidence?" Zhenya and I screamed simultaneously.

"Look at the watermark. What does it say?"

Zhenya looked at it closely and read aloud, "*Moscow Ducat Factory* ... Shit! This paper belongs to the Ducat cigarette factory near Mayakovsky Square. I cannot believe it. If someone was smart enough to try to duplicate *Doctor Zhivago* on the sly, how could they be that stupid to print it on paper with evidence pointing straight to the source?"

"What can it be then?" I wondered.

"Bloody hell! I'm afraid I know where this one is going," said Nate. "I think the KGB cooked up a few copies on their own for 'domestic' use, so to speak. They supply their informants, like Kornilov, with a copy to introduce the book into certain circles to reveal potential sympathizers, to lay bare and weed out the 'distribution chain.' Sounds plausible?"

"Holy crap!" Zhenya said, rubbing his temples. "It's impressively canny and extremely devious; nonetheless, somebody was in a big hurry and did a sloppy job selecting the paper."

"That explains it. So, what do we do now?" I asked.

"How well do you know this Kornilov guy?" Zhenya was curious. "Can you be dead certain that he is definitely a KGB fink?"

"There's not a shadow of a doubt about it," I affirmed.

"Maybe he is just an innocent pawn being used in somebody else's bloody game?" Nate pondered.

"Maybe he is a pawn, all right, but this game of chess is his. He is playing his part. He is in it knowingly and willfully. I just know it. It can't be anything else. He was just so full of it earlier ... fibbing and trying way too hard to be cogent. I have no doubt that he's a fink!"

"I have an idea," Zhenya said. "If he is a fink, report him!"

"Are you kidding me? I am not a squealer," I protested.

"Didn't you tell me just a week ago about the attempt to 'recruit' you to be one?"

"That's not funny, Zhenya. I didn't sign up." I said. "Shut the hell up!"

"No, I'm serious, Alex. What was the name of that KGB's Second Directorate colonel?"

"Shatura, Yuri Sergeevich. How could I forget?"

"You don't understand. There could be three different scenarios. Number one: Shatura is checking you out and Kornilov is his stoolie. Number two: Kornilov is not connected to Shatura, and he is somebody else's snitch. Number three: Knowing your past, all of them surmise you are somehow connected to one of the dissident groups and they're gonna watch your every step, hoping that you will lead them somewhere. You are on the hook and have no choice. It's your move now."

"Are you trying to say that my only way to get off this hook is to rat Kornilov out?" I mulled it over.

"You can't rat out a rat, Alex," Nate chuckled.

"It is your only way to get out of this pitfall and shut the trapdoor, genius," continued Zhenya. "I bet the bastards aren't counting on it. Surprise! Do you still have the colonel's business card?"

"Yes, I do."

"Tomorrow, go to your medical school early in the morning and try to get out of clinic first." Zhenya was planning on the fly. "Then get to the dean's office and ask his secretary to let you place an important phone call. If she objects, tell her that the dean knows what it's all about."

"Why does he have to initiate a call from the dean's office? A payphone isn't good enough?" Nate argued.

"You see, Shatura's headquarters are most likely monitoring all the incoming calls. A call coming from the medical school dean's office will make it more urgent and legitimate. Tell the colonel that it's a matter requiring his immediate attention and ask him to meet you somewhere. At this meeting, you will tell him that, to your great surprise, you have unveiled the source of the illegal book distribution. You will pass him the evidence and bemoan that you would never have expected it from the beloved president of your class," Zhenya concluded.

"Meanwhile, don't let anyone else touch this book," Nate warned me on my way out. "Let them discover only two sets of fingerprints on it—Kornilov's and yours. Good luck tomorrow, old man," he added, shaking my hand. "I'm eager to find out what happens at that meeting with Shatura ... to see how convincing you will be as a stoolie."

"What?" I raised my eyebrows.

"I'm only kidding, old man."

"I am not kidding, Nate. I am unsettled about this whole thing," I hurled back on my way out. "Fretful, anxious, and strung out."

Zhenya unlocked the door and gave me a hug. "Go home and chill out, genius. Everything will work out tomorrow. I can just sense it."

Chapter Twenty
Revelation

I skipped the morning clinical conference and, instead, took the school lobby elevator to the seventh floor, right to the reception area of the dean's office. Nobody was in the room except the dean's secretary, Claudia Petrovna, who was watering the potted plants parading on the windowsills.

"Good morning, Alex," she greeted me. "I don't think you have an appointment with the dean today. Did I miss something?"

"Good morning, Claudia Petrovna," I responded. "You didn't miss anything. I just have to make an urgent phone call. May I?"

"You know the rules, Alex. No personal calls allowed from the school telephones. The students have to use one of the payphones on the first floor."

"It's not personal at all," I rebuffed. "The dean knows about the nature of this call. It's a strictly official matter. I would never dare to ask you otherwise."

"Then that's totally different," she said, as if reassuring herself. "Go ahead and use the phone on my desk. Just make it brief, please."

"Thank you. You are so kind," I replied and dialed the number. "May I speak to Colonel Shatura, please?"

"Who is calling?" the person on the other end asked.

"It's Alexander Loevsky. The colonel asked me to call."

"Where are you calling from?"

"Setchenoff Medical School, Pirogova Street campus, next to Zubovskaya Square."

"One moment, please. Hold the line." I heard a few clicks followed by a moment of silence.

"Shatura here," came a familiar, velvety-soft baritone.

"Good morning, Comrade Colonel. It's Alex Loevsky from the medical school. You asked me to call you at once if I ever ran into anything peculiar. Well, I did, and I have to talk to you about it right away."

"How peculiar is it, Alex? Can it wait till tomorrow?"

"I don't think so, Yuri Sergeevich. It's very troubling."

"Are you in the dean's office?"

"No, I am in his reception room."

"You are not alone there, are you?" Shatura asked.

"No, I am not."

"My office. Kuznetsky Most Street, number

seventeen, suite eleven. See you in twenty minutes." Shatura hung up the phone without waiting for my response.

"Thank you, Claudia Petrovna," I said. "I hope I was brief enough."

"You're welcome, Alex," she replied. "You were indeed, and I'll tell the dean that you came by to make a call and that you were very polite as always."

"Don't worry; I'll talk to him myself later today. Thank you anyway," I replied on my way out.

Twenty minutes later, I was standing on Kuznetsky Most Street in front of Stalin-era twelve-story apartment building number 17. It was imposingly decorated with statues of farmers and workers diligently supporting massive columns streaming up through the full height of the front walls to the roof cornice. Like at the most of their contemporaries, different stores parading plastic groceries, books, and furniture in the gleaming storefront windows occupied the first two floors. The building was split in the middle by a three-story-tall archway leading to an inner courtyard. To my surprise, nothing about it suggested that there could be a government, police, or military office somewhere inside.

Halfway through the archway, I discovered an inconspicuous cobalt-blue enamel sign on the inner wall with a right arrow on it. "Suites 10 through 29 to the right" was written under the white arrow. I entered the courtyard and looked to my right. At the very end of the courtyard stood a two-story building with a mysterious sign next to the entrance door:

"P.O. Box 1749/2415. 2nd Dir. Restricted entry."

Aha! That's where the hornet's nest is! I said to myself.

I walked through the entrance door into a shallow vestibule and pressed the intercom button next to the "Suite 11" sign near the elevator.

"Who is it?" the speaker above the sign squawked.

"Alexander Loevsky here to see Colonel Shatura. He is expecting me," I answered.

"Take an elevator to sublevel four. Proceed to room number eleven."

The lock buzzed and the door came ajar. I walked into an elevator and pressed the "Sub 4" button. The elevator quietly dropped to sublevel four.

I walked out and followed the long, wide corridor, which was filled with the noise of ringing phones and clicking typewriters. Following the numbers on the doors and listening to the voices coming from inside, I finally stopped at the end of a corridor facing a double door with the number "11" above it. I gently knocked a couple of times.

"Come right in," the velvety-soft baritone answered.

I opened the door. "Good morning, Yuri Sergeevich."

"Good morning, Alex!" Shatura waved me in. "Come in. Sit down and make yourself comfortable."

He was wearing an imposing military uniform with a full complement of colorful ribbons and a pair of shoulder boards topped with three gold stars and two blue stripes of a colonel of the State Security. "Can I offer you a cigarette?"

"No, thank you, Yuri Sergeevich; I don't smoke."

"I know, I know," he replied, "but I do. So, how is school? You don't mind if I smoke, do you? What urgent situation brought you here? Is anything of interest happening at the medical school?"

"I really don't know how to break it to you, but last evening, on my way to the school library, someone confronted me and shoved this into my book bag." I pulled *Doctor Zhivago* out of my bag and slowly put it on the colonel's desk.

Shatura reached across his desk and grabbed the paperback. He studied it for a couple of minutes and then asked, "Who gave it to you? Do you know the person?"

"Here's the problem, Yuri Sergeevich. It's the last person I would ever have expected to approach me with a book like that. I am shocked to tell you that it was our class president, Peter Kornilov."

"Are you sure it was him?"

"Sure as one can be; it wasn't dark yet. We saw each other, and we had a short talk. It was Kornilov. I am telling you it was him."

"Why didn't you call me right away last night?"

"I was at the library. Last night, a lot of people were studying there. Peter told me what the book was before he shoved it into my book bag. I could not get this book out of my bag in public; it was too risky. I only fully realized what I had in my possession when I finally got home late last night. When I finally opened my book bag and looked at it, I was so disturbed and frightened I couldn't even fall asleep."

"What were you frightened about, Alex?" Shatura asked, pretending to be puzzled. The question sounded inquisitively cold. His searching eyes were now fixated on my face as they peeked above his thick, rimless glasses, patiently studying my expressions and body language, awaiting my reaction.

I latched onto how to play his game and took a deep breath. Then I leaned forward, lowered my voice almost to a quivering whisper, and tried to sound convincingly perturbed.

"I was worried sick that somebody somehow would find out what I had in my possession and report on me. It may sound paranoid to you, but you of all people are aware of my troubled past, and I'm sure you can understand. You have to trust me when I say that I don't want to jeopardize my future ever again. Ever!"

"Calm down. You are working with us. We are

the Second Chief Directorate, Alex. It makes a world of difference when you are on the right side. Stop worrying. I am very encouraged that you had the moral strength to do the right thing. Yes, I am encouraged and, may I say, proud of you. Rest assured your future is safe. Here is my hand to seal it."

With an accepting smile, he forcefully shook my hand and then abruptly stopped. He instantly became perplexed and quietly asked, "By the way, I'm a bit curious. When you couldn't fall asleep last night, you didn't try to read this book, did you?"

He did not catch me off guard with his sudden change in demeanor. I calculated what he did not expect to hear from me in return, but I gave it to him anyway.

"Yuri Sergeevich, it would not be sincere of me … in fact, it would be plainly dishonest of me to deny it. I am really sorry, but I have to admit that it was utterly tempting. So I did read a little, just for my own curiosity … to find out what the fuss surrounding this book was all about."

Shatura had not expected my divulgence. He tried to conceal his incredulity with an almost amateurish platitude, "Alex, my friend, temptation is common and human, but real men control their temptations. So, after you gave in to your curiosity and read it all, what did you think about all the fuss?"

He was still trying to get into my head. I took the bait and lured him in. "I am not that fast of a reader. I didn't have a chance to read all of it. To be frank, the very beginning was quite boring. I sort off glanced over the first couple of chapters, skipping most parts. But the last one, the postmortem 'Poetry of Yury Zhivago,' impressed me.

"It's a compilation of his poetic letters to Lara, the woman he loved. It was found after his death, and it was tremendously moving and immensely sorrow-ful—quite an emotional ending. It felt so private.

"I know that it is contradictory to the accepted canons of social realism. This stuff is so convoluted it could drive me nuts. I am happy that I don't write any-more. Probably because I was very partial to poetry, you know ... I did like those poems, I have to admit, but the rest of the stuff, I couldn't care less about."

I was impressed by the cool way in which I'd deliv-ered my answer, but it didn't feel as if he'd been totally persuaded by my efforts. He obviously didn't like my explanations leading him where he didn't believe he wanted to go.

He paused for a moment and then clumsily and abruptly eased his way out of my *confession*.

"Alex, I want to thank you for your honesty. It is reassuring and comforting to see your trustworthi-ness, my friend."

"Yuri Sergeevich, what should I tell Kornilov when he asks me to return the book? How should I react?"

Shatura was caught off guard without a ready answer. "He won't ask you to return it. Leave it to us. We'll take care of this Kornilov guy." He inadvertently confirmed my suspicions and revealed to me what I'd wanted to find out. "Just act normally, like nothing ever happened. Good job, Alex! You were very helpful. Keep your nose to the ground and your eyes wide open. You can go now," he rushed to finish.

"Have a nice day, Comrade Colonel. I'm glad I could help." I walked out into the corridor and closed the door behind me.

"Son of a bitch," I whispered, clenching my fists. "Kornilov is his stoolie. Nate was right." I took a deep breath of relief and cautiously smiled to myself, feeling grateful that my intuition had not failed me and that everything transpired the way we thought it would.

I started walking back to the exit. Once again, I moved through the unsettling sounds of stuttering typewriters and random voices coming from a few open office doors.

Suddenly, I came to an abrupt stop, feeling as if I'd just been hit right across the face. I heard the voice coming from the door to the right; the voice was so painfully familiar. I began moving very slowly down the corridor and, just to be sure, glanced through the threshold.

My head spun, and blood rushed to my face. I could not believe it. I remembered that I'd passed a men's room on my left only a moment before. I turned around, ran into it, and fought the sudden and over-whelming wave of nausea. I entered the empty stall, fell to my knees, hugged the toilet bowl, and vomited violently again and again until nothing was left in my stomach; there was just the constant remaining spasm of the gagging reflex squeezing my throat.

Finally, I managed to pull myself together. I got to my feet, walked over to the sink, opened the faucet, and shoved my face under the cold-water stream. It took some time to clean my face, wash my mouth, and quench my sudden thirst with a few rapid and full gulps of the stinking, heavily chlorinated drink.

I was eventually able to calm myself down. My legs were still weak, but my head had stopped spinning. In utter mortification, I entered the corridor again to hear the same voice reverberating through the par-tially open door ahead and to the right of me. I took a few more quiet steps and briefly looked through the opening once more.

The young woman seated at the desk was deeply immersed in a heated and intense phone conversation. The sound of her voice instantly covered my skin with goose bumps. The tightly pulled-back aureate hair was curling against the collar of her military uniform with the epaulets of a second lieutenant of the State Security. I started to feel asphyxiated and nauseous again. I needed to get out immediately, so I rushed to the elevator door.

I crossed the courtyard, walked briskly through the archway, and dove into the bustling noises of Kuznetsky Most, where I quickly melted into the crowd. My heart was rapidly beating, as if it was trying to get out of my chest in a hurry. For the next twenty minutes I had aimlessly rushed through the streets, madly crisscrossing the intersections, ignoring the traffic lights, and frequently changing direction without any particular reason. I felt hopelessly lost, bouncing like a wild pinball in an endless maze. I did not know where I was going and how I could get out of this *underside of beyond.*

What a total fool I was! What an idiot!

Slowly, one sobering rational thought had started to form in my head coming out of this incidental encounter with unexpectedly revealed horrific, gut-wrenching betrayal—I still had enough time to figure out what to do and how to act. It was pure luck that Svetlana hadn't looked up and seen my face through the threshold of her slightly opened office door.

Chapter Twenty One
The Plan

Instead of taking the trolley back to Zubovskaya Square, I decided to take an hour-and-a-half-long walk to the school—down Kuznetsky Most, across Ochotny Ryad and Theater Square, and through the Old Arbat neighborhood—to calm myself down and to sort everything out.

I had painfully realized how stupid I was by succumbing to the lustful obsession over a made-up Muse, while real, sweet and loving Lara, the true friend and the core essence of my life, has been waiting at my side for me to come to my senses. I was angry for being such an idiot, for convincing myself that stupid, childish, baseless infatuation over nothing had paralyzed me. I was foolishly trying to protect Lara from myself. I was scared to open up, to shake that witless daze off way earlier. I had concocted a fantasy that was completely devoid of any attributes of actuality to the point where it was too hard to separate reality from fiction, and I had allowed myself to be manipulated by the sneaky and seductive KGB operative.

The mere fact that Svetlana had been attending the School of Jurisprudence should've raised the red flag of caution a long time ago. If only I'd known then what I'd learned later.

The practice of law in the Soviet Union was quite unpopular and not at all lucrative for most of the flock. Only a handful of geeks became lawyers; the rest of the graduating class proudly aimed for careers as detectives or interrogators in police departments or as white-collar crime investigators at the Interior Ministry. However, most of them eagerly hankered for recruitment to the coveted ranks of the Committee for State Security.

From the very beginning, Svetlana never talked to me about herself; she only told me that she was older, but I never knew her age. Come to think of it, I knew very little about the real Svetlana. Had our introduction at the start of my association with New Word been an accident, or had it been a setup? Had her reappearance in my life been accidental, or had it been planned? Her sob story—had it been real or concocted?

I wasn't sure about our distant past, but I was quite confident now that her sudden visit to the clinic and the fact that her appointment had been scheduled with me at the end of the day were utterly suspicious and really stank of a setup. I now saw her eagerness to get close to me, her insatiable desire to find out details about my circle of friends, and her attempts to pry into my private affairs in a completely different light.

I was sure that I had been quite cagey with her at all times and hadn't divulged any sensitive information, but I wasn't completely certain if I had been vigilant and reticent enough not to compromise the security of my friends.

It was annoyingly disappointing to realize that I had been used as a pawn in someone else's chess game. Hadn't Aunt Anna warned me so many times to be careful?

You have to think over every move and every step you take far in advance to avoid the traps and pitfalls placed there by your ruthless opponents. Evaluate the danger. Do not get trapped. This game can be deadly if you lose.

Too much was at stake. I had to discuss the situation with Aunt Anna, but before anything else——Lara is my life... Losing was not an option. I had to man up, tell Lara the whole truth, level with her about everything, and then beg her to forgive me.

When I finally walked into the school lobby, I looked at the wall clock. It was three o'clock. I had not realized how quickly the time had flown by. I was now calm, and I felt much more confident. The I-am-sure-of-what-to-do feeling was finally back. It only took me a few minutes to find Lara in the library.

"Hi. Something is different about you," Lara whispered, studying me with her eyes. "Honestly, is everything okay?"

"Honestly? Everything couldn't be better," I whispered back. "What time are you done? I need to talk to you."

"I'm done now. Let me return my book."

"Great! I have to make a quick stop at the dean's office. Let's meet in the entrance lobby in ten minutes," I said and pecked her on the cheek.

"I'll see you at the cloakroom downstairs," Lara whispered, caught off guard.

I left the library and went upstairs to the dean's office.

"Good afternoon, Claudia Petrovna," I greeted the dean's secretary. "Is Dean Dubinin available?"

"Hi, Alex!" She gave me a smile. "I've seen you twice in one day. What a pleasure! Unfortunately, Dean Dubinin is in a long meeting right now. Would you like to leave a message for him?"

"Sure, Claudia Petrovna. Can you tell him that I was at Comrade Shatura's office today as the dean requested earlier? I had to miss the clinic, and I would like the dean to give me an official excuse for today."

"Don't worry, Alex. I already informed our dean that you stopped at the office and asked my permission for an official phone call this morning and that you left right after in a hurry. I'll make sure you get an excuse for today. Go and do whatever you have to do now. Goodbye, Alex."

"Goodbye, Claudia Petrovna, and thank you," I said before running downstairs to meet Lara.

Lara was already waiting for me.

"How long will this talk be?" she asked.

"Long," I answered and swung the door open. "Let's go. Do you mind if we walk to Aunt Anna's place? Whatever I have to tell you can only be discussed outside of the school grounds, in strict confidence, and away from any eavesdroppers. Let's walk through the park; there are very few pedestrians there."

We entered the park, and I turned around to face Lara. I raised her coat collar, took a deep breath, and said, "I know I am a couple of weeks late to respond. Forgive me, please, if you can. I love you, Lara! I love you dearly. I love you more than life itself. I cannot be without you. I realize what a gigantic part of my life you have become, and I want to become a part of yours. I want to be with you forever because I love you... and about that other girl... "

"I do not want to know about the other girl..." Lara interrupted.

"It was a dream... It was a nightmare... It is over..."

"Stop. I told you, I do not care about her, silly. Ask me better if you can kiss me now?"

"Can I kiss you? Now?"

Lara just nodded, and I kissed her ... and again ... and again ... After a while, she moved her face away from mine and said with a soft smile, "Why didn't you tell me before that you were such a great kisser? And, about that other girl, I couldn't care less about her. You are mine, and you will never find anyone better."

"I know, and I stopped looking the moment I saw you at the entrance exams."

We hugged each other, kissed again, and stood still for a few minutes.

"So, that's what you wanted to be kept in strict confidence? Can I tell my parents at least?"

"You can tell the whole world about us if you wish," I answered. "There is a lot more I have to tell you, but I wanted to tell you the most important part first."

"Okay," Lara said. "Now tell me the rest of it."

"Do you remember the last night at the dorm when we studied together with Paul and Andrew, and I ventured out for a walk in the middle of the night?"

"I do. I was worried about you. That was a cold and strange night."

"You had good reason to worry," I said. I recounted to her in detail about the murder in Alexander Gardens, the phone call I made, and meeting the dissidents and at the Bonners' apartment. I then told her about the list of three hundred and forty-six dissidents locked in the psych ward, the brass key, Eugene Baras and Nate Krimsky, our search for the locker, and my introduction to Colonel Shatura.

At that moment, we were standing at the entrance to Aunt Anna's apartment. I cut myself short and rang the doorbell. Aunt Anna opened the door.

"I hate eating dinner alone!" she greeted us. "I'm glad we can eat together. Come right in. Lara, can you help me peel some potatoes? Alex, go to the lower left cupboard near the door of the library, pick a bottle of red wine, and open it, please."

"Aunt Anna," Lara said, grinning from ear to ear. "Guess what? Alex just told me that he loves me, finally."

"Is that all he told you?" Aunt Anna asked in return.

"He told me a lot more than that, and I think he wants to reiterate it to you himself. Am I right, Alex?"

"You are always right, my dear," I said as I put the already opened bottle of wine on the kitchen table.

"I guess he told you about the other girl ..." Aunt Anna commented and quickly smiled in my direction while pouring the wine into the three burgundy glasses.

"He did," Lara responded, "but I couldn't care less about it. I didn't even care before he told me it was over. So be it! He also started telling me what he encountered in the last few days, but he couldn't finish and had to stop because we were already standing at your door. I want him to go over everything he told me so far, so you can hear it for yourself, and then I would like for him to tell both of us the rest of the story. Can we all sit down, please?"

We all sat down at the kitchen table, and I repeated everything I had told Lara so far. I then took a swig of wine. As Aunt Anna and Lara remained silent, I continued to describe my strange encounter with Kornilov, the fake copy of *Doctor Zhivago*, and, finally, the earth-shattering discovery during my visit to Colonel Shatura's office on Kuznetsky Most Street.

"What a bitch! What a frigging snake!" Lara gasped in disgust.

"I can't believe it … What was the name of that doctor from the Serbsky Institute who was murdered in Alexander Gardens?" Aunt Anna suddenly asked. "Did you say Levitt?"

"Yes. His name was Mark Levitt. Did you know him, Aunt Anna?"

"No, I did not know him personally, but I've heard his name before," she said, rubbing her temples. "I think I know what is in that locker …" Aunt Anna picked up her wine glass and slowly sipped some of its contents.

"Alex, if you recall—as I did tell you—the night before she was murdered, Masha Simyavsky went to a meeting with someone by the name Levine or Levitt to hand him her notebook containing the full transcript of Andrey's trial to be smuggled abroad for publication."

"You did tell me that, Aunt Anna. I remember," I replied.

"I'm almost sure that this someone was Mark Levitt, and if it was him, I have no doubt that Masha's notebook is in that locker!" Aunt Anna stated affirmatively. "It can't be just a coincidence. Do you have any clue where the locker is located? We have to find it before it's too late."

"The last time Eugene, Nate, and I talked about it, we came to the consensus that it was probably somewhere in the vicinity of the Leningradsky Railroad Station. I have the key, by the way. It's always on me; I do not let it out of my sight." I reached into my pocket and retrieved the key.

"There is a locomotive symbol on one side and the digit '1' on the other. Looks like the rest of the number had been ground off." Lara said, studying the key.

"The phone number I'd dialed that night had begun with the Leningradsky District exchange—251. I think that 1251 could be that locker number," I explained.

"Interesting thought… A part of that phone number, ha? Locker 1251… What if it is?" Lara said. "Why don't we go there and check it out now?"

"Let's finish dinner first," Aunt Anna said, "and then

the two of you can go to the Leningradsky Railroad Station and do some reconnaissance. But do not get close to that locker. The whole place could be under surveillance."

Lara and I literally swallowed our food because we were in such a hurry to get to the Leningradsky Railroad Station. Right before we left, Lara asked, "Aunt Anna, do you by any chance have an unmarked paper-carrying satchel that you don't need?"

"Going through so many manuscripts a year, I obviously have quite a few messenger bags. But why do you need it?"

"We could look suspicious walking across the halls of the railroad station without any luggage. It would be great if you could also give us a stack of blank paper to add some weight to it … you know, so it won't look empty."

"Great idea, girl!" Aunt Anna left in the direction of her study and soon returned with two messenger bags of different sizes, both of which were filled with stacks of blank typewriter paper. "Two is better than one," she explained. "Now both of you will look like legitimate passengers. Please be careful, kids. I'll be waiting for you."

"Don't worry, Aunt Anna. We'll just take a look, and we'll come right back. See you soon," I replied on our way out.

It was past nine o'clock when we walked into the majestic, ornate building that housed the Leningradsky Railroad Station. In front of us was a long corridor leading to the train platforms with rows of ticket stalls along both walls. To our right was a three-story waiting hall with elaborate, vaulted mosaic ceilings and inlaid marble floors covered with a labyrinth of circular rows of heavy wooden benches. The second floor, which was open in the middle, looked like a gigantic circular balustraded balcony resting on a dozen heavy Corinthian columns. Underneath the balcony, almost encircling the waiting hall, stood banks of gray storage lockers of different sizes.

I looked around and saw nothing suspicious. Some passengers were sleeping on the benches, some were reading, and some were eating snacks. A disheveled bum was panhandling between the benches. Nothing was out of the ordinary.

We approached the lockers and, on the upper left end found one with the number 1251 on the door. I checked the hall and looked up at the balcony. Nobody was watching us.

"It better be the right locker. Otherwise, the key will not fit, and we will be back at square one."

"Come with me quickly," Lara said and pulled me out of the waiting hall to the corridor with ticket stalls. "I have a plan."

She approached one of the stalls and came back with a token for a storage locker.

"Did you notice some lockers have keys sticking out of the lock and some don't?" she asked.

"Of course, I did. The ones that are taken are locked, and the others have keys in them. Simple."

"I got the simple part, but that's not what I was talking about. Twelve fifty-one is the first locker on the left side of the row, and twelve sixty is the last on the right. Twelve sixty has a key sticking out. Stay here, and do not move," Lara said, and before I could open my mouth, she went straight to the lockers.

She deposited her token into 1260, opened its door, and locked her messenger bag in it. She then turned the key twice, pulled it out, and returned to me.

"Let's get out of here. How long did it take?" she inquired, walking next to me as we headed to the exit.

"Less than a minute, but why did you do that?" I asked, puzzled.

"How else could I get the key out of the locker door? Now, we can compare that key with the one you have. If we are at the right train station, the keys from twelve fifty-one and twelve sixty should be the same kind and look almost identical," Lara explained.

"Smart!" I said. "I never thought about that. But why did you lock your bag inside?"

"That's the second part of my plan. If we are at the right place, we want to be sure that nobody is watching us. Regardless, they would be watching for the people taking stuff out, not for the ones locking their stuff in. However, if we want to safely open locker twelve fifty-one and retrieve whatever is inside, we need a decoy."

"Lara, I am amazed by you. How many spy books did you have to read to make a simple thing so convoluted?"

"It may be convoluted, but remember how concerned Aunt Anna was about this notebook? If my recollection is right, somebody beat the living shit out of you some time ago to find out where Masha's notebook was. How quickly we forget! Nothing has changed, Alex. Nothing! We all have to be vigilant."

"Lara, my dear Lara. I did not forget anything. I witnessed Mark Levitt losing his life inside Alexander Gardens not long ago over this key. It's still a deadly chess game, as Aunt Anna put it. You're right about being vigilant. Tell me about the decoy, please."

"Tomorrow, you have to get in touch with that snitch bitch, Svetlana. Let her know somehow, quite nonchalantly, that you will dispatch someone to retrieve some important papers from locker twelve sixty located at Leningradsky Train Station tomorrow night. Make up some story to make sure she bites.

"Tomorrow night, we will find one of the panhandling bums over there and offer him twenty bucks to retrieve the contents of locker twelve sixty. We will be on the balcony watching everything unfold. I bet the moment he opens that locker, he will be stopped and taken away. Immediately after, I will rush downstairs to locker twelve fifty-one, empty it, and then meet you at the subway station at the train. Is that a plan?"

Instead of answering, I hugged her and gave her a kiss.

"Let's return to Aunt Anna's place and tell her about your plan," I said.

"Let's compare the keys first," Lara replied, holding up her key.

I pulled mine out of my pocket. We looked at both keys. They looked identical.

Chapter Twenty Two
Diversion

I thought all day long about every possible way to lure Svetlana into our trap. Obviously, I had to talk to her, but a face-to-face meeting was out of the question. I would not be able to keep my cool and pretend that nothing had happened. It would be close to impossible to conceal my real feelings about her now.

At the same time, I did not want any subtle changes in my demeanor to set off any alarm bells. A phone call was my only available and relatively safe option. I figured she would be home at around five or six o'clock. At six, I dialed her number.

"Hi. It's me—Alex. How have you been? We haven't seen each other for at least a couple of weeks. I miss you," I lied right off the bat.

"I miss you too, but I figured you were probably caught up at the clinic or the library, getting ready for your finals. I didn't want to be a pest. Are you doing anything tonight? Why don't we have a late dinner together? Just talking to you is making me feel aroused … Come over to my place. Are you game?" She was one smooth operator.

"Hold on. Svetlana, can you wait for just one

second?" I had partially covered the mouthpiece with one hand and pretended that somebody was interrupting our conversation. "Are you fucking crazy? Can't you see I'm talking to someone right now?"

I then changed my voice and answered myself in a hoarse tone, as if I were impersonating someone else. "I have to split now. Did I get it right? Tonight at nine, Leningradsky Railroad Station, locker twelve sixty? I have to take everything from the locker and bring all that stuff to the meeting? Am I on the mark?"

I changed my voice back to my own and replied in an undertone, "Yes, you're right. Enough already! Just go!" I took my hand off the mouthpiece.

"Svetlana? Sorry for the wait——" I continued.

"Who were you talking to?" she interrupted me.

"One of the sophomores," I said apologetically. "Some dudes over here have no manners. They can't wait. They have to cut in just to borrow a coin to make a phone call. Get your own coin, pal!

"Anyhow, about dinner tonight, I would love it more than anything, but I'm stuck at the library studying. Can I take a rain check? I took a short break a minute ago and came downstairs to a payphone just to touch base with you and to tell you that I'm looking forward to next week when finals are over. Then we'll be able to spend a few days in a row together, just like old times ..."

"That would be awesome; I can't wait," Svetlana answered.

"Love you," I said.

"Love you too," she responded.

The receiver nearly slid out of my hand as I hung up. My palms were sweating, and my heart was racing. *Did she take the bait? I guess Lara and I will find out tonight around nine o'clock.*

At nine, Lara and I were at the Leningradsky terminal.

"Go upstairs and wait for me on the balcony. I don't want anyone around here to see us together," I said to her. After she left, it took me less than a few minutes to "make friends" with the first bum I ran into. He was mildly drunk, but that would make things easier.

"Hey, man! What's your name?"

"What's your problem, dude? You want to be my friend? Pick a name. Who cares what it is? You can call me Sam if you want to keep it simple. I could use some money. You have any to spare?"

"Sam, what if I offer you twenty bucks to get a small bag from a locker for me?"

"Did you say twenty bucks? Did I hear you right?"

"Yup! Twenty crisp ones. Whaddya say?"

"Why can't you get your bag yourself, man? Is it too heavy for you to carry? Twenty bucks is a lot of money. Do you know how much booze you can get for twenty bucks?"

"It's not heavy at all. I made a bet that I could get someone else to do it for me."

"A bet? What's in it for you?"

"Fifty bucks!" I said.

The bum shook his head and started to haggle with me. "You're such a tight motherfucker! You'll get fifty bucks, but I'll do all the work and I'll only get twenty? No fucking way! I want half. Twenty-five for you and twenty-five for me. Just to be fair. Not a penny less! Do we have a deal?"

"Okay. You win," I said. "I'll give you ten bucks now and the rest when you bring the bag to me."

"Bring it where?"

"Right here. I'll be waiting for you right here. Is that okay?"

"Give me fifteen now, man."

"Not a chance." I stood firm. "Ten now, fifteen when you get back."

"You sure drive a hard bargain, dude," the bum responded. "Fine then! Give me ten. What locker is it in?"

I pulled out the key. "Look, Sam, do you see that number on the key? Twelve sixty. That's the locker number. Get there in ten minutes, open the locker, retrieve the bag, and bring it back to me. Here's your ten bucks."

"Dude, have some mercy. The liquor stores are closed now. I will have to get my vodka from the taxi cab drivers, and they charge extra after hours! Give me twenty when I come back. Can we shake on it?"

"Okay, screw you, Sam. I'll give you what you want. See you in ten minutes right here with my bag."

"You're a tough motherfucker, dude. See you in ten. Have my twenty ready."

I entered the terminal through the side door and went to the second floor, where Lara was waiting for me.

"Your ex-girlfriend did her job. Look downstairs."

I carefully peeked through the balustrade. A few dozen visibly wound-up men, all of whom were anxiously scanning the hall as if trying to locate someone, occupied the benches across from the lockers. None of them had any luggage.

"It was a totally different picture last night," I said.

"This isn't even a weekend. It shouldn't be that crowded."

"Those guys are so transparent."

"They do look odd. Did you find someone to do it?" she asked.

"Yep, we agreed on thirty bucks. I gave him ten upfront. Looking downstairs, I don't see him being able to collect the other twenty tonight though. Look, look … there he is going down the hall and looking at the locker numbers."

Sam approached locker 1260, looked around, and inserted his key into the lock. He then opened the locker door hesitantly, suspiciously waiting for something to happen. The moment he retrieved Lara's messenger bag, all hell broke loose.

He was instantly jumped and pushed to the floor by the agents positioned around that area. Unwilling to part with the messenger bag and, thereby, forfeit his upcoming reward, Sam fought vigorously as he tried to free himself. Everybody else fled the waiting hall immediately; nobody wanted to get involved or implicated. Poor Sam was finally separated from his bag, handcuffed, and dragged away deliriously screaming expletives to his captors on the way out.

Not a single soul was left in the waiting hall. Lara hesitated for a moment and then immediately took off running downstairs. I watched from above as she rushed to the locker and tried the key. Hallelujah! The key fit! She rotated it twice and opened the locker door. She retrieved a large envelope from the locker and stuffed it into her messenger bag. A second later, she bolted to the exit.

I left the balcony and went down the stairs to the side exit door. Just a few pedestrians were here and there, and the street in front of me was pretty quiet. So as not to alert anyone, I continued at a normal pace to the subway station, where I paid the fare and took the escalator to the train platform. Lara was shivering on the corner bench.

"Are you okay?" I asked.

"I'm scared shitless," she answered.

"You are, by far, the bravest person I've ever met," I said.

"I'm not sure about that," she grimaced in response. "I need to go to the restroom. Now!"

"There's one at the Old Arbat station. It's five minutes away. Can you hold it?"

"Do I have any other choice?" she replied. "I'll do my best. Let's hurry up and get there. Can you carry this for me, please?"

She handed me her messenger bag, and I took her by the arm and helped her to the train.

We were the only two people in the car.

"Old Arbat," announced the loudspeaker a few minutes later. We walked out.

"Turn to the right," I said. "The restrooms are at the end of that hall."

Lara rushed to the restrooms, and I went to an opposite wall where I saw a few payphones. I dialed Eugene's number.

"I'm glad you're home," I said.

"Where else am I supposed to be at ten o'clock? Of course, I'm home. Nate and I are working on something."

"I'm around the corner, at the Old Arbat subway station. Can we come over right away?"

"Is everything all right?"

"Better than just all right. We finally found what we were looking for."

"Who are we? Who are you with?"

"Someone I can trust with my life. Her name is Lara. She's the girl I'm going to marry."

"You know what the wise man said? *Marry in haste, repent at leisure.* Alex, were you drinking?"

"Not yet, but I hope the four of us will have a drink after I introduce Lara to you and Nate."

"How much does she know?"

"She knows a lot. Not everything, but a lot. You can tell her the rest when you feel like it."

"Alex, please …"

"I'm dead serious, man; she's one of us, all the way."

"Let me run it by Nate," Eugene said and took a short pause. "Nate said okay. See you in a few minutes, genius."

"Thank you, Zhenya. We'll be there shortly."

Lara came out of the restroom with a sigh of relief. "I didn't think I'd make it. I've never been so scared before, and it wasn't even for myself; I was terrified about Masha's notebook … or whatever is in that envelope."

"Guess what," I said, "we're going to see Eugene and Nate right now. They're waiting for us."

"Did you say *us*?"

"Yes, I said *us*. I want to introduce you to both of them, and I want all of us to see what you brought back from that locker. I bet you'll like these guys."

Chapter Twenty Three
Two Pieces of a Puzzle

E ugene opened the door.
"Alex, come right in! Is this the girl you told me you're going to marry?"

"Zhenya! Easy, man! Easy ..." I tried to protest. "Her name is Lara."

"Please come in, Lara. I'm Eugene, and I live here. My friends call me Zhenya. Make yourself at home."

"Thank you, Zhenya," Lara answered and shook his hand.

"Let's go to the kitchen," offered Zhenya. "That's where we usually congregate."

As we entered the kitchen, Nate got up from the table and introduced himself.

"Nate ... Nate Krimsky, Associated Press."

"Hi, I'm Lara. Nice to meet you, Nate."

"I am very pleased to meet you indeed. Alex kept you away from Eugene and me. I understand now why he was hiding you away. You're too pretty for him, and he's afraid that one of us might steal you."

"Not a chance," Lara replied.

I noticed an open bottle of Johnnie Walker on the kitchen table.

"You couldn't wait for us? What's the occasion?" I asked, looking at Zhenya.

"Nate brought it from *Beriozka* ... the store for foreigners. We just had one drink," he said apologetically and put two more glasses on the table. "You indicated to me that Lara knows a lot. Did you tell her about the murder you witnessed at Alexander Gardens and about Mark's list?"

"Yes, Zhenya. Alex shared it with me," Lara answered.

"Nate held a press conference earlier today," Zhenya explained, "with members of at least seventy-five families whose loved ones are locked up at numerous psych wards, like at the notorious Serbsky Institute in Moscow, where they are being injected with powerful psychotropic drugs against their will. Mark Levitt's list was instrumental as solid proof of that gruesome practice.

"Their families appealed to the free world for help. Almost all the accredited members of the foreign press corps showed up. Tomorrow morning, the news about the punitive use of psychiatry to silence political and ideological dissent in the Soviet Union will flood the front pages of all major Western newspapers." Zhenya poured whiskey in our glasses.

"You did it, Nate! Congratulations!" I said, raising my glass.

"I only facilitated the press conference," Nate replied, raising his glass. "Kudos to you, my friend. You were the one who saved Mark's list and brought it to us. Today's events couldn't have happened without you." Nate took a sip of his whiskey. "Please, forgive my inquisitiveness—and no offense to Lara—but I have to find out what information Lara became privy to and under what circumstances."

"Lara is the one who saved my life after I was nearly crippled by a KGB major at the medical school dorm," I said. "I don't know how I would have survived my imprisonment, trial, and the last few years of medical school without her help. I did tell her about you two, but she didn't ask and I didn't tell her about the people I met at the apartment the night after Mark was killed or anyone else who I became acquainted with through Zhenya or you."

I spent over an hour recounting to both of them what had happened to Lara and me from the day we'd met until now. Zhenya and Nate sat quietly listening to our story.

When I paused, Nate shook his head and said, "That's some powerful stuff, old man. One day you'll have to write it all down for your future children so they can learn the ugly truth about our times."

"Maybe one day I will, Nate. In the meantime, let me finish by telling you how my Aunt Anna got a hunch about what could be inside the locker we were looking for, Lara's plan to get it out, and how it all came to fruition just a couple hours ago."

After finishing my story, I reached for the messenger bag, opened it up, and put the large, thick envelope on the table in front of Nate and Zhenya. Nate tore the envelope open. We all froze, staring at the green leather-bound notebook.

"Masha's notebook ... Aunt Anna was right..." I gasped.

Nate opened the notebook and looked through a few pages. "I'll be damned! This is the transcript of Andrey Simyavsky's trial. We knew that it existed, but when Andrey's wife was murdered by the KGB, we thought they'd seized it and it was lost forever. Mark..." Nate continued, raising his eyes to the heavens, "God rest your soul, mate. You came through one more time. Thank you, my late friend. This one is to your memory."

We all took a sip of whiskey and sat quietly for a moment.

"What will we do with the notebook, guys? Any ideas?" Zhenya broke the silence.

"Aunt Anna told me that Masha was supposedly going to pass the notebook to Mark and that Mark knew somebody else who promised to smuggle it out of the country to Andrey's Swiss publisher," I said.

"I don't know who Mark's contact was or why the notebook was sitting idle in that locker for a few years," Nate said. "Maybe something didn't work out according to plan ... who knows? The important thing is that it's in our possession now, and I know the right people at the embassy who can get the notebook out by simply slipping it into a diplomatic mailbag. I'll deliver the notebook to them tomorrow. In a week, it will be in the right hands in Switzerland. Trust me, it will be done."

"I can't believe how intricately all this had been intertwined," I said.

"You're right. In the last few years, life around here has become a huge, convoluted puzzle," answered Nate. "We're struggling to solve it and searching for the missing pieces every day. I think we've got what we were looking for. First, it was Alex, and now it's you, Lara ... Like two missing pieces, you fit perfectly. Welcome to our cabal, Lara. I'm glad you're with us, finally."

"Thank you, Nate. I'm glad that I could help," Lara responded humbly.

"From Masha, to Mark, to Alex ... then to Lara with her plan, and now here we are. Was it just a coincidence, or was it divine providence? It's simply awe-inspiring and mind-boggling at the same time," Zhenya added. "Now that Nate and I have finally learned the rest of your life story, can I ask you a kinda personal question? When are the two of you planning to say 'I do' to each other? I love weddings—"

"Zhenya, there you go again! Take it easy, man!" I objected. "You're in dangerous territory now. Do you really want to embarrass me? What if Lara says 'never'?"

"Why would I do that?" Lara looked at me with a soft smile in her eyes, and her cheeks blushed all of a sudden. "Are you asking me to marry you? Are you?"

"What if I am?" I mumbled timorously.

"If that's what it is, my answer is ..." Lara slowly got up. "My answer is ... yes!"

I jumped to my feet, awkwardly stumbling over my chair, and darted to Lara, who was looking at me as she stood at the opposite end of the table. I only remember that we almost melted into each other's arms.

"So, when is the wedding?" Nate interrupted us.

"Let's get married before we graduate," I said.

"I wouldn't mind." Lara smiled. "We've known each other long enough ..."

"What's the rush, genius?" Zhenya was laughing at me from behind the table.

"Yeah, what's the rush, old man?" Nate echoed him, smiling from ear to ear. "Are you that afraid that I might steal her away from you? But all jokes aside

… Congratulations to both of you! I was touched and honored to witness this beautiful moment."

Zhenya poured the rest of the Johnnie Walker into our glasses and said, "I am speechless, which is a very unusual state for me. Whatever happened is simply surreal. I wish Rosa were here to see with her own eyes what took place at our kitchen table tonight, because I know I'll be asked to repeat the whole story over and over again. I want to raise my glass to your happiness and to your children harvesting the fruits of freedom, the seeds of which all of us are sowing today."

Nate raised his glass. "Well said! To your happy life together… Mazel Tov!"

Chapter Twenty Four

The Breakup

Despite the late hour, Lara and I went to Aunt Anna to give her the news that Masha's notebook had been rescued and would be smuggled out of the country. It would be on the way to Zurich, Switzerland, in merely a couple of days.

"There's something else we have to tell you, Auntie," I said. "Let's sit down."

When the three of us were seated, Aunt Anna gave me a conspiratorial smile. "You're getting married, aren't you?"

"How did you find out?" Lara and I jumped to our feet and shouted.

"Alex proposed to me only an hour ago, Aunt Anna. How did you figure it out? What's your secret?" Lara exclaimed in utter disbelief.

"There's no secret, my dear," Aunt Anna replied. "Take a look at each other. What do you see there? Love, happiness, and marriage—all of it is written upon your faces. And you've been holding hands since you walked in. I am not clueless. When should we begin planning the wedding?"

"We better get married before graduation," I said.

"That soon? Are you afraid Lara will change her mind?" Aunt Anna smiled, still playing with me.

"It's not that, Auntie. Believe me; I've put a lot of thought into this. There's a new directive from the Department of Higher Education. Instead of a diploma, each of the graduating class will receive an official assignment to practice medicine for three years in one of the underserved remote areas of the Soviet Union. Only after successful completion of that assignment will our diplomas be issued to us.

"The other week, Doctor Plotkin, head of the Department of Surgery and my professor of orthopedics, offered me a clinical faculty position that I should accept right before my graduation. If Lara and I are married by then, the same directive prevents the assignment process from breaking families up. They could not separate us and send Lara far away while I'm working here in Moscow.

"We still have to find a suitable position for Lara here, but at least we won't be separated, and we'll find her a job in the long run. I don't know how sincere Doctor Plotkin's offer was though. After that, he told me that, as a precondition, Dean Dubinin required that I write a letter of apology and pledge my allegiance to our institution in the school's journal. I doubt I can trust him at all."

"You can trust him. Boris Plotkin is a good man,"

Aunt Anna said unhesitatingly. "He's known to be one of the top orthopedic surgeons in the country. Being under his tutelage for a few years would be priceless for you.

"You're right; we should always be vigilant about whom we can trust and never forget that a dangerous chess game is being played with our lives. Just sacrifice another pawn—write the damn letter. Make it as waggish and as sarcastic as you can so the journal will refuse to accept it. Time it right and do it at the last moment. Dubinin wants it for his own reason, to cover his ass. Let him choke on it; it will be too late.

"Your Doctor Plotkin happens to be a 'member of the tribe' and a close friend of the general. Pavel and I had dinner with him not long ago. Boris Plotkin can be a funny guy after a couple of drinks. By the way, he gave us his assurances that Lara will also be assigned to the clinical faculty of the Emergency Medicine and Surgery Department on the same day as you. Are you both happy now?"

"Aunt Anna, I'm speechless! You are our guardian angel indeed." Lara's eyes were filled with tears as she stepped up to Aunt Anna and embraced her.

"I love you, my dear girl," Aunt Anna said, wiping away her own tears. "Stop doing this to me. Anyway, are you two staying over tonight?" she asked nonchalantly.

"If it's okay with you, Auntie," I answered.

"Then I'm going to my bedroom, and you two can figure out for yourselves who sleeps where…"

"Good night, Aunt Anna," Lara said as her cheeks turned red.

"Sweet dreams, kids." She blew us a kiss and closed her bedroom door behind her.

Elated and exhausted, we eventually fell asleep in each other's arms at around four o'clock in the morning. I'm unable to describe what Heaven is and what it feels like, but I'm certain we were there that night. A couple hours later, I woke up and tippy-toed out of the guest bedroom so as not to disturb Lara. She was smiling in her sleep.

That day was the last day of my obstetrics and gynecology clinical rotation, and I had to be there a bit earlier to complete my paperwork and sign all the delinquent charts. I hated that part of my career the most, but today I felt upbeat and happy to do anything. I couldn't stop smiling.

At some point, Poline, our grumpy head nurse, asked me if I could give her some of the "happy pills" I was taking.

"Poline, those pills won't help you, my dear," I replied.

"Hey, Baby Doc, can you stay with us a bit longer? Maybe whatever it is will rub off on me," Poline said, rewarding me with one of her exceedingly rare smiles. "I had to add one more patient to your schedule today.

358

I promise it will be your last patient... not a one more. You'll be done at four—still an hour earlier than usual. Am I good to you, or am I good to you?"

"You're always good to me, Poline. I swear I'll miss you."

"Promises, promises..." Poline carped on her way out.

The day flew by effortlessly, until Poline brought me the chart for my last patient.

"I do not want to see her," I pleaded with Poline. "Give her to Doctor Rubin, please."

"She didn't want to disclose the nature of her problem to me, but she insisted on being seen only by you. She is kinda a pain in the ass, but she's your last one for today. Just deal with her and be done. I'll bring her in," Poline said and left the room.

Svetlana walked in with Poline right behind her. She looked jittery and nervous.

"Please, nurse, can you leave us alone? It's a strictly private matter," she said.

"I have to be present during your exam," Poline insisted.

"There will be no exam, Poline," I said. "Can you leave us alone for a few minutes?"

Poline shrugged her shoulders and left the room.

"You promised to call me and never did," Svetlana said, biting the corner of her bottom lip.

"What are you talking about, Svetlana? We talked on the phone just two nights ago."

"Yes, we did, but you promised to call back."

"I said in a couple of weeks, after my finals. Don't you recall? You were a student at some point. You know how it is during finals."

"What is happening to us? You sound cold and distant all of a sudden."

I looked at her and took a deep breath. "Kuznetsky Most Street, number seventeen. Does that ring a bell to you?"

"What about it?" she asked almost innocently.

"I saw you there…"

"So what? I was visiting my girlfriend who lives there on the fourth floor."

"Do you have to wear your uniform when paying your girlfriend a visit, Comrade Second Lieutenant?"

Svetlana's face turned pale, and she began shivering. "I am employed by the State Security," she said very quietly. "I couldn't disclose it to you. How did you find out?"

"Do not underestimate me, Svetlana." I responded as enigmatically as I could muster. "Did it ever cross your mind that we may report to the same boss? Comrade Colonel Shatura. His office is down the hall from where you are. Suite number eleven."

"Alex, I am stunned. I wasn't aware of that, and if

you think that I was spying on you, you're dead wrong. I was not! I could not... because... I am in love with you."

"I was not sure if you were spying on me or not. I wanted to check it out, so I decided to lure you to a locker at the Leningradsky Railroad Station terminal. I rented it, put a satchel filled with blank paper inside, and hired a bum to open it. Stop lying. You know the rest. Whatever we had or had not... Sorry, but it's over now." I got up, ready to leave.

"It can't be over. Don't do this, Alex, please! Stop!" Svetlana cried out.

"Give me one reason. Just one!" I said, putting my hand on the door handle.

"I love you," she said.

"Go fly a kite, Svetlana. I loved you too... at some point..." I opened the door and walked away.

Chapter Twenty Five
Two Weddings

A month before our graduation, Lara and I got married at the regional city hall. We were standing in front of the People's Deputy, who was officiating the ceremony. Across her oversized chest, the woman wore a wide red sash with a golden imprint of the Soviet Union's coat of arms.

Zhenya, who was a witness, stood to my right. Since Nate, being a foreigner, was not allowed to serve as a witness, Lara's brother Valery took his place to the left of his sister. Both sets of our parents, Zhenya's wife Rosa and their son Jake, Aunt Anna, and a few of our friends stood slightly behind us.

The People's Deputy pompously read her standard fifteen-minute speech about the importance of the family as a building block in the foundation of our glorious communist future. At some point, her soliloquy, which was filled with clichés and platitudes, and her grotesque delivery became almost circus-like. She sounded so fake and annoying that Lara and I looked at each other a few times and could not hold back our chuckles any longer.

The People's Deputy paused, looked at us with

anger and disdain, and then gave us a stern warning: *If our demeanor did not change immediately, she would cancel the entire ceremony.* Lara and I stopped laughing, apologized, put serious expressions on our faces, and tried to maintain them for as long as we physically could.

The People's Deputy rushed to finish her speech and, without even looking in our direction, concluded the ceremony. "Long live our glorious Communist Party, its distinguished Central Committee, and its General Secretary Leonid Ilyich Brezhnev! By the authority vested in me, I now pronounce you husband and wife. You can pick up your marriage certificate at the reception window on the first floor."

Lara and I got our certificate, walked outside, and then gave each other a long kiss as we stood on the steps of the city hall. Then, surrounded by family and friends, we exchanged our wedding rings and broke into incessant laughter.

"Can anything in this country ever be done normally?" asked Nate. "Why was that woman in charge—the one with the red sash over her oversized bosom—acting as if you were her subjects? Why did the two of you have to be treated with such contempt? Why was the happiest occasion of your lives—getting married—transformed into a disparaging mockery? Why? You don't have to answer; these are just rhetorical questions ... But it's truly mind-boggling to me."

"Everybody, please come to our apartment," announced my dad. "We have to welcome the newlyweds and raise a toast or two to their happiness. I can't promise that it will be fancy, but Mom has put all her love into everything she's cooked and baked over the last few days."

"Who cares about the fancy part?" Aunt Anna added. "The wedding reception is nothing more than a fancy gift wrap for the priceless gift of love. The gift wrap is always discarded, but the gift itself should last a lifetime. Let's go and celebrate! Hey, sis, do you mind if I bring a couple of friends? The kids already know them, and I bet they would be very happy to see them at the table."

"The more the merrier," my mom responded. "Bring them along."

"Who are you bringing, Auntie?" I was curious.

"Pavel and Boris, if you don't mind."

"The general and the professor?"

"Yes. They both asked if they could be included."

"I'm honored. What a surprise!" I said.

"I'll be delighted to have them with us," Lara added. "Thank you a thousand times for being in our life, Aunt Anna. This day would not have happened without you."

"In more ways than one could ever imagine..." I added.

Right after the wedding, Lara's parents persuaded us to move into Lara's old bedroom in their log cabin in Obiralovka. The room was snug but cozy, and Lara's folks were warm and friendly. The only difficult part was the long commute to our new workplace, which was actually the same place where we had studied medicine for seven years.

Despite the fact that the medical school journal had declined to publish my apology letter, Dr. Plotkin had kept his word. A day before graduation, Lara and I were appointed to the clinical faculty of the medical school's affiliate, the Pirogova Hospital complex, and our busy lives started to regain some semblance of normalcy. We loved what we were doing, and, most importantly, we loved each other beyond belief. Seemingly, everything was okay; yet, something was missing.

"We are so lucky to be where we are. Just enjoy it," Lara said to me one day.

"I love you dearly," I replied, "and I know that we were destined to be together. We both worked our asses off to get where we are, but what's really troubling me is that it feels like we didn't deserve it … like nothing rightfully belongs to us … like we didn't accomplish anything on our own. The truth of the matter is that if not for Aunt Anna and her friends, we could never even have survived let alone achieved anything. Life is still like a frigging game of chess! Aren't you tired of it?"

To make matters even worse, one day *Voice of America* brought us the great news that Andrey Simyavsky would soon complete his sentence and would be set free. But immediately thereafter, we learned that he had been stripped of his Soviet citizenship, issued an exit visa, and put on a plane to France, where he would settle somewhere in a small town near Paris. God only knew if I would ever have the chance to see him again.

Instead of a late honeymoon, Lara and I took a short train trip to Vilnius, the capital of the Soviet Republic of Lithuania, located on the shores of the Baltic Sea. Zhenya and Rosa had invited us to the full-fledged traditional Jewish wedding of a couple of their friends. It was the first time that Lara and I were exposed to the "real thing," as Zhenya put it. The ceremony was so mystical, endearing, and beautiful that I promised myself that, one day, Lara and I would stand under the *huppah*, the wedding canopy, and would be married the *right* way.

We also learned that a large number of Lithuanian Jews were immigrating to Israel. After the ceremony, Zhenya introduced us to a young couple that had gotten married less than a year before and were now expecting their first child. In a few days, they were set to leave the Soviet Union for Jerusalem, where they would settle for good.

"Do you have any family there?" I asked. "Some friends, maybe?"

"No," they replied, placing their arms around each other's shoulders. "We have no relatives there. Not even a friend, strictly speaking ... But there are five million fellow Jews living in Israel. They are our family. Like every family, we might be dysfunctional at times, but also like every family, we always care for each other. We grew tired of being treated like unwanted stepchildren. That's why we're leaving everything behind to start a new life."

"It's so precariously frightening," Lara said. "I hope everything will turn out fine for you."

"Hope?" the young lady retorted. "Hope has nothing to do with it; it's about confidence! It is confidence in God's promise to bring his people home. Confidence, my friends!"

"But you are expecting ... Aren't you afraid?" Lara persisted.

"No, we are not afraid! What do we have to lose? We were anxious for the whole year while we waited for our exit visas. Now we are scared that we might be stopped at the last minute. We are terrified of letting our children experience the horror of institutional hatred and bigotry that our parents and we had to endure every day of our lives. We are not afraid of the freedom to be who we are. One day, when you have nothing to lose, you will be making the same decision. Do not be afraid!"

"Easier said than done," I said. "All the best to you, guys,"

"Good luck to you too! Don't be afraid to be free," they answered.

On the way to our hotel, I said to Zhenya, "That young couple was so amazing. They are leaving in a few days, but they've already started their new lives. Did you notice their demeanor? They were so optimistic and full of conviction."

"They are lucky. Rosa and I were the same. Rosa was pregnant with Jake when we got the refusal to our first emigration request. What those guys said was right. The confidence that we will be able to get out of this hell one day is what has kept us alive. Do you mind if we all walk back to our hotel? I need a cigarette," Zhenya asked.

"Not at all," Lara said. "The night is so beautiful."

"But how does the whole thing start, Zhenya?" I continued. "Where do the people apply, and why is it that just a few can do it?" I tried to understand.

"The Soviets," Zhenya explained, lighting his cigarette, "are toying with the growing Western demands for the reunification of the families separated by war.

To apply, one needs to receive an official invitation—a reunification request or so-called *vyzov*—from a relative residing abroad. Take this couple you just met, for example. If you wanted to receive a *vyzov*, you would give them your name and address, and upon their arrival in Israel, they would pass your information to the Israeli immigration agency, the *Sohnut*. In a few months, the *Sohnut* would 'locate' your far-removed 'cousin'—the one you never knew existed before—who would, in turn, sign that vyzov and send it to you through the official channels with the full complement of governmental seals and ribbons."

"Would that distant cousin be for real?" Lara asked.

"Most likely not, but nobody cares, including the Soviets. Every case is decided individually, and the Soviets use the number of emigration permits issued as their bargaining chips to squeeze from the West whatever they are in dire need of at any given time. It could be Canadian wheat today, American corn tomorrow, or Dutch cheese next week ... They don't give a shit."

"And then what?" I asked.

"Take my case. After I got my *vyzov*, I went to OVIR, the department responsible for processing emigration permits and providing exit visas, where I registered and received all the necessary application forms and the list of documents I had to submit. After getting everything together—a task in and of itself—I paid the required duty and submitted the documents. I had to renounce my Soviet citizenship and pay a fee for that. If I do not want to be a citizen, I am a traitor.

"Then comes the trap—the requirement to obtain the character affidavit from your place of employment and the statement from your residence superintendent, encouraging your employer to fire you and to make people around you aware of what this particular 'traitor' is up to. Then there are numerous mandatory collective meetings between you, your coworkers, and your neighbors to stigmatize you as a renegade Zionist.

"So, I was officially branded an 'enemy of the people' and had to wait three long months for the response to my application. Then my application came back with a red stamp *REFUSED* across the front page. You know the rest. After you have learned what it takes to go through all that, you should clearly understand why so few among us are brave or desperate enough to do it."

"It boggles my mind how tortuous and conniving the system is." I was baffled and frustrated.

Not a word more was said until we walked into the lobby of our hotel; we were full of thoughts and emotions brought back from that wedding night. We wished Rosa and Zhenya good night and went to our room.

"I can't stop thinking about that pregnant girl emigrating in a couple of days," Lara said.

I tried to cheer her up. "If everything goes well for them, their kid will be born an Israeli citizen."

"Lucky kid," Lara sighed. "Unfortunately, ours won't be that lucky."

"Don't be such a pessimist," I said. "You never know."

"I'm not a pessimist, and I do know ... It's just not enough time." She looked at me and smiled.

"Why not?" I asked, clueless.

"Come closer, silly, and give me a kiss," Lara said. "I'm pregnant."

Chapter Twenty Six

The Last Drop

When our son was born, we named him Vladimir —Vlad for short—to honor the memory of my hero brother who had lost his life fighting Nazi Germany in the war and whom I had never met. When I looked at our little bundle of joy for the first time, I knew right away that our son would grow to be everything we could wish. He would become a reflection of us: the pride of our present and the hope for our future. I wished, most of all, that he would grow up to be more than just a son to me; I hoped that he would become my brother, my confidant, and my closest friend.

Maybe it was an attribute of every parent—or maybe it was just me—but almost every day, I repeated the same promise I made to myself the day he was born: I would do everything and anything possible and impossible to make his life, in general, and his childhood, in particular, better and brighter than mine had ever been. I took an oath that he would never experience hunger. I would teach him how to be proud and strong, even when confronted by blatant and causeless hatred. I promised to guard him from the calamities and misfortunes I had experienced while growing up.

When Vlad turned two years old, we lucked out; we managed to get a small, one-bedroom condo in the Sokol neighborhood of Moscow. Soon thereafter, we moved from Obiralovka back to the city. It was an *enormous* upgrade from our nine-by-nine room at my in-laws' log cabin. We genuinely enjoyed the luxury of our condo and having our own living room, kitchen, and bathroom.

Even the everyday struggle to put food on our table was no longer the same. We didn't have to spend three hours commuting, so we now had three extra hours a day to stand in line procuring groceries. For the most part, everything was going according to plan ... until a few months after we celebrated Vlad's fourth birthday.

That day, I was coming home from the hospital. As always, I stopped at the daycare center to pick Vlad up and take him home. He was already waiting for me inside the courtyard. I gave him a big hug and tried to put him on my shoulders for our walk back home. That had been our tradition lately. This time, he didn't want to do it and started to cry.

"Did I hurt your arm, my little man? I'm sorry," I said.

He looked at me with eyes full of tears. "It's not my arm, Daddy. I just don't want to be a fucking Jew anymore," he quietly announced and started to cry.

"What did you say?" My jaw dropped. "Where did you hear that word?"

"At lunch. Varvara Stepanovna, my teacher, called me a fucking Jew today when I didn't want to eat pickled herring. You know, Daddy, it's not my fault. When I eat pickled herring, I always throw up. Why did she say fucking Jew so many times? What does that word mean? Does it mean I'm a bad kid?"

"You're a great kid. What she said isn't even worth talking about. Do not repeat it. Only stupid people say those things."

"But the other kids started making fun of me, saying the word over and over. No one wants to play with me anymore. They said they hate me because I'm a Jew. I don't want to be a Jew! Help me, Daddy! Please, help me …"

"Let's make a deal, Vlad." I kneeled down in front of my little man. "You are not going back to that place. Done. Try to imagine that it never happened. Mommy and I will talk it over tonight and decide what to do next. Is that okay with you, bud?"

"Okay. But *what* are we going to do next, Daddy?" Vlad stopped sobbing.

"Next, we are going home, and we'll have dinner together … all three of us—you, me, and Mommy."

"Can I have an ice-cream cone after dinner, please?" Vlad pleaded with me.

"Of course, you can, sweetheart."

"Even if Mommy says no?"

"I'll tell Mommy that it was totally my fault because I had already promised you one," I reassured him.

"I love you, Daddy! You're the best!"

"You're the best, my buddy," I said. "Will you climb up on my shoulders now?"

"Yep! Let's do it, Daddy. Pick me up, please."

I put Vlad on top of my shoulders, and we walked home together, pretending that nothing had happened.

I will never forget that day—the day when Lara and I were confronted with the most critical and life-shattering decision we had ever had to make. When Vlad went to bed, the two of us sat at the kitchen table, and I was finally able to tell Lara about what had transpired at the daycare center earlier that day.

"Oh my God! I knew this would happen sooner or later. What are we going to do?" Lara asked. "Today is Friday. We have the weekend to figure out what to do with Vlad's daycare. Maybe I can talk to one of our neighbors.

"Do you remember Asya Vasylevna, the widow who lives on the third floor? She babysat Vlad on a couple of occasions last year. She enjoyed being with him so much that she even refused to be paid for it. I will talk to her tomorrow to find out if she can do it on a regular basis now and agree to be paid this time around."

"Do you know," I said to Lara, "this is like a frigging curse? I clearly remember when I was a couple years older than Vlad ... maybe I was five or six ... I had exactly the same conversation with my Dad. He told me then that I had to learn how to cope."

"Not to fight, just to cope? For God's sake!" Lara shook her head.

"Listen, he was trying to convince me that since we can't change the world, we have to conform to it. You know better than anybody that I didn't listen to his advice."

"I do," Lara said, "and you ended up in jail."

"Maybe my dad was right," I answered.

"He did not have another choice then. Everybody was just trying to survive," Lara replied in my Dad's defense.

"Those were different times," I said. "Stalin was still alive, and everyone was indoctrinated or beaten into submission to believe that the world was the same everywhere and that we, living in the Soviet Union, made our part of the world much better than anywhere else. Like the descendants of the French revolutionaries of Robespierre's time, while the opponents of the regime were being imprisoned and executed in great numbers, the brainwashed and underfed masses blindly believed in the utopian promise of *Liberté, Egalité et Fraternité* for 'everyone' and eagerly agreed to conform.

"We know it was just a slogan. We learned a thing or two since Stalin's death. When knuckleheaded Nikita Khrushchev let the freedom genie out of the bottle, we had a chance to open our eyes and look around. We knew by now that, in some places, the world is really good—way better than ours. The most important part of it is that we, the Jews, are no longer the homeless pariahs. We have our place in the world that we can call home. We have Israel now!

"In the last few years, Brezhnev and his cohorts succeeded in rolling back most of Khrushchev's changes. This country of ours will always be the proverbial shit hole of the world. It will never allow its own people to learn what freedom is. For as long as the communists poison the mood of the populace and keep it hungry and in the dark, nothing good can ever happen here. Maybe we don't have to change this world; maybe we just have to change what part of the world we have to be in."

"Are you talking about what I think you're talking about?" Lara's eyes were wide open.

"You and I have had enough of that poison," I

continued. "Do we really want to conform to it—to stay here and make Vlad live his life like we did? Do we really want him to inherit the same crap, trying to merely survive each and every day? Screw our limited, selfish aspirations! Do we have the guts to put everything on the line so he can prosper?"

"I think we do ..." Lara replied.

"I'm sure we do. It's all about our son ... our only son. What do you say? There's a place somewhere in the free world where he can achieve everything he's capable of. We have to leave everything behind and take him there. Isn't that why we brought him into this life?"

Lara was sitting quietly and staring at me. "How long do you think it would take?" she finally asked.

"Could take a year, maybe longer. Look at Zhenya, Rosa, and Jake ... God forbid."

"But we are not nuclear scientists. How many state secrets do we know? Why would they refuse us?"

"Because they can. They don't need a reason."

"Do you think we'll be able to survive?" Lara asked.

"As long as we have each other," I answered. "Look at what the two of us have already survived."

"It's not about us," she said. "It's all about Vlad and his future. I say it's worth a try. I don't want our son to suffer for the rest of his life. He will understand one day if we fail, but he will never forgive us for not trying."

"Let's hope that day will never come," I said.

"Hope?" Lara asked suddenly and got up. "Do you remember what that pregnant girl said to us in Vilnius?"

I rose to my feet as well. "Please remind me …"

Lara grabbed my shoulders and drove her response right into my head. "She said that hope had nothing to do with their decision; it was all about confidence! It is now about our confidence in God's promise to bring his people home. What do we have to lose? The freedom we never had?"

"And what do we have to gain?" I asked her in return.

Lara and I looked at each other for a moment and answered in the same breath, "The freedom we never had!"

Chapter Twenty Seven

Vyzov

The next morning, I showed up at Zhenya's apartment unannounced. Zhenya, Rosa, and Jake were sitting at the kitchen table, eating breakfast.

Zhenya answered the door. "Good to see you, genius. What, you couldn't figure out how to use the phone?"

"I did try to call you, but your line was busy."

"I was on the phone with our friends in Vilnius. You remember the Kuritzkis whose wedding we were invited to not long ago?"

"Of course, I remember them, Zhenya. How could I forget that wedding?"

"What happened to your sense of time, my dear husband?" Rosa asked. "Not long ago? It's been almost five years! Are you losing your mind, Eugene Baras? Alex, grab a chair and have a cup of coffee with us."

"Five years ago ... Really?" Zhenya mumbled.

"I'm positive!" I said, joining them at the table. "That's when Lara told me she was pregnant."

"Wow! Time flies. It feels like it was just yesterday. Anyway, believe it or not, the Kuritzkis are leaving for Israel next week."

"Then the timing is perfect," I said. "Believe it or not, we've had enough of things here as well. Last night, Lara and I decided that it's time for us to get out of here ... and the sooner, the better. Can you call the Kuritzkis before they leave and ask them to procure a *vyzov* for the three of us when they land at the Ben Gurion Airport in Tel Aviv next week?"

"I knew you would finally come to it." Zhenya smiled. "Mazel tov! I'll call the Kuritzkis right away. Can I ask you what tipped the scale?"

"I don't want to give you all the ugly details in front of Jake. It's all about Vlad's future."

"Are we going to Israel with Vlad? That's awesome, Uncle Alex!" Jake jumped in his chair.

"I hope that's the case, Jake," I replied.

Zhenya was already working the phone in the next room.

"Write down your full names, dates and places of birth, and your mailing address as well. I want it exactly as it is on all your documents!" he yelled through the open door.

I wrote down everything Zhenya asked for on a piece of paper and gave it to him. He was off the phone within a few minutes.

"Done!" he said. "In about three months, give or take, your *vyzov* should arrive in the mail. Now we have to work on your 'legend.'"

"What legend?" I was at a loss.

"The story of how your family is related to the person sending you that *vyzov*. You will have to explain that in your application. Since official public records didn't come into existence here until the late nineteen twenties, it's always better to start from far back—like before the Bolshevik Revolution or the Civil War—so nobody can trace and substantiate the validity of your claim," Zhenya explained.

"Didn't you tell me some time ago that the authorities couldn't care less about that?"

"I think I did, in general terms, but with you, it's too personal, and it's better to be ready for anything. Why would we give them another reason to reject your application?"

"You will have to coach me in all this. You have quite extensive experience," I said.

"Unfortunately, I do," Zhenya replied. "Anytime you wish. Do you want to start tomorrow?"

"Let's do it," I said. "Now, I have to break the news to Aunt Anna and my parents. It won't be easy. Wish me luck," I said, and then I went to talk to Aunt Anna first.

"Good morning!" Aunt Anna gave me a hug. "Are you by yourself? Can I offer you some coffee? Where is the rest of the Alexander clan?"

"Lara and Vlad are on their way to Obiralovka to

see Lara's parents. She has to talk something over with them."

"She's not pregnant again, is she?"

"No, she's not, Auntie."

"Vlad is such a delightful kid. You should have another child."

"It's not the right time now, Aunt Anna."

"I don't get it. Why isn't it the right time?"

"That's what I came to talk to you about … Lara and I have decided that we have to apply for an emigration permit."

Aunt Anna's face turned pale.

"Are you okay, Auntie?"

I saw her arms drop. I rushed to help her as she slumped into an armchair and started to cry. I gave her a glass of water, kneeled down next to her, and tried to calm her down.

"I knew it was coming sooner or later! I just knew it!" she wept. "When you and Lara came back from that Jewish wedding in Vilnius, you were so excited when you were telling me what you experienced there and about the people you met. You witnessed first-hand the start of the new exodus. I just knew that you caught the bug right then. I was terrified that, at any moment, you would come up with an exit strategy … and now here we are, nearly five years later…"

"It's not so much about Lara and me. We have

survived so far and probably could endure some more. It's mostly about Vlad. Why do I have to subject my only son to a future filled with the ugliness of baseless hatred in a country that denies him even the basic freedom to be what he is and achieve what he's capable of achieving?"

"Alex, you're right, and it's so unfortunate. I can't blame you for your decision, sweetheart. It's an enormous burden by itself, but you shouldn't subject your son to that kind of future if you have even a small chance of giving him the life he deserves. You, of all people, have already tasted enough of our regime's poison. But my heart is torn. All three of you are the light of my life, and without you nearby, it will be dark and worthless."

"Auntie, I swear we won't be apart for too long. Regardless of how long it will take for us to get out of here, I will never stop fighting for you, Mom, and Dad to reunite with us wherever the three of us will be."

"What do you mean, 'wherever'?" Aunt Anna asked. "Wouldn't Israel be your final destination?"

"'Wherever' means that the most important goal for us at this stage is to cross the Soviet border. Our exit visas will state that we are leaving the Soviet Union for permanent residency in Israel, but in full compliance with the tradition of blatant, convoluted mockery, the regime will only allow us to purchase our fare to Vienna, Austria. There, 'the traitors will be left on their own.'

"Well, not so fast, bastards! Luckily, I was told that, right at the Vienna airport, the representatives of the *Sohnut*, the Israeli immigration service, and HIAS, the Hebrew Immigrant Aid Society, worldwide Jewish resettlement assistance agency, should be waiting for us. A whole new free world will be opened to us. For the first time, we will have a choice; nobody will even attempt to force our decision.

"Most likely, we could end up in Israel, but there are so many other Jewish communities, in the United States, Canada, Australia, you name it, working relentlessly to get the Jewish people from the Soviet Union to the other side of the Iron Curtain and to help every new immigrant start a new life wherever they wish. We will work out all the details later. The main goal for us now is to survive the waiting game and try to stay employed."

"I saved some money and will help you to survive if you or Lara get fired."

"Auntie, this is not a matter of money. A new 'anti-parasite' decree was issued secretly less than a year ago. If anyone is not gainfully employed for more than ninety days, the authorities have the discretion to declare that person 'a societal parasite,' to place him or her under arrest, and to commit 'the parasite' to the forced labor camps for a period of five to ten years. That was done to discourage the Jews from applying for emigration permits."

"They thought of every possible obstacle, every roadblock. Rotten scoundrels! There is no limit to how low they will go and how cruel their regime can become. But I still think most of my real friends, like Doctor Plotkin, won't let you down and will do anything to keep you and Lara employed for as long as it takes," Aunt Anna said. "After the three of you leave, I will have nothing else holding me back here. Promise me that you'll do everything you can to make sure we're reunited as soon as possible."

"Auntie, you mean everything to me. I will never rest till all of us are together again." I gave Aunt Anna a big hug, and we stood embraced for a few moments in unsettled silence. "I have to talk to Mom and Dad now," I finally said. "Wish me luck."

"No, you're not going there. I know how to handle your mom, and she knows how to handle your dad. Leave it to me. You have a lot to worry about. I'll take care of it. I love you. Go now ..." Aunt Anna gave me a kiss and opened the door.

Lara and Vlad came back home at around three o'clock. I just looked at them, unable to ask how everything had gone on their end.

"My parents asked me to vow that we will all be

reunited in a couple of years. I did. What about your folks and Aunt Anna?" Lara asked.

"I talked to Aunt Anna and promised her the same. She insisted that I let her deal with my parents on her own. I gave in. She knows what she's doing. Aunt Anna told me that she is confident that Doctor Plotkin will help to keep us employed for as long as it takes," I said.

"Let's hope it won't take too long," Lara replied.

Two and a half months later, I was going through our mail when I saw the large green envelope. Inside was our *vyzov*, decorated with colorful ribbons holding the red glossy wafer of the seal of the State of Israel. I set it down and suddenly broke out in tears.

I didn't know why, but I just lost it. Maybe it was the realization that from this point, there was no way to turn back, or maybe it was the fear that all three of us would become refuseniks. After clearing my head, I realized the source of my tears. Amid the tribulations of the unknown, I felt an overwhelming sense of pride that I was holding in my hands the promise of our future, secured by the red seal of the State of Israel.

Chapter Twenty Eight
Hotel National

A lmost a year had passed since we had applied for emigration permit and submitted all the required documents to OVIR. Typically, the decision to grant or refuse emigration permission would be rendered in three to four months. In our case, the delay was unusual and nerve-wracking. Every extra day of waiting for the answer was becoming increasingly torturous. After five months, I began to call OVIR's office every couple of weeks to inquire about the status of our application. The answer was the same every time: *Your case is under review. You will be notified when a decision has been made.*

I was staring into the bone-chilling abyss of the unknown …

"It's kinda strange, but at least you didn't get a refusal. I know that shitty feeling," Zhenya said to me one day. "I experienced it a few years back. But lately the tide is starting to change. There is a very strong movement erupting in the Western world right now to compel the Soviets to abide by the provisions of the Helsinki agreement they signed on the issue of freedom of emigration and the reunification of the families separated by war.

"Keep your fingers crossed because anything could happen soon. In the meantime, listen to my advice: Live day by day, and try not to think about it if you don't want to lose your mind. Just numb yourself to it. It's all designed to break your spirit. Do not succumb to it. Deep inside, keep your dream alive, and try to hold on to your job for as long as you can. Things can always get worse."

"Zhenya, I love you, man, but your sense of optimism is mortifying!" I replied.

Fortunately, as Aunt Anna had predicted, Dr. Plotkin was true to his promise to keep Lara and me employed. The Emergency Department and its surgical team were chronically short-staffed, which meant that Lara's position was somewhat secure, as long as she was willing to work extended shifts and some weekends. To secure my employment, Dr. Plotkin personally hand-picked what sorts of patients were assigned to my service. I was given an exclusive stream of celebrities, elite athletes, and Communist party apparatchiks.

For mostly selfish but practical reasons, no one else among our staff wanted to deal with that specific group of *prima donnas* anyway, since all of those patients were the highly demanding, pain-in-the-ass, hard-to-deal-with individuals, and any little mistake or legitimate complication could become a career breaker. So my colleagues were happy with Dr. Plotkin's choice and almost sympathetic and grateful to me for sifting the unpleasant and burdensome responsibility away from them.

Time and again, the head of our HR department, Ivan Salupo, a known KGB liaison, applied pressure on Dr. Plotkin to get rid of me. Dr. Plotkin always used the same excuse: *The continuity of medical care for the distinguished Comrade X could not be jeopardized, and if Comrade Salupo himself were brave enough to assume personal responsibility and accept the inevitable liability, he was free to do so on his own volition.* Salupo, as a true bureaucrat, did not have the guts to assume any responsibility and cautiously backed off every time impatiently lying in wait for the next opportunity to strike.

The month of April finally brought to Moscow that long-awaited spring breeze, liberating us from the frigid doldrums of the hungry and seemingly endless winter. In spite of this, countless long lines still encircled the bakeries and grocery stores as people waited for the erratic bread deliveries. The warmer weather helped to unfreeze the endless crowds, making them more vocal and animated. The unhappy buzz hanging in the air grew increasingly louder, assigning the blame for the miserable wheat crop that had befallen the motherland for the last three years on everything possible and everyone in charge.

The news that, back in January, the new President of the United States Gerald Ford had signed into law the Jackson–Vanik amendment to the Trade Reform Act caused a ruckus and resentment among the unsettled and frustrated proles. This amendment was meant to enforce the restrictions on commercial interaction with the Soviet bloc countries. It made the trade concessions and low-interest loans contingent on their governments' respect for the right to emigrate. It was the trigger point to start blaming the shortage of bread, the staple food of the nation, on the so-called *selfish Jews, who wanted to stir up trouble with their undeserved egocentric emigration rights* when the homeland was being victimized by mother nature, and couldn't gather enough bread to feed their own hungry populace.

Never mind the inept communist centralized planning system, the fractured and disinterested agricultural workforce, and the failed utopia of collective farming on the previously expropriated and presently dilapidated lands ... *The Jewish conspiracy*, like the proverbial scapegoat, was expediently blamed for any and every calamity. On countless occasions, "patriotic" anti-Semitism was used as a pressure release valve to be opened or closed at the whim of the few who ruled the country at any given moment.

May started with four days off—the first and second of May due to May Day, a national holiday, followed by Saturday and Sunday. Lara, Vlad, and I were at home that Thursday evening when our phone rang. It was Zhenya.

"Hey, genius, would it be okay if Nate and I came over in twenty minutes or so? Something is going to happen soon, and we have to talk it over. Last night, I discovered that my apartment is bugged. I'll check if your place would be safe for us to meet."

"Of course, it's okay. Come right over; we're waiting for you."

By the time Zhenya and Nate arrived, I had put a bottle of Ararat, the Armenian brandy, and a tin of Red October chocolates on the kitchen table. It had all come from the accumulated stash of booze and sweets that our patients at the clinic handed to each of us every other day as a customary sign of gratitude. Lara cut a couple of lemons into thin slices, placed them on a plate, and sprinkled them with sugar and ground coffee. That simple brandy chaser, named *Nicholashki* after Czar Nicholas II who reportedly came up with the recipe during his reign, had become very popular among our friends.

Meanwhile, Zhenya was inspecting our wall outlets, lighting fixtures, and our two telephones and checking them out with a small electronic device of his own design.

"All clear. Your place is not bugged ... yet," he finally announced.

I poured the Ararat into the shot glasses.

"Let's have a drink in honor of our four-day mini vacation," I said. "Today is Thursday, tomorrow is Friday, and then Saturday and Sunday will follow. Four days off ... It's like a dream come true!"

"There's another reason to celebrate," Nate said somberly. "Yesterday, US Ambassador Graham Martin and the remaining eleven US marines left Saigon, lifting off from the US embassy roof. The Vietnam War is officially over."

We all emptied our shot glasses and chased our brandy with Nicholashki.

"That was heavenly!" Zhenya exclaimed. "However, Nate and I came here to slightly alter your plans for this weekend."

"What a surprise!" I responded with a smile. "Luckily, Lara and I don't have any set plans. What's up?"

"This morning, I got news that the US congressional delegation, accompanied by high-ranking officials of the US Commerce Department, are arriving in Moscow as we speak to hold top-level trade negotiations with the Soviet Politburo for the next three days," Nate started to explain. "My contact at the US embassy told me that during last January's negotiations in connection with the Jackson–Vanik amendment, our side was stone-walled by the Soviets, who had repudiated our claim that a significant number of Soviet Jews were denied permits to emigrate to the State of Israel, and they vehemently rejected the existence of refuseniks.

"Our side could not win the argument. We had the facts, but we didn't have the hard, verifiable evidence in our hands to prove it. I was asked to help find out on short notice if a list of refuseniks did exist and, if so, to figure out a way for a someone from that group to deliver the list directly into the hands of the members of the congressional delegation or their staff."

"I talked to the Bonners already," Zhenya added. "They keep such a list, and it's constantly being updated. Their group is verifying the number of the most recent entries, and the entire list of more than three thousand family names will be finalized and ready by noon tomorrow."

"We have to find a way to pass this list to the members of the delegation," Nate continued, "so they can present it to the Politburo as evidence and shove it right into their lying faces. I doubt if anyone would be able to approach the members of the delegation directly; the KGB will tightly guard them at all times. But, according to my source, the congressional staffers will be staying at the Hotel National in Manezhnaya Square, where the security won't be as tight."

"To make a long story short," Zhenya said, "I know someone at that hotel who is in charge of janitorial services. His name is Misha Gubkin, and he owes me a favor. A couple years ago, I used to tutor his son in preparation for the university physics exams, and he passed them all with flying colors.

"Misha knew the predicament I was in, and he knew that I always needed a job. Occasionally, when the hotel was short of janitors, he would call me for help on short notice, and I always delivered. I talked to him earlier today and asked for his help. He was happy to give me the job for two or three weeks because a couple of his people were on vacation and another couple had called in sick.

"Since I already have the hotel uniform, I just have to report for duty as soon as tomorrow morning. I want you to go to the Bonners around noon tomorrow and wait there for the list. When the list is ready, you have to bring it to the Hotel National. Stay in the lobby and I'll find you there. Can you do that?" Zhenya and Nate were looking at me, waiting for my answer.

"Of course, he can," Lara jumped in without even giving me a chance to respond. "Am I right, Alex? Can I do anything?"

"But of course." Nate got up and gallantly bowed in response. "Can you fill our shot glasses afresh, *Milady*, if you do not mind? This brandy is on par with some bloody French cognac ... and, of course, your Nicholashki ... Nothing could beat them, *Milady*."

"Oh, Nate." Lara shook her head. "You are so full of it, *Milord*. You never take me seriously. You're lucky this *Milady* started to get your sense of humor some time ago; otherwise, *Milord*, your *lordship* would be in big trouble."

"I concede, Lara. You're the toughest gal I know. But, seriously speaking, leave that part to us. Vlad needs you more now. This is the biggest lucky break you guys could ever have. Let's not screw it up," Nate said, raising his shot glass for the second time.

"To our success! To your freedom!"

The next afternoon, at two o'clock, I entered the Hotel National lobby. The list of 3,118 families was securely stuffed inside a plastic pouch, which was under my belt at the small of my back, hidden beneath my shirt and jacket. I sat at the lobby bar and ordered a double espresso. I slowly sipped it while looking around and studying the lobby.

The area was moderately busy. Some people were checking in, and some were leaving. The busboys were whisking by, carrying luggage carts in and out. Nothing was out of the ordinary.

Almost an hour went by, and then I noticed

Zhenya, dressed in his hotel uniform, across the lobby. He was changing the plastic liner inside a trash can. He saw me at the bar and briefly pointed his index finger in the direction of the men's room across from the elevators.

I asked for my check and left a couple of rubles and some change on the counter. I strolled leisurely across the lobby and entered the men's room. I stopped at a sink, turned on the faucet, and started to wash my hands.

The door swung open, and Zhenya entered the room behind his rolling janitor's cart. He checked every stall to make sure that we were alone.

"Did you get the list?" Zhenya asked.

"It's right here," I said, pointing to my back, "safe and sound. How is everything on your end?"

"Squeaky clean." He smiled. "I heard that the morning shift had to sweep the entire fourth floor, and it was closed to all guests. The personnel have been forewarned to stay away from the fourth floor unless specifically assigned there. I bet that's where the Americans will be staying.

"I happen to have the spare key for the back stairs. The doors leading to the back stairs are located at the far end of the hall. If you take the back stairs to the fourth floor, you'll bypass the security desk located next to the elevator at the opposite end of the hall."

"Did I hear you right? You want *me* to go there? I've never been inside this hotel before. Are you serious, Zhenya?" I was startled.

"You bet I'm serious. You're the perfect choice. Look, you're five foot seven and average build. I'm six foot four with bushy red hair. Which one of us is less noticeable?"

"I think I am," I answered. "Okay, so it will be me. What room do I have to go to?"

"Nobody knows yet. You have to call Nate from a payphone in a couple of hours. It is down the hall, to your right, and around the corner. Do not leave the building; they're already beefing up security at the doors.

"Nate is waiting to be briefed by his contact at the American embassy. Tell him I got the key for the back stairs. After you talk to him, stay here in the men's room. Just keep changing stalls from time to time. I'll come back later to find out what Nate told you. I have to go now. Duty calls. Stay awake, genius."

"Yeah, thanks for the warning, buddy. I've never tried to fall asleep on a commode while being sober before." I squeezed a smile and looked at my watch. It was five o'clock.

The two hours passed slowly. At five minutes to seven, I left the men's room and went to the payphone.

"Hi, Nate. It's Alex."

"Are you inside the hotel, old man?"

"Yes, I am. Zhenya shoved me into a men's room stall a couple hours ago."

"Don't complain, old man. That stall could've been inside the lady's room."

"At least it would have been more entertaining," I said. "Zhenya is full of surprises today. By the way, he wants you to know that he got the key for the back stairs."

"Bloody excellent!" Nate exclaimed. "I assume he passed that key to you, right?"

"He did … Wait a minute … Were you in on it with him from the start?"

"We were all in on it, old man. I got the word from the embassy; Congressman Vanik's assistant, Milton Sussman, will be staying in room four twenty-one. He knows that you're delivering the list, and he's expecting you. Listen to his plan step by step.

"In the next hour, Mr. Vanik and a few members of his staff will start a dinner meeting in the restaurant on the second floor of the hotel. At the end of dinner, they'll order drinks and will leave the restaurant to finish their meeting over their drinks in Mr. Sussman's room. They'll be accompanied by Mr. Vanik's security detail, and they'll exit the elevator on the fourth floor at ten o'clock sharp.

"At that time, you should take the back stairs to

the fourth floor and wait behind the door. When they pass the security desk, Milton Sussman will stumble into one of the staffers and drop his glass on the floor. At one minute passed ten on the button, Zhenya must get there with his janitorial cart and start cleaning the mess before the lady at the security desk calls for help.

"Mr. Vanik and his entourage will continue walking in the direction of room four twenty-one, leaving their security detail behind. When the congressman and his staff enter the room, Sussman will rush to the back stairs door and knock on it. That's when you unlock the door, and Milton will lead you back to his room. In the meantime, Zhenya and the congressman's security detail will provide cover by obstructing the view from the security desk down the hall.

"At the conclusion of the meeting, Congressman Vanik will leave the room. A couple of minutes later, you will take the back stairs to the first floor. Mission accomplished. You got it?" Nate asked at the end.

"I got it, Nate. Thank you," I replied.

"Go back to your hideaway, and tell Zhenya about his role. Let's check the time; it's seven ten now."

"Got it," I answered and went back to the men's room.

Zhenya showed up thirty minutes later.

"Did you talk to Nate?" he asked.

"I did. Let's check our watches, and here's his plan . . ."

I was nervous and sweaty. The time was not moving quickly enough. I was changing stalls every twenty minutes. At a quarter to ten, I left the men's room and went down the hall to my right. There were two sets of doors at the very end. I inserted the key in the lock and tried to turn it a few times. I froze when the key did not move. I tried it one more time with no result. I was terrified.

Suddenly, the door swung open, and I bumped into Zhenya pulling his janitor's cart out and looking at me in utter disbelief.

"This is the janitor's closet, genius. Read the sign! I just restocked my cart in there. The door you're looking for is to your left, for Pete's sake. Wake the fuck up!"

I felt so embarrassed that I didn't answer. I just unlocked the door Zhenya was pointing to and ran up the back stairs in total darkness. After climbing eight flights of stairs, I slid my hand along the doorjamb and finally flipped the light switch. I saw an oversized "4" stenciled on the door.

I looked at my watch; it was three minutes to ten. I tried to slow down my breathing. Ten minutes later, I heard a knock and opened the door. I was greeted by a long-haired guy wearing blue jeans and a club jacket over his pink dress shirt.

"Nice to meet you, Alex. I'm Milton Sussman. Follow me. Fast!" he said and rushed me through the open door across the hall. In the room, five people were staring at me. One man, who was wearing a black suit and a bow tie, got up.

"Alex, I am Charles Vanik, member of the House of Representatives of the United States Congress. This is my wartime friend, Hank Douglas; he is the Head of security from our embassy. Please accept our deepest appreciation for meeting with us on such short notice."

The rest of the guys got up and introduced themselves to me one by one.

"I can't thank you all enough for your involvement," I replied. "It's pretty tough surviving the fight for freedom on our own. Here's the list of refuseniks you asked for." I reached behind my back, pulled out the plastic pouch, opened it up, and carefully removed the pages.

"Here are the names of 3,118 families who have been denied emigration permits for no legitimate reason over the last seven years. They are all living in hell. They're called traitors, parasites, enemies of the people—anything but humans—and they're treated as such. Without your help, they have no future, and their very lives are gravely endangered. They are all begging you to get involved and help them to get out of this proverbial pit."

"I was briefed about your particular case, and I now know who you are, Alex. I learned what you went through, and I can understand why you are fed up with your life here. Do you consider yourself a refusenik?" the congressman asked.

"I never got the formal refusal, sir, so my family's name is not on that list. I applied for the emigration permit over a year ago and simply did not get any answer."

"Here's what I want you to do," the congressman said. "Write in yours and your immediate family's names at the end of this list. I, myself, consider you a refusenik, and I will personally challenge the members of the Politburo tomorrow to let you out. And when you are finally out of the Soviet Union, accept my open invitation to come to Cleveland, Ohio, my hometown. There is an exceptionally vibrant and strong Jewish community back home. It may very well become your hometown as well."

"Thank you, Congressman, but if I may," I said, "the names of Eugene Baras and his family are on that list, sir. He is my friend who's a physicist and one of the first refuseniks. He and his family have been struggling to survive for seven long years. Their petition for emigration was rejected when they were expecting their first and only child. His name is Jake, and he will turn seven next month. They were refused the right to emigrate three times. Eugene is somewhere in the hotel right now. He is the one who is mostly responsible for facilitating our meeting."

"Just write down his name next to yours, and I will do everything I can to deliver. I wish all of you the best, Alex. Thank you again for supplying our delegation with this formidable ammunition. Here is my pen." I took the congressman's pen and added the requested names to the list. "Excellent! See you in Cleveland next year ... What do you think?" He got up, smiled at me, folded the list, and put it into the inner pocket of his jacket. He shook my hand firmly before leaving the room.

"Man, oh man," Milton Sussman said. "It couldn't have played out any better. Thank you very much again for your effort. Let me check the hallway." He opened the door and immediately shut it. "Shit! There are two men standing over there studying the back stairwell doors," he whispered. "Somehow, we'll get you out of here safely, Alex. Do not worry."

"Hey, Milt," Hank Douglas said. "Did you get your luggage?"

"I got it this afternoon, Hank. Why do you ask?"

"You and Alex are almost the same size. Do you have an extra pair of blue jeans and a sweater?"

"I happened to put that stuff in my luggage. What do you need it for?" Milton asked.

"Get it out and let Alex change into your jeans and sweater. Then all six of us will walk as a group, staying tightly together, right down the hall and to the elevator," Hank continued. "When we reach the first floor, we will zip out in the same formation from the elevator. My security detail, waiting downstairs, will lead us right through the front door, and into the embassy van parked at the entrance.

"It's pretty dark outside, and I don't think the KGB will have enough time to detect Alex among us since they don't anticipate him being here in the first place. And even if they do, they won't dare do anything as long as we all stay together. We'll ride along to his place and make sure he gets home safely. In case we'd spot the tail we would turn around and bring him inside the embassy. Then, we all have to deal with the rest of it tomorrow."

"Sounds like a plan," Milton said before giving me his oversized sweater and a pair of Levis. "I think it will fit you just right."

"It really does," I said when I was done.

"Here's my Cleveland Indians baseball hat," Milton said. "Sorry, it's kinda worn out... Put it on."

"What do you think?" I asked after getting dressed.

"Awesome," Hank answered. "Now you really look like one of us. Let's roll."

We passed the security desk. The woman on duty behind the desk smiled and waved goodbye to us. We walked into the elevator.

"So far, so good," Hank said. "Looks like she didn't have a clue."

We crossed the front lobby, flanked by Hank's security detail, and got into the black embassy van that was idling right outside the front door.

"Get to the backseat fast," Milton hurried me. Everyone followed and the van started to move steadily in the direction to the American embassy.

"Is anyone following us?" Milton asked.

"Be patient..." Hank responded slowly, studying the traffic. Not a word was said for a few minutes. "Lights off! Sharp to the left, now!" he suddenly barked to the driver, and a second later the van crossed the oncoming traffic and scooted off into the darkness of the night.

"All clear," Hank announced shortly after with a sigh of relief. "I think we pulled it off."

I could only see the lights of the Hotel National slowly fading away behind us.

Chapter Twenty Nine
The Final Call

T he next few weeks were nerve-wracking. Nothing bad happened, but I was still unconvinced that we had "pulled it off," as Hank Douglas had put it during our ride back home inside the American embassy van. It had all seemed unreasonably easy. But when Milton Sussman had spotted a couple of men checking out the doors leading to the back stairs, I had sensed that someone could've been on my heels.

It was simply naïve to believe that we'd left the Hotel National unnoticed and without a tail. I could accept the notion that we had outmaneuvered the hotel security on our way out, but I also knew that the hotel security couldn't hold a match to the KGB's army of informants and their ability to monitor everything and everyone at any given time. They were also quite skillful at retracing any event step by step until they found what they were looking for. Still, the remote chance that we were simply lucky that night was too slim to calm my mind.

Finally, Nate broke the news that all the state-owned newspapers had purposely ignored. He informed us that the American congressional delegation had prevailed at May's negotiations with the Politburo. In the end, the Soviets had succumbed to American demands and made a few concessions to secure the biggest grain deal of the century. The Soviets were not exactly ecstatic about the outcome, but the country would have enough bread for quite a few years to come.

"In the long run, they got what they wanted, and we got a few thousand Soviet Jews. Not a bad deal. After all, it's all about the brain power, if you know what I mean." Nate chuckled. "I wonder how many hundreds of bushels of wheat we had to give up in exchange for you and Zhenya. Just kidding, old man, just kidding. I still hope it was enough."

"You better hope it was enough, Nate. Now they're gonna gang up on us. We have to get out of here ... and the sooner the better. I still doubt I left the hotel undetected that night. Something inside tells me that we were tailed. I am worried sick that we haven't seen the end of it yet."

"It's a classic case of 'postpartum' paranoia, Doctor. Just take two aspirins and call me in the morning."

"I'm not joking, Nate."

"Seriously speaking, everything should work out fine. Trust me. You're not alone anymore. The United States Congress is on your side now. That's nothing to scoff at, believe me. God willing, you'll be out of here soon, my friend."

"Thank you, Nate. Your friendship means a lot to me."

"Same here, old man."

The next couple of weeks came and went uneventfully. My fears started to melt away little by little, and then I got a hair-raising phone call one night.

"Hello?"

"Hi, Alex. This is Svetlana. Don't hang up on me, please. I know that you don't want to talk to me, and that's okay… I understand. You don't have to talk; just listen to what I have to say, please. I learned today that the people in charge of our headquarters at Lubyanka know that it was you who handed the Americans that list …"

"Why are you telling me this?" I interrupted her.

"For the sake of our past, Alex, I just wanted to give you a heads-up."

"We have no past, Svetlana."

"Maybe you don't, but I do … and I'm terribly sorry that I fucked it up. I implore you to be extra vigilant from now on. It's a dangerous game, Alex. It could turn deadly at any point—"

I hung up.

A day later, on Friday, June 20th, I received a summons in the mail. I was commanded to appear at Lubyanka headquarters at nine o'clock on Monday morning, and according to the rules of the proceedings, I was to surrender to the custody of the chief investigator, Colonel Froloff, in connection with criminal case number 78-621/1966. Upon my arrival, I would be required to turn over all my existing ID's, my selective service registration, and my employment verification record book.

It did not look good at all. The case number mentioned was the same one I was tried under previously. *So, the KGB had never closed my case,* I thought when I called Nate.

"I'm in deep shit, Nate. Out of the blue, I received a strange phone call from Svetlana a couple days ago. She wanted to warn me that the KGB knows who delivered the list of refuseniks to the Americans. I just hung up on her. To make things even worse, I just got a summons to appear and a subpoena for all my documents. They even assigned to me the same old case number. I'm afraid I'm gonna be taken into custody by the KGB on Monday morning, and that will be the end of it all. I'll never see the light of day again."

"Do not panic," Nate said. "In the next fifteen minutes, I will notify my bureau chief at the Associated Press and my contacts at the US embassy. Then I'll get in touch with the Consulate of the Embassy of the Netherlands. Since, in the absence of direct diplomatic relations, they represent the interests of the State of Israel in the Soviet Union, I'll ask them to get involved. I can assure you they will all scramble to help. Stay strong, and I'll come over to see you as soon as I'm done."

I spent the rest of the day with my parents and Aunt Anna. God only knew when I would see them again.

When I got home, Nate and Lara were sitting at the kitchen table. On the floor under the table was an open case of Stoli, which had obviously been purchased by Nate at the Beriozka store for foreigners. A partially finished bottle was already on the kitchen table. Lara got up and gave me a hug.

"Everything will be okay," she said. "Please, don't be discouraged. Vlad wanted to stay with Asya Vasylevna overnight, so I took him there. Do you want a shot of Stoli? Nate and I already had some. Nate got a case of it for us at Beriozka. He also bought a huge jar of Norwegian herring, and I've boiled some potatoes. Let's have a feast."

"Why not?" I said. "Let's do it."

Zhenya and Rosa came an hour later. One by one, our friends started to trickle in, and in a couple of hours, our apartment was full of visitors. Professor and Mrs. Bonner came at midnight, just for a moment, to express their support, but they ended up staying for an hour. At around three o'clock on Monday morning, our friends reluctantly left us alone. Rosa and a couple of her girlfriends cleaned up our place so it looked like we hadn't even entertained. They then took the garbage with them on their way out.

Lara and I were totally worn-out and went straight to bed. It all felt like a weird and prolonged wake that had lasted through Saturday and Sunday.

At 6 on Monday morning, Vlad woke us up. We'd had only a couple hours of sleep. I started to prepare all the requested documents while Lara made breakfast.

"Daddy is going on a business trip," Lara said to Vlad when he finished his oatmeal. "Give Daddy a goodbye kiss now."

"When are you coming back, Daddy?" Vlad asked.

"As soon as I can, buddy," I answered, trying to hold back the tears.

"Please be safe, Daddy. Mommy and I will be waiting for you," Vlad said, giving me a hug and a kiss.

I hugged them both and then opened the door.

"I love you. Be safe, Alex," Lara added.

"I love you too. Keep your head up! I'll try to be back soon," I said and closed the door behind me.

I was at the Lubyanka KGB headquarters at nine o'clock. I showed my subpoena at one of the checkpoint cubicles. After I surrendered all my documents, I was escorted to a room on the first floor, where I had to empty all my pockets. Nothing was explained to me, but all the contents of my pockets—my handkerchief, apartment keys, and my five rubles and some loose change—were taken away and stored in a brown paper bag.

I was then handed over to a pair of armed guards and ordered to place my hands behind my neck. I was waiting to be handcuffed, but strangely, it didn't happen. The elevator took us to the seventh floor, where I was placed in an empty room with a single chair in the middle. The door was shut behind me.

It looked as if I had been arrested, yet I hadn't been handcuffed. I still had my belt on, and my wristwatch hadn't been taken away. It all seemed odd and out of place. I had not even been formally processed, which was the usual procedure for incoming arrestees.

I remembered what a prison cell looked like, and this room didn't look like one. An interrogation room would have had a cement or linoleum floor, and the walls would have been spotty and washed out. Here, the parquet flooring had been freshly waxed, and the wallpaper looked clean and new. But if it wasn't an interrogation room, what was it then? At noon, I got up and knocked on the door. A guard opened it and looked at me without saying a word.

"I need to go to the men's room," I said.

"You have to hold it," he answered. "I'll take you there in an hour."

He slammed the door shut. I walked in circles around the room, trying not to wet myself. I was trying to figure out the predicament I was in, but nothing was making any sense. In an hour, the door suddenly opened, and another guard walked into the room.

"Put your hands behind your neck and follow me," he ordered.

At the end of a long corridor, we stopped at a door with the letters "WC" on it.

"Five minutes," the guard stated.

Unable to hold my bladder any longer, I bolted inside the bathroom before he had even finished the word "minutes."

I was taken back to the same room, where I spent another three and a half puzzling hours. I had no clue what to make of it or how it would all turn out. None of it was logical; nothing made sense. Finally, my mind went numb, but I knew that this situation could not persist for too long.

It was four thirty, according to my watch, when the door flew open, and a colonel and a captain walked into the room, followed by two guards. The colonel held his hands behind his back and studied me for a few moments as he rocked back and forth on the heels and toes of his shiny boots.

"Aha! So this is what you look like, you cocksucking kike. The captain and I would love to rearrange your fucking face right now, but we'll leave that for another occasion. So, you got what you wanted?"

I stood there looking down, not knowing what to answer.

"Look at me when I'm talking to you, asshole!"

I raised my head and looked straight at him. He sneered, looking at me with disgust through the narrowed slits of his eyes while still holding something behind his back. For a moment, I saw the corner of a large manila envelope sticking out.

Wait!

There were no manila envelopes in the Soviet Union. They did not exist! I had only ever seen one once when our friends in Vilnius had received their final travel documents from the Dutch consulate. Suddenly, I felt a hint of unexplainable relief. Is that what this sadistic son of a bitch was hiding behind his back?

"I'm sorry, Colonel. I didn't understand your question. Can you repeat it, please?"

"Go fuck yourself, smart-ass!" He pulled the yellow envelope from behind his back and threw it at me. "You have five days to get the fuck out of here."

"Five days?" I said. "Do I still have to pay for surrender of citizenship, exit visas, diplomas, airfare—"

"You bet your fucking ass you have to pay for it!" he interrupted me. "You have to pay for every fucking thing down to the last penny."

"I need a little more time. I need to sell my condo to raise some money. It's impossible to do all of it in just five days."

"Too fucking bad!" The colonel laughed in my face. "In five days, you're out of here. You will go to the West, or to your stinking Israel, or, if you're not gone by then, we will arrange your 'relocation' to the East, to our Siberian labor camps. It's your choice now. Got it, Jew boy? You have till Friday! Guards! Take him downstairs."

My heart pounded joyfully inside my chest. It was as if it wanted to jump out and start dancing along with me all the way down the stairs because of this unpredictable turn of events.

At the checkpoint, I got back the paper bag with my stuff. The five rubles were gone, but I had enough loose change for a bus ride.

"I'm sorry; I don't see the rest of my documents. Will I need them, miss?" I asked with a smile.

"All your documents were confiscated," the young lieutenant attending the checkpoint said. "You should have everything you need inside that yellow envelope. Proceed to the exit." She was looking at me with a hint of a smile. "Good luck to you," she mouthed.

I walked out of the building and ran to the bus stop on the other side of the street.

An hour later, I stepped inside our apartment.

Everything looked like it had the previous night. It was almost surreal. It was as if I had never left the place and the last twelve hours had never happened. All our friends were there, and Lara was standing in the middle of the room, holding Vlad in her arms. A deafening, eerie silence filled the room as everybody looked at me and froze in disbelief.

Vlad was the first one to break the silence. He ran away from Lara and jumped into my arms, screaming, "Daddy, you're back!"

Lara rushed to me and clung to my face, peppering it with kisses. The whole place began to go wild. Our friends became loud and animated. They pulled the three of us into the middle of the room and started plying me with questions, trying to find out what had transpired since they'd seen me last.

I raised the large manila envelope above my head, and everyone instantly went silent like they knew what's in it. Looking straight into my wife's tired and puffy eyes, I quietly said, "We're leaving on Friday!"

Chapter Thirty
Checkmate Run

Everything looked different that Tuesday morning. There was no sunshine, and ordinarily, one would feel like the skies over the city—gloomy and gray. Yet, I couldn't keep my emotions under control; I was smiling inexcusably. It was almost impossible to explain the weightless euphoria of almost palpable freedom—freedom that was just a couple of days away. But there were still a few hurdles left to clear.

As I entered the crowd at the subway station, someone shoved his elbow into my rib cage and another stepped on my toes—typical morning-commute encounters.

I will not lose my cool, I reassured myself.

"What the fuck are you smiling about, you idiot?" The smell of hangover garlic breath hit me in the face, bringing tears to my eyes.

Smiling faces on the streets of Moscow were a rarity. How could I explain to this particular moron that the joy of possibly never dealing with him and his kind for the rest of my life was actually within reach? My goal was to get to my destination inconspicuously without becoming involved in any confrontation, so

I wiped the smile off my face, tucked down my chin, and moved toward the approaching train.

The crowd pushed me into the opening doors, stuffing the cars. The pneumatic doors closed, hissing a sigh of relief. The train started to move away from the station when I noticed my offender accompanied by another one dressed in a nearly identical dark gray overcoat. They quickly turned away when my eyes suddenly bumped into their stare.

Those gray overcoats had become a very familiar attribute of plain-clothed State Security agents, inadvertently blowing their cover for those who knew what they really meant. We dubbed them "collars" and tried to avoid their attention at all cost.

Now that I realized that I was being followed, I had to shake these two collars off. At the next stop, I waited for the doors of the train to start to close. Just a split second before they shut, I squeezed myself out onto the platform and watched the perplexed faces of my two pursuers disappearing into the darkness of the tunnel as they looked at me in utter disbelief. How many of them would I have to encounter that day?

I decided to shake off any possible surveillance and jumped into a train traveling in the opposite direction. After passing a couple of stations, including the station where I'd first boarded, I exited the subway and took the trolley along Boulevard Ring. I took the middle seat in the last row, which gave me an unobstructed and elevated view of the trolley cabin and the street ahead. After twenty minutes, I didn't see or sense anything suspicious. Luckily, I gave myself plenty of extra time before my appointment at the Dutch embassy.

Officially, since the Netherlands represented the interests of Israel in the Soviet Union, I had to file a request there for the Austrian transit visa to Israel. Unofficially, AP correspondent Nate Krimsky had arranged an appointment for me with the vice-consul, whom I would be asking for a loan.

We didn't have enough time to raise the twenty-seven thousand dollars we were obligated to pay for the final duty stamps on the exit visas for myself, Lara, and Vlad; for Lara's and my refund to the state for the "value" of our medical degrees; for the three applications to surrender our Soviet citizenship; and for our airfare. Our condo, if sold, could cover the equivalent of about eighteen thousand dollars, but since we were given only five days to leave, we didn't have even the slightest chance of selling it right away. My only hope was Krimsky's assurances that everything would be fine.

"Nikitsky Gates," announced the driver, and the trolley came to a stop.

I got out and took a brisk walk across the maze of short, wavy streets of Old Arbat. Apparently I wasn't being followed; busy-looking pedestrians rushed up and down the streets without paying any attention to me. I crossed the street, strolled for another couple of blocks, and quickly turned left, diving into the green shadows of Kalashny Pereulok, before briskly approaching the gates of the Royal Dutch Embassy.

As with every other embassy in Moscow, a small checkpoint guardhouse was occupied by two Russian policemen. The Dutch guards were stationed inside the embassy gates, and visitors were required to be cleared by the Russian police first.

I walked to the checkpoint and knocked on the small window. The policeman walked outside, looked me over, and remained standing in front of me in silence, waiting for me to talk.

"I have an appointment at the embassy for noon," I said.

"Your documents!" he barked in response.

I reached into my pocket, pulled out a yellow envelope, and showed him my exit visa. He grabbed the pink folded paper from my hand, opened it, and studied my attached photograph for a few long minutes.

"Wait outside," he commanded abruptly and disappeared inside the guardhouse behind a shaded glass door.

What is he going to do? Will he let me in? Can he stop me? Is that how today is going to turn out? My mind was racing, and my heart was pounding. I felt a tight knot forming inside my throat. Through the window, I could see him talking with his partner and examining my visa with interest.

Finally, he picked up the phone and spoke to someone on the other end for about three or four minutes. He then stood at attention, nodded his head a few times in apparent agreement, and hung up the phone a second later. After that, he watched me through the glass while his partner made another phone call. A few moments later, the massive door of the embassy cracked open, and I saw the Dutch guard standing inside the doors, looking in my direction. The policeman stretched out his hand with my visa through the guardhouse door and gestured to me to approach.

I stepped forward.

"They are expecting you. Take your document and go ahead." He looked at me, and I noticed a hint of subtle interest in his eyes.

I took my visa and put it back in my pocket. "Thank you," I said, trying to cough to clear my throat.

"Good luck," he snickered in return.

I turned away and walked to the open door of the embassy, where the Dutch guard awaited me. I entered the embassy and followed the guard to a second-floor reception room.

"Sit down, please," a young Dutch lady said with a

smile. "You are Alex, right? My name is Marieke. I am the vice-consul's secretary. He will see you in a few minutes. Would you like a cup of coffee? How do you take it? Cream, sugar?"

"Just black, please."

I sat and looked around. The reception room was small and cozy—white oak parquet floor, ornate cornices, intricate ceiling medallions, and dark green walls displaying a few frameless landscapes and windmills in black and white. Everything was impressively simple and warm.

Marieke brought a cup of espresso. The second sip of coffee started to calm me down, and I felt the gratifying sensation of safety caressing my mind.

The phone rang and Marieke answered. She put down the receiver and said, "The vice-consul will see you now, Alex." She got up, opened the office door, and gestured me in with a soft smile.

The vice-consul walked forward from behind his desk and greeted me with a long, friendly handshake. "It's my pleasure and privilege to meet you in person, Alex. We are all aware of what you went through to transfer the list of Jewish refuseniks to Senator Jackson and Congressman Vanik when they were in Moscow a couple of months ago. This list was a bombshell. My government and my king personally petitioned the Soviets to let you and a few others emigrate.

"Nate Krimsky told me everything about you, Alex. He is very fond of you. Devoted friends like Nate are hard to find. Sit down, please. Let's chat for a while." His Russian was flawless, despite a hint of an accent.

"You are among friends here. Please feel safe. I want to assure you that we will do everything we can to assist you to leave the Soviet Union safely and within the required time frame. Did you get the exit visas for your family?"

"Only for me, my wife, and our son, sir," I replied.

"How old is your son?"

"He'll turn six in July."

"He will be forever grateful. He will have a future, and an exceptional one with parents like his. I have no doubt about that. There are no limits to fulfilling your dreams on the opposite side of the Iron Curtain. Unfortunately, there are limits here—man-made, without any sense or logic, and without any hope in sight ... How much do you need to pay for all that required nonsense to get out?"

"About twenty-seven thousand dollars."

"And may I ask how much you have?"

"We can scrape a couple thousand between family and friends. We also have a small condo, but we don't have enough time to sell it. Nate Krimsky told me that you could help us with the money. I will try to transfer the deed for the condo to Nate, so that when it's sold later on, he can compensate you … at least partially."

"Leave it to your friends who need it. Nate doesn't have to compensate us."

He got up and walked to a wall safe hidden behind an old Dutch oil painting. A moment later, he closed the safe and returned with a large manila envelope and a few bundles of money.

"You don't have to count. It's exactly twenty-seven thousand dollars. Go and buy your way out of here, so to speak," he said with a smile as he put the bundles of cash into the manila envelope and handed it to me.

I started to feel the knot in my throat again. Trying to hold back my emotions, I asked, "How will I pay it back?"

"Just get out of here to the free world. We will figure it out later. I know people like you; you always pay your debts."

"I don't know how to thank you …"

"You don't need to." He then paused before continuing, "With this amount of cash, it will be safer if our embassy car takes you to the State Bank's central office to pay all your obligations right away. After that, my driver will take you to the State Department to finalize your exit visas and stamp all the documents.

"Then he will drop you off at the Aeroflot agency, where you will be able to unload the rest of your cash paying for your airfare to Vienna. That's the only destination the Soviet authorities will allow you to go to. Don't worry though; our people will meet you at the Vienna Airport to give you further assistance. Godspeed, Alex."

He hugged me and walked me to the door. Marieke was waiting for me in the reception room.

"Alex, I want you to meet Geert. He will take you where you have to go."

Geert was a tall, athletically built man in his late forties with a short, military-style haircut.

"At your service, sir. The vice-consul told me where we have to go. Please follow me to the garage."

We took the service stairs to the underground garage and walked to a navy blue Cadillac Fleetwood. Geert opened the passenger door. "Please, get in, sir."

The car exited the embassy garage into a courtyard. Geert signaled to the guard to open the gate. The Cadillac rolled out onto the street, made a right turn, and slowly glided past the checkpoint. The dumbstruck policeman darted inside the guardhouse to make a phone call to report what he had just witnessed.

Our first stop was the State Bank's central office. Geert parked the car across from the bank's exit doors on Kuznetsky Most, and we walked together around the building to the main entrance on Neglinka Street.

"Stay close to me," he said when I noticed that, as we approached, two policemen at the bank's entrance were studying both of us with vigorous curiosity.

"Good day, officers." Geert pushed me in front of him and flashed his diplomatic passport in their faces. Then, without a pause, he added, pointing to the manila envelope in my hand, "Diplomatic correspondence coming through." He pushed me inside the revolving door, blocking the view behind me.

The bamboozled policemen could not simply leave their post outside the bank to follow us without starting some sort of commotion. That would have been quite an undesirable thing to do to a diplomatic passport holder on a busy day at the State Bank's central office. The only thing left for them to do was to call for assistance, and it would take somewhere between ten and fifteen minutes for their reinforcements to arrive. That would buy us enough time to unload most of our cash by paying all the required fees and then exit the bank with just a few receipts to take to the next stop—the Visa Service Section of the State Department in Smolenskaya Square.

Everything happened like clockwork. In ten minutes, we exited the bank and walked straight to the embassy's navy blue Cadillac. Geert started the car, revved the engine, and leapt to the intersection. He then pivoted to the right and instantly bolted down

Tverskaya Street toward the bustling traffic of Garden Ring, leading us to the skyscraper tower of the State Department.

"You are one hell of a driver, Geert!" I noted, holding the armrests so tightly that my knuckles turned white.

"Thank you, sir. I am glad you are enjoying the ride," Geert said with a smile.

"Those poor bastards were so inept they still don't understand what just happened. But why did we have to trick them to get inside their bank to pay what they were extorting from me anyway? It doesn't make any sense ..."

"It's indeed insane, sir."

"Isn't it? When I left home this morning and went to the subway station, I bumped into a couple of plain-clothed collars. I realized that I was under surveillance, and I thought I'd been successful at shaking them off my tail on the way to the embassy. Do you think those policemen at the bank were expecting us?"

"I think they were, sir. The State Security agents were watching the embassy when we left. That policeman at the check point was dispatching them as we were leaving."

"But what do they want? It was the KGB, the Committee of State Security, who gave me five days to leave the country, Geert."

"They don't like to lose, sir. The State Department made a deal with the Americans. The KGB hates it. To them, it's a game of chess. You are a couple of moves away from calling checkmate. You are on the run, about to win, and they don't like it. It's not over, sir—not until your plane lands in Vienna. Then it's checkmate."

Geert parked the car in front of the State Department and turned off the engine.

"I'll stay in the car, sir. It's very unlikely they will attempt to mug you now since you're practically out of cash, and they won't assault you while you are at the State Department 'cause it's not under their jurisdiction. Turf war. I'll keep an eye on the entrance doors and will jump to your assistance in case of even a hint of danger, sir. Go, register your receipts, stamp your documents, and I'll keep watch outside. No worries..."

The Office of Visa Services was dusty, hot, and slow—Soviet bureaucracy in action. It took almost three and a half hours to register my receipts and get our exit visas stamped. Without those stamps, you cannot get access to a foreign travel desk at the Aeroflot agency to buy plane tickets to Vienna. Everything in this vicious circle was methodically overburdened and complicated to perfection—a total reflection of every day's collective living hell.

"Your exit visa will expire in three days. It's non-renewable. Next in line, please."

"That's it? Are we done now?"

"There is a message for you from the Dutch Consulate at the information desk."

"Message? For me?"

"Next!" was the last thing I heard on my way out.

The message read: "Geert is waiting for you at the corner of Sadovaya and Gertsena. He is in a gray Volvo with tinted windows."

"Where is the exit to Sadovaya?" I asked the girl who'd handed me the message.

"Can't you read?" she asked, pointing to the sign with the right arrow above her. "Sadovaya Exit."

I followed the sign to the State Department parking lot. I looked around and saw a gray Volvo moving in my direction. Geert opened the passenger door.

"Get in, sir. Sorry for the confusion." Geert took off and turned in the direction of the Aeroflot ticket agency.

"Where's the Cadillac? What happened, Geert?"

"I was waiting for about an hour when I noticed a couple of plain-clothed 'friends' of yours snooping around. Twenty minutes later, I saw another pair. I drove away, stopped at the drugstore, and placed a call from a payphone to a colleague of mine at the embassy.

"Twenty minutes later, we exchanged cars at

Taganskaya Square. He drove the Cadillac to the State Department, left you a message at the information desk, and returned to the embassy, taking the tail of collars with him. They're still sitting in front of the embassy waiting for you to come out."

"Do you think we'll be able to get to the Aeroflot agency before they close?"

"We need twenty minutes to get there in traffic like this. They will be closing in an hour. It's plenty of time.

The Volvo took off and darted back into the Garden Ring traffic. I had to experience Geert's driving excellence one more time. In twenty minutes, Geert parked the Volvo in front of the Aeroflot agency.

"Can I make a suggestion, sir?" he asked.

"Sure, Geert. You don't have to ask."

"You're supposed to leave in three days, correct?"

"Yep. We were ordered to leave the country by this coming Friday. Friday is our departure day."

"What else do you have to finish by Friday?"

"The only thing left is to get the plane tickets. Everything is done. We're leaving everything behind."

"If I were you, sir, I wouldn't wait till Friday. With all that commotion around, why wouldn't you try to book a flight for tomorrow morning? Do not give them a chance to stop you. Remember, it's a game of chess. Don't let them force your hand. Make your move first."

"Come to think of it, Geert, that's exactly what I'll try to do." I said, exiting the car.

"I'll wait for you here, sir."

The Aeroflot agency was still open. I showed my exit visas to an attendant who then directed me to a foreign travel desk.

"Your documents," the girl behind the ticket counter demanded.

I passed our visas through the window. She glanced at them briefly and then opened a thick flight schedule catalogue and started to scroll through the pages.

"Friday's flight is almost booked. There are only three seats still available, but they're in the first-class cabin. If you'd like to book them, each fare is fifty-four hundred dollars."

I was shocked. "Do you have anything available on an earlier flight?"

"Passengers leaving for 'permanent relocation' are only allowed on this flight," she said and kept looking at me. In her eyes, I read, *Are you totally stupid? Don't you know what to do next?*

"Can you check your records again, please?" I glanced around to be sure that nobody was looking and slid a hundred-dollar bill through the window.

"Let me check again," she said. "Unfortunately, there are no more coach seats available for Friday or Thursday. Let me see. Let me see ... Wow! You are in luck! I've found three discounted coach seats for to-morrow's flight. That'll save you four hundred bucks. Unfortunately, I will not be able to accept Soviet currency for these tickets. This fare can only be paid in US dollars. Do you have enough US dollars on you? Can you make that flight?"

I could not believe my own luck. I had more than enough dollars left to pay for those tickets. *Geert, you are genius!*

"Yes, oh yes. We will make the flight. I'll take it. Thank you so much, miss."

"You are welcome," she said without a smile. A couple of minutes later, I was leaving the Aeroflot agency with three tickets to freedom held tightly in my right hand.

I got to the car and plunged into the passenger seat.

"Geert, you wouldn't believe it." I was over-whelmed with joy. "There were no seats left for Friday or Thursday. We are leaving tomorrow! And I still have four hundred dollars left! Take it, please."

"No, no. I can't take it."

"But, Geert, listen to me, please. I already have two hundred and ninety dollars—the most we're al-lowed to take with us. What can I do with the extra four hundred?"

"I have an idea, Alex," Geert interrupted my plea.

"Let me take you to Beriozka, the foreign currency store. You can spend your four hundred dollars there."

"Geert, I am still a Soviet citizen. Beriozka is only for foreigners. They won't let me in."

"That is exactly what I'm saying. I'll go in and spend your bucks for you. What do you want me to buy?" He was already driving in that direction based on the assumption that I had no better idea to offer ... and he was right—I didn't.

"Whatever," I said, too overwhelmed by what had transpired today. "Whatever you find useful."

Five minutes later, Geert parked the car in Beriozka's parking lot. "I'll be back shortly. They are closing in fifteen minutes. Sit still and wait." He stepped out and locked the car.

As the sun set, the trees cast long shadows across the parking lot. The rays of the setting sun flickered through the tree trunks, reflecting off the windows of the passing cars. The birds gathered in the tree branches above started to rehearse their evening chirp, uniting in one huge chorus. Seemingly, everything exuded peace and tranquility.

But as the day drew to a close, the tranquility began to dissipate and was replaced with a strange and unsettling feeling. I suddenly realized that I did not belong here anymore. Everything felt incongruous, and ordinary things no longer made sense.

Somehow, we had all gotten used to the idiocy of stagnant everyday life, but my newborn awareness refused to accept it.

I looked up and saw a couple of plain-clothed collars talking to a policeman at the store's entrance. At the same moment they entered the store, Geert exited through the doors and returned to the car.

"Let's get the hell out of here," he said. "Seems like those bastards are everywhere, but I don't think those two were after us. They didn't react when they saw me leaving."

He drove to the Arbatskaya subway station and parked the car in a nearby alley that offered the perfect viewpoint of the surroundings. He probed the street with his eyes for a few minutes, and then I heard a sigh of relief.

"I don't think those two were after us … luckily," he said and retrieved the Beriozka shopping bag, which he had stashed behind my seat.

"I learned that these are the two items most coveted by your fellow Muscovites. They were exactly four hundred bucks." Geert pulled out an Ondatra—a muskrat fur hat—and a bright mohair scarf. "Try them on," he said.

"But, Geert," I protested, "It's June! Nobody around here wears this in June."

"There will be winter someday where you're

going," he reassured me. I put on the hat and threw the scarf around my neck.

"You look stupendous!" he said mockingly, before reaching into his pocket and pulling out a flask of Cherry Jeniver. "Screw it! So what if no one around here wears it in June? No one around here spent today like you did either. It's your reward for all your troubles! Let's *gulpen* to your checkmate run!" He smiled and swallowed with a loud gulp before passing his flask to me. "To the beginning of your new life!"

"Listen, Geert, there are no words to express my gratitude." It was my turn to *gulpen*. The fiery liquid tightly clutched my throat, bringing tears to my eyes. I knew I looked pathetic. Geert was laughing as I tried to catch my breath.

"Nothing can beat good old Dutch Jeniver!" he exclaimed.

We got out of the car and hugged like two old friends saying farewell to each other.

"This day wouldn't have happened without your help, Geert."

"Nothing better I could've done today, sir."

I watched the red tail lights of the Volvo melt away in traffic, and then I turned around and headed to the nearby entrance of the subway station. I was sporting my new Ondatra and bright mohair scarf all the way down the long escalator, ignoring the strange looks of the people riding in the opposite direction. *I couldn't care less,* I said to myself. *I am out of here tomorrow, and they will never see me again.*

I took a train to Sokol. People were coming in and out at every stop.

"Mayakovskaya," announced the voice over the radio. "Next station—Belorusskaya. Attention! Doors are closing."

"Belorusskaya. Next station—Dynamo. Attention! Doors are closing."

"Dynamo. Next station—Aeroport."

As the train came to a stop, I suddenly noticed a pair of plain-clothed collars entering my car through doors to my left. I froze.

"Attention! Doors are closing."

I bolted out at the last second. The train sped up to the tunnel, passing me and taking the two men into the darkness with it. They didn't appear to be paying any attention to me, but everything that had happened today had forced me to be vigilant.

I rode a train in the opposite direction, deciding to make my way to Khoroshevo station, which was only about ten minutes walking distance from my apartment. It took a couple of interchanges from one line to another, and I was finally one train stop away from my destination when a bedraggled drunk decided to strike up a conversation with me.

"Look at this motherfucker; just look at him," he spat. "Where do you think you're going dressed like that? The North Pole? Who the fuck do you think you are?"

I tried to ignore him, but he did not take it very well.

"I'm talking to you, asshole!" He pushed me in the chest. "Do you have hearing problem? Or do you think that because of that Ondatra on top of your shithead, you're so important that you can ignore us simple folk? Talk to me, motherfucker. Are you fucking mute?"

"Leave me alone," I replied. "What the hell do you want from me?"

"A lot of things," he said. "Let's start with your hat and scarf. Do you have any money?"

"I do not have any money. I just spent all my money on this hat and scarf. Why do you think I have to give them to you? Give me a reason, man."

"You need a fucking reason? Look at him," he looked around. "He needs a fucking reason ... I'll give you a reason, motherfucker!"

He hit me on the head, knocking my Ondatra to the floor, and then pulled a switchblade from his pocket.

"Is this a good enough reason for you, you fucking retard?" he screamed at me, picking up the Ondatra from the floor and putting it on. "Now, give me your fucking scarf. NOW!" While holding the knife in his right hand, he stretched the left one toward me, waiting for me to respond. I read the tattoo on his knuckles—"ALEX."

How ironic. I took off my new scarf and gave it to him. Why do I need it now anyway? It's the end of June. My goal is to get home. Period! What a paradox! Easy come, easy go. From one Alex to another. I tried to squeeze a fake smile.

Alex rolled my scarf around his neck and asked, "So, how do I look now, you fucking asshole? I bet it looks better on me than on you."

"Yes, man, it definitely looks better on you."

"Definitely better!" He looked at his reflection in the window. "Waaaay better than on you, mother-fucker. Give me five!" he said.

The train came to a stop as Alex raised his hand, giving me a high five. I gave him a high five and stepped out onto the platform, walking safely behind him. A small crowd spilled out around us and rushed to the exit. I walked slowly, trying to keep the distance.

"Hey, Alex! Are you here?" somebody shouted. I stopped and looked ahead. Two collars were stand-ing at the top of the stairs, scanning the approaching passengers.

"Hey, Alex!" one of them shouted, "Come over. We've been waiting for you."

"Are you talking to me?" Alex answered, drawing their attention. "Do I know you?"

"Get your fucking ass over here and don't ask any questions. You're coming with us."

The crowd sensed trouble and speedily melted past them and through the doorways. I backed off, taking cover behind a nearby column.

"Who the fuck are you to order me around?" Alex walked up to them. "Do I look like a fucking lavender to you? I wasn't born yesterday, you fucking fink. I was in the 'zone.' I did my time. I saw your kind over there, you fucking pile of shit. You want a piece of me? Come and get it!"

He pulled the switchblade and swung it in front of the shorter guy, scoring the front of his coat. The shorter collar dived under Alex's outstretched arm and delivered a heavy blow to his side, hitting the liver. Alex doubled over in agony, and then, with a wild scream, he sprang out of his position and delivered a short upward strike directly into the agent's groin. A split second before the knife reached its target, the taller guy grabbed Alex's wrist, twisted it around, and drove it straight into Alex's stomach. Alex fell to his knees and then slowly slumped to the ground, making growling sounds and twitching as a swelling, darkening puddle of his own blood pooled beneath him.

I froze in utter disbelief. Is that what Svetlana had been trying to warn me about? They'd gotten the wrong Alex. They'd been looking for me ... for the Ondatra hat and the colorful mohair scarf that the drunkard had taken away from me on the train. I couldn't believe my own weird and perplexing luck.

I heard the windy sound of an approaching train and watched as both assailants rushed to the platform. A moment later, the train was whisking them away, leaving behind the dead body and me.

Chapter Thirty One
Nothing to Lose

I ran upstairs, losing my breath as I tried to find the right key to open my apartment door. My hands were shaking. Suddenly, the door swung open. Lara was standing in the doorway, with Vlad sleeping in her arms.

"I was worried sick," she whispered. "What took you so long? Why are you so pale? Are we okay? Talk to me. Answer, please."

I did not recognize my own voice when I finally caught my breath and squeezed the words out of my throat. "Yes, we are okay, and we are leaving tomorrow ... first thing in the morning."

"Tomorrow isn't Friday. Why tomorrow?"

"Put Vlad in his bed. I have to explain."

I went to our tiny kitchen and put a teapot on the cooktop.

"He fell asleep waiting for you. Talk to me," Lara said, returning to the kitchen a couple of minutes later. "Why are we leaving in the morning?"

I started to describe in detail how the day had unfolded—how collars along the way had followed me, and how I'd had to try to shake them off. I told her about my meeting at the embassy, the money we had borrowed, my trip to the State Bank's central office, the three hours at the State Department, and the bribe I gave to the Aeroflot ticketing agent. I then told her about Geert, his almost military diligence, his reassuring protectiveness, our mad race through the heavy traffic of the busy streets of Moscow, and our stop at the Beriozka store.

"Hold that thought for a moment," she said as the boiling teapot started to whistle. Lara took out two teacups from an already packed carton of dishes and put them on our small kitchen table. She placed a tea bag in each cup and filled the cups with boiling water.

Something about the way she did simple and mundane things just released the tension of the moment. It used to irritate me, coercing me to lose my train of thought or the emotional intensity of what I was saying or doing at the time, but now it affected me in a different way. I took a deep breath and paused, looking at her for a brief moment of silence. Her quiet resilience made her so beautiful in that moment.

"So, what happened then? I'm listening…"

I explained Geert's analysis of the situation and his advice not to delay our departure until Friday. Then, as calmly as I could, I told her about the Ondatra hat and the colorful mohair scarf, my encounter with Alex, and the deadly scuffle that had ensued. I recounted

how I'd trembled with fear as I'd tried to find his ca-
rotid pulse after being left alone with his lifeless body
at the exit of the subway station. I told her how, in
agony and horror, I'd abandoned his corpse and run
home.

Now, I was done talking, and I instantly felt exhausted and empty.

"You are right," Lara said simply, "it was a tough
day."

"Tough day? I was nearly murdered! Can't you understand?" I exploded.

"Calm down, Alex. Keep your composure; Vlad
and I will need it, starting tomorrow. To them, you
are dead now. They will celebrate their victory tonight and file an accidental death report in the morning. By the end of the day, when the wrong ID from
the morgue arrives, we will be out of their reach.
Let's finish packing."

Her fortitude was reassuring and encouraging. She
was the only one with a cool head that night.

"Let's finish our tea first. How was your day?"
My question sounded pathetically apologetic and
rhetorical.

"It was interesting, to say the least. I was at the
hospital on my last night call till five in the morning.
At the end, I said goodbye to everyone for the last
time, returned home by six, and prepared breakfast

for you and Vlad. When you left for the embassy at seven thirty, I went to bed for a little snooze.

"Vlad woke me up an hour later, and shortly after that, I answered a phone call from our department head, Doctor Petrushko. She was telling me just how happy she was for us that we were finally being allowed to emigrate and how, at the same time, she was sad that she was losing me as one of her physicians. It was very touching, and I responded in kind that we would never forget her help and her covert support over the last year.

"We were almost done when she asked me for one last favor. She was one physician short for the day shift at our emergency department and asked me to come and fill in one more time from noon to six if I could. I couldn't say no to her after everything she's done for us. Luckily, Asya Vasylevna was home, and she took care of Vlad until I was back from the hospital at seven o'clock.

"My shift was going on like a normal ER routine—psychosomatic trauma and drunks with broken limbs one after the other—until that idiot, Doctor Torin, struck again. He admitted a patient with acute abdominal pain and made a diagnosis of ectopic pregnancy. The poor woman was almost on her way to the operating room. Her husband, a captain of the militarized border guard in full uniform, was holding her hand and sobbing uncontrollably.

"A couple of nurses were trying to separate them, to calm him down. They tried to explain to him that his wife would lose only her right ovary and that there was still a chance she could get pregnant again. Then one of them asked me to get involved since I was the only doctor present at the time and her admitting gynecologist, Doctor Torin, was nowhere to be found.

"I introduced myself, and while talking to them and holding the wife's hand, I noticed that she was quite feverish and her skin felt clammy. I asked the nurses to show me her lab tests. Her white blood count was through the roof. Her pregnancy test was positive, but I couldn't locate her HCG test results to confirm the ectopic diagnosis. I was ready to leave and was about to say something like 'She's in good hands; everything will be okay,' but the captain grabbed my arm and implored me not to leave. He begged me to save his wife and their unborn baby.

"I succumbed to his pleas and instructed the nurse to look everywhere, even to go back to the lab, to find the HCG test result. While waiting, I decided to palpate the wife's abdomen. The right lower quadrant was uncharacteristically tender and felt quite distended for an ectopic pregnancy or a ruptured ovarian cyst. When I was done with my exam, the woman vomited violently.

"Now, I had more questions than answers. It could

fit the picture of ectopic pregnancy as easy as the picture of acute appendicitis. I needed some proof to narrow down my differential diagnosis.

"When the nurse finally brought me the lab report, I saw that the patient's HCG level was very high,
consistent with normal pregnancy. In the case of an
ectopic pregnancy, HCG would stay low. Most likely,
we had a case of acute appendicitis. The poor woman's
appendix might be on the verge of rupturing! I did not
have too much time to dwell on it. She had to undergo
surgery one way or another, and I decided to proceed
with emergency exploratory surgery to rule out acute
appendicitis first.

"We rushed her to the operating room just in
time. Her appendix was enlarged, inflamed, and on
the brink of a rupture. Luckily, we weren't too late,
and her surgery went as any routine appendectomy
would.

"After she was transferred to the recovery room,
I went to tell the captain the good news. I can't begin
to describe the level of his joy when I told him that
his wife was still pregnant and that after a few days in
the hospital, they would have to follow up with her
regular OB doctor to make sure that her pregnancy
had not been affected by the surgery. I even hinted
to him to avoid Doctor Torin while his wife was still
there.

"The captain's smiling face was tired, puffy, and red. His tears of joy flowed uncontrollably; his uniform shirt was a mess. He hugged me, grabbed my hand, and started kissing it in endless gratitude, despite my resistance. Finally, when I was able to pull myself away from him, he pledged that one day, somehow, he would return the favor.

"Little did he know it could never happen. I couldn't tell him that we were emigrating in three days and would be very far away. Anyway, it was such a nice way to finish my last day."

"Wow! You are my hero. What a great day you had!" I looked at her in admiration. "I am one lucky guy to have you."

"Don't you ever forget it." She smiled in response.

Our tea was getting cold.

"Let's finish packing," Lara said, "Are you hungry? I don't think we'll have a chance to sleep tonight. You have to call Nate. He called to check on you a few times in the last three hours."

"I am too adrenalized now to think about food. First, I have to call Nate to tell him what happened and to thank him for the referral to the Dutch embassy and for all his help. We are so lucky to know him."

"Second," Lara interrupted me, "we will finish packing. We have to be ready by the wee hours. And don't argue. Period. The end," she concluded.

I went to the living room, picked up the phone, and dialed Nate's number.

"Hi, Nate. It's me—Alex."

"Well hello, old man!" Nate answered jauntily. "I've been waiting for your call for some time. I talked to my contact at the Dutch embassy, and I was told that you're leaving in the morning. I am elated that everything worked out as planned, finally."

He always called me an "old man," even though I was ten years younger than he was.

"There is something no one knows yet, Nate," I replied. "I was followed by numerous sets of collars all day long. The last pair of them was at the Khoroshevo subway station, waiting, looking for me. Accidentally thinking that it was I, they picked a fight with a drunken thug who had robbed me on the train just a moment earlier. He pulled a knife on them, and they killed him instantly. They left him in a puddle of blood and fled like a couple of pros. There was nobody around. When I checked on him, he was already dead. I made a quick exit and ran home."

"Holy shit," whispered Nate. "Are you kidding me?"

"No, I'm not kidding. I'm dead serious."

There was a brief moment of silence on his end.

"It is dead serious," he finally said. I could hear

his heavy breathing. After a brief pause, he started urgently firing off instructions.

"Here's what you do. Do not talk to anyone. Do not answer the phone. Pack light. Leave all the crap behind. Trust me; you won't need it. You do not want to be slowed down at Customs. Take just the bare necessities—just enough to get by for a couple of days. It will help you slink through check-in quickly.

"Do not call a cab. I'll be at your place by six in the morning and will drive all of you to the airport. I'll stay there until you leave. Somebody from the Hebrew Immigrant Aid Society will meet you at Vienna Airport. I'll fly to Vienna a couple days later, and I'll find you there. See you at six sharp. Take care," he finished and hung up the phone.

Suddenly, I realized just how alarmed and nervous Nate had become when I'd told him what had happened on my way home. That overwhelmingly liberating feeling of escape started to melt away, turning into exhausting anxiety. The rapid Polaroid flashes of what had transpired began flickering before my eyes. The imminent danger, which all of us were trying blindly to dismiss, was painfully real and perilous.

I instantly broke out in a cold sweat. I felt frightened and guilty. I was not totally selfless, but my fright was not for myself. I was guilty of not thinking about how Lara and Vlad's lives could've been affected first, ahead of mine.

I should've taken care to isolate them from the inescapable precariousness of the consequences before getting into a messy and unpredictable struggle with a very slim chance of victory. I had been carelessly dismissive of what could have happened to them if I had failed.

I was unable to pacify myself with comfortable shielding thoughts of a struggle for their greater good, for their future. There were not enough platitudes to dismiss the reality staring at me in its naked simplicity screaming, "Grow up! NOW!"

Suddenly, it felt as if I just had; I'd aged in an instant and abruptly realized the full weight of coming-of-age on my shoulders. At that moment, it became irrevocably clear to me that no one but I was forever responsible for Lara and Vlad, for both of their lives, for their safety, and for their future.

Lara was putting the last few pieces of Vlad's clothes in a suitcase. I grabbed her by the shoulders, turned her around, and looked straight into her tired, beautiful gray eyes.

"What now?" she said impatiently.

"Everything will work out. I'll take care of it. I promise we're going to be okay," I pleaded in response.

"I have no doubt about that ... as long as we have

each other." She smiled back and used her thumb to wipe a small runaway tear from the corner of my eye. "Now, stop being sentimental and finish packing your suitcase."

We finished packing just before we had to wake up Vlad. I looked at the cardboard boxes, packed with books, stocked in every corner of our small apartment.

We were leaving everything behind. The bare necessities, as Nate had said, were tightly packed into two brown suitcases. All the documents were in an already fastened briefcase. Ten bottles of vodka were waiting on the kitchen table, ready for the farewell party planned for two days later. I knew that all our friends would gather in the apartment, most likely that night when the news of our early departure started to trickle through the tightly knit network.

I knew that they would understand why we couldn't have spent the last night together. They would bring Aunt Anna and my parents along and would be toasting our departure with all the bottles we'd left behind, reminiscing about times past, arguing with each other about the future, and wishing us farewell ... assuming everything went according to plan.

Lara woke Vlad up. When he was almost finished eating his oatmeal, the doorbell rang, and Nate rushed into the apartment.

"Is everyone ready? It's time to go, my friends."

"Uncle Nate!" Vlad greeted him gleefully. "Thank you for saving me. I hate this oatmeal."

"I hate it too, Vlad," Nate agreed.

"Mommy told me that I won't grow if I don't eat it, but you are tall, Uncle Nate," Vlad continued.

"Mommy is always right," I interjected. "Now, here's the deal. We are on the way to the airport to catch a plane to Vienna. You have to listen to Mommy and me very carefully. Do not ask any questions. Do not talk to anyone. Keep very close to Mommy, and try to keep your mouth shut at all times. Okay?"

"Can I start talking again when we are in Vienna?"

"Sure you can, sweetheart," Lara said. "Do not scare him like that please, Alex. Nate, can you take our apartment key and give it to my brother later?"

"Will do," Nate responded. "Let's go now."

We walked down the stairs and got into Nate's minivan, which was parked on the street. Lara and I looked back at our apartment building, watching it disappear behind us as we turned down the street.

Nate drove toward the Leningradsky Highway entrance leading to Sheremetyevo Airport. The traffic was light at that time of the morning. We didn't exchange any words until we arrived at our destination forty minutes later. Nate followed the "Departing Flights" signs and came to a stop at the main entrance.

"That's it," he said. "Alex, take both of your

suitcases. Lara, take Vlad and Alex's briefcase and go to the check-in counter. I'll park the minivan, and then I'll watch you from the visitors' gallery upstairs."

"Thank you for everything, Nate," Lara said, as she reached forward and kissed him on the cheek.

Nate squeezed my hand, patted me on the shoulder, and said, "Keep your cool, old man. Do not look tense, do not grimace, and do not rush. Put a fake smile on your face and wear it. It always helps. In a few months, I'll try to mail you all the books you left behind. Good luck, brother. See you in a couple of days in Vienna. Go, now!"

"I have no words, Nate ..."

"Go! Lara and Vlad are waiting for you."

I got out of his minivan, grabbed our suitcases, and the three of us entered the terminal and walked up to the international check-in counter.

"Good morning, miss."

"What's your destination?" The female agent was anything but pleasant.

"Flight two sixty-one to Vienna. The three of us." I squeezed out a smile and put our tickets and exit visas on the counter.

She checked our tickets and examined our visas. She then looked me over and said, "How did you get these tickets? Who sold them to you? You are not supposed to be on this flight. There is a directive about permanently relocating Jewish passengers flying to Vienna. You have to be segregated to Friday's flight only." She returned our visas to me.

No wonder Nate had been so nervous about our departure and had promised to stay at the airport until our flight was in the air. At that moment, I understood that he'd wanted to make sure we weren't left behind and alone if we weren't allowed on the flight. I turned to Lara and Vlad and realized that both of them were looking at me expectantly, waiting for me do something.

I had to try anything and everything to get us on that flight. I had heard stories about bribes paid to Customs for the release of family relics or an extra piece of jewelry, but we were not at Customs yet. Fortunately, bribes did work most of the time in our rotten system, and I was desperate to do just that. What good would our two-hundred-and-ninety-dollar fortune do for us if we were left behind?

I pulled a hundred-dollar bill out of my pocket, opened my folded visa as if checking something, placed the money inside, and slid it back across the counter. "The manager of the foreign travel desk at the Aeroflot agency made a similar exemption for us the other day." I looked at her and then pointed at Vlad with my eyes. I pleaded with her quietly, "I do not have much money left … Please, have a heart …"

She looked at Vlad and then looked around. "How old is he?"

"Almost six," I replied. "I beg you, please ..."

She put her hand on top of my visa, shrugged her shoulders, and said, "I don't know. Everyone is struggling to make a living. I could've made an honest mistake as well. Whatever that manager did, I was not there to see it. I'll issue your boarding passes, but you are on your own from now on. Go to Customs and do not come back to me. I am on my break."

She then lowered her voice and said, "Take back your money. A human does not have to be Jewish to have a heart ... Any luggage?" she asked.

"No." I was embarrassed. "Just two carry-ons and a briefcase."

"Good." She passed the three boarding cards across the counter, flipped over the 'Closed' sign, and announced, "I am closed. Go to the next counter" to the people standing in line behind us. She then hastily walked away without giving me a chance to thank her.

Holding our visas, tickets, and three boarding passes, we went to Customs.

"Open your luggage," the customs agent ordered. "What do you have to declare?"

"Nothing to declare, sir."

"Any foreign currency?" he asked, going through the contents of our suitcase.

"Just two hundred and ninety dollars."

"Let me count. Where is your exchange receipt?"

"Here it is." I took out the money and the receipt. He counted it and returned it to me.

"Any Soviet currency? Any coins?"

"No, sir. None."

"Any jewelry?"

"No."

"Any printed materials?" he continued.

"A few old issues of *New Word* magazine."

"Where did you put them?"

"In the other suitcase, sir."

"Open it," he ordered.

I opened the suitcase. He started to lay all the contents out on the counter. He eventually pulled out ten issues of New Word that had been bundled together.

"Consider it confiscated," he announced.

"But my poetry is in there," I started, but caught myself just in time.

"What did you say?"

"I said that there are some poems in there that my wife likes …"

"Any articles of prohibited publications are not permitted. Anything else your wife likes that I should look for?"

Lara gave me an angry look and jumped in, "No, no, officer. I didn't mean to take it with us. I didn't know. I don't need it. I don't have anything else."

"How about that ring on your pinky? It looks like an antique jewelry item to me. Do you have the Ministry of Culture certificate of exemption?" He was on a roll.

"This was my grandmother's ..."

"I repeat, do you have the Ministry of Culture certificate of exemption?"

"I didn't know we'd need a certificate."

"We have to file an Affidavit of Confiscation," he declared.

"Officer, please," Lara said. "We don't have time for that. We can't afford to miss our plane. I'll be glad to leave it with you. Why don't you keep it? Okay?"

"It's your choice," he said, gleaming with pride at having fulfilled his duties. He had something to prove—that he was worthy of the trust the state had bestowed upon him. "If you don't have anything else to declare, we're done. Pack everything back into your luggage and proceed to Passport Control," he concluded, affixing yellow stickers to our boarding cards.

I stuffed everything back in our suitcases, and the three of us rushed out of the Customs hall.

Passport Control was located on the second floor. We took an escalator up, walked down the hall, and then joined one of the waiting lines.

After a couple of minutes, a man in front of us turned around and smiled gently at us. He then asked quietly, "Vienna? Jewish?" He had a full head of gray curls and was dressed in a black velvet sports jacket. He looked like Einstein.

I leaned closer to Lara and whispered in her ear, "Please, do not answer. Even though he looks and acts like a foreigner, it could be a setup. Just ignore him."

I gave him an I-do-not-know-what-you-are-talking-about smile in return.

He pulled a Kit Kat chocolate bar from his pocket and tried to give it to Vlad. "May I offer some candy to your child?"

"No," I said in my limited English. "No, not permitted. Sugar ... diabetes."

The man just shook his head and smiled back.

"Next!"

Now it was his turn to step up to an open booth.

The Passport Control lobby was divided by a row of glass cubicles attended by young sergeants and first lieutenants of the militarized border guard. Two captains and a major were slowly circulating between the cubicles, supervising the flow of passengers. I looked around and noticed that every passenger there was a foreigner. Foreigners looked and acted differently from Russians. En masse, they were quieter, cleaner, and more polite.

That row of glass cubicles was almost like an invisible barrier separating the two worlds—a demarcation line between our past and our future. We were just a few feet away from a dream. We could sense it now. It was just a matter of a little distance until we could feel it and breathe it in, filling our lungs, our hearts, and our souls with that priceless substance called freedom.

"Next!"

Lara pushed Vlad to an open booth. I followed them and passed our tickets, boarding cards, and exit visas to the lieutenant behind the counter. He unemotionally studied our tickets, boarding cards, and finally our exit visas. Then he stood up and looked down over the counter at Vlad. Finally, he sat back down and picked up the phone.

"There is something out of order here, sir," he reported. "I have two adults and a child at my station, sir. It is a family of emigrating Jews. They do not have any passports—just exit visas, sir. They are in possession of discounted tickets purchased with American dollars, sir. The emigrating Jews were not previously allowed to be on a regular flight to Vienna, Austria. What has changed? We only process those on the last Friday of the month. Yes, I will, sir." He hung up the phone.

"Wait here," he ordered.

Two sergeants suddenly appeared behind us. The blood rushed from my head and my knees nearly buckled when I saw a captain enter the booth and look at our documents.

Lara grabbed me by the hand and squeezed it. She pulled herself closer to me and, with her voice trembling, whispered in my ear, "It's that captain from last night at the hospital. It's him!"

"Captain," she said loudly, "do you remember me?"

He looked at Lara in total bewilderment. Then his eyes opened so wide they were ready to pop out of their sockets. "Doc? Is it you?" His uniform shirt was still wrinkled and stained. "I just saw you a few hours ago. What are you doing here? Am I daydreaming?"

"No, Captain, you are not daydreaming. It is me. How is your wife this morning?"

"She was resting comfortably a couple of hours ago, just before I came on my shift. But, hold on for a moment, Doc. I cannot believe it! You are leaving? Are you leaving for good?"

"Yes, we are leaving, Captain. We are leaving for good ... if you would help us. Please ..."

The captain pulled out a soiled handkerchief and wiped his sweating forehead. He then turned back to the young lieutenant and said, "Stamp the exit documents. All three sets of them."

"But Captain—" protested the lieutenant.

"Shut the fuck up!" the captain raised his voice. "It's an order! Stamp them!"

While the startled lieutenant hurried to stamp our documents, the captain came closer to the counter and said in a soft undertone, "Many of us here will miss you, Doc. We are even now. All the best!" He quickly walked away.

I picked up our documents from the dazed lieutenant and proceeded to our gate, where boarding was already underway. We stepped outside and entered the shuttle bus that would take us to our plane. I drew a deep, shuddering breath in total disbelief of our luck.

Einstein walked in and stood next to me. "Do not be afraid, young man." He looked left and right and then continued quietly, "I am a Jew as well. I'm from the United States. Shalom!"

I just nodded back, still too frightened and on edge to respond.

We finally boarded the plane. Lara took the window seat, I took the aisle, and Vlad occupied the middle. We did not say a word. Einstein sat across the aisle to my right.

Twenty minutes later, we were airborne.

"Flying time to Vienna—two hours," announced the pilot over the loudspeakers.

Vlad was already dozing, leaning against Lara's shoulder. I reached over and touched her trembling hand.

"Soon," I said. "Very soon now."

"As soon as we land and get off this plane ..." Lara whispered to me.

"We will be free," I whispered in return.

"If you do not want to talk, just listen." Einstein leaned over the aisle and continued, "My parents left Russia at the turn of the century. My dad was escaping the draft. I know times are different now, but I appreciate what you are going through. Thank God, my parents made it, and I made it. Rest assured, you will make it there as well.

"For the last three years, I've been traveling here and back, buying lamb pelts for my business and occasionally delivering care packages to Soviet Jews in need. I understand your worries. Do not be afraid to start over, but do what my folks did. Settle in America. An ocean of opportunity awaits you. You have to be one dumb and lazy bum not to succeed there."

I still did not respond to him.

After a long pause, he turned back to me. "If you want to be serious... Nobody goes to the ocean with a teaspoon. Bring a bucket. A big bucket! Do you hear me?"

"I do. Thanks," I answered. I leaned back, shut my eyes, and pretended to be asleep.

"Remember ... a big bucket." Einstein finally left me alone.

Our plane landed with a soft bump. As it taxied to the terminal, I saw a huge Boeing 747 with the El

Al insignia slowly moving by the window to my right. Our Tupolev TU-104 came to a complete stop, the doors opened, and a slow stream of passengers started to trickle down the tightly parked steps.

We descended to the bottom of the staircase and stood there looking at each other in wonderment and disbelief.

"I think we made it," I said, fighting a tight spasm in my throat.

"Looks like we did," Lara answered and quickly looked away.

"We are in Vienna, aren't we? Can I start talking now?" Vlad asked. "Why are you crying, Mommy?"

"Because I am happy, my love. Because I am happy." Her smiling face was covered with tears.

"I don't cry when I'm happy," Vlad asserted.

"Grown-ups do, sweetheart … sometimes …"

"Remember… A big bucket! Good luck to you all," bade Einstein as he passed us and shoved his business card into my hand. "Do not be afraid to start over!" he yelled from afar. "What do you have to lose?"

"We have nothing to lose!" I shouted back. "I'm not afraid anymore!"

I looked at Vlad and Lara standing next to me. We huddled together, and I said it again, looking straight into my wife's beautiful gray eyes, "We are not afraid to start over. So help us God …"

"So help us God," repeated Lara. "For as long as we have each other, we have nothing to lose."

The three of us walked away from the Aeroflot plane and crossed the tarmac into a new day ...

It was Wednesday, June 25, 1975.

CPSIA information can be obtained
at www.ICGtesting.com
Printed in the USA
JSHW011227240223
38181JS00001B/2

9 780991 578610